Million Dollar Baby

FORTHCOMING BY AMY PATRICIA MEADE

Ghost of a Chance

A Marjorie McClelland Mystery

Million Dollar Baby

Amy Patricia Meade

MIDNIGHT INK
WOODBURY, MINNESOTA

First Edition
Second Printing, 2006

Book design and layout by Donna Burch
Cover design and cover image by Ellen Dahl
Editing by Valerie Valentine

Midnight Ink, an imprint of Llewellyn Publications

Library of Congress Cataloging-in-Publication Data
Meade, Amy Patricia, 1972–
    Million dollar baby : a Marjorie McClelland mystery / Amy Patricia
Meade.—1st ed.
        p.   cm.
    ISBN 13: 978-0-7387-0860-7
    ISBN 10: 0-7387-0860-7
    I. Title.

PS3613.E128M55 2006
813'.6—dc22

2005049627

Midnight Ink
Llewellyn Publications
2143 Wooddale Drive, Dept. 0-7387-0860-7
Woodbury, MN 55125-2989, U.S.A.
www.midnightinkbooks.com

Printed in the United States of America

ONE

"Using poison this time?" Walter Schutt's eyebrows arched questioningly as he pushed the brown paper parcel across the counter.

"Possibly." Marjorie McClelland took the bag and removed the contents. *The Encyclopedia of Backyard Banes: An A to Z Guide to Common Poisons.*

"That is the book you requested, isn't it?"

"Yes, Mr. Schutt. Thanks so much for ordering it. How much do I owe you?"

His eyes scanned the yellowed purchase order book. "With shipping and tax, two dollars and twenty-five cents." He looked up from the order and frowned. "That's a mighty expensive book, if you don't mind me saying so."

Marjorie's stomach tightened. She withdrew her wallet from her purse and braced herself for another of Mr. Schutt's tirades. The Schutt family—Walter, the proprietor and sole clerk at Schutt's Book Nook, his wife, twin daughters, and son—were the most unpopular clan in the tiny village of Ridgebury, Connecticut. The self-anointed pillars of the community, they thought it their duty to protect their brethren from sin, foolishness, and wrongdoing.

She extracted three one-dollar bills and thrust them into his outstretched hand as if in an effort to purchase his silence. Squinting, he held them aloft against the light for close inspection, and then mumbled, "Thank you," before placing them in the ancient cash register. While removing her change from the drawer, he resumed the inquisition. "I don't mean to pry, Miss McClelland . . ."

Yes, you do, you old bat, thought Marjorie.

"But can you really afford to be purchasing books this way? I mean, given your occupation . . ."

Mr. Schutt was always referring to her "occupation" as if she were a scullery maid rather than a moderately successful mystery writer. Three of her books had been published in the past two years, and their sales had provided her with a comfortable, if not affluent, lifestyle. Her income afforded life's necessities, as well as its modest pleasures: cosmetics and clothes, permanent waves, occasional Saturday nights at the pictures, and cups of coffee or soda at the local drugstore. Given the year was 1935 and the world was in the middle of a deep economic depression, it was, she thought, a life more comfortable than many.

"And the fact you have no husband to support you," he continued. "Don't you think you should save your money? Dear girl, it is time you started thinking about your future!" His right hand smacked on the counter, punctuating the error of her ways. His left hand still clutched the seventy-five cents.

Marjorie suppressed a grin. Maybe his harangues were orchestrated to force exasperated customers to leave before being given their proper change.

"Not that I don't enjoy reading your books." A faint flush crept up his thin, sinewy neck and stained his pallid cheeks. "But a female writing such stories is not proper. Not proper at all! Women were not meant to be storytellers. Storytelling has always been a masculine pastime. Just look at history. Homer, Virgil, Dante, Milton, Chaucer, Shakespeare, Dickens. Now *those* were storytellers! And what about George Eliot? *Silas Marner* has always been one of my favorites."

"George Eliot was a woman," Marjorie checkmated.

Mr. Schutt paused only a blink. Defeat was unacceptable. "You're focusing on the technicalities, Miss McClelland. The simple fact is that you are swiftly passing your prime. A woman your age should be married and starting a family."

Countercheck. Marjorie sighed noisily. Anyone listening might have thought that Marjorie was approaching her third century of life rather than her third decade.

"Take my dear Louise, for example." Marjorie rolled her eyes. *He* could take her. If Mr. Schutt was the second most-hated citizen in Ridgebury, Mrs. Schutt took grand prize. Louise shared her husband's proclivity for giving unsolicited advice, but whereas Mr. Schutt tended to shun social functions, Mrs. Schutt basked in them. Never content in just attending the local carnivals, bazaars, or women's luncheons, Mrs. Schutt always tried to usurp power from the committee chairpersons, inciting such hostility in her peers that the most genteel of social events assumed the pugilistic air of a prizefight. Even the local church services had become a weekly power struggle, with Mrs. Schutt praying and singing louder than Reverend Price. The latest misadventure had resulted in Louise Schutt providing the church organist with musical instruction during the middle of a sermon.

"When my dear Louise was your age," he continued, "we had been married six years and were eagerly awaiting the delivery of our son

Simon." Mr. Schutt's phrasing made it sound as if Simon were an item that arrived by the morning post. "Sharon and Sheila were born four years before."

Marjorie was surprised that the odious Schutt sisters were "born"; she had always imagined them sprouting from their mother's head. "Mr. Schutt," she interrupted, before he could further expound on his familial bliss. "I would love to get married, but the opportunity has not presented itself. There are simply no men in town whom I would consider dating, let alone marrying."

"Well, what about Dr. Russell? He's about your age."

As if that were the only criteria. "I have nothing in common with Dr. Russell." Seeing an opportunity to extricate herself from the bookstore and, at the same time, have some fun with the bookseller, she turned and sighed, "The only person I've ever had anything in common with is you, Mr. Schutt." She clicked her tongue several times, and then added, wistfully, "If only I were twenty years older."

His flushed cheeks turned crimson. When the astonished Mr. Schutt dropped the change from his left hand, Marjorie scooped the coins off the counter, winked, and whistled her way out of the store, leaving the gaping shopkeeper staring open-mouthed after her.

"Smitten" aptly described Creighton Ashcroft as he gazed out of the large picture window overlooking the village common. He had entered the Ridgebury Drugstore for a cup of coffee and a sandwich, but while awaiting his lunch, his attention became riveted on a young woman emerging from the bookstore on the other side of the green. In her twenties and lovely as a finely etched cameo, she wore a black coat and matching shoes. The March wind was sweeping her unbound hair into a golden halo framing her face. He noticed that in the crook of her arm she cradled a large, rectangular object. *Ah, a book!* he thought, excited at the prospect that this was not only a goddess, but a fellow reader as well.

He was awakened from his hypnotic state by the call of the young boy behind the lunch counter, informing him that his order was ready. Creighton turned his head from the window only to realize that his nose had nearly been pressed against the glass.

The lunch counter and its line of stools ran from the front of the shop to the rear and was the only seating provided for its patrons. Creighton selected the stool nearest the front of the store and then returned his gaze to the young woman. The server, who introduced himself as Freddie, followed his customer's line of vision out of the store window, but assumed that his focus was on the 1929 Rolls Royce Phantom II Continental parked along the curb.

"Is that your car, mister?"

"Yes," Creighton answered distractedly; the goddess was heading directly toward the drugstore.

"Would you mind if I went out and had a look at it, sir? I won't touch it or nothin'."

At the excitement in Freddie's voice, Creighton turned and looked at him. The lad couldn't have been more than fifteen. Creighton smiled inwardly at the love affair that inevitably ensued between teenage boys and automobiles. Then his spirits plummeted. Unless the economy improved, Freddie, and other boys like him, might never possess such luxuries. "Freddie, my lad, you are welcome to look, touch, and sit in the car if you like."

"Thank you!" shouted the boy, donning his jacket and running out the door.

As Creighton watched him leave, he saw that his mystery lady was about to enter. He quickly snatched up a newspaper from the counter, held it to his face and pretended to read. The small bells dangling over the door announced her arrival. She passed behind him and took a seat two stools to his left.

Feigning nonchalance, Creighton sipped at his coffee without lifting his eyes from the newspaper, then almost gagged at the bitter brew. In his fascination with the young woman, he had forgotten to add cream or sugar. Shuddering slightly, he forced himself to swallow the scalding hot, pungent liquid.

Upon returning the cup to its saucer, he noticed that the woman was eyeing him curiously. He smiled. "Hello."

"Hello." Obviously accustomed to Freddie's absences, she rose from her seat and wandered behind the counter. She bent down, retrieved a cup and saucer from some hidden location and poured herself some coffee. She held the carafe over Creighton's cup. "More?"

Creighton glanced at the book she had left, face up, at her seat. *Common poisons?* "Umm . . . No, thank you."

She replaced the carafe then glanced out the window. A large crowd had gathered around Freddie and the Rolls Royce. Creighton followed her gaze. "It seems my arrival has caused quite a stir."

She sat on her stool and began adding sugar to her coffee. "They react that way over any stranger," she shrugged. "Ridgebury doesn't get too many visitors."

"Oh?" Creighton doubted that "any stranger" drove a Phantom.

"Most people just pass through on their way to New York or Boston." She picked up a spoon and dipped it into her cup. "So, where are you headed?"

"Nowhere, actually. I just purchased Kensington House this morning, so I suppose that makes me your new neighbor."

She stared at him in disbelief. "You're kidding me! *You* bought Kensington House?" He nodded his reply. "You must have a *ton* of money to buy that place! You would have to be a millionaire!"

Creighton tried to respond as modestly as he could, "Well . . . um, yes, I am."

In her excitement, she put aside her coffee and moved to the stool next to him. "But that place is huge! How many rooms are there?"

"Twenty-seven."

She leaned toward him, her emerald eyes dancing with curiosity. He found the proximity pleasant, if unnerving. "Twenty-seven! You must have a large family to need a house that size."

He was glad at the opportunity to mention his marital status. "No, just me. I'm not married."

Her eyebrows furrowed. "You mean you're going to live in that big house by yourself?"

"Yes. Although my butler and cook will probably take up residence in the house as well."

She seemed annoyed at such blatant waste of space. "But that's only two more people. Why do you need twenty-seven rooms?"

"I don't. I just fell in love with the house. It suits me."

She contemplated this for a moment, and then said suddenly, as if she had just taken note of his accent, "You're English, aren't you?" She made it sound like an explanation for his eccentric behavior rather than a legitimate question.

"Yes, I am."

"So, you're new to this country?"

"No. I've lived in New York the past few years." He pulled a small card from a gold case in his suit pocket and presented it to her.

She felt the heavy stock of the card and then took note of the name engraved upon it: *CREIGHTON RICHARD ASHCROFT III.*

Beneath it was a Park Avenue address. "I'm afraid I don't have a card to exchange for yours," she apologized.

He smiled. "A name would suffice."

"Marjorie Irene McClelland," she stated, then quickly added, "the first."

"The one and only, to be certain," responded Creighton. "Pleased to make your acquaintance."

She shook his proffered hand but did not let hers linger in his large, strong palm. "So why did you go to New York?" she asked, stirring her coffee.

"My father made his fortune in England, manufacturing airplane parts. After the war, he realized that America had a much larger market for such items, so he moved the business here. The corporate offices are in New York, but we have plants across the country."

"But Ridgebury is a three-hour drive from New York. You'd have a terrible time getting to work every day."

"Oh, I don't work in New York."

"You have an office here in Connecticut?"

"I perhaps misled you with my last statement. In truth, I don't work anywhere. I quit the family business."

She stared incredulously at him. "Quit? Why on earth would you do that?"

"Why should I work? I don't need to. I have enough money to live quite comfortably for the rest of my life and still provide for my heirs. Besides," he added peevishly, "I don't much fancy airplane parts."

"So what do you do all day?"

"Nothing. What do *you* do all day?"

Her chin jutted defiantly. "I'm a writer."

A writer! Creighton's heart skipped a beat. "What do you write?"

"Mystery novels." She stared at him, daring him to scoff.

"*Mys*tery novels," he repeated. He leaned closer, trying to recall where he had seen her before. "Excuse me, what was your name again?"

"It not only was but *is* Marjorie McClelland."

He feigned excitement and surprise. "No! Not *that* Marjorie Mc-Clelland!"

She blushed slightly. "You've read my books?"

Careful, man, thought Creighton. He resisted the temptation to claim he had read everything she had written. "I read your last one."

"*Death in Denmark*?"

Creighton nodded.

Marjorie smiled hesitatingly. "Did you enjoy it?"

He searched for an appropriately vague compliment for a mystery novel. "Enjoy it? I loved it. It was terribly clever. And that ending caught me completely by surprise." Fearing she might begin discussing the plot in detail, he quickly inquired, "When will your next book be released?"

"I'm writing it now. My publisher wants to release it this autumn." She frowned and shook her head slowly. "I don't know, though. I've been having so much trouble with it." She sat motionless, staring out the window behind him.

Suddenly, she snapped to life, her eyes wide with excitement. "I know—maybe you can help me!"

Creighton wondered what schemes were forming in that lovely blonde head. "Help you?"

"Yes. You said yourself you have nothing to do."

He was annoyed at this intrusion upon his idleness. "I enjoy having nothing to do. Besides, I'm *not* a writer."

She remained undaunted. "Oh, no, you don't have to be a writer. I just need someone to read what I've written so far and give me an honest opinion. And, since you're obviously well educated and you're familiar with my work, I thought you might be a good candidate. But, if you don't want to do it . . ."

Her head tilted downward and she looked as if she might cry. Creighton could have strangled himself for refusing. After all, discussing her book would allow him to see her again. "All right, I'll do it."

She picked up her head and beamed. "I'll need help as soon as possible. Are you moving into Kensington House today?"

"No, I can't. There's no water, heat, or electricity. Not to mention, after more than five years of being empty, it could use a good cleaning."

"So you're going back to New York?"

"No. It would be more convenient if I stayed in this area, so that I can supervise the work on the house."

"Well, Mrs. Patterson has a boarding house around the corner. The rooms are comfortable and she does a good breakfast." She hesitated, then added, "But I suppose you're accustomed to more swank surroundings."

"No, if I wanted swank surroundings I would have stayed in New York. Mrs. Patterson's sounds fine."

"Good. Then if you're staying in Ridgebury, why don't we get together tomorrow? Say, about noon?"

"Fine. Where should I meet you?"

She rose from her stool and began buttoning her coat. "My house. It's across the green and two doors down from the post office." She moved toward the door. "I've got to run now. I'll see you tomorrow."

With a tinkling of bells, she disappeared. Creighton looked down and noticed that she had not paid for her coffee. Unsure as to whether she had a running tab, he paid for both orders and slipped out the front door. The novelty of the Rolls Royce had apparently worn off, for the crowd had dispersed, except for Freddie, who was now sweeping the sidewalk.

Creighton walked around the corner and secured a room with Mrs. Patterson. His accommodations settled, he set out on his next mission. He rounded the corner, made his way across the green, and entered Schutt's Book Nook. Twenty minutes later, he emerged with a large headache, the wrong change, and a copy of Marjorie McClelland's *Death in Denmark*.

TWO

CREIGHTON AWOKE THE NEXT morning to the song of sparrows outside his bedroom window. Lying atop the covers, listening to their chattering, he became slowly aware of clinking noises emanating from the kitchen below. Gingerly, Creighton turned his head to the left and, through partially closed eyelids, glanced at the clock on the night table. Seven thirty.

He sat up, knocking the copy of *Death in Denmark* from his chest and onto the floor. Staggering into the adjoining bathroom, he inspected his reflection in the mirrored medicine cabinet. What a sight! Dark circles underscored his piercing blue eyes and yesterday's clothes hung limply about his tall frame. He splashed his face with cold water and cursed his own stupidity. His head throbbed and eyeballs ached—byproducts of either exhaustion or the bottle of port he had drunk the night before. Whatever the cause of his discomfort, a strong, hot cup of coffee would doubtlessly improve his current situation, so he donned his shoes and wended his way downstairs.

Mrs. Patterson was an elderly, pink-faced woman who was constantly in a flurry of activity. She reminded Creighton of a small bird, flitting from one place to the next, and her plump torso, carried along by a set of short, spindly legs, heightened her avian appearance. She was in the kitchen, pouring batter upon a waffle iron when Creighton entered.

"Oh! Mr. Ashcroft, I didn't expect you to be up and about so early. If you'll just wait in the dining room, I'll bring in your breakfast."

"Please, call me Creighton." He examined the kitchen and noticed a small table to his right; upon it rested a teapot and a single place setting. "If you're having breakfast here, why don't I just grab a plate and join you?"

"But the dining room is more formal. And I have the family china in there."

"Nonsense! There are only two of us in this house. Why should we both eat alone?" He glanced at the waffle iron. "And from what I can smell of those waffles, they don't need the further embellishment of fine china."

Mrs. Patterson's pink complexion grew rosier. "Well," she agreed reluctantly, "if you insist." She directed him in locating the contents of a second place setting while she retrieved a platter of waffles from the warm oven and added the contents of the iron to the top of the pile.

Creighton relieved her of the steaming dish, and placed it on the table with a gallant "Allow me," before helping her into her chair and placing a napkin in her lap. Having settled into the chair across from her, he poured tea into both of their cups.

Mrs. Patterson giggled girlishly and placed a waffle on each of their plates. "Did you sleep well?"

"Yes, I did." It wasn't a lie, for his sleep had been peaceful, if short-lived.

"Are you certain?"

"Yes. The room was quite comfortable." Realizing his disheveled appearance belied his words, he quickly added, "I didn't get to bed until quite late, but that was through my own shortcomings, not yours."

She nodded. There was a brief silence wherein they both ate their breakfast. The waffles were light and delicious, and Creighton made the point of saying so.

"Thank you." Then, as if the two subjects had anything to do with each other, she asked, "So what are your plans for today?"

"I'm to meet Miss McClelland at noon. She's asked me to assist her with her book."

Mrs. Patterson was intrigued. "Are you a writer?"

Creighton shook his head. "No. Just an avid reader."

"You've read her books, then?"

He grinned sheepishly. "Actually, I put myself in quite a spot. I told her that I had read her latest novel."

Mrs. Patterson filled in the blank. "And you hadn't?"

"No. Not until last night."

"You read the *entire* book last night?"

It was his turn to blush. "Yes, well, I wanted to be prepared for our meeting today."

"What time did you finish?"

"About four this morning."

"So, that's why you look so tired."

"That, and I think I consumed a little too much of the wine and cheese my butler packed for me."

She sounded a hearty chuckle. "I'm sorry, Mr. Ash—I mean, Creighton. I don't mean to laugh, but it never ceases to amaze me how even the most sensible men will do silly things to impress a woman."

"Yes, well, this is certainly the silliest thing I've ever done."

She flashed him a sympathetic smile and pushed the last waffle onto his plate. "Marjorie *is* a lovely girl. I've known her since she was born. Practically helped to raise her."

"What about her parents?"

Mrs. Patterson poured more tea into their cups. "Her mother was an actress. Still is, actually. Her father was an English professor. He died seven years ago." She clicked her tongue. "What miscrossed stars brought those two together, I'll never know."

A flicker of a smile crossed Creighton's lips, for he had often wondered the same thing about his own parents.

"They were married only a year before Marjorie arrived. Lorena —Marjorie's mother—seemed happy at first, but obviously, a husband and baby didn't fit in with her dreams of an acting career. One day, while her husband took Marjorie for a stroll, she packed up all her things and left."

"Did she ever try to contact Marjorie?"

"No. Every now and then her name would appear in the papers— in a theatrical review or advertisement for a new play—but apart from that, it was as if she had disappeared off the face of the earth." They had both finished their breakfasts, and Mrs. Patterson pushed the empty plates to the unused portion of the table. "I used to take care of Marjorie while her father was at work. He never remarried, so there was no woman in the house. Mr. Patterson and I never had children, so I was delighted to help." She sighed. "Poor thing. It's very difficult for a child to be without a mother."

Creighton, remembering his own childhood, nodded somberly. "My mother passed away when I was eight." The memories of his mother were distant, faded, but they were more than Marjorie would ever have.

"And your father?" Mrs. Patterson asked quietly.

"Alive and well. He and my brother run the family business." His face hardened. "They're very much alike, my father and brother: shrewd, athletic, popular. I'm afraid I've always been a bit of a disappointment."

Mrs. Patterson placed her hand on his and patted it. "If your father's disappointed in *you*, then he's not as shrewd and intelligent as you claim."

Creighton smiled, weakly. "Thank you."

She removed her hand and returned the smile. "I'm glad you're spending the afternoon with Marjorie. She could use someone her own age to talk to. I think she's very lonely."

He recalled the cheerful girl he met in the drugstore. "She didn't seem lonesome to me."

She leaned back in her chair with an air of wisdom that comes only with age. "She hasn't realized it yet. She's been typing away at those books of hers, taking pride in the fact that she's earning her own keep. Don't get me wrong. She has a definite talent, and I think she should continue writing. But mark my words, one day she will stop, look around her, and realize that something is *missing*."

"So," she leaned forward and clasped her hands together, "why did you come to Ridgebury?"

Creighton recalled the day he decided to leave New York. There he stood, in his Park Avenue apartment, alone on his birthday, watching the October rain as he took stock of his blessings: wealth, status, a successful job, and a bevy of society matrons who would be more than pleased to marry their daughters to him. Yet, despite these things, he was not fulfilled. Each passing day left him with the overwhelming feeling that life still had much more to offer.

"Why have I come to Ridgebury?" he repeated. "To find what *I've* been missing."

Creighton knocked upon Marjorie's door at five minutes to twelve, dressed in his finest navy blue suit and a black cashmere frock coat.

"Come in!" she shouted through the closed door. "It's open!"

Creighton planned on lecturing Marjorie on the dangers of leaving her door unlocked, but quickly decided against it. This was Ridgebury, not New York.

Entering the cottage, he found himself in the living room, which, despite the youth of its primary occupant, was decidedly old-fashioned, replete with overstuffed furniture and floral chintz. Creighton unbuttoned his coat and breathed a sigh of relief. City life had left him weary of the stark, bold design of modern furnishings. At last, here was true down-home comfort.

Marjorie was seated at a large secretary, upon which rested a rather dilapidated typewriter. She was busy, pecking away at the keys and, beyond granting him admittance, had not acknowledged Creighton's presence. Suddenly, she raised her right hand and beckoned him closer.

Creighton draped his coat over the arm of a plumpish love seat and obediently joined her. Upon approaching, he became conscious of a massive, mottled gray tomcat curled beside the typewriter. As he reached to stroke the animal, it greeted him with a mighty hiss.

"Sam!" Marjorie shouted. "That's no way to treat a guest. Go sit on the window ledge and behave yourself."

Sam jumped from his perch and skulked toward the window, his yellow eyes fixed upon the strange visitor.

Marjorie settled back to business. "I was transcribing my first paragraph. I tend to write things out longhand and then type them." She pointed toward the paper still in the carriage. "Here, have a look and tell me if it grabs your attention."

He bent down and placed his head adjacent to hers. However, it was not the paragraph that commanded his attention, but the fragrance of honeysuckle emanating from her hair. He inhaled deeply and allowed his eyes to wander in her direction. He thought her magnificent. She was wearing an ordinary daytime dress, but its mossy green color complemented her eyes beautifully, and the white collar made her peaches-and-cream complexion appear even rosier.

He wondered if he should place his hand on her shoulder, or attempt to steal a kiss, but thought the better of it. Removing himself from the temptation, he jerked upright and stepped back.

Marjorie's eyes grew wide. "Are you all right? You're very pale."

Away from the aroma of those alluring golden tresses, Creighton felt much better. "Yes, I'm fine."

She stood up and put the back of her hand to his forehead. "You're perspiring. Your head is hot."

He gently pushed her hand away. "I'm quite all right. Thank you." It would be difficult to maintain a professional relationship when his feelings for her were far from platonic. Perhaps it was best to be honest about his intentions. He would start by describing the feeling he had when he first saw her. "Tell me, have you ever had the sensation that you've been 'struck' by something?"

She cast her eyes upward as if in an effort to remember. A smile of recognition spread upon her face. "Oh, yes. I think I know what you mean."

It was an unexpected jolt. "You do?"

"Yes. Like the stomach flu. It comes on so suddenly, it seems to 'strike' you. I remember I had it once. Couldn't eat anything but clear broth and toast for a week."

He sighed and buried his face in his hands. *How had this become a discussion about intestinal disturbances?*

"I have some bicarbonate of soda," she offered, turning toward the kitchen.

Creighton blocked her path and guided her back to her seat. *Was she being deliberately obtuse?* "No. No, you've misunderstood. I mean like struck by a streetcar, or a subway, or a thunderbolt. Something horrible, or . . . wonderful." He knelt before her, a twinkle in his eye.

Her brow furrowed. "I think you mean a lightning bolt. Thunderbolt is a misnomer. Thunder is a sound. There's no such thing as a 'bolt' of sound."

Leave it to a writer to be so damned literal. His head was throbbing again, and he wondered if he might be having a small stroke. He stood up and walked to the window. Somehow, he must get her mind off work. "Why don't we take a walk? It's a beautiful day and I could do with some fresh air. Better yet, why don't I give you a tour of Kensington House? We can take our walk on the grounds."

She glanced reluctantly at the typewriter. "I shouldn't. I need to work on my book."

"We can work on your book after our walk. I read somewhere that Dashiell Hammett does his best writing after a day in the great outdoors."

"Does he, really?"

Creighton, hesitant to perpetuate this myth, merely nodded.

"All right," she sighed. "I'll go. Just wait here a minute."

She disappeared into another room and returned sporting the black coat and a jaunty green hat that coordinated perfectly with her dress. Creighton donned his coat and, with Sam trailing behind him, followed Marjorie out the door.

"No, Sam. You stay and watch the house," Marjorie ordered before taking off down the walk.

Creighton turned to grab the doorknob and noticed the cat, sitting a few inches beyond the threshold, glaring at him. He returned the contemptuous stare and, as if in a display of feline superiority, sounded a loud hiss of his own before shutting the door behind him.

THREE

Built in the wake of the American Revolution by a prominent Hartford family, Kensington House was a sedate three-story Georgian mansion settled amid a cluster of shade trees. Creighton navigated the Phantom down the gravel-lined drive and brought it to a halt before steps of the front portico.

"Here we are," he announced, helping Marjorie out of the car. "Home."

"Be it ever so humble." She shielded her eyes from the sun with a delicately gloved hand and took several steps back. Until now, she had only viewed Kensington House from the road. She knew it was big, but from this vantage point, the vastness of the house and the surrounding grounds was overwhelming.

In true Georgian fashion, the residence was a heavy, symmetrical, limestone structure with a central entrance flanked on either side by four double-hung windows. This pattern of eight windows repeated itself in the next two stories, the final set of eight having been dormered into a slate mansard roof.

But perhaps the most striking feature of the façade was a pair of Ionic columns that graced either side of the front entrance and sprouted forth from the stone portico like twin redwoods. These imposing monoliths, and the classic Greek pediment that topped them, supported the second floor balcony. Marjorie noticed that something had been etched into the frieze in Latin. She recited it under her breath and then chided herself for not having paid better attention during her days at Catholic school.

Overhearing her mutterings, Creighton read aloud: "'*Virtute, non astutia*.' It means 'By virtue, not craft.' I would say the founder of the house was explaining how he came into his fortune."

"Or advising future generations how to make theirs," quipped Marjorie as she mounted the stairs. "So, which one applies to your fortune? 'Virtute' or 'astutia'?"

Creighton placed his palms together and struck a saintly pose. "'Virtute,' naturally. I made my money 'by virtue' of being a wealthy man's son."

Marjorie sighed and shook her head.

Laughing, he plucked a gold key from his pocket and unlocked the front door. "As a writer I thought you'd appreciate some clever wordplay."

"I do. When you come up with some, let me know."

Creighton wrinkled his nose and ushered her into the elegant entrance hall. Constructed with rich wood paneling and parquet flooring, the room, like the façade, also demonstrated a strong sense of symmetry. A door at the opposite end of the corridor mirrored the one that they had entered. Three of the four doors that lined the wall to her right found their counterparts on the other side of the hall, the exception being the second to last door, which found its match in a wide staircase.

"Where should we start?" inquired Creighton.

Marjorie recalled the house's recent, and nefarious, past. "Upstairs, the second floor." She bit her lip and colored slightly.

Creighton raised an eyebrow and happily led her to the first room at the top of the stairs. It was an enormous room with one wall consisting almost entirely of windows. "This room was one of the main reasons I bought this house. Come here and see what I mean."

Marjorie followed him through a set of French doors, onto a balcony that spanned the back of the house. From here, one had a commanding vista of the meadows and trees that comprised the Kensington House property, as well as an aerial view of what was, once, the sunken formal garden. She stepped to the rail and, looking down, noticed the vestiges of blue tile peeking through the thick vegetation.

Shivering, she recalled the incident that had taken place just a few years earlier. "Is that a swimming pool?" she demanded.

"Yes."

Marjorie gasped. "Then *this* is the room!"

Creighton looked at her in wonder. "What room?"

"The room where *it* happened."

"What happened?"

She wondered how a man who spoke Latin could be so dense. "The *tragedy!*"

"What tragedy?"

Was it possible he didn't know? "The previous owners of this house were the Van Allens. Right after the stock market crash, Henry Van Allen killed himself." She pointed to the ground on which she stood. "He did so in *this very* house—by jumping from *this very* balcony!"

Creighton was stupefied. "Why didn't you mention this before now?"

"I thought you already knew."

"How on earth would I know that someone jumped off the balcony?"

"The real estate agent might have told you."

"Why would he do that? The real estate agent wants to *sell* the house. Telling me that someone died in the master bedroom is *not* a major selling point."

"There's no need to become angry with me," she scolded. "Even if I had told you about the suicide earlier, it wouldn't have done much good. You've already bought the house."

Creighton frowned and nodded as he gazed over the edge of the balcony. "You say he jumped from this balcony? That's awfully risky, isn't it? It's only about a thirty-foot drop. I'm not saying that I'm surprised he died, but the fall easily could have left him very much alive and with a few broken bones."

"He landed in the swimming pool," Marjorie elaborated.

"Then he drowned?"

"No. It was November. The pool had been drained."

Creighton glanced down at the blue tile. "Add another ten feet," he mumbled. "Yes, I can see where that might leave a mark."

"It did. He broke his neck." She headed back inside.

He followed and closed the French doors behind him. "Well, I don't care, I still plan to make this my master bedroom."

Marjorie was appalled. "But someone died in this room!"

"No, someone died in the swimming pool," he corrected.

"That's close enough for me."

"Marjorie, at the risk of sounding cold, people have to die *somewhere*—Henry Van Allen happened to have died *here*. In a house that's nearly a century and a half old, I'm certain that he's not the only person to have done so."

Logically speaking, he was probably correct, but his insolence galled her. "Don't you have any respect for the dead? A person who dies that way never rests—they wander the earth for all eternity. They call it 'limbo.'"

"If Mr. Van Allen is wandering the earth, it's because he's looking for a good glass of liquor. Poor man died before they repealed Prohibition."

"You mean to tell me you're not at all afraid of staying in this room? His ghostly apparition may visit you in the middle of the night. He may even try to lure you off the balcony."

"No, I'm not afraid. However, if you think Van Allen may put in an appearance, I shall leave a decanter of brandy on the balcony every night. As an offering, you see. A so-called 'spirit for the spirit.'" He flashed a toothy grin.

She sighed in exasperation and walked toward the door. "I've had enough of this. Let's go downstairs."

"Don't you want to see the rest of the bedrooms?" His eyes twinkled. "Or were you only interested in mine?"

Marjorie, turning a deep shade of pink, silently stormed out of the room.

She was on the first floor, standing in the room to the immediate right of the staircase when he caught up with her. "Ah, here you are," he exclaimed breathlessly. "This would be the library."

"Yes, I assumed that when I saw the shelves," she stated without the slightest glimpse in his direction.

The room was art nouveau in style, lined with walnut bookcases separated by intricately carved panels that stretched from floor to ceiling. On the wall opposite the door, amid the bookshelves, was a stunning stained-glass window depicting a riverbank surrounded by flowers, mountains, and trees. Marjorie walked toward it, admiring the arrows of colored light it sent darting about the room. "How lovely."

"It's one of those Tiffany windows that were so popular before the war."

She stood before the scene it portrayed. "The colors are so vivid; it's as if you're actually part of the scene."

"Hmm, it is serene, isn't it? But it doesn't really go with the rest of the house."

She turned, sharply, to look at him. "You mean you're going to get rid of it?"

"No," he reassured her, "I like it too much to do that. Besides, I would be foolish *not* to keep it. Not only would I have a devil of a time removing it without inflicting any damage, but now that Louis Tiffany is gone, the value of that jolly hunk of glass is only going to increase."

She shook her head. "It's odd, isn't it? How we only fully appreciate a piece of art after its creator is dead."

As if he were suddenly reminded of something, Creighton walked toward the corner to the left of the window and pointed a finger heavenward. "Speaking of odd, there's something in this room that's a bit unusual."

"Something more unusual than you?" she smirked.

He made an attempt at a laugh before giving in. "Yes. All right, I suppose I deserved that. Are you feeling better now?"

Marjorie, grinning from ear to ear, nodded vigorously.

"Good, then I shall rephrase the statement. There is something in this room, other than yours truly, that is unusual."

"Oh? What is it?"

"A lift."

Her eyes narrowed. "A what?"

"A lift," he repeated. He pushed on the corner panel with his elbow, thus generating a loud click. As Creighton backed away, Marjorie noticed that a portion of the wood had swung outward.

She peered inside the recess made by the open door. The hollow was about two-and-a-half feet high and approximately two feet in depth and width. A wooden board served as the bottom, but it was evident from the gaps around it that the space continued downward. There was a pulley mechanism on the right. "Oh, a dumbwaiter."

"Dumbwaiter. Lift. Have it your way. As expected, there's another one in the dining room, but it's not disguised as well as this one."

Marjorie pushed the door shut; the seams were barely discernable. "Whoever created this door did a wonderful job." She paused a moment. "I can understand why you said this was odd. One doesn't usually see a dumbwaiter in a library."

"No, one doesn't. Whoever requested that it be built must have spent quite a bit of time here. Or at least enough time to request refreshments be brought up from the kitchen."

"I can see why someone might spend their time here. It must be very nice," she said dreamily. "Sitting here by the fireplace on a cold, snowy day, curled up with a good book, light filtering through the tinted glass, and someone serving you tea or coffee . . ."

"Or hot chocolate with gobs of fresh whipped cream," added Creighton.

She snapped from her reverie and smiled at him. "I thought you would have suggested brandy."

He escorted her out of the library and an impish grin crossed his face. "No, don't you remember? The brandy was for the *bedroom*."

Damn him! As she felt her hands become clammy and her face grow gradually warmer, she wondered if there had ever before existed a man as bedeviling as Creighton Ashcroft.

Creighton and Marjorie, continuing their tour of Kensington House, viewed the remaining first floor rooms and then, via a back staircase, descended to the basement where they inspected the pantry, kitchen, and, a few steps beneath them, the wine cellar. With the perusal of this subterranean area complete, they departed through the kitchen door and climbed an exterior cement stairway that led back to ground level.

At the top of the steps, they encountered a wide gravel-lined driveway. "Is this the way we drove in?" Marjorie asked, disoriented.

"No," explained Creighton, "this is the service entrance. It lets out on the main road a few yards away from where we entered. It was positioned in such a way that it could only be seen from a few vantage points within the house; that way none of the residents or guests would be disturbed by the sight of a cart or lorry making a delivery."

He led her away from the driveway, onto an overgrown path that led to the back of the mansion. There they resumed their walk past the infamous swimming pool to a stone staircase that led to the gardens below. From the steps, Marjorie had an impressive view of the floral parterres, but it was now impossible to determine what shape they once took. The boxwood, still green, had broadened into unruly shrubs, and the planting beds were overgrown with tall, brown weeds that, though quashed by the winter frost, hung over the garden paths.

Creighton rushed ahead and, pushing the unwelcome growth aside, cleared a trail for Marjorie to follow. "I can hardly wait to restore this to its former glory. The only plants I've seen for the past thirteen years are window-ledge geraniums." He asked, over his shoulder, "Do you have a garden?"

"Yes, I have a small one in the backyard."

"Backyard banes?"

She laughed. "Oh, the book you mean? No, I don't usually grow anything that exotic, just the standard tomatoes, lettuce, and beans. Although, maybe you have an idea there. You never know when some digitalis might come in handy."

"Remind me never to have salad at your house," Creighton quipped. They had reached the end of the path, and were standing in a small clearing facing a narrow section of woods. To the right was a vast meadow. "We can cut through the trees," he pointed straight ahead, "to go to the stables and the orchards." He nodded to his right. "It's quicker than the route through the fields."

Marjorie, thankful that she had worn her low-heeled walking shoes, agreed, and they moved forward. The woods provided not only a shortcut, but a picturesque diversion; the canopy of bud-lined branches high above shone red in the afternoon sun and the forest floor was blanketed with dainty, purple blossoms.

"Oh!" exclaimed Marjorie. "Look at all the crocuses! My father always said they were a sure sign that spring was coming."

"From the number of them, it looks like spring's already here."

Unable to resist the charms of the delicate blooms, Marjorie stooped to gather a miniature nosegay. "They spread quickly. Plant one of these, and before you know it, your whole yard will be covered." As she crouched down, an odd rock formation a few feet away caused her to take a second glance. *How strange! That rock over there looks like a . . . My God! It is!*

She dropped the flowers from her hand, and opened her mouth as if to scream, but the only sound she could muster was a high-pitched squeal.

It was enough to summon Creighton to her side. "What's wrong?"

Marjorie, wide-eyed and ashen faced, pointed frantically at the object on the ground before them.

Creighton leaned down to examine it. "Oh, yes. That rock does look rather like a skull doesn't it?" He leaned downward and wiped away some of the surrounding soil before taking a giant leap backward.

"What is it?"

"I think it *is* a skull."

Marjorie opened her mouth again. This time the scream was clearly audible.

"Now, now," reasoned Creighton. "We mustn't panic. We'll call the police. They'll know what to do." He placed a consoling arm around Marjorie's shoulder. "Are you all right?"

She nodded, then abruptly recoiled at his touch.

"What's the matter?" he asked, moving toward her.

She snatched a heavy stick from the ground and wielded it like a baseball bat. "Don't come any closer!" she shrieked.

Creighton was bewildered. "What?"

"Don't act so innocent with me!"

"You think *I'm* responsible for this?" he pointed at the bony remains. "That's impossible. It—it flies in the face of logic. How could I possibly have buried this person when I arrived here only yesterday?"

"I don't know how and I don't know why," she stammered. "But it seems strange that nothing *ever* happens in Ridgebury, then you come along, and 'poof!' we find part of a skeleton!"

"Coincidence. Sheer coincidence."

"Oh really?" she snorted.

"Yes, really. And what do you mean 'nothing ever happens in Ridgebury'?" He hiked his thumb in the direction of the house. "A man jumped to his death from *that* balcony. I would call that *something.*"

"That's different."

"Different? I tend to think Mr. Van Allen might disagree with you."

She hoisted the stick higher. "See! There's that cavalier attitude toward death again. You're enjoying this. It's all part of your sick game. You might not have murdered this person, but you knew his skeleton was here and you wanted me to find it. It was *your* idea to come here today, and it was *your* idea to take a shortcut through the trees. You even slipped me a hint upstairs, when you said you were certain that Van Allen wasn't the only person to die in the house."

"I swear to you, I never knew this was here. And, as for murder—aren't you jumping to conclusions? For all we know, this could simply be some sort of Indian burial ground."

"Oh, don't give me that story! If it were an Indian burial ground, someone would have found the body when these trees were planted. Besides, the skull has a big hole in the side of it, like . . . like . . . someone . . ."

Creighton, eyeing Marjorie and her weapon, completed the sentence. "Hit it with a big stick?"

She gasped. "Are you accusing *me?*"

"Accusing? No. I'm just showing you how silly you're being. If anything, I should be suspicious of you. *You* have lived here all your life, and, unlike *me*, could have been present when this person was killed. *You* write mystery novels, and, therefore are well versed in the various ways in which to do away with someone. *You* have a morbid curiosity, which manifested itself in your interest in the site of Mr. Van Allen's demise. And, might I say, of the two of us, *you* are the one with violent tendencies."

Her jaw dropped in disbelief. "Violent tendencies?"

"Correct me if I'm wrong, but I'm not the one who looks like Babe Ruth approaching the batter's box."

"But I couldn't have done it!"

"Oh? Why not?"

"Because I *know* I didn't, that's why."

"Yes . . . that's a ringing endorsement." He held his head. "This whole conversation is ridiculous. You're obviously unhinged right now. Let's just go and call the police."

She took a step backward. "You go in the house, I'll wait here."

"I can't call from the house," he explained. "I don't have a phone yet. We'll have to drive back to town and call from there."

"What do you mean 'we'? I'm not getting in the car with you."

"But you drove here with me."

"That was before all this happened," she explained.

Creighton was tired of arguing. "Fine, stay here then. But, here's some food for thought. Let's assume that this person was murdered. Now, if *I'm* telling the truth and *I* didn't kill that person, and *you* didn't kill that person . . . that would mean that someone else *did*."

She huffed impatiently. "That's obvious."

"Well, that person might be some vagrant who took up residence while the house was vacant. A vagrant who may very well still be lurking about the grounds." He turned around and trotted off toward the garden.

Marjorie scanned the area nervously. The woods would provide wonderful cover for any number of dangerous villains. "All right," she shouted. "I'll go with you. But I'm bringing my stick, and if you so much as look at me funny, so help me, I'll let you have it."

Creighton stopped walking and whirled about to face her. "Miss McClelland," he stated, as if suspicion of murder had brought their relationship back to a last-name basis, "I am in earnest when I tell you that I have no desire to touch you." He pulled a face and added quickly, "At least, not with the intention to inflict bodily harm."

Satisfied with this proclamation, he turned on one heel and the two of them marched, single file, back to the Phantom.

FOUR

MARJORIE, HER FEET RESTING on a hassock and her shoulders covered by a hand-crocheted afghan, was sitting in the back sewing room of Mrs. Patterson's boarding house, suffering through the tongue lashings of the establishment's proprietress.

"I still can't believe you threatened that poor young man!" exclaimed Mrs. Patterson as she poured tea from a heavy stoneware pot.

Creighton had accompanied the police to Kensington House to show them the location of the skull, and Marjorie, left behind to await questioning, now wished that she had gone with them. "Mrs. Patterson," she sighed, "I already told you I would apologize to him. I admit that I was wrong. It's obvious that he had nothing to do with the body. But I was frightened and I panicked. You might have done the same thing if you were in my place."

"But he's so nice," she persisted, as she handed Marjorie a cup of the steaming beverage. "How could you suspect him of anything so terrible?"

"'Nice' doesn't enter into it. Don't you read the papers? That's exactly what Leopold and Loeb's neighbors said about them. 'They're such nice boys! They wouldn't hurt a fly!'"

Mrs. Patterson dismissed this comment. "Oh, but those two were such odd-looking fellows," she shot Marjorie a sideways glance, "whereas Creighton is rather handsome."

Marjorie stirred some sugar into her tea and reflected upon this comment. She had never really taken note of Creighton's appearance, but she supposed he was good-looking, in a well-bred sort of way. He was tall, lean, and ever so polished, from his neatly trimmed chestnut hair to his shiny black shoes. However, possibly his greatest assets were those pale, cerulean eyes; she tried not to think of them as she begged the question. "Is he really? I hadn't noticed."

Seated in a cushioned armchair at a right angle to Marjorie's, Mrs. Patterson replied, "No, of course you haven't noticed. You're so busy writing descriptions of dead men that you don't pay attention to the live ones."

Marjorie took exception to this comment. She was about to argue when they were interrupted by the sound of car doors slamming. Mrs. Patterson sprang from her chair, and as if she were hosting an intimate social gathering rather than a police investigation, declared, "That must be Creighton and the other men. I'll go fix some coffee and sandwiches." She nervously smoothed her dress and hair and then scurried off toward the kitchen, leaving Marjorie alone with her thoughts.

It was true, Marjorie realized. She had treated Creighton miserably. He had shown her nothing but kindness since his arrival. He had volunteered to help her with her book, although he had work to do in preparing his new home. He had given her a tour of Kensington House, despite the fact that he had been suffering from the stomach flu. And though he had enjoyed teasing her, he had never been anything less than a gentleman the whole time they were together. And how did she repay him? She nearly clubbed him to death.

She cringed as she pictured herself brandishing the tree limb and wondered if a verbal apology were sufficient for an offense of such magnitude. Perhaps a grander gesture was necessary. She could, she thought, express her regret in a letter. But she dismissed this idea as too formal. She could acknowledge him in her next book. But that was several months away. She could bake him a pie or cake. But he might not like sweets. She could sire out Sam and give him one of the kittens—but the offspring might inherit its father's personality.

"There must be something I can do to make it up to him," she stated aloud as she placed her untouched cup of tea on the small table next to her. Trying to formulate a plan, she rested her head against the back of the chair and closed her eyes. When she opened them again, minutes later, all thoughts of Creighton Ashcroft rapidly dissolved.

There had emerged, in the sewing room doorway, the figure of a man. He was in his thirties, of average height and build, but the rest of him was far from ordinary. He was, in fact, what one might call movie-star handsome. Lush, undulating waves of dark hair crowned a pleasing countenance: cleft chin, classic nose, perfectly formed lips, and soulful, chocolate eyes lined by thick, sensuous lashes.

Marjorie suddenly learned what it meant to be rooted to the spot, for all she could do was stare, her mouth agape, as he entered the room and sauntered toward her. With a sympathetic smile, he introduced himself, "Detective Robert Jameson, Hartford County Police.

I'm in charge of the investigation regarding the body you found in the woods." He leaned downward and offered her his right hand, but Marjorie, intently studying his face, was too preoccupied to notice.

He drew his hand back and perched on the edge of the chair previously occupied by Mrs. Patterson. "I know you've had a terrible shock, but I do need to ask you some questions," he retrieved a pencil from his jacket pocket and poised it over the notebook he had brought in with him. "First, the formalities. Let's start with your name and address."

Marjorie did not answer; the information he wanted was there, in the forefront of her memory, but she was unable to impart these facts verbally, as if the power to formulate words had temporarily escaped her.

"You're still upset aren't you?" he asked rhetorically while imparting a look of pity. "I'll just go and let you rest a little while longer."

She bolted upright in her chair, but still, she could not utter a sound.

"I'll send Officer Noonan in later."

She wanted to scream, *No! No, don't go! I don't want Officer Noonan! I want you!*

But he was already halfway out the door, and as soon as he was no longer visible, her voice, though weak, miraculously reappeared. "Wait!" she exclaimed breathlessly, "Come back! I'll tell you my name! It's . . . it's Marjorie . . ." Realizing her opportunity had passed, she flopped, angrily, back in her chair and sighed, "Marjorie . . . the village idiot!"

*   *   *

After a few moments of solitude, Marjorie perceived the sound of men congregating in the front parlor. Her inquisitive nature taking hold, she pushed her chair closer to the door and settled in to listen to the police encounter that, by all indications, was guaranteed to be less pleasant than hers.

The gruff voice of Officer Noonan spoke first. "Okay Mr. Ashcroft, I need to fill out my report, so let's just make sure I have all my facts straight. I have your last name as A-s-h-c-r-o-f-t," he spelled the surname aloud.

"Correct," replied Creighton.

"And your first name is spelled C-r-a-y-t-o-n."

"No," interceded the Englishman, "It's C-r-e-i-g-h-t-o-n."

Noonan had gotten lost after the first three letters, "C-r-e-y?"

"No, not 'y,' 'i,'" he repeated the spelling of his name, this time more slowly.

Noonan recited the letters after him, "e . . . i . . . g," he paused, "'G'?"

"G," confirmed Mr. Ashcroft.

"Humph, go figure," mused the detective. "What type of name is that anyway? German?"

"Yes," he answered facetiously, "I'm a nephew of the Kaiser."

Marjorie, relieved that Creighton had found a new soul to torment, tried hard to suppress a giggle.

Noonan, on the other hand, was unfazed. "Oh, I thought so. You don't sound like you're from around here." He continued with the questions. "So, Cretin, your address is Kensington House?"

"That's Creighton," he corrected, "and yes, that's my address, but I'm staying here until I move in."

"So if we wanted to contact you we would call here."

"Yes."

"Got the number, Cretin?"

"Creighton," he corrected more adamantly, "and yes, I do." He recited the number cautiously so that the policeman could write it down.

"You got a daytime number I can call you at? You know, a telephone at the job."

"No."

"You don't have a phone?"

"No, I don't have a job."

"Don't tell me you were laid off, too."

"No, I wasn't laid off."

"Then, what are you retired? I mean, how old are you, Cretin? Thirty-one? Thirty-two?"

"Thirty-four," Creighton responded. "Is this essential to the investigation?"

Noonan didn't answer, but remarked to the other officer in the room, "Get a load of this, Palutzky! He's thirty-four, retired, and he owns that great big house we were just at."

Marjorie flinched at Noonan's description of Creighton. He had stated the facts simply, without embellishment, but there was a sharp edge in his tone. It was an edge honed by years of economic hardship, an edge that Marjorie had heard before in descriptions of the wealthy. If the Depression had affected class distinctions in any way, it was only to broaden the dichotomy between them: the rich remained rich while the poor became poorer. Certainly, there were stories of people who fell from riches to rags, but those with sense understood that "rags" was just a euphemism; there were no former millionaires to be found waiting in bread lines, experiencing malnutrition, or suffering from dust pneumonia.

Of course, Marjorie had not experienced any of these demons either, but this did not mean that the town of Ridgebury had remained unscathed. In the months following the crash, several local families had left town; some moved in with relatives, others traveled in search of greener pastures—though Marjorie was unsure as to where those greener pastures may lie. Men took any odd job to help feed their families, from mowing lawns to patching roofs. Women took in laundry or sewing. Families started growing more of their own food, and neighborhood gardens had expanded, in some cases to encompass nearly the entire backyard. Some citizens had even begun raising chickens, and though currency was still the preferred method of payment, it was not unusual to overhear neighbors bartering a basket of beans for a fresh young roasting hen and a dozen eggs.

The Depression had left no one untouched. With book sales plummeting to an unprecedented low, the high and mighty Mr. Schutt had been forced to convert part of his shop into a library, where, for a nickel, a person could borrow a book for one week. And Mrs. Patterson, out of a need to supplement her savings, was spending her golden years lodging total strangers. Even Marjorie, who considered herself very lucky, knew that less than a decade earlier, her books, those small volumes over which she agonized, would have earned seven times what they did now.

No, it was little wonder to Marjorie that Officer Noonan harbored bitterness toward Creighton Ashcroft. For Creighton, with his luxurious mansion, fancy automobile, and finely tailored suits, represented those vanished halcyon years of the twenties: that decade of prosperity and growth, easy money and fast living; that decade for which they were now paying dearly.

Noonan's bitterness was no surprise, but it was irritating. Irritating because it was grossly unfair: Creighton could not be held responsible for the world's financial plight. And yet, had she not fallen prey to this prejudice herself? She wondered how much of her suspicion at Kensington House had been spurred by envy of his wealthy status and mistrust of the era he symbolized. Was this also why she stubbornly refused to view him as anything other than an assistant? Disturbed by this thought, she shut her eyes tightly, as if to squeeze the idea out of her head.

In the other room, the voice of Creighton rose above the chuckles and mutterings of the two policemen. "I'm so glad to have provided entertainment for you gentlemen, but can we please get this over with?"

Noonan sounded almost apologetic, "Sorry, Cretin."

He shouted it this time, "That's Creighton! Cray-ton," he sounded it out syllabically. "A 'cretin' is a mentally retarded person of diminutive size."

She heard footsteps moving toward the front parlor and then the voice of Detective Jameson. "Are you gentlemen finished harassing Mr. Ashcroft?"

Noonan attempted to defend himself. "We're not harassing him. The guy's a crackpot."

"If I held that against everyone, you'd be out of a job," Jameson retorted. "Palutzky, go in the kitchen and get yourself some coffee. Noonan, go and question the girl. I'll take over here."

At this reference to her, Marjorie jumped from her seat, returned the chair to its former position, fell back into it and tried to assume an air of casual indifference.

Noonan, a short, stocky, red-faced man in his mid-forties, entered a few moments later. He plopped into the chair adjacent to Marjorie's and after obtaining her name, address and telephone number, asked, "So what's your story?"

"My story?" she repeated. "Oh. How I found the body. Where do I begin?"

"Try the beginning," Noonan retorted.

"Oh, okay. Let's see . . . well, I met Creighton yesterday in the drugstore, the Ridgebury Drugstore. It's around the corner from here and it faces the green. I always go there for coffee, and I went there yesterday and Creighton was there drinking coffee too, which I thought was odd, because he's English, and I thought they only drink tea. But apparently, I was wrong because he was drinking coffee. So I got my cup of coffee and we started talking and it seems that he's a big fan of my books," she leaned closer to him. "I'm a mystery writer. You know, detective novels. Oh, but don't worry, the policemen in my novels are very intelligent. Maybe you've read my books. *Death in Denmark, Murder in Morocco*? Anyway, Creighton is a big fan and he offered to help me with my next book, *Fear in Finland*. It's supposed to be published this summer, but I'm having a terrible time with it. So Creighton met me at my house today to help me with the writing, but I had writer's block and he had the stomach flu, so we decided to take a walk, thinking that the fresh air would make him feel better and maybe help me to write, because that's what Dashiell Hammett does. You know Dashiell Hammett, don't you? He wrote *The Dain Curse* and *The Maltese Falcon*. Did you read them? Oh, and he wrote *The*

Thin Man, which they made into a movie. Did you see the movie? Myrna Loy was in it. I love Myrna Loy . . ."

Noonan silently made his way to the doorway, where he paused, leaned into the hallway and shouted, "Palutzky! We got another crackpot!"

FIVE

CREIGHTON SPENT ANOTHER SLEEPLESS night under the Patterson roof. His restlessness was caused by fear, not of ghosts or of corpses, but of falling property values. In the twenty-four hours since he purchased his new home, he had learned of two deaths associated with the estate, and he knew that this could only have a negative effect on his investment. He prayed that no other bodies would be found as the police excavated the woods, for with his luck, he half expected to learn that Kensington House had once been used as a potter's field.

As daylight began trickling in through his bedroom window, Creighton was flooded with an overwhelming sense of relief—the sunrise marked the final minutes of a darkness that had seemed to last for an eternity. As if rejuvenated by the sunshine, he sprang from his bed, went about his morning ablutions, and hearing noises from downstairs, decided to join Mrs. Patterson for breakfast.

He entered the kitchen to find the kindly woman standing over the stove, stirring the contents of a large pot. "Good morning," she cried cheerfully. "I'm making oatmeal for breakfast."

Creighton had experienced an aversion to oatmeal since his child-hood, but he tried to smile enthusiastically, "Mmm. Yummy."

Mrs. Patterson waved a hand in the direction of the breakfast table, "Oh, before I forget, there's a note for you."

He looked down at his place setting. Propped against his teacup was an envelope upon the front of which had been written, *To C.A.* "When did this come?" he inquired.

Mrs. Patterson shook her head, "I don't know. It was lying on the floor by the front door this morning, as if someone had pushed it through the mail slot."

He tore open the flap of the envelope and removed its contents. The note, written in neat, cursive letters, read:

Ashy,
Need to discuss case with you. Please come to my house
ASAP.

M^2

M²? Oh, yes, Marjorie McClelland. He chuckled to himself; Marjorie had certainly inherited her mother's flair for the dramatic. He won-dered if she shouldn't be writing plays rather than novels, since she had, quite adeptly, made yesterday's events sound like a cloak and dagger affair. She had even gone to the trouble to provide them both with code names, although Creighton took umbrage at his. Wasn't it bad enough that he had argued with Officer Noonan about his first name? Did she have to desecrate his last name as well?

He wondered if he should take the issue up with her. It was, after all, rather presumptuous of her to assign him a nickname. It was even more presumptuous to demand that he meet her at her house, particularly after she had threatened to bludgeon him to death.

I won't meet her today, he thought. *That will teach her a lesson!*

However, as time passed, and he consumed his thick clumps of oatmeal, his resolve weakened. As much as he hated to admit it, he needed to see her more than she needed to see him. Despite his reluctance, he knew that he would be knocking upon her door a few minutes later.

No, he acknowledged, it was futile to resist. She could summon him to the gates of hell with a dog whistle, and he would still obediently follow.

As predicted, twenty minutes after breakfast found him on Marjorie's front stoop, waiting to gain admittance.

Unlike the previous day, she greeted him at the door. "Hi. I'm glad you're here. I wasn't sure if you'd come."

She was resplendent in a long, slim, crimson skirt and matching jacket with peplum, and Creighton wondered if it might not be the best dress in her closet. Her lips and nails had been painted to match the color of her suit, and upon her head nested a fashionable, "Robin Hood" hat into whose band had been tucked a scarlet feather.

"Aha! The notorious 'Lady in Red,'" Creighton commented. "No wonder Dillinger met his end."

Giggling, she ushered him inside. "Here. Let me take your coat."

As Marjorie manipulated the garment onto a wooden hanger, Creighton took note of a small girl sitting on the loveseat in the living room. She was petite and fair-skinned, with dark, wavy hair and brown eyes that were doe-like in their innocence. From her size, he might have estimated her to be about four years old, but facially she appeared older. On her lap was a doll in a tattered dress.

Creighton leaned downward in an attempt to make his height seem less intimidating, "Hello, there. My name's Creighton. What's yours?"

The girl merely stared through him as if he were invisible. And, Marjorie, busy trying to find space for Creighton's coat in the closet by the front door, was of no assistance.

He tried on his most dazzling smile. "That's a very pretty baby you have there. She looks like you."

The girl still said nothing, but this time thrust her tongue in Creighton's direction.

Creighton's smile turned to a smirk. In a world full of foolish inconsistencies, the effect of the Ashcroft charm was annoyingly predictable. Regardless of whom he plied it on, be it young women, small children, or household pets, they all reacted with something akin to contempt.

The little girl, fed up with Creighton's conversational shortcomings, rose from her spot on the sofa, and with her doll trailing on the ground behind her, shuffled to the front door.

Having temporarily tamed the clutter of the coat closet, Marjorie spotted her as she made her exit. "Are you leaving now?"

Without looking up, the child nodded her reply.

"All right, then. I'll watch you walk home." She followed the girl to the front door and, after shouting her goodbye, waited there for approximately a minute before she closed it and joined Creighton in the living room.

"Delightful child," he remarked.

"Her name's Mary. She lives two doors down the block. She comes and visits every now and then. Sometimes she has breakfast with me, other times she just comes to play with Sam."

He wanted to comment on the similarities in disposition between Sam and the little girl, but instead he asked, "Her parents let her wander about?"

"Parent in the singular," she corrected. "Her mother passed away a couple of years ago and her father . . ." She bent her elbow in that universal gesture that conveyed alcoholism. "Most of the time he's passed out on the couch."

"Doesn't he have a job?"

"No, he lost that about the same time he lost his wife. It's a shame. He's really a good man."

They observed a moment of silence before Marjorie spoke again. "Please, sit down. Can I get you anything? Coffee? Tea?"

He marveled at her sudden attentiveness; yesterday he might have coughed to death before she offered him a lozenge. "No, thank you," he replied as he positioned himself in the seat vacated by Mary.

As she sat at the other end of the small sofa, her face colored slightly. "I want to apologize for my behavior yesterday. I'm afraid I wasn't very nice to you."

Oh, he thought, *so that's why she's being so courteous. She feels guilty. That explains the outfit, too. She's using her feminine wiles to gain my forgiveness.*

"I've never acted that way before," she continued, "I just don't know what came over me. Please say you'll forgive me." She looked at him with eyes that were wide and pleading.

Should he let her off the hook so quickly? It might be fun to drag out this little scene. He could even try a bit of extortion: *I'll forgive you if you kiss me* or *I'll think about it over dinner.*

She didn't give him the opportunity. Accepting his silence as a form of acquiescence, she grabbed his arm and exclaimed, "Oh, good! I'm so glad we can be friends again. And now that that's over with, I have a proposition for you."

"Proposition?" His curiosity was piqued.

"Yes, I was up all last night thinking about it. You know it's not often that people like us have a dead body dropped in our laps."

"People like us." His voice was quizzical.

"Yes, literary people. I'm a writer and you're an editor."

"An editor? Have I been promoted?"

"Well, what would you call yourself?"

A sucker, a patsy, a chump . . . "I don't know. So many other words come to mind." He shook his head, "Don't bother . . . just continue."

"I was thinking that we should write a book about our discovery in the woods. You know, one of those 'true crime' works."

"A book? We only have enough information for a short story."

"Well of course that's all we have *now*," she explained testily, "but we'll find out more as time goes on."

"And how do you suggest we do that?"

"We work with the police, tag along on their investigation."

"And what if they find that this person died of old age?"

"Then I go back to writing *Fear in Finland*, and you go back to being my editor. But if this ends up being a big story, we could wind up as co-authors of a best seller. Just think of it! Fame! Fortune!"

He shot her a doubtful glance.

"Okay," she said, "so those aren't incentives for you. But they are for me, and whether you decide to join me or not, I'm still doing it."

He pondered the situation and had to admit it was convenient. Long days of investigating combined with long nights of writing, doubtlessly, would bring them closer together. "All right," he sighed, "I'll do it."

As Marjorie let out a whoop of joy, Creighton calmly cupped his hand around his ear and squinted as if he were listening for something. Looking at him as if he were quite mad, she inquired, "What's wrong?"

He brought his hand back to his lap. "Nothing. Nothing. I just thought I heard a dog whistle."

SIX

THEY DROVE TO THE one-room structure that served as headquarters for the local division of the Hartford County Police. The station, located at an isolated site seven miles from the Ridgebury village center, functioned as the outpost of law enforcement for both Ridgebury and the neighboring community of Exeter.

After parking in the unpaved lot next door, they maneuvered their way through the entrance of the cabin. Inside, they found Detective Jameson alone in the squad room, poring over paperwork at an aged wooden desk. At the sound of their entrance, he looked up. "Mr. Ashcroft," he stated as if they had been lifelong friends, "How are you?" He rose from his seat and met Creighton halfway between the door and the desk.

"I'm all right," he replied as they shook hands. "At least I'm a sight better than our skinny friend back at the house."

Jameson chuckled, "Aren't we all?"

Creighton remembered his manners. "I'm not sure if you met yesterday," he began, "but this is . . ." He gestured to his left, believing that Marjorie had been standing beside him. Glancing around in search of her, he noticed that she had not followed him into the room, but had, instead, draped herself rather seductively in the doorway. She was leaning on the interior of the frame, with her right forearm extended above her head. Her right leg was crossed over the left and poised to show a bit of a curvaceous ankle, and her left hand was planted firmly on one hip.

Creighton shook his head; he should have known better than to think that she had dressed that way to impress him. "The young lady acting as a doorstop is Miss McClelland."

She cast a nasty look in Creighton's direction and then, turning her attention toward Jameson, pasted on a radiant smile.

The detective, of course, was drawn to her like a moth to a flame. Walking toward her, he exclaimed, "Miss McClelland. I trust you're feeling better today." He took her hands in his. "You certainly look wonderful."

"Thank you. Yes, I am feeling better, and I owe it all to you," she said fawningly.

"Me?"

"Yes, you. Yesterday you granted me those few extra minutes of rest, and it ended up that they were exactly what I needed to pull myself together."

"You mean to pull together your plan," Creighton muttered under his breath.

Marjorie turned to face him. "What?"

Creighton smiled, innocently. "I said it's silly for us to *stand*," he cleared his throat. "May we sit down?"

The detective apologized. "Oh, yes. I'm sorry. How rude of me." He escorted Marjorie to the chair facing his desk and then resumed the position he had been in before they had arrived. Creighton, finding no other seats in the immediate area, stood with his back against the wall directly behind Marjorie.

As befitted a rural building used solely by men, the station was reminiscent of a hunting lodge, with wainscot paneling, gun racks, and taxidermist's animals. On the wall upon which Creighton leaned had been mounted the head of a large, antlered deer. He immediately felt a sense of empathy for the creature, as if they had somehow befallen the same fate. He stared into one of its lifeless glass eyes and whispered, "Lost your head over a woman, too, eh?"

Marjorie and Jameson, meanwhile, were absorbed in each other, chatting away as if in some secluded bistro. Creighton, left to watch the nauseating scene, might as well have been invisible. He wondered if he shouldn't just hop in his car and drive away, leaving her here with her schemes, her books, and her beloved detective. However, as he fingered the car keys in his coat pocket, he felt a tiny spark, fueled by spite and sheer determination, ignite within his chest. *No*, he thought, firmly setting his jaw, *I'm not giving up that easily. If it's a game she wants, it's a game she'll get!*

"As much as I hate to break up your coffee klatch, Marjorie," Creighton spoke up, "aren't we going to tell the detective about our project?"

She seemed startled, as if she had forgotten that he was still there. "Oh . . . oh, yes. Of course."

Creighton moved closer to Marjorie and placed his hands on the back of her chair. "You may not know it, Detective, but our Marjorie here is a very talented mystery novelist," at this compliment, the young woman blushed. "And she has appointed me as her editor. Naturally, as so-called 'literary people,' we are always looking for new ideas for novels; we think that the body we found in the woods would be an interesting subject for our next book."

Jameson looked puzzled. "What does this have to do with me?"

"Well," Creighton explained, "You see, it's a nonfiction work, so we would need all the details surrounding the case."

"So you want me to check in with you and tell you how the case is progressing."

"More than that," Marjorie replied. "I would need physical descriptions of witnesses and snippets of actual dialogue. Therefore it would probably be more helpful if we joined you on your investigation."

Jameson shook his head. "I don't know how the department would feel about civilians interfering with police work."

"We won't interfere," declared Creighton. "We'll just observe."

Marjorie leaned across the detective's desk. "And you would be the main character of the book."

Creighton was caught off-guard. *Main character of the book? Had she planned this all along? Or was she just using it as a ploy to convince the policeman to cooperate?*

The detective was equally bewildered. "Main character?"

"Yes," interjected Creighton, "that was my idea." He heard a sharp intake of breath come from the chair in front of him. "Marjorie's original idea was to fictionalize the whole account; she said she needed a dashing detective as the central character and wasn't sure you fit the bill. I told her I thought you'd be fine as the lead, but she was afraid that you wouldn't be attractive to readers, said you were too dull."

"That's not true!" shouted Marjorie as she whirled about in her seat, her eyes tiny daggers.

"Marjorie, you needn't be embarrassed. Detective Jameson doesn't strike me as the type who is easily offended. Are you offended, Detective?"

"No."

"See that? He's not offended. So you needn't be embarrassed," Creighton offered in a comforting tone, "even if you did say that he lacked charisma and that his ears were too big."

Marjorie, her face as red as the ensemble she wore, was simmering by now. Creighton, trying hard to avert her icy stare, asked, "So, Detective, will you help us?"

"Okay," he agreed reluctantly, "I suppose we can try it for a couple of days and see how it works out. But I have to warn you, police work isn't easy, and sometimes it isn't pretty, either. And it might just be that after all our hard work, you may not have a story."

"We understand that. But nothing ventured, nothing gained," Creighton philosophized. "Right, Marjorie, old girl?" He smiled down at her.

She returned his smile with an artificial one of her own. "Right, Creighton, old bean," she replied through clenched teeth.

"Good, as long as we're all clear on that," responded Jameson. "Just give me a minute to call the medical examiner, and then I'll let you in on our findings."

"We'll give you some privacy. Let us know when you're done." He took Marjorie by the arm and led her to an unobtrusive spot by the front door.

As soon as Jameson was no longer watching them, Marjorie struggled free from Creighton's grasp. "What do you think you're doing? It was my idea to write the book from Jameson's point of view."

"Yes. And it was very kind of you to discuss it with your editor first," he said facetiously.

"Poetic license," she replied smugly.

"No, predatory nature. You didn't tell me of your intention to place Jameson as the protagonist because it would have given away your plan."

"Given away my plan? You already knew that I was writing a book."

"Writing the book is a means to an end; the end is to cozy up to Detective Jameson. And you're using me as some demented version of Cupid!"

She raised an eyebrow, "Cupid?"

"Yes, Cupid. You didn't have enough nerve to come here yourself; it would have been obvious what you were up to. So you dragged me along to introduce the two of you, open up the conversation, bring you both together," he emphasized this last action with a clap of his hands. "Well, I'm telling you here and now, I don't want any part of it!"

"So you're not going to help me with my book."

"I'll help you with your book, but I will *not* help you to play a spider to Detective Jameson's defenseless housefly."

"Will you stop it? You make me sound like a lioness out on the hunt. Besides," she added, self-importantly, "how is it any of your business what I do with Detective Jameson?"

"It isn't," he nearly choked on the words. "I just don't appreciate being used."

"I'm not using you," she responded coolly. "Nor am I interested in Detective Jameson." She thrust her nose in the air as if to demonstrate her indifference.

"Really? Is that why you posed in the doorway like you were about to perform the Dance of the Seven Veils?"

She made a low, growling sound as her glacial demeanor yielded to her quick temper. "You know, I really should have coshed you on the head when I had the opportunity."

He pointed a finger at her. "See, I was right."

"Right about what?"

He was wearing a complacent grin. "Violent tendencies."

Jameson hung up the receiver and beckoned Creighton and Marjorie to return. Marjorie repositioned herself in her chair; Creighton perched his lanky frame on the edge of the detective's desk.

"The medical examiner is still in the process of writing his report, but I managed to get some information out of him." Jameson picked up the yellow legal pad on which he had scrawled some notes from the conversation. "The body is that of a middle-aged man roughly five feet, nine inches tall. From the level of decomposition, it's estimated that he's been dead for approximately five years. Cause of death was a gunshot wound to the right temple; the angle of the shot indicates that it was not self-inflicted. The doctor found the bullet during the examination. Came from a standard, army-issue Colt revolver."

"The hole we saw in his skull was made by a bullet?" inquired Marjorie.

"Yes," responded Jameson.

"But it appeared too big to be a bullet wound. We thought perhaps he had been struck with a blunt object." She shot a warning glance at Creighton.

"Yes, the examiner explained the reason for that. The gun was fired at an extremely close range, causing the bone surrounding the area of impact to shatter."

"Did the examiner also happen to explain who this person was? I mean, did he find any identification?" asked Creighton.

"No, he didn't." He paused, as if choosing his words carefully. "But I have a good idea as to who it might be. The examiner is comparing the dental and bone records now. So far they look like a match."

"Well?" prodded Creighton.

"When we took the body to the morgue yesterday, I pressed the examiner for some preliminary information. All he could tell me was that the victim was male and had been dead anywhere between three and eight years. I came back here last night and pulled all the missing person reports for men during that time frame."

"And?" It was Marjorie's turn for prompting.

"And I found one file to be particularly intriguing." Jameson leaned back in his chair and folded his hands on his lap.

Creighton was growing impatient with the detective's reticence. "We're not making a film, we're writing a book. There's no need for your dramatic pauses. Just tell us who the devil was buried in my yard."

Jameson's face bore the expression of a small boy returning to school after summer break. He removed a manila folder from one of the desk drawers. "Victor Bartorelli," he replied as he opened the file and began scanning its contents. "His wife reported him missing on December 14, 1929. He was forty-six years old at the time of his disappearance, and approximately five feet, nine inches tall." He looked up, "Fits the description, huh? Listen, it gets better. His occupation is listed as a gardener. His employer? Mrs. Henry Van Allen, Kensington House, Ridgebury, Connecticut."

"December of 1929," Marjorie repeated, "That was only a few weeks after Henry Van Allen's suicide. Wasn't it considered odd that a member of the staff would go missing so soon after that?"

"Yes and no," answered Jameson. "I wasn't at this precinct at the time, but from what I can see from his file, Bartorelli was not your ordinary servant. He had spent most of his life in and out of trouble with the law. Petty larceny schemes, mostly. His last prison stint ended in 1925. When he went missing in 1929, and didn't turn up, it was assumed that he had gone back to his previous profession."

"So the theory was that Mr. Bartorelli, who had stayed on the so-called 'straight and narrow' for four years, had suddenly gone back to his life of crime?" Creighton shook his head, "I'm no criminologist, but that seems a bit shaky."

"On the surface, yes, but not if you consider the circumstances. After her husband's death, Mrs. Van Allen decided to put the Kensington property on the market. She closed up the house on December first and, with the exception of her personal servants, dismissed the entire Kensington House staff, leaving Bartorelli, among others, unemployed. By the end of '29, it was difficult enough for an honest man to find a job, never mind an ex-convict. It seems logical then, that Bartorelli, finding no use for his gardening skills, would use his other talents to provide for himself."

Marjorie was perplexed, "But what about his wife and family? Wouldn't he have wanted to provide for them, too?"

"Mr. and Mrs. Bartorelli were husband and wife in name only. She and their two children lived in a cold-water flat in Brooklyn. Bartorelli stayed in the caretaker's cottage over at Kensington. Seems he had pulled the disappearing act before, and that was the reason for the couple's estrangement."

"If she didn't live with her husband," inquired Marjorie, "then how did she know he was missing?"

"Victor had promised her money for the children's Christmas presents. When he didn't deliver, Mrs. Bartorelli called the police. The missing person's report was made, not out of concern for her husband's well-being, but to send the police breathing down his neck. She knew her husband's behavior well enough to realize that if he skipped town, it was because he was involved in some illegal activity—she so much as told the police that."

"Hell hath no fury like a woman scorned," commented Marjorie.

"Did the police investigate Bartorelli's disappearance, or did they take the wife's word that he was up to no good?" asked Creighton.

"They did as much as they could," replied Jameson. "They checked out his cottage on the estate—not surprisingly, it was empty. After that, they tracked down the other servants and questioned them. They all concurred that Bartorelli was optimistic about his future. Said he actually bragged about 'having something lined up' after his gardening job was finished. Last time they saw him was December first. He had packed up his belongings in a neat and orderly fashion and joined the rest of the staff inside the house, where Mrs. Van Allen handed out the final paychecks and said her last farewells. After Mrs. Van Allen took her leave, Bartorelli and the staff proceeded down the driveway and exited through the front gate, never to return again." He gazed up at Creighton. "Does the story meet your approval, Mr. Ashcroft?"

Creighton apologized, "I'm sorry, Detective. I didn't mean to come off as questioning police methods; I just wanted to get a feel for the case. After hearing the whole story, I must concede that I would have made the same assumption the detectives on the case made, had I been in their shoes."

Jameson sighed, "Unfortunately, we're not in their shoes, are we? They had a nice, simple missing person's case. We're left with a homicide whose trail of clues is over five years old."

Creighton rose from his position on the edge of the desk, and stood with his arms folded next to Marjorie's chair. "Well, there's one thing we know for certain. If the body in the morgue is that of Victor Bartorelli—and we are fairly confident that it is—then he didn't leave Kensington House with the other servants. At least, not for good."

Marjorie was still fixated on the image of the wife done wrong. "What about Mrs. Bartorelli? Isn't it possible that she killed her husband? She had motive enough: he left her alone to raise two children. If I were in that situation, I might be tempted to murder my husband. And I'm mild-mannered, so just imagine what a person with a temper might do."

Creighton stared at her in disbelief. *Mild-mannered?*

Jameson, meanwhile, appeared to be ruminating over her theory. "It's possible, but not very likely. What would Mrs. Bartorelli gain from killing her husband? With him dead, she would have lost a second source of income, however sporadic that income might have been."

"What about a life insurance policy?" she thought aloud.

"I can check it out, but I doubt it. He didn't support his family when he was alive, what would make him want to do it after he was dead?"

"Maybe she just snapped," she shrugged as if this were the only explanation she had left.

Jameson smiled at her tenacity. "'Snapped' would describe someone who shoots another person in the heat of an argument. Not a woman who travels three hours from Brooklyn to Connecticut to kill her husband and then bury him. Besides, if she did kill him, why would she call the police and send them out looking for him? It wouldn't make sense."

"What about a gang?" she asked, hopefully. "You said he was an unsavory character; maybe some of his hoodlum friends killed him. Or possibly a loan shark?"

"This wasn't that type of crime," answered Jameson. "Gangs don't cover up their killings, they advertise them. Use them as a warning to others." He looked up at Creighton, who had returned to his spot on the edge of the desk, and appeared to be lost in thought. "What are you thinking?"

He was staring off at some unidentified spot in the distance. "I was just wondering why anyone would wish to kill a gardener."

Jameson's face was a question, "Hmm?"

Creighton turned his attention to the detective and the young woman. "What I mean is, if we look at Bartorelli's death as an isolated incident, it doesn't quite gel. Who are the main suspects? His wife? The two of you did a good job of exonerating her. The underworld?" He nodded toward the man at the desk. "That idea's been scratched." He clasped his hands together and brought his forefingers to his chin, meditatively. "Who else then?"

Marjorie and Jameson were silent.

"No one," Creighton announced as he held his hands outward, like a magician demonstrating that he had no cards up his sleeve. "You're left with nothing." He raised his left index finger. "Nothing, except one nagging question: why would anyone wish to kill a gardener?"

"Maybe he was in the habit of trimming things too short," Marjorie deadpanned.

Jameson laughed, but Creighton seemed to be giving credence to the idea. "That's a clever theory. I'll keep it in mind in case we find a dead barber." He continued his previous train of thought. "No, the only way Bartorelli's death makes sense is if it's connected to something else."

"You mean the Van Allen case?" offered Jameson, wearily.

"Yes, the Van Allen case. What else? Two men who live on the same property both meet violent deaths within weeks of each other. I think that's a bit too much to dismiss as mere coincidence."

Marjorie was skeptical, "I agree that the timing is extremely odd, but how could a murder be linked to a suicide?"

"I don't know," admitted Creighton. "It could be anything. Maybe Van Allen killed himself because Bartorelli dug up his prized roses. Maybe Bartorelli squirted a garden hose at Van Allen's mourners. Or maybe someone was just irked at Bartorelli for having drained the pool. I can't tell you how the two are related. But I can tell you that it's something worth investigating." Creighton turned to the detective, "What do you think?"

Jameson walked across the room and pulled a folder out of the drawer of a tall, metal cabinet. He walked back to his chair and plopped the file on top of his desk; it was nearly an inch thick. "I think we have some reading to do."

Creighton looked at the folder, "The Van Allen file?"

Jameson, settling back into his chair, nodded.

The Englishman smiled. "I knew you'd come around to my way of thinking."

The detective had divided the file into three sections; he handed a stack to Creighton. "Did I have a choice?"

* * *

63

They had been reading for nearly half an hour, and Creighton found that his job was growing more tedious by the second. Each page he read might as well have been a carbon copy of the page before it, for they all bore the same information. There were several reports describing Henry Van Allen's last hours, his frame of mind before his death, and the grisly scene at the swimming pool. Though a different person might have completed each form on a different day, using a different turn of phrase, the stories they told were identical.

He was suddenly distracted by the sound of Marjorie rifling through the pages she had placed, face down, on the desk after reading them. She plucked one page from the stack and then settled back in her chair. After a few minutes, she spoke up. "Creighton."

"Hmm?"

"Creighton, you're familiar with New York City."

"I should hope so."

"Do you know where Liberty Street is?"

"Liberty Street in Manhattan? Yes, it's in the middle of the financial district. Downtown, near Wall Street. My broker had an office on Liberty Street, before the crash."

"How tall are the buildings there?"

"How *tall*?" He stretched his right arm as high above his head at it would reach. "Oh, about this tall, give or take several hundred feet."

Marjorie was in no mood for joking. "Please. Just answer the question."

Creighton lowered his arm. "It depends on the building."

"On average."

"On average probably about ten stories. Why?"

"Oh, nothing. At least, nothing concerning Bartorelli. Just a bit of a riddle regarding our friend, Henry Van Allen. Maybe you boys can help me solve it." The men looked at her, their curiosity piqued. "Why does a man who owns a ten-story office building commit suicide by jumping off a second-floor balcony?"

SEVEN

Marjorie folded her arms across her chest and glanced from one man to the other. She was satisfied with the effect her question had on her two companions, but she was even more pleased with her powers of deduction. She had uncovered an anomaly in the case that, despite the efforts of the Hartford County Police, had theretofore gone unnoticed. *She* discovered it, not them. The thought of it made her smile.

Creighton, naturally, was the first to answer her query. "It was there."

Marjorie's face was a question. "What was there?"

Creighton rolled his eyes as if the answer were obvious. "The balcony. The balcony was there at Kensington House. The office building was in New York. Van Allen happened to be at Kensington House when he decided to end it all, so he jumped from the most convenient point of elevation: the balcony. It's the same principle as a man who hangs himself with the bed linens rather than going to the hardware store to buy a rope. Though a rope is a more foolproof device than a knotted, wrinkled bed sheet, a soul who is intent on doing away with himself is not going to bother with such formalities. Likewise, if Van Allen was determined to kill himself on that particular night, he wouldn't travel all the way to the city just so he could jump from a taller building."

Marjorie was excited. "That's right!"

Creighton's brow wrinkled in confusion. "Wait one minute. You're agreeing with me?"

"Absolutely. It *doesn't* make sense for Van Allen to drive from Ridgebury to New York in order to jump from a taller building." She smiled, "But it makes even *less* sense for him to drive from New York to Ridgebury in order to jump from a shorter one, which is *exactly* what he did!" She pulled a page from the file on her lap and began to read. "According to his secretary, Van Allen arrived at his Liberty Street office somewhere around ten minutes after nine that morning. He stayed there all day. Didn't even go out for lunch. The night security guard reported that he left a few minutes before seven o'clock that evening. His body was found at Kensington House at approximately 10:17 that night."

Jameson chimed in, "Meaning that he must have driven to Kensington house directly from his office."

Marjorie completed the thought. "And killed himself soon after arriving. So soon after arriving, in fact, that it would seem that he drove there with that intention."

"But," explained Jameson, "we've already ruled out that possibility."

Marjorie nodded. "So why did Van Allen go to Kensington House that night?"

Creighton yawned. "I fail to see what's so odd about his going there. It was his weekend home, wasn't it? He obviously planned to take a few days off."

Marjorie shook her head. "That's just it: he *didn't* plan it. He drove there on the spur of the moment. He didn't notify the Kensington House staff to prepare for his arrival. He didn't inform his wife of his departure, and he didn't instruct his secretary to cancel his appointments for the next day." She stared at the stack of paper in Creighton's hand. "Don't you have any of this information in there?"

"This?" Creighton lifted the pages and then cleared his throat. "I'm a slow reader."

Marjorie raised a skeptical eyebrow.

"Well," Creighton continued, "It would appear that our friend Henry was in dire need of rest and relaxation and didn't wish to be disturbed."

"Yes," Marjorie conceded, "I'll admit that does have a ring of truth to it. But why did he leap off of his bedroom balcony immediately upon arriving?"

Creighton shrugged. "He was already depressed. His condition probably worsened during the drive there. He had time to consider the gravity of his financial situation. It was dark. It was quiet. He was alone." He paused a moment, stared off into the distance and then returned his attention to Marjorie. "Have you been on the Boston Post Road at night? Very sobering experience. A person can drive for miles without seeing another human being. And dark?" He whistled to emphasize the extent of this darkness. "Blackness all around you. Like someone has a velvet shroud over your car. Ghastly."

Jameson was trying, unsuccessfully, to hide his amusement. "Should I seek an arrest warrant for the Works Progress Administration?"

Marjorie, meanwhile, was staring at Creighton incredulously. "So Van Allen was pushed to the edge of despair by the Boston Post Road. That's your theory?"

Creighton seemed to be contemplating his answer. "Umm . . . well . . . yes, it was."

Jameson looked at him. "You're not sure?"

"Well," Creighton explained in a plaintive tone, "it just sounded more plausible when I said it."

"All right, Creighton, we'll stop picking on you," Marjorie said in a condescending fashion. "We'll assume, for the moment, that your theory is correct. Van Allen arrives at Kensington House intent on committing suicide. He runs up the stairs and hurls himself off the balcony. Why?" She looked at Creighton. "As you said yesterday, he couldn't have been certain that the fall would kill him. Why not use a knife, or poison? Surely, he could have found either one of them lying around the house."

Jameson breathed a heavy sigh. "What are you getting at, Miss McClelland?"

"I think you should reopen the case," she responded matter-of-factly.

"Reopen the case?" he repeated. "Why should I do that? Everything you've mentioned so far has been pure conjecture. The hardcore facts remain the same: Henry Van Allen was having financial trouble, he wrote a suicide note and he jumped from his bedroom balcony. End of story."

Marjorie looked to Creighton for support but found that he had resumed his reading efforts. Suddenly a thought occurred to her. "That's strange . . ."

Jameson did not reply, but leaned his elbows on his desk and buried his face in his hands. Marjorie recalled that Creighton had made a similar gesture the day before. *Was it possible that the detective was also coming down with the stomach flu?* Determined not to become distracted from her goal, she pushed the thought aside. "Van Allen supposedly killed himself over financial concerns. Yet, his secretary reported that he spent his last day working furiously, reviewing numbers, dictating letters, scheduling appointments, et cetera. He even skipped lunch. To me, that sounds like a man who is trying to keep his business afloat, not a man who is planning on cashing in his chips."

Creighton looked up briefly, "'Cashing in his chips'? What sort of films have you been watching lately?"

Jameson held his ground, "Miss McClelland, you don't understand. I'm not disagreeing with you. I'm just looking at this from the point of view of my superiors; if I go to them and ask to reopen a five-year-old case, I need good reason. So far, everything that you've mentioned could easily be accredited to Van Allen's irrational state of mind. Besides, I am supposed to be investigating the Bartorelli case, not the Van Allen case. Your questions, although very good, have not concerned Bartorelli in the slightest."

Creighton concurred. "He's right, Marjorie. You haven't found anything to link Bartorelli with Van Allen's death."

Marjorie stared through him. *Lousy traitor! You're supposed to defend me, not the Hartford County Police!*

Creighton smiled, "I, however, have."

Marjorie lunged from her chair and joined Creighton on the edge of the desk. She struggled to read the report over his shoulder. "Where is it? What did you find?"

"It's a timeline of the events of Henry Van Allen's last day." He pointed to the item of interest. "Look at that."

Marjorie read the line aloud. "Ten seventeen p.m.—body found at bottom of backyard swimming pool by Victor Bartorelli, gardener." Upon realizing the importance of Creighton's discovery, she kissed him firmly on one cheek and exclaimed, "Oh, Creighton, you're wonderful! This is exactly what we're looking for!"

Creighton knitted his eyebrows together as if deep in thought. "Hmm . . . a kiss for a tidbit of information." He shot Marjorie a sideways glance, "What do I get for solving the case?"

Marjorie blushed as it occurred to her that she might have acted too hastily. "Nothing. You've already gotten more than you deserve." She turned her attention to Detective Jameson, "There! What do you think of that?"

"I think you did a great job of placing Bartorelli at the scene of Van Allen's death. But it still doesn't prove anything."

Creighton sprung from his spot on the desk, nearly upsetting the stack of papers he had placed beside him. "Oh, come on, Jameson! Bartorelli was the first on the scene of Van Allen's suicide. Combine that with the fact that Bartorelli bragged about his future prospects, and I would say that Bartorelli knew something about Van Allen's death that no one else knew. Something that got him killed."

Jameson's head was tilted downward, as if it were suddenly too heavy for the rest of his body to support. "I get paid not to jump to conclusions."

"You also get paid to solve crimes, but I don't see you moving on this case at all. To be honest, I'm really beginning to wonder about the efficacy of this police department. First, we nearly have to twist your arm to read the Van Allen file. Then, when we do, Marjorie notices a number of unusual circumstances surrounding the case that were never investigated. Finally, when we find a link between the two cases, you're reluctant to pursue it. What's going on here? Are you afraid the

Van Allens won't purchase tickets to the next Policemen's Ball? Or do they have a courtesy card from the Hartford County Police?"

Jameson glared at Creighton, his eyes cold as steel. "They might as well have. When you were marveling at the shortcomings of the Hartford County Police, did you ever ask yourself why Noonan, a man ten years my senior, holds a lower rank than I do? Well, I'll tell you why: the Van Allen family. The Van Allen family who uses their wealth and privilege like some people use a fly swatter." He paused a moment as he suddenly recalled the status of his visitor. "I'm sorry Mr. Ashcroft, but I'm just telling the story as I see it."

Creighton shook his head. "No need to apologize. I've been in the company of 'polite' society long enough to know that they very seldom live up to the description. Please, continue."

"Noonan was in charge of the Van Allen case. He declared it a suicide, but he also noticed the same inconsistencies as Miss McClelland did. Noonan investigated them; he questioned the family, secretary, servants."

Creighton commented, "They mustn't have liked that too much. Hard to sweep a suicide under the rug when the police are always lurking about the house."

Jameson nodded. "Exactly. I don't know what sort of connections the Van Allens have, but soon afterward, Noonan was informed that the case was officially 'closed' and that he was being accused of harassment. The Van Allens wanted Noonan to be thrown off the force, but fortunately the top brass kept their heads and merely had Noonan demoted."

Marjorie was looking at Jameson sympathetically. "And you're afraid that if you reopen the Van Allen case, the same thing will happen to you."

"Yes, I am. Part of me wants to get to the bottom of this, but the other part is very hesitant to open what might prove to be a can of worms."

Creighton had been staring off into the distance, but Jameson's words had snapped him from his reverie. "But you don't have to worry about that," he stated reassuringly.

Jameson was puzzled. "I don't?"

"No, you don't. Because you have something that Noonan didn't have."

Jameson's puzzlement was now mixed with something akin to fear. "I do? What's that?"

Creighton threw his arms outward. "You have me."

Jameson and Marjorie exchanged worried glances. "With all due respect, Mr. Ashcroft, I fail to see how you're going to help me."

Creighton looked at Jameson as if he were a dullard. "Don't you see? If the Van Allens can use their money and prestige to close a case, I can certainly use mine to have it reopened. Bartorelli's body was found on *my* property, policemen are tramping through *my* woods, and disturbing the sanctity of *my* life. I'll just call your superior and demand that the case be solved by any means necessary, even reopening the Van Allen case, if need be. I'll take full responsibility. If the Van Allens are upset at the reopening of the case, you can point the finger at me. If they decide to charge you with harassment, I'll get you the best attorneys money can buy."

Jameson shook his head. "That's very nice of you, but you don't seem to get it. Even if we manage to reopen the case, the Van Allens aren't going to talk to the police. And if they do, they're certainly not going to surrender any personal details to a flatfoot."

Creighton was undeterred. "No, they won't talk to *you* very readily, but they will speak to a 'member of the club.'"

Jameson was reluctant to respond. "You?"

"Yes, me. I just bought their house; it seems only natural that I might 'pop' in on them for a social visit. I'll go over there and dig around. If I don't find anything . . ." He shrugged his shoulders. "But if I do . . ." He flashed a boyish grin.

Jameson glanced at Marjorie again. She raised her eyebrows, tilted her head and sighed. "It might work."

"Of course it will work," Creighton exclaimed. "It's a great plan. A bold and daring plan." He wandered toward the mounted buck and began speaking to it. "There never was such a plan! Wouldn't you agree?"

Jameson leaned toward Marjorie and inquired, sotto voce, "Is he serious about all this, or is he just crazy?"

Marjorie turned and watched Creighton, now heavily engaged in conversation with the stuffed animal. She swiveled back toward Jameson. "I don't know him well enough to answer that question, but from what I've seen so far, I would say . . . both."

EIGHT

AFTER A BRIEF PHONE call from the county coroner's office confirmed that the body found at Kensington house was, indeed, that of Victor Bartorelli, it was decided that the trio separate to commence their respective investigations.

Jameson, in one of four squad cars, was to drive to Kensington House and check on the progress of the ground search. From there, he would travel to Hartford to review the medical examiner's final report. The last lap of his journey would bring him to Brooklyn, to notify Mrs. Victor Bartorelli of her husband's death.

Creighton and Marjorie, meanwhile, were to make the trip to Manhattan in order to ingratiate themselves with Mrs. Van Allen. They climbed into the Phantom and took off down the thoroughfare that eventually led into the now-notorious Boston Post Road. Marjorie was unusually quiet; she sat gazing out the passenger side window, frowning.

Creighton misinterpreted her silence. "Don't worry. You'll see Detective Jameson later. We're meeting him downtown for dinner."

"I'm not thinking about him," she dismissed. "I'm worried about meeting Mrs. Van Allen. How do you plan to get in and see her?"

Creighton replied. "That's easy. I'll give her my calling card."

Marjorie was skeptical. "That's it? That's your plan?"

"Yes. I'm sorry if it's not exciting enough for you. Feel free to climb through a window if you wish, but don't expect me to post bail."

She ignored him. "You mean that will work? You're going to walk up the front steps, ring the doorbell, flash a bit of cardboard, and they'll let you in?"

"Well, not exactly like that, but you have the general idea."

She shook her head and then muttered to herself, "Sounds like a speakeasy." She returned her attention to the car's driver. "Are you sure she won't be upset with us? We don't have an appointment. Won't she think that we're rude, dropping in unannounced?"

"Visiting is a favorite pastime of the wealthy. It's quite common-place for people who have never met to call upon each other. As long as you are a member of a respectable family, you will be received." He glanced at his passenger. "In fact, Mrs. Van Allen would be considered rude *not* to receive us after we've traveled this far to see her."

"So it's not rude of us to barge in," mused Marjorie, "but it would be rude of Mrs. Van Allen to deny us entry." She narrowed her eyes as if trying to make sense of it all. "I'm glad I was born a peasant," she declared. "High society seems to have so many silly rules and regulations."

She looked at Creighton and studied his profile. His features were those of a mature man, steady, strong; yet there was something about them—the twinkling eyes, the upturned mouth—which hinted at the mischievous schoolboy that still lurked beneath the surface. "I have to say, I can't imagine you in that sort of environment, high society, I mean."

"Thank you," he replied. Marjorie, thinking that he was joking, began to giggle. Creighton guaranteed her that he was, indeed, in earnest. "No, I mean it. Thank you. That's the nicest thing anyone has ever said to me."

"Is it really?"

"Yes, it is." He glanced at her; she was staring at him in astonishment. "You needn't worry. I know you didn't intend on paying me such a lofty compliment." Creighton chuckled. "And I won't tell a soul that you actually said something kind to me."

Marjorie was offended. "Do you really think that I'm that cruel?"

Creighton moved his head from side to side. "No, I don't think you're 'cruel.' I think you're honest." He quickly amended his statement. "*Brutally* honest. If I ever *do* receive a compliment from you, I shall hold it in very high regard, for I shall know that it is sincere."

Marjorie appeared placated with this explanation. She restored her gaze to the scenery flickering past the passenger window, but after a few moments her frown returned, this time gloomier than the one that had preceded it.

"What's wrong now?" Creighton asked.

"Well, we know how *you're* going to get in and see Mrs. Van Allen, but what about *me*?"

"You'll follow me inside, of course. Did you think I might leave you at the curb?"

"No, that's not what I meant. You said yourself that you're a 'member of the club.' I, however, am not. Isn't she going to notice that?"

Creighton grinned, "Why? Do you have a label on your forehead that reads, 'Commoner'?"

She sighed. "I don't think I need one. Just look at my clothes . . ."

"You look perfectly lovely. Very stylish."

"This old thing? It was very cheap."

"Can't tell by looking at it. Fits you very well."

"And my hair . . ."

"Wonderful. Blonde is the rage right now."

"But not this shade of blonde . . ."

"Yours looks more natural."

She turned on him suddenly. "It *is* natural."

He shrugged. "All the more reason for Mrs. Van Allen to be envious."

She paused a moment. "The way I speak . . . that will be a dead giveaway . . ."

"Your diction is flawless."

Despite Creighton's reassurances, Marjorie was determined to wallow in self-pity. She slouched in her seat, threw her hands up in the air, and brought them down, noisily, on her lap. "It's no use. The entire time I'm there, I'll feel as if I don't belong."

"Good," pronounced Creighton. "That will make two of us."

Marjorie was doubtful. "*You* won't belong there? But you were raised in that atmosphere."

"That doesn't mean I enjoy it or that I feel comfortable in it. Why do you think I moved to Ridgebury?" He answered his own question. "To get away from that sort of crowd, that's why. And if you're the sort of woman I think you are, after today you'll want to stay away from that sort of people, too."

"But," she argued, "you always seem so confident, so self-assured."

"Acting," he responded. "I was always taught that true nobility lies in bearing, not in breeding. If you behave as if you're an important person, you'll be treated as if you're an important person. You should try it."

"I'm not very good at that sort of thing."

"Oh, come now," prodded Creighton. "Didn't you ever participate in a school drama production?"

"Yes, one. Hamlet."

"Ah, yes," Creighton exclaimed, wistfully. "The fair Ophelia. She was a tragic character—a bit over the top—but she *was* of noble birth. Pretend that you're Ophelia for the day. Just promise me you won't jump into the East River."

"I didn't play Ophelia," she replied testily. "That role went to the daughter of our drama coach."

"Nepotism," he commented briefly. "So you were Hamlet's mother, then? Even better. She was the queen. Can't get any more regal than that—"

Marjorie interrupted him. "I wasn't Hamlet's mother."

"You weren't Ophelia and you weren't Gertrude . . ." Creighton was thinking aloud. "I give up. What part did you play?"

"Polonius."

"Polonius? Who did the casting for your play? A blind man?"

"I went to an all-girl school," she explained. "They needed students to volunteer for the less than glamorous roles, so I obliged."

"Yes, well, you did a bang-up job. You can't get much less glamorous than Polonius, can you? Still, he was a rather noble character. And a little bit of Polonius might come in handy today." A devilish grin appeared upon his face. "I can picture it now: 'Mrs. Van Allen, did you know Victor Bartorelli?'" He raised his voice a few octaves, "'No, I did not.'" He resumed his normal speaking voice, "'Are you sure, Mrs. Van Allen?'" Again, in a high-pitched tone, "'I've already told you, I never heard his name before today!'" His voice was lower again, but this time it took on a preaching tone, "'Very well, Mrs. Van Allen. But just know this: you may be able to lie to your family, your friends, and the police, but you can't lie to yourself. Remember: to thine own self be true.'"

Marjorie was laughing. "I think you've misinterpreted that line a bit."

Creighton was laughing, also. "Yes, I know I have, but at least I've managed to put a smile on your face."

When the merriment had died down, Marjorie spoke up. "Creighton, you said before that if I were the sort of woman you believed me to be, I wouldn't want anything to do with high society. Exactly what sort of woman *do* you think I am?"

"You are the sort of woman," began Creighton eloquently, "who has more grace and charm than all the society 'cats' of New York thrown together."

Marjorie's eyes opened wide. "Oh, Creighton! I . . . I don't know what to say," she stammered. "Thank you."

"It's nothing, really."

"No, it isn't *nothing*. It would seem that you've not only repaid my compliment, but you've bettered it."

"You needn't go on about it."

"But no one has ever said anything like that to me before," she argued. "Why shouldn't I go on about it?"

His devilish grin had returned. "Because I said that *you* were honest. I, however, am not above the use of shameless flattery."

"Ugh!" Marjorie shouted. "You—you—you creep!" She hit him on the back of his head with her purse, sending the hat he wore tumbling to the car floor.

Creighton could not help but snicker with delight.

* * *

80

The Van Allen residence was a stately single-family dwelling located on Eighty-fourth Street, between Park and Lexington Avenues, in that exclusive Manhattan neighborhood known as Carnegie Hill. Creighton brought the Rolls Royce to a halt by the curb in front of the house and then accompanied Marjorie up the wide granite steps that led to a pair of intricately scrolled metal doors.

Creighton rang the doorbell and then leaned toward Marjorie. "Just follow my lead," he whispered. "What I do, you do. Understand?"

She nodded.

"And for heaven's sake, try not to talk too much. You might give away the true reason for us being here."

Marjorie reassured him, "Trust me. I'll be so nervous about meeting Mrs. Van Allen, I don't think I'll be able to put two words together to form a coherent sentence."

Suddenly, one of the wooden main doors swung inward to reveal a gray-haired man. He peered through the glass and filigree work of the storm doors, and then, turning the handle, opened one of them just far enough to expose his nose and one eyeball. "May I help you?"

Creighton had retrieved a calling card and a fountain pen from his jacket pocket. "Yes. We are here to call upon Mrs. Henry Van Allen."

"Is Madam expecting you?" inquired the man in the black suit who, quite apparently, was the butler.

Creighton was in the act of taking the pen to the card. "No, I'm afraid she isn't. But if you might present her with this." He handed the bit of paper to the butler. He had scratched out the Park Avenue address and beneath it had scrawled, *Kensington House, Ridgebury, Connecticut.*

The butler took the card and read it. He raised his eyebrows and scrutinized Creighton suspiciously. "I'll be back in a few minutes. You may wait right here."

Creighton, interpreting the butler's instructions to wait outdoors as a bad omen, interrupted him before he could shut the door. "Before you go, do you think it's quite safe to leave my car parked here?" He stepped aside to allow the butler a glimpse of the Rolls Royce. "I think the time limit on parking in this neighborhood is one hour." He checked his watch in exaggerated motion that showed off its shiny gold band. "Perhaps I should move it. Is there a garage nearby?"

Creighton's display of conspicuous consumption had worked, for the elderly man smiled. "I assure you, nothing shall happen to your automobile, sir. But, if it will ease your mind, I shall instruct the chauffeur to move it to Madam's private garage." He glanced at the sky, which had become quite overcast. "It appears we might be in for some rain." He opened the storm door wide. "Please. Do come in."

He ushered them through both sets of doors and into the foyer of the townhouse. Upon reaching this entryway, the pair found themselves in a world devoid of color. The ceilings and walls, both painted white, supported stainless steel light fixtures. The floor was a checkerboard of black and white Italian marble tile; this same white marble covered the second-story staircase, which also sported a black carpet runner and a stainless steel handrail. The whole lavish production reminded Marjorie of the set of a Busby Berkeley musical—she half-expected Ginger Rogers and Fred Astaire to come gliding down the steps.

"May I take your coat, miss?" inquired the butler, interrupting Marjorie's overactive imagination.

She removed the garment and handed it to the elderly man, who promptly draped it over his arm. After doing the same with Creighton's frock coat, the butler led them to the door just to the right of the entrance. "If you would just have a seat in the drawing room, Madam will be with you in a few moments." Creighton and Marjorie stepped inside and the butler closed the door after them.

Keeping with the theme of the front hall, the drawing room was outfitted in art deco style. However, whereas the foyer had been enlivened by the addition of black in its color scheme, the drawing room was entirely monochromatic—white walls, white carpet, and white furnishings. Even the floral arrangements—calla lilies in large, frosted urns—did nothing to alleviate the antiseptic atmosphere of the space.

"Charming place," Creighton commented facetiously. "Very warm and inviting." He approached a futuristic-looking chair constructed of chrome-plated steel tubing and white canvas, located against the wall to the left of the doorway. Gingerly, he lowered his body into the odd contraption.

Marjorie watched with interest. "Looks like some sort of newfangled torture device."

The chair was quite low to the ground, leaving insufficient space for Creighton's long legs. "Yes, I rather think it is." With his feet planted on the floor, his knees were level with his chest. He tilted forward a bit and rested his chin on them. "If Henry was forced to sit in this thing, I can see why he might kill himself."

Marjorie pointed at a boxy sofa with a low back, situated perpendicular to the chair. "Why don't you sit there? It looks more comfortable."

Creighton heeded her advice and moved. "Yes. That's better. Not like my wing chair at home, mind you. But it will do."

Marjorie crossed the room and stood by the unlit fireplace, leaning an elbow on the mantle. Creighton patted the sofa cushion beside him. "Relax. Have a seat."

She looked at the sofa reluctantly. "I'm afraid to sit on that."

"This seat's fine. It's that thing you have to look out for." He gestured toward the metal structure.

"I'm not afraid *of* the sofa, I'm afraid of what I'm going to do to it. I already told you this dress wasn't very expensive. With my luck, I'll perspire out of sheer nervousness and leave a giant red spot on the cushion."

"Then, by all means, *do* sit down. The place could use a little color."

She capitulated and positioned herself beside him. As she sat, she felt the rumbling of her empty stomach. "Do you think Mrs. Van Allen will serve us some refreshments? I'm famished."

"Liquid refreshments, most likely." He glanced at his watch. "It's already twenty minutes past four o'clock; too late for lunch and too early for dinner."

She screwed her face up at him and looked away in disappointment.

"Come now, you don't have to wait too much longer. Once we leave here, we'll go directly to the restaurant to meet Jameson."

"If I don't faint before then." She slumped against the rear bolster of the couch and pulled her purse onto her lap. "Maybe I have a piece of candy in here," she thought aloud as she rummaged through the handbag.

"If you happen to find two pieces, pass one my way. I'm getting rather hungry myself."

She nodded and proceeded to call out an inventory of the contents of the purse. "Lipstick . . . comb . . . mirror . . . hankie . . ." She continued, and when the roll call was finally complete, she declared, "Nothing." As she withdrew her hand from the purse, her fingertips met with something hard and sticky. *Wait. What's this?* She peered through the opening and squinted in an attempt to distinguish the item at the bottom of the bag.

It was a lemon drop that had somehow worked its way out of its plastic wrapper and adhered itself to the lining of her purse. She gazed at it and then glanced at Creighton to ensure that he wasn't watching her. *It wouldn't do to meet a grand dame of New York society with a growling stomach.* She glanced at Creighton again—he wasn't looking. Hastily, she pried the candy loose and popped it into her mouth.

The drop had no sooner reached her mouth than Creighton turned to look at her. Realizing she had been caught, she gasped, inhaled the sugary morsel, and immediately began to choke. Thinking quickly, Creighton hit Marjorie on the back, dislodging the confection and sending it shooting across the room.

"What the devil were you doing?" Creighton blurted.

"Eating a lemon drop," stated Marjorie, her voice raspy.

"Is that what sailed past me?" His eyes narrowed. "But I thought you said you hadn't any candy."

"I didn't," she answered.

"Then where did that come from?"

"I found it," she replied, sheepishly. "It was my last piece."

"I see. And you didn't want to offer it to me, so you tried to eat it without my knowing about it."

She left her place on the sofa and knelt down upon the floor. "You wouldn't have wanted it anyway."

"How could you be so sure?" he persisted.

"Because, if you must know, I found it stuck to the bottom of my purse." She dropped down on all fours.

"Good God, woman! I said I would buy you dinner." He watched, bewildered, as she crawled along the drawing room floor. "What on earth are you doing now?"

"I'm looking for the lemon drop," said the small voice from behind the sofa.

"Why? Are you going to put it back in your mouth?"

She stuck her head up from behind the sofa and glared at him. "Very funny. I don't want it to stick to the rug or the furniture."

"Did you happen to notice where it went?" he asked.

"No," she answered sarcastically. "It's difficult to be observant when you are choking."

"The last I saw it, it was heading in this direction." He pointed to the area slightly to the right of where he sat. "So it should be somewhere on this side of the room. You look near that metal chair thingamabob. I'll check under the sofa." Still seated, he bent down toward the floor and, with his head between his knees, began peering beneath the large couch. Marjorie crawled toward the canvas chair and analyzed the rug beneath it.

Their search, however, was called short by the sound of a door handle turning and then of a woman clearing her throat. Creighton automatically sprung to his feet. Marjorie followed suit, but not before creating a loud, reverberating clang as she accidentally struck her head on a tubular chair rail.

Mrs. Van Allen's appearance was as dramatic as that of the house in which she lived. She was dressed in a black, crêpe de Chine, floor-length gown with a high mandarin collar, tight-fitting bodice and extravagant bell sleeves. Her raven hair, clearly color-treated, had been clipped short and, with the exception of a dark curl strategically placed in the middle of her forehead, was pin straight. In stark contrast to both hair and dress, her face had been covered in pale powder until the natural tint of human flesh had almost disappeared and her features looked as if they had been carved from alabaster.

"Mr. Ashcroft," she purred from lips painted a deep cerise, "am I to assume that you are the new owner of Kensington House?"

"Yes, I am."

"Then I am honored to welcome you to my home." She thrust a bejeweled hand in his direction.

He grasped her fingers and made a slight bow. "The honor is all mine, Mrs. Van Allen."

"Please, call me Gloria," she insisted. "I *do* hate such formality among contemporaries."

Contemporaries? Marjorie could hardly believe her ears. *That woman is fifty years old if she's a day!*

Creighton smiled politely. "Very well, then—Gloria."

Her lips broadened into a simper. "And who is this *charming* woman? Your wife?" she inquired as she caught glimpse of Marjorie standing in the background.

Marjorie had never known the word "charming" to be anything other than a compliment, but from the mouth of Gloria Van Allen, it was a demeaning term.

"No, just a friend. Mrs. Gloria Van Allen," he began his formal introduction, "I would like you to meet Miss Marjorie McClelland."

Marjorie smiled and nodded. "How do you do?"

The older woman did not reply but merely repeated the young woman's name. "McClelland . . . McClelland . . ." She shook her head. "I can't say that I know the name. Who are your people?"

"My people?" Marjorie echoed.

Creighton interceded. "Miss McClelland is what you might call a 'self-made woman.' She's an author, a scholar, and the founder and president of the Connecticut Women's Literary League."

Marjorie looked at him in awe. How could the man utter such fabrications and still manage to maintain a semblance of integrity?

"The Connecticut Women's Literary League?" Gloria reiterated. "What type of organization is it?"

Marjorie had expected Creighton to provide an answer, but the Englishman was oddly silent. Frantically, she racked her brain for a plausible scholastic crusade. "We distribute books to those in financial difficulty," she finally blurted.

Gloria Van Allen raised a finely penciled eyebrow. "Isn't that why we have public libraries?"

"Public libraries have only been established in large cities; those who live in rural areas do not have access to them," she explained. "Previously, such people could purchase reading materials from their local bookstore, but with our present economic crisis, these families can no longer afford to buy shoes, let alone books. That's where our organization comes in. We feel that every person is entitled to inherit the legacy of great literature." She took a deep breath, confident that her explanation was successful, for she had nearly convinced herself of the group's existence.

Gloria nodded. "Yes, I suppose they are entitled to great literature, if they can understand it. I must commend your organization for undertaking such an arduous task. It must be difficult to educate the masses."

Marjorie felt the vein in her temple begin to throb. "Yes, it is difficult," she agreed, biting her tongue, "but highly worthwhile."

"Then," Mrs. Van Allen declared, "I shall write you a check before you leave."

"A check?" Marjorie asked, startled.

"Yes, a check," she affirmed. "Your organization might be non-profit, but you still need money. You know—to purchase books and things." She waved her hand as an indication that she hadn't the slightest idea what these other "things" might be.

"Yes, we could do with some new books," agreed Marjorie. "We've had some special requests recently. Like the works of Karl Marx, for instance," she added slyly.

Creighton kicked Marjorie's shin with the toe of his shoe.

"Yes, yes," Mrs. Van Allen replied impatiently. "Whatever you want to buy. You know what they like." She waved both hands, as if brushing away the present topic of conversation and directed her guests to be seated.

Creighton commandeered the sofa, and Marjorie sat alongside him. Mrs. Van Allen eased herself into the tubular chair and began stroking its arms. "This is my favorite seat in the house," she declared. "It's a Wassily chair. I paid a fortune for it, but it's worth *every* penny. Very comfortable. My dog likes it, too; I usually have to chase him out of it."

As if on cue, a small, white, powder puff of a dog ambled through the doorway and plopped down at his mistress's feet. "Oh!" she exclaimed. "Here he is now. His name is Mal—that's short for Marshmallow. He's a purebred bichon frisé."

"Adorable," commented Creighton.

"Yes, I know," cried Gloria. "The minute I saw him, I just *had* to have him!"

Marjorie wondered if the woman's enchantment with the dog had been fueled by the need for companionship or the desire for a unique accessory to her monochromatic décor. In either event, she was certain that if Mal's fur had been any color but white, he would still be in the pet shop window.

Mrs. Van Allen leaned down and patted the dog's head. "It's frightfully damp outside. Can I get you something to chase away the chill? Tea? Sherry?"

"I'll take a sherry, if you don't mind," replied Creighton.

Marjorie was about to opt for tea, and then recalled Creighton's instructions before entering the house. "I'll have sherry, also," she declared.

Mrs. Van Allen rose from her chair, walked to the corner nearest Marjorie, and grabbed the bell pull to summon the maid. Mal, anxious of being away from his mistress for even a moment, trailed obediently behind her.

Marjorie watched the endearing creature with delight. However, delight quickly changed to dismay as she noticed a flash of yellow every time the pooch wagged his tail. Silently, she nudged Creighton with her elbow and drew his attention to Mal's hindquarters. There, at the base of the rear appendage, in a tuft of matted fur, clung the missing lemon drop.

Creighton's face took on a pained expression. "How in blazes did that get there?" he whispered.

"I don't know," she replied quietly. "It must have been somewhere in the rug and he sat on it. What do we do now?"

"I'll handle it," he stated with aplomb and lurched forward in anticipation.

Gloria followed the path back to her chair; Mal, as predicted, followed. As the dog passed him, Creighton sprung into action. With lightning-quick reflexes, he reached down, gripped the candy, and pulled.

The operation was a success; the offending sweet had been expunged from the animal's rump, but not without removing a tangle of silky white hair in the process. The unfortunate beast yelped and then scampered from the room.

Mrs. Van Allen shouted after him. "Mal! Mal! Come back!" She stared at Creighton and Marjorie in bewilderment. "He's never acted like that before. I don't know what's gotten into him."

Creighton shrugged, innocently. "Don't know. Perhaps 'Mal' should be short for 'Malcontent.'"

"Yes, perhaps," Mrs. Van Allen tittered abstractedly. "If you'll excuse me one moment, I'll go check on him."

As she made her leave, a plain-faced young woman in a dark dress and white apron appeared in the doorway. At her entrance, Mrs. Van Allen's attention was immediately diverted from her dog. "Oh, there you are, Doris. I've been waiting *ages* for you."

"Sorry, ma'am," Doris mumbled.

"Please fetch us *three* sherries," ordered Gloria, displaying the same amount of fingers. "That's *three*."

Doris nodded.

"And *do* be quick about it. Stupid girl will find some way to louse it up," she muttered as she returned to the Wassily chair—the topic of Mal completely forgotten.

Once she had comfortably resettled herself in her seat, the heiress beamed at Creighton. "I must say, when I heard that the new owner of Kensington House was here to visit, I didn't expect to meet someone like you."

"Oh? What did you expect?" he asked.

"I don't know . . . someone older, I think . . ."

Marjorie wanted to blurt out, *You mean someone closer to your own age.*

"Stodgier. No one as witty as you." She batted a set of fake eyelashes. "And certainly no one as attractive."

Marjorie wrinkled her nose and quietly harrumphed.

Creighton's shoe met her shin again. "Thank you," he replied modestly, over Marjorie's yelp of pain. "Although I don't understand why you expected me to be old and stodgy."

The sound of clinking glasses flowed through the open door of the drawing room. Doris had returned, balancing a decanter and three drinking vessels full of sherry on a round, silver tray.

"It's the house, I suppose—it's nearly prehistoric," Gloria exaggerated. "And God only knows, there's no nightlife in Ridgebury. More the sort of place an elderly person would reside."

Doris placed the decanter on the table in front of her mistress and served the first glass of sherry to Marjorie. She took a sip, and finding it quite palatable, drank the rest of the liquid in one gulp.

"But," argued Creighton, "*you* lived at Kensington House, and you're certainly not elderly." He looked up to see the maid hovering over him with his glass of sherry. As he took it from her hand, he flashed her a luminous smile. "Thank you, Doris." The young woman blushed and smiled coyly in return.

"Doris," demanded Mrs. Van Allen, "Miss McClelland's glass is empty. Please fill it." The young woman dutifully reached for the decanter, but her attention was still riveted on the brilliant blue eyes of the gentleman caller.

Gloria Van Allen, meanwhile, had returned to the subject at hand. "I never spent much time at Kensington House. I didn't like it much.

It was Henry's folly, not mine. He bought it without even consulting me."

Marjorie held her glass out, and the maid, after unstopping the decanter, began to pour more liquor into it.

"Henry was always like that," Gloria continued. "Impulsive. Even in death."

At that, the maid's hand slipped, splashing sherry into Marjorie's lap.

"Doris!" shrieked Mrs. Van Allen as she leapt from her chair. "You insipid little cow! Look what you've done!"

Doris immediately snatched a tea towel from her apron and, apologizing profusely, began blotting the damp spots on Marjorie's skirt. Marjorie grabbed the young woman's hand. "It's all right," she reassured her. "I've always been rather clumsy. The drink would have ended up there eventually, anyway. You just saved me the time and effort of having to do it myself."

Creighton, attempting to lighten the situation, laughed loudly at Marjorie's comments.

Mrs. Van Allen, nevertheless, was still not amused. "Go, Doris! Find something else to do!" She added, in an attempt at martyrdom, "If I want more sherry, I'll just have to pour it myself."

Doris, her limpid gray eyes rimmed with tears, fled as quickly as her legs would carry her. As she made her escape, a middle-aged man stepped into the drawing room. She shoved past him and through the door, slamming it behind her.

The man appeared to have been entertained by the scene he had just witnessed. "Terrorizing the servants again, Gloria?"

Mrs. Van Allen had been unaware of the man's presence, but at the sound of his voice, she whirled around to face him. "Bill!" she cried out. She ran to him and kissed the air beside his right cheek. "How nice of you to stop by. Do, have some sherry with us."

The man declined. "No thanks. I already did my drinking at the club." He eyeballed the couple standing in front of the couch.

Gloria followed his gaze and, taking his arm in hers, led him closer to the sofa. "Miss McClelland. Mr. Ashcroft. This is my brother-in-law, William. He's Henry's brother," she explained. "Bill, this is Miss Marjorie McClelland and Mr. Creighton Ashcroft."

William Van Allen was not an extraordinarily handsome man. He was in his middle forties and of average height and build, with a bit of a paunch. Nevertheless, his salt and pepper hair, neatly trimmed mustache, and impeccably tailored clothes gave him a distinguished appearance. At his introduction, he bowed before Marjorie and then shook hands with Creighton.

Marjorie managed a halfhearted greeting; her thoughts were still focused on Doris. The expression that had registered on the maid's face was fear of something greater than the sharpness of her mistress's tongue.

"Well," announced Mrs. Van Allen, "now that we all know each other, why don't we make ourselves comfortable?"

Marjorie saw an opportunity to excuse herself from the room. "Actually, Gloria, if you don't mind, I think I'll visit your powder room and wash the sherry out of my dress."

"By all means," the heiress replied. "You wouldn't want that *lovely* outfit to be stained, would you?" In Gloria's language, the word "lovely" had a connotation similar to that of the word "charming." "The powder room is down the hall, fourth door on your left."

"Thank you." She finished the contents of her glass and left the drawing room, quietly shutting the door behind her. Doris was in the hallway, standing over a metal console table, polishing it morosely.

Marjorie placed a hand on the girl's shoulder. "Doris."

The maid jumped and spun around in surprise. "Oh," she declared breathlessly. "It's you, miss. You startled me."

"I'm sorry."

Doris's eyes grew wide. "Oh, no, miss! If anyone should be sorry, it's me! I hope I didn't ruin your dress. It's so pretty. I'll help you clean it. If you follow me, I have some soap powder—"

The girl's ramblings, combined with the sherry, were making Marjorie dizzy. "Stop, Doris!" The maid instantly fell silent. "I didn't come out here for you to clean my dress. I wanted to see how you were feeling. I was worried about you."

The young woman was quizzical. "Miss?"

"You seemed so upset, I was concerned you might do something rash." Marjorie stared at the drawing room door contemptuously. "The way that battle axe treats you is terrible."

Doris jumped to her mistress's defense. "Oh, but you mustn't call her that," she flustered.

"Why not? It suits her. The way she sailed into you, why it—it made me want to pop her one." Emboldened by the alcohol, she swung her fist. "Right in the nose."

The maid bit her lip and suppressed a laugh.

Marjorie smiled. "It's safe to laugh, Doris. The Dragon Lady can't hear you." The girl complied with a nervous titter.

Seeing that she had gained the young woman's trust, Marjorie returned to the objective of her mission. "But, enough about her. How are you?"

Doris's cheeks colored and she cast her head downward in an effort to avert the other woman's inquisitive gaze. "I'm okay," she said, more to her shoes than to Marjorie. "Mrs. Van Allen just rattles my cage sometimes."

"I can understand that," Marjorie empathized. "Although you seemed to be upset even before she yelled at you."

With an intensity that surprised Marjorie, the young woman answered, her face hard and her voice full of venom. "Darn right, I was upset. I was fine when I first walked into the room, but then I heard her talking about Mister Henry. I hate the way she talks about him." Marjorie half-expected the girl to spit upon the floor, in demonstration of her disgust. "And the poor man dead in his grave, unable to defend himself. She makes it sound like he was crazy and that it was the craziness that killed him. Well, I'll tell you, it wasn't craziness that killed him, it was her. She killed her husband! She killed her husband as sure as if she had pushed him from that balcony!" She gasped, as if stunned by her own words, and her face instantly softened. "I'm sorry, miss. I shouldn't be telling you this. You being her friend and all."

Marjorie guffawed loudly. "Me? Her friend? No. I wouldn't even say we're good acquaintances. I've only just met the woman today, and as far as I can guess, I don't think she'll be wanting to see me again any time soon."

"Oh, I just thought . . ." Doris trailed off.

"Forget what you thought," Marjorie instructed. "Mrs. Van Allen and I have absolutely nothing in common. Why, I'm practically penniless compared to her. That drawing room is nearly as big as my entire house. And we certainly don't move within the same social circle. You can rest assured that she will never hear a word of what you say to me today." She tried to steer the conversation back to the topic of Gloria and Henry's tumultuous relationship. "So, with that said, why don't you tell me more about Mr. and Mrs. Van Allen? Was their marriage terribly unhappy?"

"Yes. They—they didn't get along." Her eyes darted about the room, nervously. "I should go now."

Marjorie, ignoring Doris's feeble attempt to extricate herself from the conversation, pursued her next line of questioning. "What did they argue about?"

"I—I don't know. All I know is that I can't talk to you anymore." She glanced from side to side and then added, in a near whisper, "It isn't safe to talk here. The walls have eyes and ears."

Marjorie looked around her as if the sensory organs might be visible. "You're probably right," she agreed. "We'll meet somewhere else and discuss it over coffee."

"Oh, I—I'm awfully busy around here," Doris stammered.

Marjorie had pulled a scrap of paper and a pen from her purse and was recording her name and telephone number. "But you get a day off, don't you?"

Doris's cooperation as a witness was rapidly waning. "Yes, b-but I use that day for personal errands."

Marjorie's eyes slid surreptitiously toward the drawing room door. There was one way she could convince Doris to talk. She folded the scrap of paper that bore her name and telephone number and handed it to the maid. "Well, if you think of something you'd like to discuss, call me at that number and Mr. Ashcroft and I will meet you as soon as possible."

Doris's face brightened. "Mr. Ashcroft? You mean the gentleman you were with?"

"Yes," Marjorie answered casually.

Doris folded and unfolded the piece of paper with Marjorie's number and licked her lips eagerly. "He'd . . . um . . . be joining us?"

"Yes, naturally. Wherever I go, he goes." In truth, it was the other way around, since Creighton possessed an automobile and she didn't, but in the words of Mr. Schutt, she was focusing too much on technicalities. "We're partners, of sorts."

"Oh," Doris replied despondently, and turned her gaze once again to the floor.

"*Business* partners," Marjorie elucidated.

"Oh." The maid looked up again and recommenced with her paper folding. "Is he also . . . um . . . like us?"

"What do you mean, 'like us'?"

"Is he part of Mrs. Van Allen's circle? Or is he practically penniless too?"

"Creighton? Nope, he's loaded. Oodles of money."

"Oh." She thrust her hands, still clutching the piece of paper, into the pocket of her apron and yet again gazed, disheartened, down at the floor.

"But you needn't worry," Marjorie consoled, "he's quite egalitarian."

"Huh?"

"He's very down to earth," Marjorie paraphrased.

Doris's gaze turned from the floor to the hem of her apron, which she began nervously pleating and unpleating between her nimble fingers. "I think he's dead handsome," she blushed.

"He has his merits, I suppose." She grinned, a fiendish glint in her eye. "I'm sure he'd be the perfect catch for *some* lucky girl."

"But I'm just a maid," Doris sighed.

"What does that have to do with anything?" Marjorie demanded as Creighton's words came flooding back into her memory. "I was always taught that true nobility lies in bearing, not in breeding. Why, from what I've seen, you conduct yourself with more grace and charm than Mrs. Van Allen and all her friends thrown together."

"Really?" the maid beamed.

"Absolutely."

"I—I think I will meet with you. My day off is Wednesday." The sound of footsteps emanated from a location somewhere further down the hall. The young woman glanced behind her. "I should get back to work. I'll call you."

Marjorie watched as Doris scooted down the hallway and admonished herself for her behavior. She had wheedled her way into Doris's confidence. Naïve, gullible, frumpy Doris! The thought made her slightly nauseous. She moped into the lavatory and closed the door. Standing before the pedestal sink, she examined the sherry stains on her skirt and wondered if they weren't somehow symbolic of the smudges of dishonor upon her soul.

She heaved a melancholy sigh and looked up to view her reflection in the mirror. Same blonde hair, same fair skin, and same rosy cheeks. Yes, she was the same person. Her face broke into a wide smile. Her ethics may have been slackening a bit, but she was turning out to be a damn good detective.

NINE

"So now I'm Mata Hari," Creighton asserted. He and Marjorie had left the Van Allen residence and journeyed downtown to The Pelican Club, a popular restaurant and nightspot. They were seated in a cozy, semicircular booth not far from the dance floor, discussing their Wednesday meeting with Doris.

"I would hardly call you that," Marjorie contradicted.

"Oh no? What else do you call someone who has been asked to seduce the enemy in order to gain information?"

Marjorie clicked her tongue. "No one's asking you to seduce anyone! Besides, Doris isn't the enemy. She's just a maid who might be a valuable witness."

"Perhaps," Creighton argued, "but she's a maid to Gloria Van Allen, which makes her a member of the enemy camp." He paused for a few moments. "And if you're not asking me to seduce the girl, what exactly *are* you asking me to do?"

"Nothing," she cried. "I'm asking you to do nothing other than to be present at our meeting."

"So I'm supposed to sit there like a boob?"

"No," she nearly sang the word. "Be polite, say hello, smile. Whatever it was you did today that she found so irresistible."

"Well, what was that?"

Marjorie shrugged. "Don't ask me. I'm not the one drooling all over you."

Creighton winced. *As if I need to be reminded.* "Speaking of drooling," he peeked at his watch, "I wonder what's keeping your dreamboat, Jameson."

Marjorie ignored him and took an exaggerated interest in her dinner menu.

"Oh, well. As they say, absence makes the heart grow fonder." He picked up his own dinner menu and perused it before speaking again. "I have to tell you, Marjorie, I'm not exactly happy with this whole Doris business."

Marjorie looked up from her bill of fare.

"I feel as if we're toying with the girl's emotions. Leading her on, so to speak."

"Then don't lead her on. Act naturally. Be yourself."

"Yes, but I'm afraid that my mere presence will be enough to lead her down the garden path. She's only meeting us because she anticipates that some great romance might develop. The poor girl's going to be awfully disappointed if I leave the meeting without asking to see her again." He frowned, and then suddenly his eyes grew wide. "I know what I'll do. I'll make myself unattractive to her. That way, she'll be relieved when I don't make a move in her direction."

"What are you going to do? Glue an artificial wart to the end of your nose?"

"Not *physically* unattractive," Creighton corrected. "Unattractive personality-wise. You know—behave in an irritating manner."

Marjorie smirked. "In other words, be yourself."

"Miss McClelland, do I sense hostility?" he asked playfully.

"No." She turned up her nose.

"You're lying," he accused. "You're still upset over that comment I passed earlier, in the car."

"Maybe." The writer looked away and fiddled with an earlobe.

"No, not maybe. You're angry with me." He grinned. "I don't know why you're so incensed. I merely remarked that I wasn't above the use of flattery. I never said that I was using it at that particular moment."

Marjorie cast him a sideways glance. "Well, were you using it?"

"Using what?" Creighton asked dumbly.

"Flattery!" she nearly shouted.

"That depends."

"Depends on what?"

"On which one of us is buying dinner tonight."

Marjorie stuck out her tongue.

Creighton smiled and then glanced over her head. "You'd better put that away." He gestured toward the sliver of pink protruding from her mouth. "Here comes lover boy."

Jameson hurried toward the table. "Sorry if I've kept you waiting."

"No bother," assured Creighton. "We were just discussing the dinner menu. Marjorie was considering ordering the tongue."

She wrinkled her nose at Creighton and then slid to the center of the rounded booth to enable Jameson to sit beside her. "How did everything go with Mrs. Bartorelli?"

Jameson sat down and took a deep breath. "If you consider a woman who throws herself on the ground screaming to be a positive sign, then my visit was an overwhelming success."

"She did all that, did she?" asked an amused Creighton.

"And more," the detective answered. "Although I think I brought on some of it myself."

"How?" Marjorie inquired.

"When I told her that her husband was dead, she started to cry. She said she'd never find another man like Victor, so, of course, I asked her if that was such a bad thing."

"Oh, no," mumbled Marjorie and Creighton in unison.

"Oh, yes," Jameson affirmed. "She screamed at me in Italian, and then fell to the ground in hysterics—kicking, shrieking, crying, wailing." He brought his hands to his temples. "I'll never understand people. I thought she'd be happy to be rid of him."

"Talk about your love-hate relationships," Marjorie commented.

"Hmm," agreed Jameson.

"Did Noonan's men find anything at Kensington House?" asked the Englishman.

Jameson pulled a face. "No, I'm giving them one more day. If they don't find anything by dusk tomorrow, I'll order them back to the station. This way you can have your house back."

Creighton was indifferent. "I never really had the house in the first place."

Marjorie interjected, "Did you get anything new on Bartorelli?"

Jameson shook his head—that, too, was a washout. "How was your afternoon? Better than mine, I hope."

"Yes," Creighton responded. "Although not quite as entertaining."

"What did you learn?"

"Aside from the fact that Mrs. Van Allen wasn't as passionate about her husband as Mrs. Bartorelli was about hers, not much." He recounted the events of their meeting with Gloria Van Allen.

"Did you mention Bartorelli?"

"Yes, when I was alone with Mrs. Van Allen and her brother-in-law. Other than not recognizing the name at first, they showed little or no reaction."

"So your afternoon was about as successful as mine."

"As far as information is concerned, yes. However, we did make some inroads. Gloria invited us to a party she's throwing on Friday."

"Correction: she invited *you* to the party," rectified Marjorie.

"Yes, but she told me to bring a guest. That would be you."

"She doesn't want that guest to be me. She's probably at home right now, wishing that I come down with the grippe."

Jameson smirked. "Is it safe to assume that you and the Widow Van Allen didn't get along well?"

"Like oil and vinegar."

"I wouldn't go that far," Creighton differed. "You may not like the woman, but I don't think she totally abhors you. After all, she did give you that check before we left."

"She only wrote that check to get rid of me. She doesn't want to hear about the Ladies Literary Whatchamacallit again."

Jameson pricked up his ears. "A check?"

"Yes," Marjorie laughed. "It's actually kind of funny. Creighton introduced me as the head of some hoity-toity charitable organization. The Ridgebury Women's Book Club or something like that. Well, he must have been very convincing, because she sent me off with a contribution."

"You mean you accepted a donation from her?" Jameson asked in disbelief.

"I had to," stated Marjorie matter-of-factly. "If I had refused it, I would have given away the whole charade."

"But you can't take money from these people," the detective argued.

"It's only a little bit of money," Creighton stated dismissively.

"No it isn't. It's five hundred dollars." Marjorie removed the check from her handbag and passed it to Creighton. "Here. Have a look."

He took the piece of paper and examined it. "Hmm. Gloria mustn't have remembered the name of our group either. She wrote the check out to you." He handed it back to her. "That means you can cash it."

"No, you can't cash it," Jameson exclaimed.

Marjorie placed her hand on the detective's arm. "I know how you feel. I was uncomfortable about accepting it at first, too. But then I realized that she can well afford it."

"That's not the point. The two of you conned her out of that money."

Marjorie gasped. "We did not! She gave us that money quite willingly. We never asked her for a dime!"

"It doesn't matter. You misrepresented yourselves; that constitutes fraud. I could have you both arrested for this."

"Well! That's a fine note of thanks, isn't it? After we spent all afternoon doing your dirty work."

"I never asked you to do my dirty work. You offered to visit Mrs. Van Allen." He looked to Creighton for aid, but the Englishman held up his hands to show he had nothing to offer.

"That makes it even worse!" Marjorie raged. "You threatening to arrest two good-natured volunteers!" She took a deep breath and looked at Jameson with moist green eyes full of hurt. "Really, Robert, I expected more from you."

The use of his Christian name, combined with Marjorie's adroit rearrangement of the facts had left Jameson looking as if he had survived a cyclone. Creighton watched the detective with amused pity. He hadn't doubted for an instant that Marjorie would emerge from this struggle victorious.

"I'm sorry," the policeman muttered, "I didn't mean to be ungrateful."

Marjorie pouted for a moment and then tried on a bewitching smile. "That's all right, I forgive you. And as a show of my esteem, I'll tell you about my visit with Doris."

"Doris?"

"The maid." She went on to describe the encounter in the Van Allen hallway.

"Quite a scoop," Jameson commented when she had finished. "But be careful—Doris's judgment might be clouded by dislike for her boss."

"Yes," Marjorie agreed. "I had wondered about that myself, but then I remembered the expression on her face. The fear I saw there was very real."

"Well, in either event, you'll find out more when you two see her the day after tomorrow."

"And, even if she tells us nothing else of interest, she has, at least, shed some light on an interesting prospect."

"What prospect is that?" the detective asked.

"That Henry was murdered," answered Creighton.

Marjorie expounded upon this concept as Jameson held his head and groaned. "Look, before you pooh-pooh the idea, just think about it. Doris said that Mrs. Van Allen killed her husband as surely as if she had pushed him. What if he had been pushed? We've already found some flaws in the suicide theory: his work practices that day, the trip from New York to Ridgebury, and the height of the balcony."

"You're forgetting the suicide note," the detective countered.

"The note is irrelevant. It would have been quite easy for Gloria, or anyone else with a sample of Henry's handwriting, to have forged it."

"Refresh my memory, Jameson," Creighton requested. "What did the note say again?"

"'I can't go on,'" he replied.

"You needn't be so dramatic," Marjorie chided. "He only asked a question."

"I'm not being dramatic. That's what the note said: 'I can't go on.'"

"Oh," she responded comprehendingly.

"Was it signed?" Creighton asked.

"Yes, with his first name and nothing more."

"So we're talking about a handwritten document containing five words. Five very simple words, nonetheless. I would say that unless this note was witnessed by a notary public, it's wide open to suspect."

"Let me get this straight," Jameson imposed. "Not only do you think that Bartorelli's death is linked to Van Allen's, but now you're assuming that they were both murdered."

"You have to admit," Creighton cajoled, "it makes more sense that way. A murder linked to a murder rather than a murder linked to a suicide."

Jameson shook his head. "I don't know. It doesn't—"

"Oh, look!" Marjorie interrupted before Jameson could argue. She pointed toward the dance floor; the band that had been on break was filing back into their seats. "I hope they play something good. It's been ages since I've danced."

At that, the orchestra soared into a rousing rendition of "The Continental."

Marjorie cooed with delight. "Oh, I love this song!"

Creighton, interpreting Marjorie's declaration as a hint for a dance invitation, declined. "Don't look at me. I don't dance."

Jameson hopped to his feet and extended his hand toward the young woman. "Fortunately, I do. Shall we?"

Beaming, she placed her hand in his and followed him onto the dance floor.

Creighton, left behind to observe, took solace in the fact that "The Continental" was a lively, sprightly tune, rather than a soft, romantic ballad. As Jameson twirled Marjorie about the room, Creighton examined their dancing positions for any sign of impropriety. He heaved a sigh of relief as he noticed that the couple stood about a foot apart from each other and that the detective's right hand was in a safe position on the small of Marjorie's back.

His comfort was short-lived, however. He recalled that "The Continental" had been played at the numerous holiday parties he had attended during the previous season. He also recalled a section in the song wherein the participants of the dance were spurred to share a kiss.

Creighton immediately leapt from the booth. He sprinted across the dance floor and tapped Jameson on the shoulder. The policeman politely nodded and then stepped aside so that the Englishman could adopt his place opposite Marjorie. The writer, placing her left hand on Creighton's shoulder, was perplexed. "I thought you said you didn't dance."

"I don't, but I thought it might make a nice companion poster for the film *Anna Christie*. You know, 'Garbo talks! Ashcroft dances!'"

Marjorie laughed, and Creighton might have thought it to be the most wonderful sound in the world if his concentration weren't focused entirely upon his feet. Creighton was not a very good dancer. He could muddle through the slow numbers, but quicksteps and their frequent chord changes had always intimidated him. Not knowing what else to do, he broke into a choppy box step, hopping from one foot to the other as if there were an imaginary divider between his legs.

As the string section flew into a lilting melody, Creighton, in a burst of bravado, spun Marjorie about several times, and then, grabbing her firmly around the waist, took off in a steady trot to circumnavigate the dance floor. Marjorie, panting, struggled to keep pace with him.

The singer took his position at the microphone and began to croon. "*Beautiful music . . . dangerous rhythm . . .*"

Creighton prepared himself for the next line of the song.

"*You kiss while you're dancing . . .*"

At the sound of the singer's words, all the men on the dance floor leaned forward to kiss their partner. Creighton eagerly puckered up and followed suit, but Marjorie, turning her head at the last second, left him with a mouth full of hair.

"*You sing while you're dancing . . .*"

Marjorie, expecting Creighton to respond to these lyrics as well, firmly clamped her hand over his mouth. They both laughed and set off for another dizzying sprint around the room.

When the song ended, Creighton accompanied Marjorie back to the table, his arm still encircling her waist. "That was an interesting dance," Jameson commented upon their arrival.

"It's called the 'Society Two-Step,'" Creighton replied.

"Funny. It didn't look like a two-step."

"It's a misnomer. Like the word 'thunderbolt,' for instance."

"Well, I personally wouldn't have cared if we had done the cakewalk or the black bottom," Marjorie declared. "It just felt good to dance again." She returned to the seat beside Jameson; Creighton slid in after her.

No sooner had they sat down than a waiter surfaced to take their drink orders. Jameson checked his watch. "I'm off duty. I'll have a scotch and soda."

Marjorie was about to ask for a cup of coffee when Creighton submitted his order for a bottle of vintage Montrachet and two glasses. The waiter hurried off to fill his customers' requests.

"I don't know if I should drink that," Marjorie stated in reference to the wine. "I have a screaming headache."

"Little wonder," remarked Creighton. "I thought for certain you would have stuck to drinking tea this afternoon. What, in heaven's name, possessed you to choose the sherry?"

"You said to follow your lead," Marjorie snapped. "I thought, perhaps, sherry was more fashionable than tea."

"It is if you're accustomed to drinking it," he answered sharply. "When I told you to follow my lead, I was referring to words and actions, not beverages."

"Well, I thought that since you opted for the sherry that I should do the same."

"Yes, but I opted for the sherry once, not four times."

Jameson, who had been selecting an entrée from the dinner menu, looked up. "You drank four glasses of sherry?"

"Yes," Marjorie replied sheepishly, "but they were very small glasses." She held up her thumb and forefinger as to indicate the size of the glass.

Jameson sighed and threw his menu onto the table.

"What's the matter, Jameson?" Creighton asked. "Are you going to berate us for drinking while on duty? We're not policemen, remember."

"I know you're not policemen, but you are representing the Hartford County Police Department. You might try to remember that the next time you're out snooping around."

"No one knows the police sent us," Creighton argued. "As far as they're concerned, we popped in for a social visit."

"Yes, but just imagine my report." He looked out into the distance, as if he were actually reading the document from across the room. "'Miss McClelland and Mr. Ashcroft, during an afternoon of heavy drinking—'"

"It was not an afternoon of heavy drinking!" Marjorie avowed.

"That's right," Creighton concurred, and then added, sotto voce: "At least not for *me*." He winked and nodded in Marjorie's direction.

"Thank you, Mr. Volstead," she stated sarcastically.

Jameson, meanwhile, was in the process of verbalizing his doubts about allowing his tablemates to work with him. "This is what I get for recruiting civilians: using bribery to reopen a case, committing fraud, drinking on the job . . ." The list of injuries went on and on.

Creighton and Marjorie glanced at each other in commiseration. The band began to play "Prisoner of Love." Creighton rose to his feet and summoned loudly, "Marjorie, would you care to feather step?"

"I'd be delighted," she replied with obvious relief. She slid out of the booth after him.

"Wait one minute!" Jameson bellowed. "We're having a discussion here."

"Not now, Jameson!" He held his hand to his mouth in a secretive gesture. "The lady wants to feather step."

"I thought you didn't like to dance," the detective responded.

"I don't," Creighton confessed. "But the more you talk, the more appealing it becomes." He grabbed Marjorie, and in an exaggerated version of the tango, the couple danced away from the table.

TEN

CREIGHTON RESTED COMFORTABLY THAT night, lulled to sleep by thoughts of Marjorie: the sensation of holding her in his arms as they danced, the smell of her perfume, the sound of her voice as they sang along with the radio during the long drive home. It had been an idyllic, if somewhat flawed, evening. The first and principal defect had been the distracting presence of Robert Jameson. He liked the detective well enough—he was an honest, hardworking, affable chap. However, there was something, be it jealousy or insecurity, that made Creighton want to throttle the man.

The second and lesser flaw lay in the fact that, in all of their fourteen hours together, Creighton had not once managed to steal a single kiss from Marjorie. His attempt on the dance floor of The Pelican Club had been easily thwarted. And a bid for a farewell smooch on Marjorie's front stoop had nearly resulted in his nose being broken as the young woman slammed her door shut. Still, Creighton remained optimistic; he might not have tasted those tantalizing red lips, but neither had the good detective.

He awoke a few minutes after eight in the morning, and after a prolonged period spent stretching and yawning, he rose from his bed and threw open one of the heavy canvas window shades. The morning loomed gray and stormy, the sort of uninspiring day that made Creighton loath to relinquish the comfort of his pajamas. Fortunately, lodging with Mrs. Patterson meant that he didn't have to dress for breakfast. It was a distinct advantage over staying at the Ritz.

He plucked a plaid dressing gown from its place in the closet and donned it, taking care to conceal his bare chest, for his sleeping ensemble consisted only of pajama trousers, never the jacket. As he slid his feet into his slippers, he caught a glimpse of himself in the mirror and frowned. The plaid pattern of his robe clashed most dreadfully with the bold stripes of his pajama bottoms, his hair was quite tousled, and upon his face grew a heavy layer of stubble.

Vanity nearly got the better of Creighton, but then he remembered the gentlewoman downstairs. Staying at the boarding house was similar to visiting the home of a grandmother or an elderly aunt—there was no need to keep up appearances. Bearing this in mind, Creighton headed for the kitchen feeling well rested and utterly at ease with himself.

It was, therefore, much to his alarm that he found Marjorie, perfectly outfitted in a cream-colored blouse and brown skirt, seated at the breakfast table sipping coffee. She looked him over from head to toe. "Good morning," she greeted, a hint of a snicker in her voice.

Creighton clutched at the top of his robe with one hand and began smoothing his hair with the other. "Good morning," he replied. "I, um, didn't expect to see you here this early."

She was scrutinizing his costume and smiling. "Yes, I can see that."

Mrs. Patterson was in her usual spot by the stove. "Good morning, Creighton. Breakfast will be ready soon. Why don't you and Marjorie keep each other company in the meantime?"

Creighton heeded this suggestion and took his seat at the place opposite Marjorie. A small, stenographic notebook rested on the table in front of her. "What's that?"

"I'm making a list of people associated with the Van Allen case," she replied, before taking another swallow of coffee from her earthenware cup.

His own cup had been placed upside down on its saucer; Creighton righted it and then lifted the coffeepot from a trivet in the center of the table. "A cast of characters?" He poured himself some of the dark, fragrant fluid and then topped off Marjorie's cup.

"Thanks," she remarked absently, as she diluted her drink with a drop more milk. "I guess you could call it that, but I'm afraid the roster is a bit short at the moment. Tell me if I've missed anyone. So far, I have Gloria, William, Doris, and Henry's secretary. I think her last name is Hadley."

Creighton tilted backwards on the rear legs of his chair and pensively combed his hair with his fingers. During the silence, Mrs. Patterson deposited his breakfast on his plate. "*Pain perdu*," he stated as he returned the chair to its proper position.

Marjorie looked at him in confusion. "Who?"

"Not who. What. Pain perdu is what the French call French toast," he explained as he drizzled maple syrup over the slices of egg-soaked bread.

"You know, I had often wondered about that. It would be rather redundant for the French to name it 'French toast,' and it would sound too possessive if they referred to it as 'our toast.'" She reached across the table and, with the spoon she had used to stir her coffee, removed a bite-size portion of bread from his plate. "What does *pain perdu* mean anyway?" she asked when she had finished chewing.

"It translates to 'lost bread,'" he replied as he watched her steal two more mouthfuls.

"Lost bread, that's an odd thing to call it." She raided his dish again. "How did they come up with that?"

His plate was now half-empty. "I don't know," he replied as he spied her spoon returning for yet another assault. "But I suspect it originated with a person who shared his table with the likes of you." He fought off the attack by poking her hand gently with his fork.

"I can make you a slice of your own, Marjorie," Mrs. Patterson offered from the other half of the kitchen.

"No, thank you," she declined. "I had breakfast before I left the house."

"If its not too much trouble, Mrs. Patterson," Creighton appealed, "I'll take another piece."

"Of course it's not too much trouble."

"Three slices?" Marjorie remarked. "My, but you're hungry this morning."

"Yes. Watching other people eat has always had that effect on me."

She glared at him and picked up the notebook. "So, can you think of anyone else to add to my list?"

Mrs. Patterson returned with the lone slice of French toast and then settled in to enjoy her own breakfast. Creighton hunched over his plate to guard his new acquisition. "No, I think you mentioned everyone thus far," he answered as he stabbed a piece of the fried bread with his fork. "Unless there's someone here in Ridgebury to whom Henry was close."

She shook her head. "No, the Van Allens never socialized with the townspeople. Everything they needed was up at the house. The servants ran errands and did the shopping."

"Except," Mrs. Patterson interjected, "for the times that Mr. Van Allen visited Walter's shop."

"That's right," the young woman cried, "I had nearly forgotten about Mr. Schutt."

Creighton looked up from his food. "Mr. Schutt? The old busybody who owns the bookstore?" No sooner had the words left his mouth than he realized his mistake.

"How do you know Mr. Schutt?" Marjorie immediately questioned.

Mrs. Patterson, who had been in the act of sipping tea, froze on the spot. She stared at Creighton from behind her steaming cup.

"Well . . . um . . . Mrs. Patterson told me about him, of course."

"Oh."

Mrs. Patterson, visibly relieved, replaced her cup on its saucer and sighed.

Creighton made haste to move the conversation along. "So Henry and Mr. Schutt were fast friends, then?"

"I wouldn't say 'fast friends,'" Mrs. Patterson countered, "but they got along all right. That is, until the book dispute."

"Book dispute?"

"As I said before, Mr. Van Allen frequented the bookstore. One day, he mentioned to Walter that he was searching for some rare book."

"A first edition of *David Copperfield*," Marjorie editorialized.

The elderly woman nodded. "That's right. He said that he would be very grateful if Walter could track down a copy for him. Said he would pay three times whatever Walter paid for it."

"Sweet deal," Creighton commented, as he dabbed the corners of his mouth with his napkin.

"That's what Walter thought," Mrs. Patterson continued, "so he located a copy of *David Copperfield* and purchased it with his life savings, confident that Mr. Van Allen would reimburse him, with interest."

"But he didn't," Creighton presumed.

"No. He called Mr. Van Allen and they agreed to meet at Kensington House to make the exchange. When Walter arrived at the house, Van Allen had an appraiser there with him. The appraiser examined the book and valued it at far less than what Walter had anticipated. Mr. Van Allen rescinded on his original offer and said he would only pay what the book was worth. Needless to say, Walter was livid. He refused Mr. Van Allen's offer and tried to sell the book elsewhere, but no one wanted to pay the price he asked for it. Eventually, viewing half a loaf as better than none, he went back to Mr. Van Allen and offered it to him at the price the appraiser had suggested. Mr. Van Allen simply laughed at him and told him he was no longer interested in the book." She shook her head in empathy for the pitiable Mr. Schutt. "Walter had gotten in way over his head. He was only a small town shopkeeper. What did he know about first editions?"

"Did Mr. Schutt contact an attorney?" Creighton asked.

"He couldn't afford a lawyer, but he did seek some legal advice. He was told that he didn't have much of a case since all he had with Mr. Van Allen was a verbal agreement, and not a written contract."

"True," the Englishman observed. "It would have been one word against the other, and the majority of people would have believed Van Allen over a lowly merchant." He pushed his empty plate aside and further pondered the situation. Gazing across the table at Marjorie, he asked, "Are you thinking what I'm thinking?"

She nodded. "That losing one's life savings is a very good motive for murder."

"Oh, no!" Mrs. Patterson cried. "You can't think that Mr. Schutt—he may be abrasive and difficult, but *murder?*"

Marjorie placed a comforting hand on the woman's shoulder. "Mrs. Patterson, we have to look into all the possibilities. I personally don't believe Mr. Schutt is capable of hurting a fly." She looked away suddenly. "*Mrs.* Schutt, on the other hand, is a different story."

"Not Louise!" the boarding-house owner gasped.

"You have to admit she's a tough lady," Marjorie prodded.

"Yes, she's tough," Mrs. Patterson acknowledged. "But I'll have you know that underneath that tough exterior is a very religious, family-oriented person. Why, she's simply devoted to her husband."

"Yes, very devoted," Marjorie agreed. "All the more reason for her to harbor a grudge against Henry Van Allen."

"Add their names to the list," Creighton directed as he gestured toward the notepad. "Is there anyone else you ladies can think of?"

Mrs. Patterson somberly shook her head, but Marjorie stated boldly, "Yes, Reverend Price."

The elderly woman stared at her, aghast. "Marjorie, no!"

"It will eventually come out in the open. Everyone in town knew that there was no love lost between them."

"Who's Reverend Price?" Creighton inquired.

"Reverend Price is the minister over at the First Presbyterian Church. It's down on Ridgebury Road." She pointed in an easterly direction. "At the other end of the green. It's the second-oldest building in town, Kensington House being the first, of course. Well, it goes without saying that a building of that age requires a great deal of maintenance. In order to pay for that maintenance, the parish sponsors a variety of fundraising activities, but the most popular event is a fair they hold the first weekend of June. It's your ordinary church fair: flower competition, bake-off, kissing booth, pony rides for the children. But the highlight of the whole thing is a drawing in which the church raffles off a percentage of the weekend's earnings."

She took a deep breath and then continued. "One year, the fair and the drawing were held as usual. Everything seemed to have come off quite smoothly. However, on Sunday night after everyone had left, Reverend Price sat down to count the proceeds and found that he had quite a bit less than he had anticipated. Someone had made an error in arithmetic; as a result, the church had raffled off more money than it could afford."

"Bit of bad luck," Creighton commented.

"It gets worse," Marjorie responded. "That year, the church was in dire need of a new roof. Reverend Price was beside himself. He didn't feel it was proper to ask the winners of the drawing to return their money, so he did the only thing he could conceive of doing. He went to Henry Van Allen and asked for the money to pay for the roof. Since Henry had already donated some money to the church that year, the Reverend thought it feasible that he might give more. But, when Reverend Price explained what had happened, Henry accused the Reverend of misappropriation of church funds and reported him to the local presbytery."

Creighton quipped in the manner of a proud father, "That's our boy Henry, always taking time to make new friends."

"If that's your idea of friendship, then Mr. Van Allen and the Reverend were very chummy. Reverend Price was temporarily removed from his pulpit while the classis investigated the charges against him. He was only restored to the parish after Henry's death. Seems that Mr. Van Allen was the only person in town who had a complaint against the man. With him out of the way, there was no reason the minister shouldn't continue his work in Ridgebury."

"So Henry's demise was very convenient for the good vicar," he commented.

Marjorie smiled. "One might even be tempted to call it heaven-sent."

Creighton mused, "As my nursemaid used to say, 'What the good Lord doesn't provide, we must provide for ourselves.'"

"Reverend Price is a man of the cloth! I will not have you two speaking about him in such a manner!" Mrs. Patterson turned her wrath toward the girl seated beside her. "Especially you, Marjorie Mc-Clelland! Your father raised you to be a God-fearing young woman and here you are, talking heresy."

"I am a God-fearing woman, but Reverend Price isn't God; he's a human being who represents God. And human beings, no matter how divine, are capable of terrible things if they're desperate enough, particularly where love or money is concerned."

"So you're going to add his name to the list," Mrs. Patterson concluded grimly. "And what, if I might be so bold to ask, do you plan to do with this list when it's finished?"

"Review it with Detective Jameson," Marjorie admitted.

"Detective Jameson!" Mrs. Patterson shrieked.

"This *is* Detective Jameson's case."

"But you're going to turn the Schutts and Reverend Price over to the police?"

"We're not turning them over to the police. We're advising Detective Jameson of the situation."

"You may call it 'advising.' I call it betrayal."

Creighton reached across the table and placed his hand on Mrs. Patterson's in a soothing fashion. "I understand how you feel, Mrs. Patterson," he began diplomatically. "These people have been your friends and neighbors for several years. They're probably like a second family to you. It's only natural that you should wish to protect them, but keeping silent isn't the solution. In fact, it would probably make matters worse."

The elderly woman cast him a doubtful glance. Creighton leaned in further and followed his line of reasoning. "The whole village knew of Henry's disputes with Mr. Schutt and Reverend Price; if we don't tell Detective Jameson about them, it's only a matter of time before someone else does."

"Fine. Then the blame will be on that person's head, not mine."

"Yes, but don't you see? If Jameson gets this information from someone else, he'll immediately know that Marjorie and I have been holding out on him. It will appear to him that we concealed the truth because we believe that either Mr. or Mrs. Schutt or the Reverend Price is the guilty party. Not to mention, he'd most likely dispatch Noonan or Palutsky or another one of his goons to interrogate the poor souls. You know how they treated me during a routine questioning; imagine what they'd do to your friends."

"On the other hand, if Marjorie and I tell Jameson, we have more control of the situation. We can downplay the animosity between Van Allen and your neighbors, we can vouch for their character, and we can insinuate ourselves into being present at their questionings."

The elderly woman stared at Marjorie, searchingly. "It's in their best interest, " the writer corroborated.

Mrs. Patterson nodded solemnly. "I just hope they see it that way," she sighed.

With her loyalty no longer in dispute, Marjorie turned her attention to Creighton. "How much time do you need to, um, pull yourself together?" She ended her question with a tiny chortle.

"Half an hour, at most."

"Good," she proclaimed as she rose from her chair. "I'll call Detective Jameson and tell him to meet us at the bookstore in thirty-five minutes."

"The bookstore?" he inquired in alarm. An interview with Mr. Schutt was bound to reveal that Creighton had visited the shop on the afternoon of his arrival. His pulse quickened; somehow he had to find time to meet with the bookseller alone and secure his silence.

"Yes. Once I explain everything to Jameson, I'm sure he'll want to speak to the Schutts and Reverend Price as soon as possible."

"Why?" he asked in an effort to bide time.

Her eyes narrowed at his sudden lack of perceptiveness. "So that we can hear their stories firsthand. Right now, we're relying on gossip. Plus, we need to find out their alibis for the night of Henry's death."

"Oh," he remarked in a dimwitted fashion. "Well, you don't have to call Jameson this instant, do you? Sit down. Relax. Have another cup of coffee." He held up the coffeepot and posed with it, smiling.

"I don't want another cup of coffee. Besides, Jameson told us that morning was the best time to call him; he usually spends his afternoons out of the office." Marjorie left her side of the table and started in the direction of the kitchen door.

Creighton, realizing that she was headed for the telephone in the front parlor, stood up and blocked her path. "M-M-Marjorie," he stuttered. "I-I-I'm having second thoughts about telling Jameson."

She was wild-eyed. "What? We just finished having this discussion. Only a few seconds ago, you loved the idea."

"Yes, but I've realized that we've been acting rather hastily. This issue needs careful consideration; we should take our time. Sleep on it, if necessary."

"Sleep on it? You just woke up."

"I know," he complained, "but I'm not feeling particularly sharp today. Definitely not sharp enough to make a decision that might alter other people's lives. Why, just look at what I'm wearing. Do I look like the bastion of sound judgment?" He held out his arms and modeled the garish ensemble. "Let's give it one more day. If, by tomorrow morning, our opinion on the matter hasn't changed, we can drive out to the station and speak with the detective in person."

"We won't have time for that; we'll be out of town all day tomorrow. We're meeting with Doris, and after that I thought we'd try to track down Henry's secretary."

"Then we'll talk to him first thing on Thursday."

"Someone might spill the beans by then. We can't take that chance."

"All right, then. Go ahead and call Jameson, but I think it would be best if he and I went to the bookstore alone."

Marjorie raised a single eyebrow. "Oh? And why shouldn't I join you?"

Why . . . why? "Conflict of interest," he blurted. "These people are your neighbors."

"They're your neighbors, too," she quickly pointed out.

"True, but they've been your neighbors a lot longer than they've been mine."

"Are you saying you don't think I'd be able to remain impartial during the interrogation?" she challenged.

"I'm not doubting your objectivity. I'm trying to protect you. You've known these people your entire life. It may prove difficult for you to watch them being treated as suspects in a murder case."

"I can handle it," she assured him. "I'm not as fragile as you think I am."

Unless it had become a synonym for single-minded and stubborn, fragile was not a word that came to Creighton's mind when he thought of Marjorie. He was about to announce this fact when the young woman placed her hand upon his unshaven face, causing him to lose all train of thought.

"I thank you for your concern, though," she said softly. "It's very sweet of you." She gave his jowl a playful pinch before waltzing out the kitchen door.

Creighton, his heart a mixture of emotions—pleasure, guilt, anxiety—stared after her.

Mrs. Patterson, who had witnessed the entire scene from her seat at the head of table, spoke up. "Ah, what a tangled web we weave."

Creighton looked at her. "As appropriate as that cliché may be, can't you offer me something a little more hopeful?"

Mrs. Patterson chewed this over a moment and then shrugged. "Here goes nothing?"

Creighton nodded his approval and then repeated the elderly woman's words with a sigh. "Here goes nothing, indeed."

ELEVEN

THE RAIN CREPT INTO Ridgebury, arriving in the form of a gently soaking mist. Huddled beneath a large black umbrella, Creighton and Marjorie braved the drizzle and cut a path across the green to Schutt's Book Nook. As they stepped foot off the common and traversed the section of Ridgebury Road that accommodated westbound traffic, Creighton noticed a man emerging from the front door of the bookshop. He was close to Creighton's age and dressed in an erudite fashion: brown tweed suit with leather elbow patches, red bow tie and thick glass lenses. At the sight of Marjorie, he called out a greeting. "Hello! What brings you out on such a soggy day?"

"Research," Marjorie stated. "A new book waits for nothing, not even the weather." They stepped up onto the sidewalk and stood before the man. "Creighton," Marjorie presented, "I'd like you to meet Dr. Benjamin Russell."

Dr. Russell interrupted before Marjorie could complete the introduction. "Say, you're the new owner of Kensington House aren't you? Mr. Ashcroft, isn't it?" He extended his right hand.

The Englishman accepted it and gave it a hearty shake. "That's right, but how did you know?"

"Are you kidding? You're the talk of the town. The whole village is buzzing with the news of your gruesome discovery."

"Terrific. I'm a local celebrity because I discovered a body in my yard."

"I wouldn't feel bad about it. The townspeople feed on rumor and intrigue. If you hadn't found the body, they would have circulated stories of their own: that you've been married seven times, or that you have fifteen illegitimate children, or that you earned your money through bootlegging . . . that sort of thing. To be quite honest, the body has served you well. It's taken the focus of their gossip away from you."

"Lovely. I shall have to go to the morgue and thank him. So, Doctor, what is it like to be the local physician?"

"Oh, Dr. Russell doesn't practice medicine," Marjorie interposed.

The doctor chuckled and smoothed back a wayward strand of dark blonde hair. "No, the only people in my office have been dead thousands of years. My doctorate is in archaeology, specializing in Egyptian antiquities."

"Really? Would you mind if I paid you a visit some day?"

"Not at all." His pale eyes widened. "You've studied Egyptology?"

"No. However, I've always found the subject fascinating. One of my most vivid memories as a lad is of going to the British Museum and seeing the Rosetta Stone for the very first time. As a grown man, I can appreciate its scientific significance. But, back then, as a schoolboy suffering from poor penmanship, I was more impressed by the fact that someone had managed to carve the inscription so neatly, and not just in one language, but three." He smiled in embarrassment. "But here I am running on about it when I'm sure you've seen it for yourself."

"Yes, I have." Dr. Russell smiled indulgently.

"So you've been to London, then?"

"No, I saw the Stone while it was on loan to the Egyptian Museum in Cairo."

"Too bad. You'd love the British Museum; the Egyptian antiquities department has expanded quite a bit since I was a boy. Someone actually told me that there are now more artifacts there than what's left in the whole of Egypt."

"That's a bit of an exaggeration, but not much." Dr. Russell's last words were interspersed with the sound of tires splashing through the newly formed puddles that dotted Ridgebury Road. The trio gazed down the street at the approaching vehicle and recognized its black and white exterior as that of a Hartford County police car. The vehicle veered adjacent to the curb and came to a stop a few yards away from where the group was standing.

Dr. Russell commented at the sight of the automobile, "It looks as if your presence is requested elsewhere. Goodbye, Marjorie. Nice meeting you, Mr. Ashcroft." He bid adieu and retreated toward the green.

Detective Jameson, accompanied by the lumbering Officer Noonan, disembarked from the squad car and took up the spot on the sidewalk recently vacated by Dr. Russell. After a brief exchange of greetings, the detective inquired, "Are we ready?"

Creighton envisioned the fate that lay waiting for him behind the bookshop door. "As ready as I'll ever be," he answered fatalistically.

"Good," Jameson proclaimed. He grabbed the handle of the bookshop door and propped it open to allow the others admittance. Marjorie entered first, after a brief struggle with her umbrella; Creighton trailed closely behind.

Inside the shop, they found Mr. Schutt standing upon a narrow ladder, rearranging the contents of a high shelf. He descended from his lofty perch. "Good morning, Miss McClelland," he greeted, and then spying Creighton standing behind her, declared, "Mr. Ashcroft, how nice that we should meet again—"

"Yes!" Creighton interrupted loudly, successfully drowning out the word 'again.' "It is nice to meet you." He grabbed the shopkeeper's hand and pumped it vigorously.

"Why in heaven's name are you shouting?" Marjorie reprimanded. "Mr. Schutt isn't deaf."

"I'm sorry." Creighton laughed nervously as he relinquished the older man's hand. "I'm so excited. I've never been this popular before. Dr. Russell's right, I must be the talk of the town."

She eyed him askance. "Unfortunately, this isn't a social call, Mr. Schutt." She motioned toward the two men standing behind her. "This is Detective Jameson and Officer Noonan from the Hartford County Police. They'd like to speak to you about Henry Van Allen."

Mr. Schutt was surprised. "Henry Van Allen? Why, I haven't heard that name in quite a while. Does this have anything to do with that body you folks found up at Kensington House?"

"It has everything to do with it," Jameson explained. "'That body,' as you called it, happens to belong to Victor Bartorelli, the Van Allen's gardener."

"You're wasting your time here, then," Schutt argued crabbily. "I don't know anything about this Bartorelli person."

"But you did know Henry Van Allen," Officer Noonan interjected.

"I did, but he never mentioned his gardener, or anything else having to do with horticulture, for that matter."

"Well, you can just tell us what you *did* discuss," Noonan persisted.

"I fail to see how that information could possibly help you," the bookseller contended.

"Mr. Schutt," Jameson implored, "we have reason to believe that Bartorelli's death is somehow connected to Van Allen's. Therefore, *any* information you can give us might be helpful."

"Connected? But the person Miss McClelland and Mr. Ashcroft found was murdered, and Henry's death was a suicide, wasn't it?"

"Yes, that was the ruling," Jameson answered evasively.

"That *was* the ruling? You're questioning it?"

"No, we're exploring all the possibilities," Jameson stated abruptly. "Now, if you don't mind, it's time we ask *you* some questions." He scanned the area. "Is there an office or someplace where we can sit down?"

Mr. Schutt shook his head, "We all can't fit in the office; I'll bring some chairs out here." He shuffled behind the counter muttering to himself and anyone else who would listen, "Nothing better to do than to sit here and chat all day . . . waste of time, that's what it is . . . waste of time and taxpayers' money . . ."

"I'll lend you a hand with those chairs," Creighton volunteered. He followed Schutt through a pair of heavy woven curtains that served to partition the office from the rest of the shop. Once safely concealed behind the drapes, he grabbed the man by the shoulders. "Mr. Schutt, I have a favor to ask of you," he whispered frantically.

"A favor?" the merchant repeated. "What sort of favor?"

"Marjorie mustn't find out that I was here the other day."

"Why not?"

Creighton should have realized that this was not going to be easy; Mr. Schutt needed to know the why and wherefore of everything. "I want to surprise her."

"Surprise her how?"

"I'm sending Marjorie's book to a publishing friend of mine in England."

Schutt's forehead wrinkled. "Why?"

What would the man ask next? "Why is the sky blue?" "Where do babies come from?" "I hold Marjorie's work in very high regard. I think she would be a great hit there." He studied the older man's face. "Can I count on you to keep quiet about this?"

"I don't like to lie."

"You're not lying," Creighton cajoled, "you're just not telling her everything."

"That's a sin of omission."

"Yes, but look at the big picture. You'll be helping a local writer to become an author of world renown."

Schutt yawned in apathy.

Creighton sighed. *So much for altruism.* "I tell you what. I'll sweeten the pot. If you cooperate, I'll throw in a little bonus for you."

The man's eyebrows twitched. "Bonus? What did you have in mind?"

"I don't know. You tell me. Just name your price: money, books, a night on the town, anything you want."

While Mr. Schutt mulled over the offer silently, Creighton realized that his companions on the other side of the curtain were probably growing anxious. "Well?" the younger man pressed. "Will you do this for me?"

The merchant nodded reluctantly.

"Good man," Creighton proclaimed while patting him on the back. "And when you figure out how I can repay you, just let me know."

Mr. Schutt hoisted a pair of folding chairs from their position against the office wall. "Don't worry," he assured, tucking a chair under each arm and pushing his way through the drapes, "I will."

Yes, Creighton thought, *that's what I'm afraid of.* He inhaled deeply, grabbed the upholstered desk chair and a tall, wooden stool, and followed the older man back to the public area of the shop.

"What happened to you? You were gone forever," Marjorie commented upon the return.

The two men deposited their cargo and arranged them in a circular formation. "We were scrounging around for a fifth seat," Creighton explained as he moved the upholstered chair beside Marjorie and motioned to her to be seated. "Alas, we didn't find anything."

With Marjorie's comfort ensured, Creighton looked for a seat for himself, but found that they had all been occupied. Schutt and Jameson were stationed in the two collapsible chairs, and Noonan had positioned his bulky frame rather tenuously upon the wobbly stool. Seeing no other place to roost, Creighton leaned an elbow on the back of Marjorie's chair. "That's all right," he gibed his fellow men, "don't get up on my account."

Jameson flashed a guilty look at the Englishman and then began the interrogation. "So, Mr. Schutt, when did you first meet Henry Van Allen?"

"I remember it plain as day. It was January 1929, a couple of days after New Year's. We had just been hit by one of the worst snowstorms on record. Shut down everything—roads were blocked off, train tracks were frozen, and the whole town was without electricity." He took a deep breath before continuing. "The morning after the storm, I came down here to open the shop."

"You were open for business in spite of all the snow and the fact that the power lines were down?" interrupted Jameson.

Mr. Schutt chuckled. "What do you mean 'in spite of'? I opened the store *especially* because of all the snow and the power lines being down. The situation was a boon to my business. Snow-blocked roads meant that people couldn't go to Hartford for a movie, and no electricity meant that people couldn't listen to the radio. In those circumstances, what else can one do to entertain oneself, other than read a book?"

"There's always a game of cards," Creighton offered helpfully.

"So you opened the shop," Jameson prodded.

"Yes, I opened the shop and who do you think was the first person to come through the door?"

"Henry Van Allen," Creighton answered.

"That's right. You guessed it in one!"

"And they say guessing games are strictly a sport for children."

Marjorie looked up at him and grinned. "And you've disproved that theory how, exactly?"

Creighton bared his teeth in a mock snarl.

Mr. Schutt carried on with his tale. "Well, you could have knocked me over with a feather. That's how surprised I was. The Van Allens didn't make a habit out of coming to town, and they certainly never associated with ordinary townsfolk. To see Henry Van Allen standing in my doorway was quite a shock."

"What did he want?" Jameson inquired.

"Nothing, except maybe a reprieve from his boredom. He told me that he and his family had come to Ridgebury for the holidays. They were scheduled to return to New York when the blizzard struck and left them stranded. Like everyone else in town, the Van Allens were without electricity, so Mr. Van Allen decided to take a walk into town to pass the time. It was then that he first saw my shop. Being a book collector, quite naturally, he was drawn inside."

"So, he told you right away that he was a collector of old books," Noonan commented, his voice questioning.

"I guess he figured it would open up discussion: favorite books, favorite authors . . ."

Noonan nodded. "Is that when he mentioned his interest in first editions?"

"He mentioned them in passing, yes."

"Did he mention a *particular* first edition?"

Mr. Schutt's mood immediately soured. "I know what you're getting at, Officer. You want to know if Henry asked me about the copy of *David Copperfield*. If you've heard the whole story already, then why are you bothering me?"

"It's like you said, we got nothing better to do with our time."

Schutt scowled at the officer. "From what I see, I'm right."

Creighton leaned his head next to Marjorie's. "Watching these two is like watching the eleventh round of Baer and Carnera."

Jameson intervened. "Mr. Schutt, we're here because we want to hear your version of what happened. When a story gets spread around as gossip, the truth very often gets lost."

The older man conceded this point grudgingly. "Then to answer Officer Noonan's question, no. Mr. Van Allen did not mention the first edition of *David Copperfield* during our initial meeting. It would be several months before he finally broached that subject."

"And during that time a friendship developed," Jameson postulated.

"I wouldn't use the word friendship. That would imply a certain degree of intimacy. It's more accurate to say that an 'acquaintance-ship' developed. He'd stop by every few weeks and make idle conversation: the weather, the economy, the latest authors. He never spoke of his personal life, and I never spoke of mine."

"So, when did he ask you to obtain the first edition for him?"

"Saturday, September sixteenth," the shopkeeper answered flatly.

Jameson was startled by such a rapid and precise response. "You remember the exact day?"

"Yes, I recall it vividly because my wife and I were hosting an engagement party in honor of my daughter, Sheila, and her future husband." Schutt paused a moment and then added, offhandedly, "My other daughter, Sharon, is still at home." He cleared his throat and continued. "Anyhow, I planned to close shop early that day in order to help my wife with the preparations for the party that evening. Just as I was locking up, who should come wandering by but Henry Van Allen. He was surprised to see me leaving work so early and asked if I was ill. I assured him that I was fine and then told him of the party and of Sheila's betrothal. It was the only personal bit of information we ever exchanged."

"How did he react?"

"He was polite; he was always polite. He congratulated me heartily, and then remarked that his timing could not have been better. I asked him what he meant, and he explained that he had come to me that day with a business proposition. I informed him, very nicely, that I wasn't interested in any business other than the bookstore. He laughed and then told me that his business and my business were very closely related."

"His business being the acquisition of a rare book," Creighton commented.

"That's right."

"What, specifically, did he tell you?" Jameson queried.

"He told me that he possessed a first edition copy of nearly every major work by Charles Dickens. The only two books missing from this collection were *Little Dorritt* and *David Copperfield*, and he thought that perhaps I could find them for him."

"And you told him you could?"

"No, I told him he was out of luck. I had never dealt in first editions. I never had that kind of clientele."

Creighton spoke up. "A man like Van Allen wasn't going to let you off the hook that easily."

"You got that right. He told me that I stood to earn a great amount of money out of the deal, and then proceeded to remind me that my daughter was getting married. How nice it would be if I were able to provide her with a beautiful wedding or a new home as a wedding gift."

"And that's when you agreed," Jameson surmised.

Schutt, glassy-eyed, nodded. "I wanted those things for Sheila. I want those things for all my children. What parent doesn't?"

"It's true," a whiny voice concurred. The group was surprised to discover that the foreign sound had risen from none other than Officer Noonan. The police officer's eyes were damp and his naturally ruddy complexion was now a deep crimson.

"We all want to give our children the things we never had," his voice cracked. Massive teardrops streamed down his cheeks.

Creighton pulled a starched white handkerchief from his jacket pocket and handed it to the sobbing man perched beside him. "Here," he ordered irritably. "Pull yourself together. You're frightening Mr. Schutt . . . not to mention me."

Noonan tilted his head downward and blew his nose into the handkerchief, exuding a honk that made the frail legs of his seat tremble violently.

Marjorie drew a hand to her mouth to hide her amusement.

Jameson tugged awkwardly at his tie and cleared his throat. "I realize that this is a difficult subject." His eyes slid to Noonan, who was using the white cloth to wipe his brow. "But what were the terms of your arrangement with Henry?"

Mr. Schutt, still mesmerized by the hypersensitive Officer Noonan, was only half-listening. At Jameson's question, he jolted out of his awe-stricken state. "Terms? What terms?"

"For starters, how and when were you to deliver the book to Mr. Van Allen?"

"He didn't specify a date or a time by which he needed the books. I was instructed to call him as soon as I had either book in my possession."

"So you were to purchase the books on your own, and Mr. Van Allen would reimburse you," Jameson concluded.

"Correct."

"And how much money did he offer you to do this?"

Schutt laughed bitterly. "Henry Van Allen was the consummate businessman. He said to make him an offer, but he hinted that it wasn't uncommon for a good dealer to add a 200 percent markup on an item."

"So he led you to believe that you would triple your investment," Jameson interpreted. "Did you happen to get any of this in writing?"

"No, I didn't," Schutt answered as he sunk lower in his chair.

"You agreed to pay money out of your own pocket and trusted that this man would make good on his side of the deal?"

"Yes," Schutt nearly shouted. "Yes, I trusted him. I realize now that I was stupid. But Henry Van Allen was a wealthy and well-respected man. I had no reason to think he would go back on his word."

Jameson nodded morosely. "What happened next?"

"I went searching for the two books. I couldn't find *Little Dorritt* anywhere, but I did manage to locate a copy of *David Copperfield* so, as per Van Allen's instructions, I purchased it and immediately placed a call to him. He arranged for us to meet at Kensington House the following weekend."

"And when was this?" Noonan asked as he poised a pencil over his reporter's notebook.

Schutt cast his eyes toward the ceiling as he searched his memory. "Umm, around the middle of October."

Noonan jotted down the information as Schutt continued his story. "I went to the house as scheduled, showed him the book and named my price. Do you know he actually brought an appraiser with him? As if I were going to swindle him. Me! A simple store owner! As soon as I stated my price, he called his appraiser into the room. They examined the book and then went off to discuss the findings in private. When they returned, Van Allen declined my offer. He said that his so-called expert claimed that the price I wanted was for a book in 'very fine' condition, but that the copy I was offering was only in 'fine' condition."

"Did he make a counteroffer?" Creighton asked.

"Yes, but it was only slightly more than what I had paid for it. In hindsight, I should have accepted that offer. At least I would have broken even, but instead, I lost my temper."

"You lost your temper," Jameson repeated, his curiosity aroused. "What did you do?"

"I grabbed the book, called Van Allen some choice names, and left."

"Did you see him again?"

Schutt folded his arms across his chest. "Yes, I saw him a few days before he died, when I paid a visit to Kensington House."

"You went to Kensington House?" Jameson's eyes narrowed. "Why? Did Van Allen summon you?"

"No, going there was my idea. I wanted to make amends."

"Why? Did the better angels of your nature suddenly take hold of you?"

"No," Schutt rejected with a chuckle. "I'm not that big-hearted."

I can certainly attest to that, Creighton sneered to himself.

"I was looking out for my own interests. After the scene at Kensington House, I tried to sell the book elsewhere. When I couldn't find a single taker, I decided it was time to swallow my pride and try to renegotiate a deal with Van Allen."

"Was he receptive?" Jameson asked.

"He was polite, as usual. He welcomed me inside and even offered me a drink. I declined and got straight down to business. I apologized for my behavior during our previous meeting and explained to him that, in my inexperience in dealing with first editions, I had misjudged his offer."

"How did he react to all of that?"

"He was silent for a very long time after I had finished, and then he started to laugh, softly at first, and then with more and more zeal. Finally, after laughing himself red in the face, he spoke. I'll never forget his words. He said, 'You're very much the tragic hero, aren't you Walter? And like the tragic hero, hubris has been your downfall.'"

"Hubert?" Noonan spoke up. "Who's Hubert?"

"Hubris," Marjorie corrected. "An exaggerated sense of pride."

"If you ask me," Creighton remarked, "Van Allen sounds a bit balmy, evoking Homer to cover up his own transgressions."

Noonan looked up from his notepad, his eyes wide.

"Don't get your knickers in a twist, Noonan. Homer is a poet, not a suspect."

"I wouldn't be so hasty there, Cretin," Noonan chided. "In my experience, it's always the person you least suspect."

Jameson rolled his eyes and moved along with the interrogation. "How did you respond to those remarks?"

"I didn't have a chance to respond. Van Allen ordered his butler to escort me out of the house. Looking back, he must have realized why I was there, but he wanted me to say it. Wanted the pleasure of hearing me admit that I was wrong. Wanted to relish the moment when I got down on my knees and begged him to accept my offer."

"How much money did you lose, Mr. Schutt?"

He replied in a near whisper, "Five hundred dollars."

"Where were you the night Henry Van Allen died?"

"At home with my wife and daughter. Why?"

Jameson barreled forward. "How did you feel when you heard about his death?"

"I wasn't upset about it, if that's what you mean, but I wasn't happy, either."

"Why not?"

"Because he died before the world could learn what he was really like. The newspapers glorified him, made his life into one of virtue." Schutt fell silent, and then added softly, "*He* became the tragic hero."

With that, the shop door opened as if thrown wide by an ill wind. A beefy woman clad in a black coat and an absurd-looking rain hat stood in the doorway. "Walter! Walter! I brought your lunch!" She immediately noticed the group gathered before the counter, and approached them. "Walter, what is going on? I thought you were doing inventory today."

"I was, but I had some unexpected guests," the man answered as he gestured at the seats around him.

The woman closely examined the disruptive group; upon seeing Marjorie, she swiftly turned up her nose. "Hello, Miss McClelland," she hissed. The identity of the gang's ringleader was now evident.

Marjorie affected a smile. "Hello, Mrs. Schutt. How are you?"

Mrs. Schutt grunted her reply and looked questioningly at the other participants in the meeting, all of whom had since risen from their seats.

"Darling," Mr. Schutt began on cue, "this is Detective Jameson and Officer Noonan from the Hartford County Police."

Mrs. Schutt stared at them haughtily. "What business could you possibly have with my husband?"

"Police business," Noonan answered in an attempt to bait Mrs. Schutt. "But don't worry, you're not excluded from this party. We need to speak with you, too."

"Me? Why do you need to speak to me? What is this all about?"

"Henry Van Allen," Jameson rejoined.

"Henry Van Allen? What questions could you possibly ask about him?"

Mr. Schutt leaned close to his wife. "Detective Jameson here believes that the body that was found up at Kensington House might be somehow linked to him."

"Henry Van Allen's been dead nearly five-and-a-half years now, and that body was found just recently. I fail to see how the two could possibly be connected. Just seems like a big waste of time." She gestured to Creighton, who was leaning against a bookcase and trying, very earnestly, to blend into his surroundings. "You there! Are you the 'chief' or 'captain' here?"

An archaic smile registered upon the Englishman's face. "No. I'm Creighton Ashcroft, your new neighbor."

"Oh, I'm sorry! I didn't know." She quickly plucked the rain hat from her head, exposing a snarl of straw-colored hair. "I'm Louise Schutt," she stated abjectly as she thrust her hand at the newest member of the community. "It's so nice to meet you Mr. Ashcroft. It is 'Mr.' Ashcroft isn't it? It's not 'Sir' or 'Lord'?"

Creighton took her fleshy hand in his and bowed slightly. "Just 'Mr. Ashcroft.'"

"Oh well. You're still a person of quality. Lord knows, that's a lot more than I can say about many young people these days." She nodded in Marjorie's direction.

Jameson interrupted. "Ma'am, if you don't mind, we'd like to ask you those questions now."

Mrs. Schutt's round face grew pink. "I don't see how I can possibly help you. I never met Henry Van Allen. He dealt exclusively with Walter."

The detective knitted his eyebrows together, "But you knew *of* him, didn't you?"

"Well *of course* I knew who he was. The man swindled my husband, after all."

"So you weren't sorry to hear of his death," Jameson asserted.

"No, I wasn't sorry he died. I was only sorry for the way in which it came about."

"You mean the suicide?"

"No, not that. I mean that Henry Van Allen died as a result of a broken neck. It all happened very quickly. He should have suffered more."

"Mother!" Mr. Schutt admonished. "Remember yourself!"

Mrs. Schutt turned to her husband, frostily. "I realize the cruelty of my words, Walter. However, there's truth to be found in them. Henry Van Allen deserved a fate far worse than the one he received."

Marjorie mouthed a silent "I told you so" to Creighton.

With the matter of motive settled, Jameson posed the crucial question. "So where were you the night of Van Allen's death?"

"At home. Mr. Schutt and I don't go out much. We were just about to retire for the evening when the commotion started: police sirens, flashing lights, cars speeding down the road."

"Were you and Mr. Schutt alone all evening?"

"Alone? Heavens, no! Our daughter, Sharon, was there."

"Was she with you the entire night?"

"Yes, why do you ask?"

"I need to account for everyone's whereabouts," the detective answered evasively. "You're sure she was at home the whole evening? She didn't leave at any point to go out on a date or to meet with a couple of girlfriends?"

"No. Sharon is very particular about the kind of company she keeps."

Jameson cleared his throat. "What about your other daughter? I believe her name is Sheila."

"Yes," Mrs. Schutt chirped in adoration, "Sheila. She was out of town that week, visiting her future in-laws." She added quickly, "The trip was quite proper. I made sure that she was under a watchful eye at all times,"

"I'm sure," Jameson answered distractedly. "Do you have any other children?"

"Yes, a son, Simon. He hasn't lived at home for years, though. He went to school in New York and decided to stay there after graduation. He's very successful. Works in radio."

"Oh," Jameson replied with mock interest. "Did you know of anyone by the name of Victor Bartorelli?"

"No. Should I?"

"Not necessarily. I just thought it possible, since he lived nearby. He was the Van Allen's gardener."

"The gardener, you say? Come to think of it, I believe I might have encountered him. It was in the local hardware store. I went there one day to buy some mothballs, and I noticed a small, dark, foreign-looking man at the counter, purchasing a variety of lawn tools. I had never seen him before. When he left, I asked the clerk about him."

"And the clerk told you it was Bartorelli?"

"I think so. I remember it was some Italian name." She pronounced the word Italian with a long 'I.' "I'm positive, however, that it was someone who worked and lived up at the house."

"Did you speak to him?"

"Of course not!" Mrs. Schutt replied, horrified. "Do you think it is my wont in life to start up conversations with strange men?"

"No, of course not," a chastened Jameson replied haltingly.

Mr. Schutt took advantage of the detective's discomfiture to give voice to his weariness. "Say, are you almost done? I have to get back to my inventory."

"As a matter of fact, I only have one more question, and it's for you, sir."

Mr. Schutt peered over the half lenses of his glasses. "What's that?"

"Did you or your son ever serve in the Army?"

"No. Simon went off to college directly after graduating high school, and naturally, he was much too young to have fought in the war. As for myself, I was too old to register for the first draft of the war; the age limit was thirty. When they raised the age limit to forty-five the next year, I put my name in, but I was never called."

"And what about your father? Did he ever serve?"

"No, Detective Jameson, I come from a long line of civilians."

"Then I can safely assume that you don't possess an army issue Colt revolver."

"Yes you can. In fact I don't own any guns. Never have." He turned quizzical, "But what does the gun——"

Jameson cut him off. "Well, I think that does it for now. If we have any other questions, we'll contact you. Thank you for your time, Mr. Schutt." He nodded at the merchant's wife. "Mrs. Schutt."

Noonan tipped his hat in salute and followed his partner to the front of the shop, leaving Marjorie and Creighton to their goodbyes. "Good day, Mr. and Mrs. Schutt," the writer offered as she prepared for her departure. "I'll be seeing you soon."

"Yes," Creighton concurred, "we'll all be seeing each other again soon. It was very nice meeting you. *Both* of you. It was very nice meeting *both* of you." He gave a farewell wave and, keeping close at Marjorie's heels, moved to join the policemen waiting by the door. Once there, he congratulated himself on his successful coup. *I did it,* he thought. *I did it! Marjorie has no inkling that I was here the other day. True, I owe the old man a favor, but how bad could that be?*

His effervescence, however, was swiftly weighed down by the booming voice of Louise Schutt. "Mr. Ashcroft! Mr. Ashcroft, wait!"

Creighton and his companions paused near the front door and reluctantly returned to the rear of the shop. "Yes, Mrs. Schutt," Creighton replied with a polite smile.

"Mr. Ashcroft, will you do us the honor of having dinner with us tonight?"

"Dinner? Tonight?"

"Yes, at our house."

"I don't think so. I might not finish up with the police until late."

"Oh, yes, of course. My invitation is rather last minute isn't it? It's very rude of me to assume that you'd have nothing planned." For some reason, she didn't think it rude not to include Marjorie on the invitation. "How about tomorrow night, then?"

For this, Creighton had a legitimate excuse. "I have an appointment in New York tomorrow. Probably won't be back till late."

Louise was relentless. "Thursday?"

"Oh, I don't know." He tried to come up with another pretext for not attending.

"Sharon will be there. I know she'd be thrilled to meet you."

Mr. Schutt had resumed his inventory and was scratching figures onto a white piece of paper; at the mention of his daughter's name, he looked up over his clipboard. "That's right, Sharon will be there. If the two of you hit it off, you can take her to the Bijou after dinner. There's a film playing there that's she's dying to see."

"Dinner and the cinema? I'm not sure—"

Mrs. Schutt stared at him admonishingly. "Why? You're not married are you?"

The Englishman gave a jittery laugh. "Me? No, I'm not married."

"Good," Louise proclaimed. "Then there's no reason you shouldn't meet her."

"I'm not very fond of blind dates."

"Mr. Ashcroft," urged Schutt from his place before the counter, "don't think of it as a blind date. Think of it as a favor to an old man."

Creighton felt a cold spot develop in the pit of his stomach. "Favor?"

Schutt flashed a sly smile. "Yes, a favor. You know how it works. You do a favor for me and, someday, I do a favor for you."

Oh, hell! Was he cashing in on that already? "Well, when you put it that way, how can I possibly say no?"

"Delightful!" declared Louise. "Then we'll see you at our house at half past six on Thursday. Mrs. Patterson can tell you how to get there."

"Oh, and Mr. Ashcroft," Mr. Schutt added as he pulled his wallet from his pants pocket. "So that you won't consider this a blind date." He drew out a photograph and handed it to Creighton.

"Sharon?" he asked as he took it in his trembling hands.

The bookseller nodded.

Officer Noonan and Detective Jameson now flanked Creighton on either side; the three of them gazed down at the photo simultaneously. The portrait was that of a moon-faced girl with a piggy nose and slightly protruding front teeth.

Jameson cringed and then moved to stand beside Marjorie, his mouth a tiny 'O.' Noonan's eyes were still glued to the snapshot.

"So," Schutt prompted, "what do you think?"

"She's, umm, umm," Creighton struggled to find a complimentary word.

"She's womanhood's fairest flower," Mr. Schutt stated grandiosely.

Creighton pointed a finger at Walter Schutt. "That's it," he announced. "You took the words right out of my mouth. She's a flower. A blossom. A sweet-smelling blossom."

Noonan, whose attention had heretofore been riveted on the spherical countenance in the photograph, roused from his inert state. "Yep," he said flatly, "she sure does stink."

TWELVE

THE MORNING MIST HAD graduated to a steady falling rain since they had entered the bookstore. Marjorie opened her umbrella and turned a scornful eye heavenward. Normally she enjoyed rainy days, perhaps even reveled in them: skipping over puddles, listening to the sound of the raindrops as they splashed against the roof, watching the storm clouds as they passed overhead. Today, however, the wet weather only served to exacerbate her already foul mood—a mood that had sprouted the moment Creighton accepted the Schutt's dinner invitation. Or, more precisely, the moment he agreed to a blind date with Sharon Schutt.

Marjorie had always loathed the Schutt sisters, and the Schutt sisters had always loathed Marjorie. It was an animosity that could be attributed not to any single event, but rather to a general divergence in personalities. The Schutt sisters, self-centered and vainglorious, possessed the two traits that Marjorie found most abhorrent in other human beings, and Marjorie, clever and determined, was the antithesis of what the Schutts believed a "proper" young lady should be.

In recent years, by what many considered an act of God, Sheila had managed to find a husband and had subsequently relocated to another town. Marjorie rejoiced at the news that Ridgebury would be one Schutt lighter—rejoiced, that is, until she beheld the effect the marriage had on Sheila's sister. With the departure of her sibling, Sharon became the sole recipient of her parents doting and coddling—consequently growing more self-absorbed with each passing day. If she were now to receive the attentions of a handsome millionaire, the young woman's arrogance would become insufferable.

Sharon's complete lack of humility was enough to extinguish even the brightest of spirits. However, Marjorie's state of mind was blackened by something more than a mere dislike of Sharon Schutt. Creighton's decision had evoked within her a profound sense of disappointment; not because she wanted the man for herself, (how could she want such an irritating scamp?), but disappointment at the prospect that *he might not want her.*

As if he had been conjured by her thoughts, the Englishman materialized at Marjorie's side and stooped beneath the protecting brim of the umbrella. "Is something wrong?"

She kept her focus on the ground, under the pretense of avoiding puddles. "No. Why do you ask?"

"It looks like you're brooding over something."

"No, I have a bit of a headache, that's all."

"Would you like me to stop in the drugstore and get some headache powder?" he offered.

"Thank you, no," Marjorie rejected waspishly. "That won't be necessary."

"Are you certain?" he asked again, his voice tinged with worry. "You look a bit peaked."

"Yes, I'm fine," she managed to spit back.

"Well, if you need anything, let me know."

She sensed his eyes upon her and, feeling as if she were suffocating under their penetrating gaze, she was struck by an overwhelming need to escape. Fortunately, Creighton's offer had provided her with a means to do so.

"What I need," she announced, "is to get out of this dampness." Having thus pardoned herself, Marjorie broke away from her escort and tore down the road, heedless of the pools of water that splashed about her feet. By the time she reached the rectory of the First Presbyterian Church, her shoes and stockings were soaked through. Thinking nothing of her soggy condition, she folded her umbrella, scaled the slate entrance stairway and stepped inside the unlocked door.

The front vestibule offered Marjorie a moment's refuge from the rain and her own emotions. She slouched against a fieldstone wall and, swallowing her own saliva, attempted to dislodge the lump that had formed in her throat. She had never been the sort of person easily given to weeping. However, she now found herself struggling to hold back her tears. *What am I doing?* she admonished herself. *Why should I care what Creighton does with his personal life? We've only just met. I have no designs upon him and he has no designs upon me.*

Yet, the truth remained that she did care, considerably, and that the image of Creighton and Sharon walking arm-in-arm was one she found quite nettling. She closed her eyes and endeavored to find a reason, other than jealousy, for her mental distress. *Illness, possibly? Fatigue?*

Her rationalizations were called short by the sounds of the men approaching the rectory steps. Marjorie took a deep breath in order to regain her composure. Under no circumstances could she allow her companions to see that she was upset, lest they believe her to be an overwrought female.

Detective Jameson's face was the first to peer through the doorframe. "Been waiting long?" he asked with a smile.

Marjorie returned the smile and quickly realized the absurdity of her behavior. Here she was carrying on over Creighton when there was a man like Robert Jameson around—a man for whose affections most women would willingly trade their eyeteeth. She gave the policeman a flirtatious look. "Yes, but some people are worth waiting for."

Creighton entered the passageway in time to intercept Marjorie's compliment. "I'm jolly glad you think so," he stated in annoyance. "The way you ran off, I expected to find that you had finished the investigation without us." He tugged at the interior door of the rectory and, holding it open, motioned Marjorie to lead the way. "Go on, then, if you're in such a hurry."

She brushed past him with a caustic glance. Inside the parsonage, a middle-aged secretary seated at a desk by the door greeted her. "Hello, Marjorie."

"Hello, Mrs. Reynolds. Is the Reverend in?"

"He's in his office."

"We'd like to see him. Is he busy?"

"No, go right in."

Marjorie thanked the woman graciously and steered her friends to an adjacent room. The door was ajar, but Marjorie nonetheless gave it a polite tap.

The Reverend was positioned in a high-backed leather chair, heavily engrossed in the act of reading. He looked up from his weighty tome. "Marjorie, how good to see you." He removed the book from his lap and placed it on a side table before rising to his feet. "So what brings you to this neck of the woods? You're not thinking of switching faiths, are you?"

Marjorie laughed. "No, I don't think Father Callahan would stand for that."

The man's brown eyes twinkled. "Well, no matter. With all the work you've done for us, I already consider you an honorary member of the parish. Marjorie runs the kissing booth at our annual fair," he explained.

"Really?" Creighton smirked. "I didn't realize you were so talented."

"It's hardly a talent. I stand there and pucker up. Anyone can do it," she squinted at Creighton, "provided they can keep quiet long enough."

The Reverend interrupted, "So, Marjorie, what *does* bring you here? And, um, who are your friends?"

She introduced her companions and the men shook hands.

"I suppose you're here to discuss my relationship with Henry Van Allen," Price asserted with a grin.

"Yes, we are," Jameson replied. "I take it, then, that you've been anticipating our visit."

"From the moment it was announced that a body was found up at Kensington House."

"And you assumed that it had something to do with Van Allen? Why?"

The vicar shrugged. "Location, first of all, and then the time frame. The paper said that the body had been there for approximately five years. That's about the time the Van Allens lived at the house."

"You're very perceptive."

"You have Marjorie to thank for that. I suspect reading her novels has sharpened my intellect." He moved behind a dark mahogany desk, and in the same manner in which he might lead his Sunday services, motioned his guests to be seated.

Jameson and Noonan grabbed the two chairs facing the desk. Creighton and Marjorie landed on a leather settee placed adjacent to the chairs to form an L-shaped conversation area.

Reverend Price sat, his back to the wall. "Do you know who the body belongs to?"

"Yes, his name was Victor Bartorelli. Did you know him?"

"Bartorelli," the gray-haired man repeated the name slowly like a magical incantation. "No, I can't say that I do."

"Are you sure?" pressed Jameson. "He was a gardener to the Van Allens. He lived up at Kensington House."

Price frowned and shook his head. "I think the Van Allens preferred their house staff to remain invisible."

"And you're positive he was never in your church?"

"Absolutely. My parish is small; I know everyone by name. If there was a new face in one of those pews, I'd notice it. Nevertheless, if you don't mind me saying, you may want to check with Father Callahan. A man with the name of 'Bartorelli' is more likely to be Catholic than Presbyterian." He swiveled his chair toward Marjorie. "You've gotten a look at this man. Do you recall seeing him over at St. Agnes?"

Marjorie squirmed uncomfortably. "Um, no, but in all fairness, I don't think he looks the same now as he did then."

"Oh?" he replied with mild puzzlement.

The young woman explained delicately, "I think he's, um, lost some weight since then."

"Oh!" the pastor started. "Yes, I see what you mean."

Creighton chuckled. "Even if he hadn't 'slimmed down,' I doubt you would have recognized him from church. I get the impression that Victor Bartorelli's concerns were more material than spiritual."

Jameson nodded in agreement. "So, as far as you're aware, you never met Victor Bartorelli, but you certainly knew Henry Van Allen."

"Know him? I don't think anyone really knew him."

"But you had the opportunity to speak with him face to face, didn't you?"

"I had the dubious distinction, yes."

"And when did that take place?"

"Nineteen twenty-nine. Right after our annual fair. I had gone to him to borrow money."

"Tell me about this fair."

The clergyman leaned his elbows on the desk and repeated, practically verbatim, the story Marjorie had told that morning in Mrs. Patterson's kitchen.

Jameson hung on his every word, listening for any incongruities in the man's statement. When the account was finished, he jumped into action. "When you learned about the mistake, why didn't you ask the winner of the raffle to return the money?"

"I couldn't do that. The man who won that prize money needed it just as badly as the church."

"What about the person who made the error? Why didn't you hold him responsible?"

"Responsible for what? Being human?"

"No. Being careless."

"Detective Jameson," Reverend Price began softly, "the people who help with these fairs are good-natured volunteers; they're not professional businessmen with ticker tape and adding machines. What occurred that day was the result of a simple error in arithmetic. It might have happened to anyone." He removed his arms from the desk and slouched back in his chair. "If anyone could be accused of carelessness, it would be me. It's my parish. I should have double checked the receipts before we held the drawing."

"So you went to Henry Van Allen for help and, not only did he turn you down, he accused you of stealing. That must have made you angry."

"No. No, I wasn't angry. I think I was surprised mostly. I hadn't anticipated that reaction."

"How about when he reported you to the presbytery? Didn't that get you a little hot under the collar? Ahem, no pun intended."

"It bothered me," the minister conceded.

"I have to hand it to you. If I were in your shoes, I would have hated Henry Van Allen."

Price remained calm, despite the younger man's baiting. "Hate is a very strong word, Detective. It's true that I disliked Mr. Van Allen, but I didn't hate him."

"Did you dislike him enough to rejoice over his death?"

The Reverend drew a deep breath. "I realize that Mr. Van Allen's passing was very beneficial to my predicament; however, I did not feel it was an occasion to celebrate. Mr. Van Allen was still a member of the human race, and as much as I disliked him, I am sure he was not without redeeming characteristics."

"You weren't at all relieved that the problem of Henry Van Allen had been solved?"

"Death is seldom the solution to anything, Detective Jameson," Price philosophized. "I think we all learned that during the war."

The word "war" provided a perfect segue for the detective. "You served in the war?"

"Yes, as a chaplain in the Army."

Another smooth transition: "Tell me, Reverend, as an army chaplain, were you issued a weapon?"

Price frowned in repugnance. "No, I was classified as a conscientious objector."

Jameson looked at Noonan in question; the officer replied in the negative. "Well then, I think that takes care of everything," the detective summed up as he rose from his chair. "Thank you for your time, Reverend. And if you can think of anything you might want to tell me, give me a call at the station."

They bid their adieus to Price and Mrs. Reynolds, and made their way out of the building. Once outside, Creighton sidled up to Marjorie, his face illuminated with a giant grin.

"Don't say it," Marjorie warned.

"Say what?" the Englishman responded innocently.

"I know you're dying to comment on my volunteering at the kissing booth."

"Yes, but not in the sense that you think."

She was mildly curious. "Oh?"

"I think it's very nice of you to volunteer your time at the fair."

She scanned his face for a sign of trickery but found none. "Really?"

"Yes, it's quite generous of you, but I do have to ask you something."

She sighed wearily, "What now?"

"Well, you're not a Presbyterian and yet you benevolently donate your lips to them."

"So?"

"So, what part of you do you donate to St. Agnes?"

THIRTEEN

MARJORIE WAS STILL A bit sullen when Creighton met her the next morning to once again make the tedious commute to New York. Doris had designated Harry's, a West Side luncheonette, to be the site of their rendezvous. As he pulled the Phantom to a halt before the dingy cafe, Creighton decided that it was, indeed, an excellent spot for their secret assignation. Not only was the luncheonette clear across town from the Van Allen residence, but its very appearance would have repelled anyone accustomed to Carnegie Hill living. To the indiscriminate palate, the luncheonette looked like just another neighborhood eatery. However, to a person with even the slightest epicurean tendencies, the thick layer of grime on the front windows and the collection of cats gathered in the side alley marked this establishment as that most contemptible of culinary villains: the greasy spoon. No self-respecting member of the Van Allen family would be caught dead in such a place.

The interior of the restaurant was even less enticing. Watery sunlight filtered by the particles of dirt covering the front window, washed over the gray linoleum floor and matching charcoal walls, revealing yellowish-brown stains—products of the combined effect of cigarette smoke and cooking grease. Seating consisted of a melee of mismatched tables and chairs scattered at random intervals about the room; some of these tables, though unoccupied, still held half-eaten plates of food, left there as if in offering to some unnamed god. In a far corner of the room, from an early-model Crosley radio, Carl Brisson sang of the virtues of alcohol in his rendition of "Cocktails for Two." Carl, however, found stiff competition in the cacophony that rose from behind the lunch counter—the placing of orders, the sizzling of fat upon the griddle, the tinkling of dishes and silverware, and the obscene utterances of the short order cook rendered his vocals nearly inaudible.

In the center of everything, like Gaea emerging from Chaos, sat Doris, waving feverishly to her guests. Creighton and Marjorie approached the square, oilcloth-covered table. "Hi, Doris," Marjorie greeted. "We aren't late, are we?"

"Oh no, miss," Doris hastened to answer. "You're right on time."

Marjorie nodded and then gestured toward Creighton. "You remember Mr. Ashcroft, don't you?"

Doris played it cool. "Yes, I think so."

"Well, I certainly remember you, Doris," Creighton responded playfully as he extended his hand to remove Marjorie's coat. Doubtlessly fearing that her unworn coat might become a host to all manner of vermin, she clung to the garment tenaciously.

Doris reacted with a start. "You do?"

"Um hmm," he replied as he then offered Marjorie the chair opposite Doris. She inspected it thoroughly, and finding it clean enough, sat down gently, taking great pains not to brush against the crumb-laden table. Creighton sat beside her, but before he or Marjorie could broach the subject of Henry Van Allen, a beefy, bleached-blonde wait-ress plopped a handwritten menu in the center of the table.

Doris's attention was riveted on the food-stained piece of paper. "I'm sorry," she apologized as she handed the list to Marjorie. "I'm hogging the menu."

"No, I don't want anything. We had a late breakfast this morning and I'm still quite full." She patted her abdomen for added effect. In truth, they had bypassed breakfast, preferring to satiate their ap-petites with a large lunch rather than a healthy portion of Mrs. Pat-terson's oatmeal.

Doris offered the menu to Creighton. He was hungry, but not hungry enough to risk ptomaine poisoning. "No, thank you, I never eat lunch."

Doris shrugged and returned her attention to the menu, her eyes hungrily skimming over each entry. Upon reaching the end of the list, she bit her lip in indecisiveness and squinted as she labored over some sort of mental tabulation. Dissatisfied with the results of her arithmetic, she pulled a small change purse from her handbag and began calculating its meager contents.

Creighton stopped her in the act. "Put that away, Doris. Your money is no good here."

The maid was taken aback. "What?"

"I said put your money away. Lunch is my treat."

Doris opened her mouth to argue, but a quick gander at her pocketbook caused her to cave. The waitress had returned to take or-ders. "Umm, a hot meatloaf sandwich and a sarsaparilla with lots of ice, please," the young woman requested.

The platinum blonde jotted the order on a small pad and then turned to Marjorie and Creighton.

"Nothing for me, thank you," Marjorie stated.

"Me neither," Creighton rejoined.

The waitress issued her ultimatum. "No eat, no seat."

"You mean we have to order something to sit here?" Marjorie asked.

"That's exactly what I mean, sister," the waitress replied as she shifted her weight from one foot to another. "So, what will it be?"

Creighton smiled. *If it weren't for such extortion, Harry's might not do much business.*

"I guess I'll have coffee," Marjorie answered hesitantly.

"I'll have the same," Creighton added.

"Big spenders," the waitress commented as she walked away in disgust.

Marjorie ignored her. "You know, Doris, I've been looking forward to our meeting all week."

"You have?"

"Why, yes. You got my imagination racing with all that talk of Mrs. Van Allen murdering her husband."

The maid panicked. "Oh, no! I didn't say she murdered him. She couldn't have *murdered* him. He killed himself."

"I know that, but you do think she's partly to blame for his suicide, don't you?"

Doris squirmed uncomfortably in her chair. "Yeah."

"Why do you think that?"

She stared at the crumbs on the table and shrugged her shoulders. "I dunno."

"Doris," Creighton cajoled, "you're holding out on us."

She looked up in alarm. "What do you mean?"

"I mean that you're a smart girl with great insight into human nature. You're not the type to jump to conclusions. So, tell us, why do you think Mrs. Van Allen is responsible for her husband's death?"

Creighton's honeyed words acted upon Doris like a truth serum. "Because, sir, they weren't happy."

"Oh? How do you know?"

"They didn't seem to get along at all. They hardly ever went out together, and they never really spoke to one another."

"I hate to burst your romantic bubble, Doris, but it isn't unusual for a couple who have been married several years not to talk to each other."

"I know that. My mom and pop don't talk to each other too much, either. They sit by the radio each night. My pop with his newspaper and my mom with her mending and sewing. I don't think they say two words to each other, but . . ."

"You know that they're content," Marjorie guessed.

The maid nodded. "But it was different with Mr. and Mrs. Van Allen. They were just plain cold-blooded."

"There are a lot of people in that house, Doris. Couldn't it just be that they didn't want other people overhearing their conversations?" Creighton suggested. "Perhaps they saved their conversations for late at night, after they had retired for the evening."

Doris blushed crimson. "No, sir, they didn't share the same bedroom."

The waitress arrived with their food. She unceremoniously plopped the dishes upon the table and, without so much as a word, moved on to spread her particular brand of sunshine to the next group of customers.

Creighton examined the food closely. The sarsaparilla, lacking the extra ice Doris requested, appeared harmless. The meatloaf, however, was a nasty bit of business. Resting upon a slice of stale bread smeared with gelatinous gravy, it resembled a dirty sponge in both color and texture. The origin of the meat was a complete mystery; it could have been anything: beef, pork, veal, horse, or even cat. Creighton recalled the confluence of felines in the side alley and promised himself to count their numbers before he left—he had a strong suspicion that there would be fewer of them now than when he had entered the luncheonette.

As for the coffee, it was an enigma unto itself. Nothing, it seemed, could allay the sinisterness of the wicked brew. Sugar appeared to dissolve upon contact. Cream poured into the fluid did not lighten the substance, but merely disappeared into a deep abyss, never to resurface. Creighton irresolutely dangled a spoon over his cup but, fearful that the coffee might corrode the utensil, returned it to the table unused.

Marjorie pushed her cup aside with nary a second glance. Doris, however, tore into her lunch with gusto.

Creighton was anxious to resume the questioning, but he knew that an informant with a full stomach was bound to be more helpful than a hungry one. He waited until her plate was clean before finally speaking. "Was everything satisfactory, Doris?"

The maid licked her lips. "Yes, thank you."

"Good, then let's get back to Mr. and Mrs. Van Allen. You said they were miserable together. Was there ever talk of them getting a divorce?"

Doris gaped at Creighton as if he were clairvoyant. "Yeah, funny you ask. It was right before Mr. Van Allen passed away."

Creighton and Marjorie exchanged glances. "Tell us about it."

"Mr. Van Allen came home early one afternoon, which was strange because he never left the office early. He was in an awful mood, too. He didn't even say hello to me as I took his hat and coat. It wasn't like him not to say hello. He asked me where his wife was. I said she was in the drawing room. He told me to open up the good scotch he had been saving and bring it to him there. I reminded him it was against the law to drink."

"I don't think that mattered much to him at the time," Creighton chuckled. "So you brought him the drink. Did you overhear the conversation he was having with his wife?"

"Yes. He must have already asked about the divorce, because Mrs. Van Allen was really taking him down a notch. She said she would never set him free, that he needed her just as much as she needed him. That he might have the money, but she had the name. Then she called him something foreign sounding."

"*Nouveau riche?*"

"That's it."

"What did Mr. Van Allen do?" Marjorie asked.

"He went off by himself to sulk. That's what he always did when his wife got the better of him. He hardly ever said 'boo' to her. That's why the whole staff was surprised when he actually asked for a divorce. None of us thought he had the gumption."

Creighton brought his hand to his chin. "Then, to your knowledge, Van Allen had never before mentioned the subject of divorce."

She shook her head. "I think he was too afraid."

"I wonder what finally pushed him over the edge," Marjorie mused.

"I can tell you," Doris offered with zeal. "He had a girlfriend."

"A girlfriend?" Creighton repeated. "You mean a mistress?"

"Yes. And I can tell you who—a maid up at their country house." Marjorie spoke up. "Kensington House?"

"Yes. Some girl by the name of Stella."

"Stella Munson?"

The maid nodded. "That's the one."

Creighton turned to Marjorie in astonishment. "You know this person?"

"Remember Mary—the little girl you met the other day? Her mother, Claire, was Stella's older sister. Stella and Claire both grew up in Ridgebury. I went to school with them."

"Since you were school chums, did Stella ever mention to you that she was having an affair with Van Allen?" Creighton asked.

"No, Stella and I weren't friends. She was a few years ahead of me, but I must say I'm not surprised. Stella was always a bit fast."

Creighton leaned back in his chair to think. After a few moments meditation, he asked, "Doris, did Mrs. Van Allen know her husband was having an affair?"

"I don't know, she might have. It's hard to tell with her."

"Jealousy?" Marjorie asked her companion softly.

"Either that or fear that her husband might divorce her and take his money with him," he replied.

Doris eyed both of them suspiciously. "What are you two whispering about? And why do you want to know so much about the Van Allens?"

Marjorie was quick on the draw. "I'm doing research for my book."

The maid, naturally, was intrigued. "Book?"

Creighton felt the blood drain from his head. *What in God's name was she doing? Doris couldn't be trusted with the truth. After all, she had sold her boss's secrets for a greasy meatloaf sandwich.*

"I don't know if Mrs. Van Allen told you, but I'm a writer. Many of the characters in my books are based on people I meet; and the stories I write are inspired by the tales they tell me. I wanted to get to know you better because I thought you might provide an interesting story for my next novel. "

Creighton relaxed; the maid was genuinely fascinated. "Novel?" she asked. "What kind of novel?"

"A mystery novel."

Doris's eyes were unblinking. "Would I be a character?"

"Doris, you already *are* a character," Marjorie deadpanned.

"Oh, but you can't do that. If Mrs. Van Allen read the book and saw my name, I'd be out of a job."

"Mrs. Van Allen won't see your name. I said I'd *base* the character on you, I didn't say it would be you *exactly*. I would use the story you gave me and embroider it a bit. Add facts, take away facts."

If such an explanation had come from Creighton, Doris would have agreed, no questions asked. However, since the tale came from Marjorie, she required further reassurance. "You're sure you won't use my name?"

Marjorie held up her right hand as if taking an oath. "You have my word as a published author in the Book-of-the-Month club."

"You were in the Book-of-the-Month club?"

"Yes. Twice."

"What was your name again?"

"Marjorie McClelland."

"Strange. I don't think I've ever heard of you before," the maid stated, as if she were the judge of literary merit.

"*Murder in Morocco? Death in Denmark?* Have you heard of them?"

"No," she replied flatly, and then with excitement, "but I've heard of Agatha Christie. I love her books. She's wonderful."

"Yes, she is."

"Have you met her?"

"No, I haven't," Marjorie answered in annoyance.

"Oh, because I love Agatha Christie. Everyone's heard of her too—very famous. Your books couldn't possibly be as good as hers, or I would have heard of you, too."

Creighton watched as Marjorie tensed her fists and knew that it wouldn't be long before she opened her mouth in retaliation. Fortunately, the waitress arrived before the writer could start a row.

"Ah, here's our lovely waitress now," Creighton said loudly. "Is there anything else I can get you, Doris? Pie? Ice cream?"

Doris blushed and bit her lip coquettishly. "I am partial to black and white sodas."

"A black and white soda for the duchess," he commanded.

"Will that be all, Your Highness?" the waitress inquired sarcastically.

"Yes, that and the check."

"As you wish," she muttered as she made her way back to the counter.

Doris, meanwhile, was tickled with her new title. "I'm not a duchess," she reproved between giggles.

"I know you're not," he pointed his finger toward the lunch counter, "but she doesn't."

"Oh, but she can tell I'm not," she persisted, still tittering.

"How? You conduct yourself very well. "

This sparked a memory in Doris's head. "You know, Miss McClelland and I were discussing this the other day."

Marjorie shook her head violently.

"Oh?" Creighton prodded.

"Yes, she said that true nobility lies in bearing, not in breeding."

Marjorie turned her head and stared off into the distance. "Oh, really?" the Englishman asked in amusement.

"Yes, and she even told me that I probably have more class in my little finger than Mrs. Van Allen and her friends have in their entire bodies."

Creighton smiled. "Really? And from whence did Miss McClelland acquire such great wisdom?"

"From a long lost friend," Marjorie answered crabbily.

"I'm sorry," offered Creighton in mock sympathy. "When did this friend 'pass on'?"

Marjorie stared at him from the corner of her eye. "As soon as we get into the car."

FOURTEEN

MARJORIE DID NOT KILL Creighton as she had threatened. As the Englishman was her only means back to Ridgebury, it was to her benefit to keep him alive. Besides, he had not taunted her as she had anticipated. On the contrary, he was quite pleasant. Having escaped the luncheonette without committing to any future social engagements with Doris, he was simply too elated to cause Marjorie any distress. He helped her, wordlessly, into the car, and then sat in the driver's seat beaming. It was not a smug or supercilious smile, but one of true gratification with just a touch of giddiness.

They pressed on to their next assignment, but not before stopping for lunch at a midtown eatery that put Harry's to shame. It was not an elegant establishment, but it was comfortable and clean, and the food proved to be excellent: generous cups of vegetable soup—hearty, rich, and wonderfully seasoned—and, on the side, slices of buttery bread stacked with thick layers of ham and cheese, slathered with spicy mustard.

They devoured the tasty repast, and having eaten their fill, paid the check and headed back to the car. As they walked past the dress shop next door to the restaurant, Marjorie spotted something that made her heart skip a beat. Displayed in the window was the most exquisite evening gown she had ever seen. It was silvery blue and made of the sheerest silk chiffon, with a matching under-slip for modesty. As was the rage, it sported fluttering cap sleeves and a beaded scoop neckline that plunged to a deep vee at the back. Dainty flowers rested on each shoulder and a thin belt differentiated the waist from the full flowing skirt.

What a perfectly glorious dress for Mrs. Van Allen's party on Friday, Marjorie thought, but then swiftly realized that it probably had an equally glorious price tag. She looked away from the window and berated herself on her excessive vanity. She already had a gown at home; she didn't need another one. Her gown, although over ten years old, still had plenty of wear left in it, and with a few alterations by Mrs. Patterson, it would be as good as new.

She stepped into the Phantom and Creighton closed the door behind her. *Yes*, she persuaded herself, *my dress is just as good as that one. And once Mrs. Patterson is done with it, no one will ever know I wore it to my high school formal.* However, as the car pulled away from the curb, Marjorie once again caught sight of the heavenly garment and knew that her own dress was hopelessly unsophisticated and out of date.

She sighed as she watched the gown disappear from her sight. *Perhaps in another lifetime.*

Despite the present economic crisis, Van Allen Industries and its most loyal employee, Evelyn Hadley, could still be found in the granite-faced building on Liberty Street, both of them serving as a steadfast reminder of more propitious times. Evelyn was a slim, highly efficient woman of indeterminate years—she could have passed for any age between thirty and fifty. She wore a coarse tweed business suit and her shoes, along with her personality, were flat and no-nonsense. She might have been pretty, but she had gone to great lengths to erase any signs of attractiveness. Her brown hair was pulled tightly into a chignon and the only distinctive feature on her cleanly scrubbed face was a pair of wire-framed spectacles similar to those worn by elderly women.

"May I help you?" she asked in a businesslike manner.

"Yes," Creighton replied, "we'd like to speak—"

Miss Hadley broke in before he could continue. "Do you have an appointment?"

"No," Marjorie answered, "but—"

"Then I'm afraid you'll have to leave," the secretary again interrupted. "Mr. Henderson is a very busy man."

"We're sure he is," Creighton agreed, "that's why I'm sure he won't notice if you leave your desk for a few moments."

"Leave my desk?" she repeated as if the notion were absurd.

"Yes," Marjorie interjected, "so we can ask you a few questions."

"You've come to speak with *me*?"

"Yes," Creighton answered, "if you can spare a minute or two of your time."

"And to what is this in reference?" she asked in perfect telephone voice.

Marjorie told of the discovery of the gardener's body at Kensington House and the subsequent police investigation.

"What does that have to do with me?"

The writer explained, taking care not to use the word "murder." "We think the gardener's death might be linked to Henry Van Allen's suicide."

"I told the police everything I knew about Mr. Van Allen."

Creighton leaned closer to the secretary. "Yes, but perhaps you could refresh our memory."

Miss Hadley gave him a cool appraising stare from over the top of her glasses. "And whose memory am I refreshing?"

He extended a hand in greeting. "Creighton Ashcroft, private detective." He motioned toward Marjorie. "My assistant, Miss McClelland."

Marjorie gave a slight curtsy at her introduction.

The secretary looked mistrustfully at each of them. "Private detective? Who hired you?"

"I'm not at liberty to divulge any names, but, suffice to say, I represent a very influential party."

Miss Hadley reluctantly capitulated. "All right, I'll tell you what you want to know." She wagged a long, tapered finger. "But I'm not leaving my desk. If you wish to speak with me, you can do so here."

"Yes, you want to be here in case Mr. Henderson needs you," said Creighton.

Miss Hadley nodded in relief. At last, someone appreciated the importance of her life's work.

"Fair enough," he assented. "I shan't deny Mr. Henderson his right arm. He is, as you said, a very busy man."

"Yes, quite."

"He's the president of the company, isn't he?"

"Yes," Miss Hadley affirmed. "He took over when Mr. Van Allen passed away."

"Surprising," he commented casually. "I thought for certain that Mr. Van Allen's brother would have assumed the position."

"William?" Evelyn scoffed. "Heavens no! He's never taken any interest in the family business. He's on the Board of Trustees—*barely*. The other board members refer to him as 'the prodigal son.'"

"Bit of a playboy, is he?"

"I think that's a fair description."

"Nice work if you can get it," Creighton remarked.

"If you enjoy that sort of life," the secretary replied. "I personally prefer to keep busy. Idle hands are the devil's workshop, you know."

He spotted a set of steel office chairs positioned against the wall. "May we?" he asked as he gestured to them.

"By all means, though I wouldn't get too comfortable. What I have to tell you won't take very long." She waited until the guests had settled into their seats and then, glaring at Marjorie, asked, "Aren't you going to take notes?"

"Oh, yes," Marjorie replied absentmindedly. She rummaged through her purse and pulled out a pencil. "Do you happen to have some paper I could use? I left my notebook in the car."

The secretary sniffed at Marjorie's inefficiency, handed her a few sheets of Van Allen Industries letterhead and then launched into an account of the events of Henry's last hours. "Mr. Van Allen was here that day. He arrived at his usual time, about ten minutes after nine in the morning. I immediately fetched him his coffee—two lumps of sugar, no cream—and joined him in his office to take dictation. We worked until noon, whereupon Mr. Van Allen dismissed me for lunch. Mr. Van Allen did not eat lunch. He was in his office when I left, and was still there when I returned one hour later. He worked alone that afternoon, going over the books and adding up figures, and was still doing so when I left for the evening at five o'clock. There were no visitors, no unusual telephone calls, and other than being

173

unusually ambitious, I noticed no difference in his frame of mind." She took a deep breath. "Does that cover everything?"

"No," Marjorie spoke up from behind her notes, "not *everything*. You said that Mr. Van Allen didn't eat lunch that day. Did he tell you that? Or did you come to that conclusion on your own?"

"Mr. Van Allen frequently worked through his lunch hour; when I came back and saw him still at his desk, I figured that's what he had done."

"So you *assumed* he had stayed in the office the whole time but, in reality, he could have slipped out during your absence and returned before you came back. Likewise, during that hour, someone could have come into the office or have telephoned Mr. Van Allen, and you would be none the wiser."

"Yes, I suppose it's possible, but I doubt it. He would have told me if that had happened. He told me everything."

Creighton jumped into the conversation. "You described Mr. Van Allen as unusually ambitious. Why?"

"He stayed late that evening."

"Did he normally stay behind after closing hours?"

"No," Miss Hadley answered, "he and I usually left at the same time."

"But, on the last day of his life, he was so engrossed in his work that he didn't leave with you," Creighton noted. "Was it common practice for Mr. Van Allen to review the ledger?"

"Yes, he did so at the end of every quarter."

"Fine, but he died on the twentieth of November. In my experience, quarterly reports are generated at the end of a month, not in the middle."

"H-he was a bit behind in his work," she stammered.

"Humph," the Englishman grunted in cynicism. "Did Mr. Van Allen have a financial manager?"

"Naturally."

"What was his name?"

"Philips. Roger Philips."

"Was Mr. Philips present to assist with the review process?"

"No, Mr. Van Allen requested that he not be there."

Creighton knitted his eyebrows together pensively. "Was that routine?"

"It had become routine during those last few months."

"But that hadn't always been the case?"

"No, it hadn't."

"Why the sudden change?"

Miss Hadley looked at him sheepishly. "Mr. Van Allen wasn't very happy with Mr. Philips. He was planning to terminate him from his position."

"Why? Didn't he trust him?"

"No, but then again, Mr. Van Allen was suspicious of everyone. He always said that I was the only person in the world whom he could completely trust." Miss Hadley smiled proudly.

"Really?" Creighton asked in disbelief. "You mean to say he trusted you more than his own brother."

"Yes," she gloated.

"More than his own wife?"

"*Particularly* his own wife."

Marjorie had been watching the secretary, noting her face as she spoke of her late employer. *It was a hunch, but she had to be sure.* "More than his mistress?"

The question brought Miss Hadley's spirits crashing down like a lead balloon. She stared down at her desk, crestfallen.

Bingo! "I'm sorry, I thought you knew. Mr. Van Allen was divorcing his wife in order to be with her. She was a maid at his home in Connecticut. Her name was Stella Munson."

"Yes, I knew about Stella," the secretary barked, "but I assure you Mr. Van Allen wouldn't have divorced his wife for her. What could he possibly have wanted with a trollop like that? She was a girl! A servant! She knew nothing about making a man happy, especially a man like Henry!"

Aha! So, it was "Henry" now . . . "Perhaps, but the fact remains that he asked his wife for a divorce just a few days before he died."

"Where did you get your information?" she challenged.

"From a very reliable source," Creighton answered cryptically.

"Reliable? Ha!" the secretary sneered. "Henry would never have divorced his wife, though he probably should have. She never treated him with even a modicum of respect." She leaned forward to exchange a bit of gossip. "Do you know she's engaged to marry Roger Philips?"

"Roger Philips, Mr. Van Allen's business manager?" Creighton asked.

"The same. She took up with him just two months after her husband died. Can you believe it? If that doesn't show a lack of respect, I don't know what does."

"If that's true, then why do you find it inconceivable that her husband might want to divorce her?" Marjorie asked.

"Because he would have lost too much if he did."

"Lost too much? Didn't Mr. Van Allen have all the money?"

"Yes, but his wife had the reputation. It was through her that he gained his most affluent business associates. If Mr. Van Allen divorced his wife, he would have lost those valuable connections."

"Maybe the business wasn't that important to him any longer," Creighton suggested.

"Not important? Blasphemy! Why, business was the most important part of Mr. Van Allen's life."

"Perhaps he found something he loved more," Marjorie suggested with a twinkle in her eye.

"What? That slip of a girl? Don't be foolish. Mr. Van Allen wouldn't let his father's company fall to pieces over her."

"Oh, come now," Creighton cajoled. "Where's your romantic streak? Can't you believe that a man might be willing to sacrifice everything to be with the woman he loves?"

"No, I'm not unromantic," Miss Hadley responded mournfully. "I've simply never had anyone love me that much."

Marjorie was swept by an overwhelming sadness. How many people, she wondered, could honestly say that they had ever known a love that strong? Very few, she fancied. Very few, indeed. More people, she was certain, spent their lives thinking that such a thing existed only in fairy tales.

The ringing of a telephone disturbed her melancholy thoughts. The secretary picked up the receiver. "Yes, Mr. Henderson?" She examined her fingernails as the gentleman gave his instructions. "I'll be right in," she promised before placing the phone back in its cradle. Evelyn Hadley looked at her guests. "I'm afraid our time is up." She excused herself as she stood up from her chair.

"We'll show ourselves out," Creighton offered. "Thank you for your time."

The woman nodded her head once and disappeared behind Mr. Henderson's office door.

When they were safely seated in the car, Marjorie was the first to speak. "It would appear that my suspect list is expanding."

"Yes," Creighton agreed, "you can definitely add Roger Philips name to the roster."

Marjorie shook her head. "I can't believe Gloria's going to marry that man. I wouldn't think he was in her class. Financial managers aren't usually wealthy."

"Not usually, no, but I have a feeling this one might be."

"Do you think he was skimming money off the top?" she asked excitedly.

"'Skimming money off the top?' If that means embezzling, then yes, I think it's possible."

"If Henry had found out about the whole racket, then Roger had one heck of a motive for getting rid of him."

"Yes, and if Roger and Gloria were seeing each other while Henry was still alive, then it's possible that Gloria was also in on the embezzlement 'racket,' as you called it," Creighton added. "That adds yet another possible motive for the widow Van Allen."

"Hmm. And then there's Evelyn Hadley."

"Evelyn Hadley? Why is she a suspect?"

Marjorie let out a deep audible breath. *Why were men so oblivious to women's feelings?* "Evelyn Hadley was in love with her boss. Wasn't it obvious?"

"It was obvious that she admired him, but in love with him? I don't know if I'd go as far as that."

"I would."

"Okay, so assuming Evelyn Hadley was in love with Henry Van Allen—why kill him?"

"Jealousy."

"Jealousy? She knew he was married."

Marjorie rolled her eyes. "Evelyn Hadley wasn't jealous of Gloria. Gloria posed no threat. Evelyn Hadley was jealous of Stella. Stella was the reason for Henry leaving his wife and possibly even abandoning his business."

"So Hadley decided she'd rather kill Henry than lose him to another woman," Creighton completed her thought.

"Exactly."

"I don't know. You're accusing her of a crime of passion, and she just seems so *passionless.*"

"Yes," Marjorie conceded, "but don't let that fool you. As Mrs. Patterson would say, 'Still waters run deep.'"

FIFTEEN

MARJORIE AWOKE AT DAWN on Thursday, and finding it impossible to get back to sleep, rolled over to view the daybreak through her bedroom window. It was yet another overcast day, and the sun rose above the horizon only to be immediately muffled by the clouds, until all that remained were a few wan, dusky beams. She watched this dim light as it glided into her room, engulfing each item it touched and tinting it with a ghostly pallor. She observed, mesmerized, as it consumed the curtains and the window seat where Sam slept, then the ceiling and walls, and, eventually, swallowed the bed itself and herself with it. Within just a few minutes, the world about her had been enveloped in gloom.

The writer shivered; she snuggled beneath the blankets for warmth and closed her eyes in hopes that she might somehow be able to relax, but she knew it was no use. It had been this way each morning since the discovery of Victor Bartorelli's body at Kensington House; awaking with the dawn, suffering from chills, insomnia, and an increasing sense of dread.

It was silly, really. She had spent her life wishing that "something" would happen in Ridgebury, and now that it had, she was having reservations about being involved in it. She enjoyed participating in the investigation, relished the opportunity to flex her sleuthing muscles, and even found some measure of joy in sharing Creighton's company. Nevertheless, each interview they conducted, each fact they uncovered left her feeling increasingly like an intruder. She was prying into peoples' personal lives, encroaching upon their private thoughts and feelings, and unearthing secrets that others preferred remain buried.

Secrets. They're what made Marjorie particularly apprehensive— secrets and the lengths to which people might go to keep them. Everyone who knew Henry Van Allen had something shameful to hide. Did anyone truly care for Henry Van Allen? It seemed that no one did. His was a world of vices, not emotions: a maelstrom of power, adultery, avarice, and perhaps even murder, and the more Marjorie learned, the more she felt herself being pulled into the vortex. How and when the storm would end she did not know, and that frightened her the most.

She looked at the clock upon her nightstand and wished that the time had passed more quickly, but only ten minutes had elapsed since she had first awoken. There were still eight more hours left before she was scheduled to meet with Creighton and Detective Jameson. *Ah, Jameson*, she thought dreamily. No doubt he would be impressed with her and Creighton's handiwork; in one day they had managed to uncover not one or two, but three more suspects in the possible murder of Henry Van Allen. She might actually be rewarded for such good work; but for Marjorie, being close to Detective Jameson and those heavenly brown eyes was reward enough. He was her ideal man:

good-looking, intelligent, charming, and, best of all, a police detective. *Imagine, a police detective and a mystery novelist!*

Marjorie sighed contentedly as she nodded off. No doubt about it, Robert Jameson was the perfect man for her.

Creighton and Marjorie arrived at the police station at the scheduled hour; Detective Jameson was working at his desk, looking more handsome than ever, if that were possible. His face lit up at the sight of Marjorie. "How's my favorite snoop?"

"Very well." She sat in one of the two chairs positioned in front of his desk.

"And your day?" he continued.

"Enlightening," she remarked enigmatically.

Creighton took the other seat. "I'm fine, too," he interjected crabbily. "Thanks for asking."

Jameson looked at him in surprise. "Oh, hello, Creighton. I didn't see you come in."

"That's because you were too busy debriefing Miss McClelland."

The detective cleared his throat in embarrassment. "Then why don't *you* tell me what happened yesterday?"

Creighton complied and, with Marjorie's assistance, told him about their conversations with Doris and Evelyn.

"Sounds like you dug up two more suspects."

"*Three* more suspects," Marjorie corrected.

"Three?" Jameson counted on his fingers. "Gloria Van Allen and Roger Philips. That's two."

"*And* Evelyn Hadley."

"Evelyn Hadley? Why is she a suspect?"

"Because, according to Marjorie, she was in love with Henry," Creighton explained.

"If she was in love with him, why would she want to kill him?"

Marjorie sighed. *Men! Really!* "She was jealous," she stated impatiently.

"Jealous of who? Stella Munson?"

"Who else?" she asked rhetorically.

"If she had been jealous of Stella, why kill Henry? Why not just bump off the competition?"

Did she have to spell out everything? "Because Henry was the person who betrayed her."

"If they didn't have a personal relationship, why should she feel betrayed by Henry's involvement with another woman?"

"In Evelyn's mind, they *did* have a personal relationship. He confided in her, remember?"

"Yes, but entrusting someone with your secrets is a far cry from romancing them. Unless you think Henry might have done something else to lead her to believe that their relationship was more than just business," Jameson suggested.

"I doubt it," Marjorie disallowed, "I've met both Gloria and Stella, and I can't imagine Evelyn Hadley being his type. Not to mention he already had two women on his hands. He certainly didn't need another one."

"I agree," Creighton chimed in. "Henry wouldn't have risked losing a good secretary if their romance soured. If he did or said anything, it was purely unintentional. Complimenting Miss Hadley on her dress or hairdo, or even her typing skills. Innocent things like that. I don't fancy it would have taken much to crank her engine."

"You needn't be crude," Marjorie chided. "So, are we all in agreement that she's a suspect?"

The two men nodded in unison. "Good," she continued, "then that brings the grand total to six."

It was the detective's turn for amendments. "Better make that seven."

"Lucky number seven, Jameson?" Creighton ribbed. "I had no idea you were that superstitious."

"Believe me, adding another suspect to this mess is not my idea of luck."

"Who's the new suspect?" Marjorie quizzed.

"William Van Allen."

"Henry's brother? What did he stand to gain by his brother's death?" Creighton questioned.

"A pretty hefty inheritance," Jameson answered, shuffling through the papers in front of him.

"I can see why money might be a motive for Gloria," Marjorie started, "but for William? He's a Van Allen; he's wealthy in his own right."

"It's a logical assumption, but a wrong one. Arthur Van Allen, William and Henry's father, left all his earthly belongings to his elder son."

"Henry," Creighton guessed.

"On the nose."

"What about his wife?" Marjorie asked. "Didn't she get anything?"

"She died before him."

"And William got zilch?"

"I wouldn't say zilch. Arthur's will stipulated that William was to be provided with a monthly allowance to cover his living expenses."

"Sounds like someone was Daddy's favorite," Creighton remarked.

"Evelyn Hadley said that William was the prodigal son," Marjorie reminded him. "Arthur was probably fearful that he'd squander his inheritance."

"Or he simply liked one son better than the other," Creighton speculated.

"He didn't forget about William completely. He just put him on the 'installment' plan."

"Only to assuage his guilt, I'm sure."

"But Henry made it up to his brother in his own will. Didn't he?"

Jameson nodded. "Henry's estate was split between Gloria and William. Gloria got the houses: Kensington House, the townhouse in New York City, and a place in Palm Beach. She also inherited two limousines and half of Henry's liquid assets: bank accounts, treasury bills, and of course stock."

"Stock," Creighton guffawed. "I think it's safe to say the old girl didn't murder her husband for that."

"I know, nowadays stocks have the crackle of Confederate money. But Gloria's stock, combined with the shares she received from her late husband, gave her controlling interest in Van Allen Industries."

"As they say in New York, 'That and a nickel will get you a ride on the subway.'"

"It's still better than nothing," Jameson pointed out, "which is exactly what she would have gotten had the divorce gone through."

Creighton pulled a face. "I suppose the arrangement offered Gloria some amount of financial security. She'd be able to continue living in the manner to which she had grown accustomed, at least as long as the company survived."

"It gave her more than that," Marjorie ventured. "If she and Roger Philips *were* dipping their hands into the till, being in charge of Van Allen Industries would give her a chance to cover their tracks."

"You seem convinced that Gloria was involved in this embezzling scheme. What if she wasn't?" Creighton hypothesized. "What if Philips was working alone?"

"Gloria might not have been in on it from the beginning, but she is now. Being the principal shareholder would have afforded her the opportunity to review the books. She looks them over, sees something hinky, realizes what Philips has been up to, and cozies up to him for a share in the loot." Marjorie paused. "Gloria has to know about the money. It's the only way to explain that strange engagement."

"My dear, Marjorie, your cynicism surprises me. Couldn't Mrs. Van Allen and Mr. Philips be madly in love with each other?"

"Gloria fall for a working-class stiff like Philips? Not very likely. That woman isn't looking for a man; she's looking for a bank account with feet."

"Marjorie," Creighton chided in false dismay, "are you suggesting that the dear, sweet woman we met is a mercenary at heart?"

"Oh, you," she wadded up a piece of scrap paper from Jameson's desk and threw it at Creighton. "You shouldn't tease like that. You could end up being her next husband."

"Me?"

"Uh huh. I noticed the way she eyed you up and down the other day."

"Are you calling me a—what was the term you used—a 'bank account with feet'?"

"If the shoe fits . . ."

Jameson stifled a laugh. "We're getting ahead of ourselves. Until I get a chance to look over those books, we can't say for certain that Roger Philips was stealing from the company. Nor can we accuse Gloria of being his accomplice." He shuffled some papers on his desk.

"Getting back to the will, Henry left the other half of his liquid assets to his brother as well as the contents of his entire collection."

"Collection?" Marjorie repeated.

"Yep, Van Allen had accumulated enough stuff to start his own private museum; paintings, sculptures, antique furniture, military paraphernalia, jewelry, and, of course, first edition books."

"Anything of particular value?" Creighton asked.

"Some paintings that were worth a couple of thousand dollars, and a few tables that I wouldn't dare set a drink on. But the granddaddy of 'em all is an eight-and-a-half carat diamond ring once belonging to Madame Du Barry, given to her by King Louis XV. Estimated value: $25,000."

"Eight and a half carats," Marjorie declared breathlessly. "Can you imagine?"

"Down, girl," Creighton mentioned aside. "Sounds like Billy Boy's ship finally came in. All he had to do is sell the collection, cop the lolly, and he's sitting pretty, for at least a little while."

"And $25,000 is a lot of lolly," Marjorie remarked.

"It is," Jameson agreed, "but William never got it."

"What do you mean, he never got it?"

Jameson picked up a piece of paper from his desk and waved it. "An insurance claim for the ring, filed on November 28, 1929. Evidently, Mrs. Van Allen was packing up the contents of Kensington House when she noticed that the ring was missing."

"Stolen?"

The detective shook his head. "The ring was kept inside a safe in the Van Allen's bedroom. Only Henry and Gloria had the combination and there was no sign that anyone had tampered with the door."

"A case of safecracking?"

"Doubtful. There were other pieces of jewelry in that safe, along with bonds and treasury notes, none of which had been touched."

"Maybe Gloria pocketed it," Creighton suggested.

"The insurance company had the same suspicion, so they conducted their own investigation."

"You mean they actually investigated Gloria for possible insurance fraud?" Marjorie was aghast.

"Naturally," Creighton replied. "What did you think they would do? Write out a check, no questions asked?"

"Well, no, but she's a Van Allen. I would have thought they'd consider her above reproach."

"Marjorie, in the case of a $25,000 insurance claim, even FDR himself isn't above reproach." The Englishman turned to the detective. "Since Gloria isn't in jail right now, I guess it's safe to assume that they didn't find anything."

"Nope, not a thing. They kept their eyes on the local auction houses and pawnshops, but nothing turned up. Eventually they were forced to conclude that Gloria actually had 'misplaced' the ring, as she said, and, therefore, the claim was valid."

"Well," Marjorie commented, "William might not have gotten the ring, but at least he got the insurance money."

"No, he didn't."

"What do you mean he didn't? You just said the claim was valid."

"It was," the detective explained, "but, as fate would have it, the insurance company went under before they could make good on the claim."

"But wouldn't another company have picked up the policy?"

"If it were a simple little homeowner's policy they might," Creighton explained, "but there are very few firms left that are equipped to handle a claim of that size. They could sue, I suppose, but it wouldn't be worth the time or effort, since, as the proverb goes, you can't get blood from a stone. And if Gloria did take the ring, she wouldn't want to drag the whole thing up again." He stroked his chin meditatively. "It seems everywhere we turn, we find another nail for Gloria's coffin. Possible murder, possible adultery, possible embezzlement, possible insurance fraud."

"Yep, she's a piece of work, all right," Jameson acknowledged, "but don't forget, that will puts William on the list of suspects, too."

"No, I haven't forgotten. However, Gloria seems to be, by far, the most multitalented of them all."

"There's someone else who might make a close second," Marjorie announced.

"Who's that?" Creighton inquired.

"The one suspect we've completely overlooked. Victor Bartorelli."

"There's a small problem with that theory," Jameson started. "He's dead."

"As a doornail," Creighton added. "You really must try and keep up, Marjorie."

She nearly screamed. "Yes, he's dead *now*, but he was alive at the time of Henry's death. And Bartorelli had a criminal record. What was he in prison for, Robert?"

"Burglary."

"Burglary," she repeated, "how convenient."

"We can't guess what you're thinking," Jameson urged.

"What if Bartorelli somehow got wind of the ring, and upon finding out about it, his old instincts kick in. He decides to steal it, so he waits until a night when no one is home. He creeps into the house, up the stairs, and opens the safe. But, as he's about to grab the ring, Henry walks in on him. Bartorelli panics. He can't go back to jail, so he struggles with Henry and pushes him off the balcony, thus killing him. Bartorelli knows that if there's a murder investigation, he'll be hauled into the police station, so he sits at the desk, writes a suicide note, and then calls the police to report his boss's death."

"There are more holes in that hypothesis than there are in all of Saint Andrews golf course," Creighton criticized.

"Such as?"

"For starters, if Bartorelli killed Van Allen, who killed Bartorelli?"

"We ruled out the possibility of Bartorelli being a member of a gang, but we never said he couldn't have a partner. He and this partner could have had a falling out and, as a result, the partner popped him one."

"The suicide note. How did Bartorelli know what Henry's handwriting looked like?"

"He got a sample of it every week," Marjorie pointed out, "the signature on his paycheck."

"Then there's the whole house thing," Creighton continued. "Bartorelli was a gardener, not a house servant. How would he have gotten into the house that night? And if he did manage to get in, how did he know where to find the safe?"

"I admit, he would have needed help there."

"And how would Bartorelli have gotten into the safe? Jameson just said that there was no signs of tampering."

"He used the combination," she replied matter-of-factly.

"And just how would he have done that?" the Englishman posed.

"The same way he found out about the ring, and got into the house and located the safe. Someone told him."

"Someone told him? Who would have that sort of information?"

"His partner must have been someone familiar with the house. Someone who knew everything going on. Someone who was on very intimate terms with the master of the house."

"Gloria?" Creighton guessed.

"No, not Gloria."

Jameson smiled knowingly. "Stella Munson. She could have sweet-talked the combination out of Henry."

"Precisely. Stella Munson."

"You grew up with Stella," Creighton spoke up. "Do you think she's capable of that sort of thing?"

"I don't know her well enough to say either way."

"Where can we find Miss Munson?" Jameson asked.

"I don't know; haven't seen her in years. But we could ask her brother-in-law, John Stafford. Mary's father," she added for Creighton's benefit. "He's my neighbor."

"Well, then," Jameson announced as he rose from his chair, "let's go pay a call on Mr. Stafford."

"Yes, let's," Creighton followed suit. "At least we know he keeps his bar fully stocked."

SIXTEEN

THE THREE OF THEM drove back into town, Creighton and Marjorie in the Phantom, and Jameson in his squad car. They parked before the Stafford house and followed Marjorie up the narrow brick path that led to the front door. Creighton spotted a small face peering at them through the window; he smiled, but the girl retained her stern expression and disappeared. A few moments later, the front door creaked slightly inward, and the pale, sad face reemerged in the narrow opening.

"Hi, Mary," Marjorie greeted as she removed her gloves. "Is your father at home?"

Mary nodded and then stared warily at the men who also stood on the front stoop.

"These are friends of mine. You met Mr. Ashcroft a few days ago, and the other man is Detect—um, *Mr.* Jameson. We'd like to speak with your dad."

Mary opened the door wide, allowing them to enter the cramped, dimly lit foyer. A man's voice bellowed from the next room, "Mary! Who is it? Who's there?"

The girl donned a worn, plaid wool coat and ran out the door.

"Mary, answer me! Mary!" A tall, dark-haired man staggered into view. He wore a white undershirt tucked into black work pants, his face was unshaven and he carried a half-empty bottle of beer in his left hand. "Oh, hullo, Miss McClelland, I didn't know you were comin'." His face reddened in anger. "Why that fool girl didn't tell me—"

Marjorie interrupted, "Mary didn't know I was coming here today. In fact, I didn't know I was coming until just a few minutes ago. I'm sorry if this is an inconvenient time for you."

John Stafford took a swig of beer and staggered back through the arched doorway through which he had come. They followed him into a faded-looking living room, where he plopped down on a threadbare chair. "That's okay, you know you're welcome here. I was afraid it was one of them ladies from the church, trying to give me their 'charity.'" He dragged the word out to show his disdain.

Marjorie sat on the sofa and bid her friends to do the same. "I'm sure those 'ladies' mean no harm by bringing you food and clothes."

"I'm sure they don't, but you know what they say about the road to hell."

"That it's paved with good intentions," she completed, "and Mrs. Schutt's pound cake."

Stafford's face relaxed into a huge smile. "So whadya come here for? And who are these fellas?"

Marjorie introduced Jameson and Creighton, in turn.

"We need to talk to your sister-in-law," Jameson explained.

"Stella?" his tone became more guarded. "What do you need to talk to her about?"

"I'm sure you heard about the body Miss McClelland found last week."

Creighton looked up sharply. *The body Miss McClelland found?* To hear Robert Jameson talk, Creighton was a kibitzer in this whole thing.

Stafford placed an unlit cigarette between his lips. "Yeah, I read somethin' about it in the local paper."

"The body belongs to a gardener, Victor Bartorelli. He worked for Mr. and Mrs. Van Allen. He died only a few weeks after his employer, leading us to believe that the two deaths might be related."

Stafford had been searching his pants pockets, unsuccessfully, for a match. Jameson took the lighter from his coat pocket and handed it to him. The man took it, cupped his hands around the end of the cigarette, ignited it, and drew a long puff. "What does that have to do with Stella?"

Creighton spoke up. "Stella worked there, didn't she? Maybe she knew Victor Bartorelli."

"Thanks." Stafford handed the lighter back to Jameson. "I can't tell you if she knew this Bartorelli fella or not. Claire and me were living in New Jersey with my mother-in-law at the time."

"Didn't she keep in touch with her mother and sister?"

"Not really." He took another drag on the cigarette. "My mother-in-law was sore at her for not moving out of Ridgebury. But Stella always did whatever she pleased. Marjorie could tell you the whole story."

"I'm sure the detective would rather hear it directly from you," the writer suggested.

He swallowed another mouthful of beer. "There's not too much to tell. My mother-in-law raised Claire and Stella here in Ridgebury, in this house. About ten years back, my mother-in-law's sister got sick— bad rheumatism. She lived alone in a big house in Nutley, New Jersey, so my mother-in-law decided to pack up the girls and move down there so that they could take care of her. Well, Stella had her mind set on staying here. She was already working up at Kensington House, and she said she wasn't gonna give up a good-paying job to take care of a sick woman. So, Stella put her foot down and refused to move. Money was no problem for her; the house here was already paid for and she got most of her meals up at Kensington. All she had to worry about was her electric and water. My mother-in-law couldn't do much about it—Stella was a grown woman, and she had a right to stay if she wanted, but it would've been nice of her to help out."

"So Stella was estranged from her mother. What about her sister, your wife?" Jameson probed.

"They kept in touch for a little while, and then suddenly the letters stopped coming." He grabbed a small dish and flicked a bit of ash into it, edgily. "Look, Stella wasn't the only person who worked for the Van Allens. There were plenty of others; why don't you go bother one of them?"

"Because no one else was in the same position as Stella," Marjorie explained delicately.

"Whadya mean 'position'? She was a maid."

Jameson dispensed with the niceties. "I'll be perfectly blunt with you, Mr. Stafford. Your sister-in-law was having an affair with Henry Van Allen."

Stafford, who had been in mid-sip, started spraying beer like a fountain. "Stella and Henry Van Allen? You're joking!"

"No. I take it you didn't know, then."

"I had no idea," he replied in earnest. "Her mother was upset 'cause she'd been hanging around some young hoodlum, but then word got back that she had thrown him over for someone else. We had no idea that someone else was Henry Van Allen." He gazed distractedly out the window to the front yard where Mary was playing. "I guess she was holding out on all of us."

"You said Stella was seeing a young man. What was his name?" Jameson prompted.

Stafford shifted his attention back into the room. "Scott. Scott . . . Jansen, I think."

"Did this Scott Jansen have a jealous streak?"

"I don't know. We never met him. We only heard about him— that he'd been in some scrapes with the law." He looked out the window again. "Henry Van Allen. I can't believe it."

"Now you know why we need to speak with Stella," Jameson started. "So tell us, Mr. Stafford, where is she?"

The man looked away in a manner that told them he was lying. "I don't know."

"Come on, Mr. Stafford. Stella isn't in any trouble, so there's no need for family loyalty."

He flung his empty beer bottle onto the sofa. "I'm not being loyal to Stella. What'd she ever do for us, except saddle us with more worries? But I promised Claire."

"Mr. Stafford," Marjorie beseeched softly, "your wife wouldn't want you to lie to the police. So, please, tell us where Stella is."

He looked at Marjorie through glassy eyes. "Stella's dead."

None of them had anticipated the answer they heard. "Dead?" Marjorie repeated in a near whisper. "When?"

"About four years ago."

"Why didn't your wife say anything?"

"'Cause she didn't want to disgrace her family."

"Disgrace her family how?"

"By telling everyone her sister took her own life."

"Suicide? My God. What happened?"

Stafford ground out his cigarette. "Like I said, Claire and Stella would write to each other, and then one day, the letters stopped. Mrs. Patterson, here in town, telephoned my mother-in-law and told her that no one had seen Stella around and that the house was empty."

Marjorie nodded. "I remember that, yes. Your mother-in-law called back a few days later and said she had traced Stella to California."

"Yep, we had. She had taken an apartment outside of Los Angeles. Claire got hold of the telephone number and called her to find out what was goin' on. Stella said she was okay, she had plenty of money to live off of, but that she'd moved in order to forget everything and make a clean start."

"What did she want to forget?" Creighton asked.

"Beats me," Stafford shrugged, "but it didn't work too good, 'cause less than a year later we got a call from the Los Angeles police department saying that they had found Stella dead in her apartment. She hanged herself."

Marjorie gasped. "How terrible."

"By that time Claire was already feeling poorly, so I made the trip to California alone, to identify the body and get Stella's belongings. When I came back, my mother-in-law suggested Claire and me move up here to Ridgebury. She knew we had always wanted a home of our own, and it meant a lot to her that her granddaughter would be raised in the same house her mother and aunt grew up in. She said it always was a happy place." Stafford's voice cracked.

Marjorie leapt from her seat and placed a comforting hand on the man's shoulder. "There, there, Mr. Stafford. I think you've told us all we need to know right now." She shot a questioning glance at Jameson, who nodded his approval. "Why don't you lie down for awhile and we'll let ourselves out."

The sobbing man nodded, and Marjorie led her companions back to the foyer and out the front door. They marched somberly down the front walk; Mary was on the side of the house, trying to replace the wheel on a rickety scooter. When they reached the curb and were safely out of earshot, Creighton finally broke the silence. "Poor tragic people. It's not fair that one family should have to go through so much. Are you okay?" he asked Marjorie. "I know you went to school with both of them."

"I'm fine. It's just a bit of a shock. When you go to school with someone, you always seem to remember them as a child. Although you might see the person every day, in your memory they never age. You never think of them growing up, or getting sick or dying. And for not just one sister to die, but both . . ." She clicked her tongue. "I always wished I had a sister. Short of mother and daughter, there's no bond quite as close."

Creighton wanted to reach out and pull her close to him, as though his arms might somehow be able to shield her from all the ugliness in the world. It was clear, however, that Marjorie did not want anyone to think she required such protection, for after only a few moments, she sniffed and resumed her role as gumshoe extraordinaire. "So what do you think about the boyfriend?" she asked Jameson. "Is he a suspect?"

"If Stella really threw him over for Henry, I guess that gives the boyfriend a motive."

"I think so, too," she agreed.

Jameson smiled. "But according to your Evelyn Hadley theory, Scott Jansen should have killed Stella for betraying him. Or do the rules of jealousy differ for men and women?"

"As a matter of fact, they do," she answered confidently.

"They do? Can you offer any proof?"

"Certainly. Let's pretend Creighton and I are married."

"All right," Creighton swung his arm around Marjorie enthusiastically. "Did we have our honeymoon yet?"

"Yes," she answered impatiently. "Now let's assume that Creighton has been having an affair with Sharon Schutt."

"Let's not and say we did."

"Am I going to take it out on Sharon?" she posed. "No. I might harbor resentment toward her, but I would most definitely take it out on Creighton." To prove her point, she jabbed him in the ribs with her elbow.

"Hey," the Englishman objected, "we were just pretending."

"Now, let's assume the sides are reversed. Creighton is interested in me, but I throw him over for you."

Creighton sighed. *Art imitates life.*

"Now, Creighton, who are you going to feel antipathy toward? Me? Or Jameson?"

"Jameson, definitely," he answered without hesitation. "Although I wouldn't kill him. I'd never wish anyone dead. However, I might wish him ill. A cold, or a nasty rash or something. Then again, I probably wouldn't do that. It wouldn't accomplish much. The thing to do would be to get him transferred to another precinct. That would give you time alone with me to appreciate my considerable charms." He added, self-consciously, "This is all *purely* hypothetical of course."

"Okay, Marjorie," Jameson conceded. "You proved your point. I'll see what I can come up with on Scott Jansen."

"And what about Stella? Do you think she might have been involved in a plot to steal the ring?"

Creighton spoke up. "I don't know if she was involved, but Stafford mentioned something intriguing in there. He said that when Claire contacted her sister in California, she assured her that she had 'plenty of money.' Stella was only a maid—even if she lived frugally, she would never have 'plenty' of money."

"Van Allen might have been paying her way," Jameson suggested.

"I don't think so. It sounds as if Henry Van Allen was one of the things she was trying to forget."

Marjorie glanced at her watch. "Speaking of forgetting things, Creighton, isn't your date with Sharon tonight?"

"It's not a date; it's dinner with the Schutt family," he balked.

"Whatever it is, you'd better get moving," Jameson advised. "It's already five thirty."

"I have plenty of time—their house is only five minutes away."

"Yes, but don't you want time to freshen up first?" Marjorie asked.

"Freshen up?"

"Well, yes; shave, brush your teeth, change your tie."

Creighton looked down at his necktie; navy blue and cream diagonal stripes. "What's wrong with my tie?"

She pulled a face. "Nothing, I guess."

"All right, I'll go, but let me walk you home first."

"I'm only two doors away. I'm well able to walk myself."

"No, it's getting dark. I'd feel much better knowing you were safely at home."

"He's right, Marjorie," Jameson concurred. "You can't be too careful nowadays. Creighton, you go and I'll walk her home."

"Oh no, old boy, you have to be getting back to the station, don't you?"

"Nope. This is my last call for the day. I'm off duty now."

Creighton spied the squad car parked in the street. "What about the car? Aren't you going to bring it back?"

"No, they let me borrow it for my own use."

"You see, Creighton," Marjorie said serenely. "I'm in very good hands. So you run along and enjoy your dinner."

The Englishman started to walk away, but paused to give his companions one last parting glance.

"Have a good time," Marjorie instructed. "I'll see you tomorrow."

"Goodnight, Creighton," Jameson added smugly.

He grunted his reply, and then walked to his car as a condemned man walks to the gallows. All he could do was listen as Jameson made his move: "I don't mean to seem presumptuous . . ." Creighton couldn't hear the rest, but he did catch the tail end of the detective's offer: "There's a movie at the Odeon at eight fifteen."

He hopped into his car and slammed the door, grinning like a Cheshire cat. After all, didn't he promise the Schutts that he would take Sharon to the movies?

SEVENTEEN

MARJORIE FOLLOWED THE MOVEMENT of Jameson's mouth, but his words did not register immediately. "I don't mean to be presumptuous. We've only just met and it's very last minute, but I was wondering if you had any plans tonight."

"Tonight?" she asked incredulously.

"Yeah, there's a movie playing at the Odeon at eight fifteen. I thought we could try to catch it. That is, if you're not busy."

"Hmm, let's see," Marjorie creased her brow, as if poring over the contents of a mental calendar. "Tonight . . . tonight . . . what do I have planned tonight?" In truth, such contemplation was not necessary, as Marjorie spent every evening alone, in her bathrobe and fuzzy slippers, reading a book and listening to her favorite radio shows. She did not, however, wish to give Jameson the impression of being too readily available. "You're in luck; my agenda seems to be open for this evening."

"Swell," he said as they strolled slowly down the sidewalk. "Are you hungry? We could grab a bite before the show starts."

"That sounds nice."

"Great. There's a little Italian place near the theater that serves a beauty of a pizza pie."

"Pizza pie? I've heard of it but I've never tasted it. What is it like?"

"It's a flat, round piece of bread covered with tomatoes and cheese. Come on," he urged, "trust me, you'll like it."

Marjorie and Jameson occupied a table in the window of Guiseppe's Italian Restaurant. The pizza was everything Jameson had claimed it would be: crispy, cheesy, and hot. Marjorie, in hunger, had polished off two slices before she chided herself on her lack of daintiness. They were now enjoying that quiet span of time between the completion of the meal and the receipt of the check.

"I have to admit," Jameson prefaced, "I was very relieved when Creighton agreed to take Sharon to the movies."

"Relieved? Why?"

"Because when I first met you and Creighton, I thought maybe you two were a couple."

"A couple of what?" she asked stupidly.

Jameson laughed. "A couple, as in married."

"Married? To each other?"

"Yes, but then I saw that your name was McClelland, not Ashcroft, so I knew you weren't married. Still, I couldn't be sure that you weren't engaged or betrothed, or anything serious like that. But when Creighton decided to see Sharon, it was clear there was nothing going on between you two."

"I don't know how you could have gotten that idea in the first place."

"A few things. First, you *looked* like you might be together. Then, you know Creighton *is* very protective of you."

"He's extremely well-mannered," she dismissed.

"Then there was the bickering. You two bicker like my parents do, only they've been married forty years."

"Some detective you are," Marjorie teased. "I'll have you know that there never has been, nor will there ever be, anything between Creighton Ashcroft and me. He's simply not my type."

Jameson fished for a compliment. "And what exactly is your type?"

Marjorie didn't take the bait. "I'm still trying to find out, but I can tell you it isn't Creighton. He and I are from two different worlds. He's a millionaire, for heaven's sake. He's probably never known an unhappy day in his life. If loneliness or misery knocks on his door, he buys it off with a new house or a new car."

Speaking of cars . . . She did a double take out the window at an automobile that looked exactly like the Phantom. *It couldn't be*, she convinced herself. *Creighton's probably still at the Schutt's, being force-fed Louise's revolting rhubarb pie.*

"What about you?" the detective probed. "Have you known many unhappy days?"

"Only my fair share," she answered vaguely.

"What does a smart, pretty girl like you have to be unhappy about?"

She shrugged evasively. "Things."

Jameson, ever the policeman, tried to pin her down. "I notice you live alone. What happened to your parents?"

"My father's been dead seven years," Marjorie replied curtly. She wished to God that Robert would find something else to talk about.

"I'm sorry. What about your mother?"

"I never knew her; she left when I was very small."

"You have any brothers or sisters?"

"No, just me."

"Sounds like a lonely existence."

"It's not, really. I have plenty to keep me busy."

"I'm sure you do."

"What about your parents?" she deftly turned the conversation away from her own background.

"They're in Boston. I was born and raised there. My pop walked the beat for the Boston Police. He retired a few years back, and now he drives my mother crazy."

"So being a policeman is in the blood."

"Yeah, though my father would have liked it better had I joined the force in Boston. Says it's 'God's country' out here."

"Compared to Boston, I suppose it is," Marjorie smiled. "Do you have any brothers and sisters?"

"Two of each."

"Two brothers and two sisters? Sounds like an *un*lonely existence."

"Yeah, we see each other a lot: holidays, birthdays, picnics. My brothers and I get together sometimes and toss the football around." He reflected a moment and then asked, "I don't suppose you like sports, do you?"

"Sports? You mean like baseball and football, and things like that?"

Jameson nodded.

"Not really," Marjorie said, then eagerly added, "I love radio quiz shows—if a sports question comes up on a quiz show, I can answer it, but apart from that, I really don't like sports much. However, I do love to read. Do you like to read?"

"I read enough at work," he dismissed. "What about the outdoors? Are you a nature lover?"

"Oh, yes. Actually, I just invested in a collapsible chaise lounge so that I can do my reading outdoors in the nicer weather. This way I can listen to the birds and soak up some sun."

He laughed and shook his head. "No, I meant more along the lines of hiking."

"Hiking? Yes, I suppose you could say I hike. At least, I enjoy taking long walks. I could walk for hours on end. It helps me think."

"I get paid to think all week long. I don't like to do it in my spare time, but I still enjoy hiking. I go to the Berkshires a lot in the summer, just for the day. Maybe you'd like to join me some time. That is, if having me around wouldn't interrupt your thinking."

"I'd love to," she replied and then chastised herself for appearing too eager.

The waiter deposited the check on the table. Jameson paid it on the spot with instructions to "keep the change." Rising from his chair, he shoved his wallet back in his pants pocket and put on his heavy trench coat. "Shall we?" he asked. Marjorie nodded, and Robert pulled her chair away from the table and helped her into her coat. Then he offered her his arm, which she readily accepted, and they walked out of the restaurant and down the street toward the local cinema.

The evening had turned cold and windy, and Marjorie huddled close to Jameson for warmth. She scanned the faces of the people they passed on the street, hoping to encounter someone she knew—an old schoolmate, a neighbor, anyone—to see her out walking with this dashing young man, someone who would go green with envy at the sight of them together.

Her wish was interrupted by the movement of something in her peripheral vision. It was the Rolls Royce again, this time driving away from her and toward a dark intersection. She blinked in order to clear her vision of the strange image; when she opened her eyes again, the car was gone.

What was she doing? She had been looking forward to this evening ever since meeting Robert Jameson, and now it was being ruined . . . by *him*! She had thought about him during the car ride to the restaurant, she had discussed him during dinner, and now she was hallucinating about him, too.

Upon reaching the Odeon, Marjorie stared up at the marquee and heaved a sigh of relief. She thought of the flickering black and white screen, the aroma of popcorn and she and Jameson holding hands in the darkened theater. A movie was just the thing to get Creighton Ashcroft off her mind.

Creighton brought the Rolls Royce to a stop at ten minutes after eight o'clock, in a spot just a few yards away from the movie theater. He could have been at the theater earlier, but he had spent the past ten minutes scouting the area for a glimpse of Jameson's patrol car, as it was Creighton's only means of knowing whether the other couple had followed through with their plans. After circling it several times, he finally spotted the vehicle near an Italian restaurant down the street.

Sharon, thankfully, was too absorbed in conversation to notice Creighton's circumnavigation. A reader of film star magazines, she had been chattering away about her favorite actors and the latest Hollywood gossip. These topics held no interest whatsoever for Creighton, and the monotonous drone of her thin, reedy voice might have driven him to a nervous breakdown had it not been for her comical appearance. She was wearing a ridiculous black felt hat, which sat, rather precariously, on the back of her round head. The upturned brim of the hat was covered in a plethora of champagne-colored ostrich feather plumes, and on top of the small, helmet crown was wired an artificial bird, which bobbed up and down with the slightest vibration. When Sharon spoke animatedly, the faux-feathered creature seemed to go into epileptic fits.

Creighton helped Sharon out of the car and jogged ahead to the ticket window. With the tickets safely in hand, he led the way to the theater entrance, Sharon and her short, stubby legs struggling to match pace with his long, elegant steps. He paused a moment so that she could catch up, and watched as the wind made the bird on her hat appear as if it might take flight. If the bird did succeed in taking wing, he only hoped it possessed enough strength to carry Sharon off with it.

"Come on," he urged. It was essential that they enter the theater before the lights went down.

Giggling, she waddled past him and through the open door and then stopped to catch her breath.

"Where shall we sit?" Creighton asked, searching for Marjorie and Jameson among the members of the audience.

"Why don't we sit here, in the back?" the moon-faced girl tittered salaciously.

"No," he rejected coolly, "you'll strain your eyesight. Let's sit up front."

Sharon grabbed his arm possessively and they strolled, slowly, up the left-hand aisle. They had only gone a few paces when Creighton's eyes picked out the swirl-patterned hat and blonde tresses of Marjorie McClelland. She and Detective Jameson were seated smack-dab in the center of the theater in an otherwise unoccupied row of seats.

"There," he pointed. "That row looks empty."

He dashed off, dragging Sharon along with him. When he neared the line of seats, he called out, "Marjorie! Jameson! Fancy meeting you here!"

The couple looked up in surprise. "So it *was* you," Marjorie muttered to herself.

Creighton felt an elbow nudge him in the ribs. "Who's that?" Sharon whispered, gazing at Jameson longingly.

Was no woman safe from Jameson's spell? "Miss Schutt, this is Detective Jameson. Detective Jameson, this is Miss Schutt."

Jameson rose partially out of his seat. "Nice to meet you," he acknowledged. Sharon replied with an embarrassed cackle.

"Hello, Sharon." Marjorie addressed the girl with a cordial nod of the head.

"Marjorie," the girl spat back contemptuously.

"We didn't know you were coming here tonight," Jameson stated.

"We didn't either," Creighton explained, "but we wanted to take in a movie, and this theater lets out earlier than the Bijou."

"I wasn't aware Sharon still had a curfew," Marjorie remarked cattily.

"I don't," the plump girl whined. "I haven't had a curfew since I was twenty-one. And now I'm nearly twenty-three."

"The show's about to start," Creighton stated, looking at his watch. "Would you mind if we sit with you?"

"Not at all," Jameson offered.

"Why did you ask if we could sit with them?" Sharon whispered to her date. "I can't stand that Marjorie."

"Sharon, dear, we don't want to be rude to Jameson. He's the detective who questioned your parents at the store the other day. We wouldn't want to get on his bad side, would we?" He flashed her a disarming smile. "I know. I'll sit next to Marjorie, this way you won't have to talk to her."

"You would do that for me?"

"Anything for you, Sharon," he replied through clenched teeth.

She squeezed his arm, cutting off the circulation. "Oh, Creighton! You're aces!"

"Yes, well." He awkwardly sidestepped the compliment and slid in next to Marjorie.

"Thank goodness," she whispered. "For a moment I thought Sharon was going to sit next to me."

"She was going to, but I convinced her to switch places with me. I know you don't like her very much, and I thought it might ruin your evening if you had to spend it sitting next to Sharon."

Marjorie smiled. "Thank you, Creighton. You're very sweet."

He returned the smile. "Anything for you, Marjorie."

The lights dimmed and, as the film projector started to roll the most recent newsreel, a head suddenly appeared between Creighton and Sharon. "Excuse me, miss, but could you please remove your hat? The bird is blocking the picture."

Sharon swiveled about to peer behind her. "There are plenty of empty seats, why don't you sit somewhere else?"

"Because my wife and I are comfortable the way we are."

"Well, I'm comfortable the way I am and that includes wearing my hat," she declared obstinately.

"Lady, if you don't take the hat off, I'll take it off for you!"

Creighton could see this escalating to the point where they might be ejected from the theater. "Just take the bloody hat off, Sharon," he insisted.

"Okay, okay," she grudgingly agreed, "you don't have to yell."

The man thanked Creighton and sat back as Sharon made the removal of her feathered hat a major production. "I don't see why . . ." she grumbled to herself. "He could have just moved . . . but no . . ." She stuck the hatpins into the brim of the bonnet and balanced it, along with her purse, on her lap. Only a few seconds elapsed, however, before her ample belly pushed both objects to the floor.

Creighton, weary of the girl's escapades, snatched the hat from the ground and placed it on his own lap. "There." he proclaimed in a loud whisper. "Now be quiet."

The newsreel had ended, and Betty Boop flitted across the screen in her latest romp, "Baby Be Good." Sharon eased back in her chair, grinning like a mollified child.

Creighton, like the parent of a rambunctious youngster who has finally gone off to sleep, took a deep breath and stretched his legs out as far as he could. After several minutes, he found that he had calmed down considerably and was even starting to enjoy himself. The animated short had provided him with a few chuckles, and the serial, Gene Autry in part five of *The Phantom Empire*, was entertaining in a far-fetched sort of way. However, the best part of all was being so close to Marjorie. For in the dark, in that kingdom where fantasy reigned, he could temporarily block out the existence of Sharon and Jameson and have Marjorie all to himself.

But, as the serial ended and the audience was shown highlights from the next episode, he spotted something that reminded him that his was merely a fantasy. Detective Jameson, after an overstated stretch, was proceeding to slide his arm around Marjorie's shoulders.

Creighton grinned. The detective was a smooth operator, but he was sharper. Slowly, he drew one of the long pins from the brim of Sharon's hat, and pricked the tip of the policeman's finger as it appeared above Marjorie's shoulder. Jameson flinched slightly, then carried through with his invasion.

I must stab him harder, Creighton thought, adopting a siege mentality. Wielding the pin like a miniature spear, he plunged the weapon, harpoonlike, into the back of Jameson's hand, and then quickly withdrew it. In reflex, the detective pulled his arm away, accidentally clobbering Marjorie in the back of the head and knocking her hat down over her eyes.

"Ow!" she cried.

"Sorry," Jameson whispered apologetically.

"Say, what did you do that for?" she asked as she pushed her hat back into place.

"I didn't mean to," he explained as he surveyed the back of his hand. "I think something must have bitten me."

Erstwhile, Creighton had palmed the hatpin and was watching the opening credits of the feature attraction, his arms folded across his chest. When he saw the title of the film, he couldn't resist taking a shot at his romantic nemesis. "Oh, look, Jameson," he pointed out innocently. "It's a movie about your insect attacker: 'Captain Blood.'"

"Where are you off to now?" Creighton inquired when the movie let out. "Are you getting some coffee? Or maybe a soda?"

The foursome exited the theater lobby. "Home," Jameson answered. "I've got to go to work tomorrow."

"*I* could go for a soda," Sharon interjected.

"No, it's getting late," Creighton refused. "High time I take you home."

"Well, then," the detective concluded, "I guess this is goodbye." He grabbed the other man's hand and shook it. "'Night, Creighton. Nice to meet you, Miss Schutt," he added with a tip of his hat.

Again, the pudgy girl cackled idiotically.

"So long, Jameson. Thanks for letting us tag along." Creighton took Marjorie's hands in both of his, and gazed deeply into her eyes. "Goodnight, Marjorie," he bade softly.

She met his gaze and swiftly turned her head. "Goodnight Creighton," she murmured, releasing her hands from his grip. "Bye, Sharon."

"*Marj*orie," the young woman hissed.

Creighton watched wearily as Marjorie and Jameson walked down the street, arm in arm. He had managed to waylay most of the detective's advances toward Marjorie, but he knew that this was just one battle in a long and vigorous war. The road ahead was fraught with many perils, the most immediate of which was Jameson's attempt at the goodnight kiss.

"I'm cold," Sharon snapped. "Can we go now?"

"Hmm?" he answered distractedly. "Yes, of course." He helped her into the passenger compartment of the Phantom and walked around to the driver's side door. All the while, his mind pictured Marjorie and Jameson, their arms entwining each other in the moonlight. *Well, it wasn't going to happen. Not on his watch!*

He jumped into the driver's seat and started the engine. As he watched Jameson's squad car drive past him, a plan began to take shape in his head. The plan's success, however, was dependent upon him taking Sharon home as soon as humanly possible. He pulled away from the curb and followed the police car through the crowded streets of town.

Sharon had resumed her discourse on Hollywood celebrities, this time including the stars of the film they had just seen. "Olivia de Haviland was just beautiful, don't you think? Mother says I look like her. Do you think I look like her?" She didn't wait for an answer. "I read somewhere that she brushes her hair five hundred strokes a night. Five hundred strokes a night! Can you imagine?"

Creighton concentrated on the scene outside the front windshield. They were out of town now and had reached a portion of straight, open road. He shifted gears and applied steady pressure to the accelerator.

"And that Errol Flynn," Sharon went on. "Why, he's just a peach. Not as peachy as you, though."

Creighton glanced over at his passenger, who was watching him with a twinkle in her eye, and immediately floored the gas pedal. He swerved onto the left side of the road, passed the police car and then moved back into the right lane, all the while maintaining speed.

Sharon, for the first time all evening, was silent, her head having been thrown back against the headrest. "You're going awfully fast," she indicated nervously.

Creighton wondered whether his plan might have the added benefit of frightening off the ardent Miss Schutt. "Fast? I always drive this way."

"You didn't earlier."

"That's because I had just eaten. Food makes me sluggish."

"Y-your friend might give you a ticket."

"Jameson? No, the most he'd do is give me a warning." He glanced in his rearview mirror. "Look behind us. He hasn't even given chase."

Sharon turned around and looked out the rear window. "I don't see him."

"That's because we've outrun him," the Englishman replied as he maintained constant speed.

Within a few minutes, they were outside the Schutt home. Creighton left the car idling and walked Sharon to the front door.

"Good night, Sharon, pleasant dreams," he wished her hastily.

"Nighty night, Creighton." She closed her eyes and puckered her mouth.

"I'd better not," he hedged. "I'm coming down with a cold." He validated his statement with a fake sneeze.

She opened her eyes. "You've been fine all night."

"It's this night air," he waved his hands to include the space around him. "Plays havoc with the sinuses, you know. Which is why you should get inside," he pushed her stout frame toward the doorway. "Wouldn't want you to catch a chill."

She opened the front door and stepped inside, giggling. "Oh, Creighton, you're so thoughtful."

"Now, now, none of that," he reprimanded. "Off to bed with you."

She complied, still tee-heeing, and quietly shut the door. Creighton took off like a shot down the front walk, hopped in the car and drove, hell for leather, toward Marjorie's house.

The writer and the detective were standing on the front stoop of the McClelland homestead, poised for their farewells. The wind had died down and the moon had poked its glowing face from beneath the clouds. Marjorie watched the orb's reflection in Jameson's eyes. "Thank you, Robert," she said quietly. "I had a very nice time."

"I did, too. Maybe we could do it again sometime."

"Maybe," she replied, determined to maintain a semblance of aloofness.

"Soon?" he pressed.

"I think we could work something out."

He tilted his head close to hers. "Goodnight, Marjorie."

"Goodnight, Robert." She angled her neck upwards and shut her eyes in anticipation of his lips meeting hers.

The next sensation she experienced, however, was not the taste of Jameson's mouth, but the blast of a car horn. *Toot-toot!*

The couple looked up to see Creighton driving past them, waving out of his car window dementedly. When he had vanished down the street, Marjorie asked, "What was that all about?"

"He's probably happy to have gotten rid of Miss Schutt." He leaned his head toward Marjorie's again, but it was too late. The moment had passed. Giving her a chaste peck on the cheek, he bid adieu and walked back to his car.

Marjorie stood in the frame of the open front door and watched him drive away. When he had gone she slammed the door shut in furor, sending Sam scuttling from his position on the windowsill.

"I hope you sleep well, tonight, Mr. Ashcroft," she shouted. "Because tomorrow, boy, are you ever going to hear it from me!"

EIGHTEEN

Marjorie let herself into Mrs. Patterson's back kitchen door around eleven o'clock the next morning. The elderly woman was there, leaning over the sink and scrubbing at the last of the breakfast dishes.

"Good morning. Is Creighton around?"

"No, he had an errand to run over at the post office, but he should be back shortly, if you want to wait." As if on cue, the boarder appeared at the back door, his arms loaded to capacity with a multitude of boxes. "Why, here he is now." Mrs. Patterson hastened to open the door.

He thanked Mrs. Patterson and placed the parcels gently upon the kitchen table. "Ah, Marjorie," he acknowledged the younger of the two women. "Just the person I wanted to see."

"What a coincidence. I wanted to see you, too."

Creighton ripped the lid from the first box and withdrew from it a pair of men's black patent leather shoes, polished to an immaculate shine. "What did you want to see me about?"

"Last night," she answered coolly.

He placed the shoes on an empty area of the table.

"Creighton!" Mrs. Patterson shouted from the sink area. "Take those shoes off the table. Don't you know it's bad luck?"

"Sorry." He moved the offending objects to the floor beside his feet, and removed the top from another package. "Yes, I had a good time last night, too. Thanks again for letting us join you."

"I didn't come here to tell you I had a good time," she snapped impatiently. "I wanted to talk to you about what you did after the—" She stopped in mid-sentence as Creighton pulled out a silver beaded evening bag. "What is all this stuff?"

He grabbed a shoebox-shaped package. "I had these things shipped over for tonight. You remember—Gloria's party."

Picking up the evening bag, she teased, "They're not going to let you in with this purse. It doesn't match your shoes."

Mrs. Patterson giggled and came to the table for a closer look.

"No," he replied calmly, "but it matches yours."

"No it doesn't. My shoes are black."

"Not anymore they aren't." He opened the shoebox to reveal a pair of high-heel silver pumps with a strap across the vamp fastened by a rhinestone buckle.

The shoes were lovely, exactly what she would have chosen for herself, but there was one problem. "I can't wear these. They don't go with my dress. My dress is black crepe."

"No, it isn't," Creighton argued. "Your dress is silver."

He really was the most impossible man. "I know what color my dress is. My dress is—"

Her voice trailed off as Creighton opened a large box to unveil a silver evening gown. "As you were saying?"

Marjorie fell silent as she took the stunning gown in her hands and examined it. The fabric, luminous silk, was cut on the bias, with numerous pleats and tucks to flatter every curve. Designed in the halter style, the upper part of the dress was backless as well as sleeveless and held in place by a slender strap around the neck. The bodice boasted a plunging v-neck whose opening was modestly fastened together by three rhinestone-encrusted x-shaped embellishments. A fitted waist, secured with a slender belt, flowed into an angle cut skirt culminating in a flounced hem.

"My, but it is lovely," Mrs. Patterson exclaimed, then pulling her hand to her mouth and frowning, "but it's awfully bare. No sleeves, and no back. Marjorie would be sure to catch her death."

"I had a feeling you'd say that, Mrs. Patterson." He opened another garment size box. "That's why I got this." It was a matching full-length opera coat, lined and trimmed in the purest of white fur.

"Oh, how grand!" Mrs. Patterson cried.

Marjorie was still speechless.

"I know it's not the dress you were looking at," Creighton apologized.

"The dress I was looking at?" she asked in astonishment.

"Yes, the one in the shop window when we went to see Miss Hadley," he stated matter-of-factly. "I caught you admiring it, but the head of the Connecticut Women's Literary League wouldn't buy a dress displayed in a shop window."

"That's why you bought all this? To keep up appearances?"

"Yes," he paused, "and so that Mrs. Patterson wouldn't become a slave to her sewing machine."

"You thought my dress was inappropriate?"

"Marjorie," Mrs. Patterson interjected, "wearing that dress to your high school dance was one thing, but this . . . *this is Gloria Van Allen.*"

Marjorie looked again at the whole ensemble. It was indeed beautiful, but it must have cost a fortune. She shook her head, "I'm sorry, but I can't accept all of this. It's too expensive."

"You're not *accepting* anything," Creighton argued. "These things aren't gifts. They're items necessary to the continuance of this investigation and, hence, the writing of your book. This is all strictly business, and any money I might have spent should be viewed as an 'operating expense.'"

"Fine," she responded, inexplicably annoyed that Creighton had found her unworthy of a gift. "Since this is strictly business, you can't possibly be insulted if I reimburse you."

Mrs. Patterson shuffled back to the sink in disgust. "I'll never understand young people these days," she mumbled to herself.

"Fine," he spat back. "If that's the way you want it, you can pay me back out of the proceeds from the book."

"Fine." she agreed, grabbing the dress from the table. "Now, if you don't mind, I'm going to try this on. I not going to pay for something that doesn't fit."

"It fits."

"How can you be so certain?"

"Because it was made precisely to your measurements."

"How did you get my measurements?"

The elderly woman inched quietly from the sink toward the hallway door. Marjorie spotted her before she could break away. "Mrs. Patterson, you gave my measurements to a perfect stranger!"

"No, dear, I gave them to Creighton. *He* gave them to a perfect stranger," she replied innocently, before leaving the room.

"Did you hear that?" Marjorie accused Creighton as one parent might accuse another. "She's beginning to sound like you."

"I never claimed to be a good influence," he commented as he packed the evening clothes back into their boxes. "Now, are you taking this stuff or not?"

"Yes," she responded frostily, "I'll take it."

He stacked the boxes into a neat pile. "Shall I help you carry these home?"

"No, I can manage." She scooped the pile into her arms and strode toward the back door.

"Oh, what was it you wanted to talk to me about?"

Marjorie stopped, her hand on the doorknob. She turned around, slowly. "I wanted to tell you that I didn't appreciate you honking your car horn last night."

"I'm sorry. I didn't realize I interrupted . . ." He raised his eyebrows. "*Something.*"

"You didn't." She blushed. "Robert and I were having a deep philosophical discussion, that's all."

Creighton cleared his throat. "Hmm. Yes, I've had a few of those myself. Of course most of them were during my college days and took place in a rumble seat."

"Are you doubting me?" she cornered him.

"No, no, not at all. I'm sure Detective Jameson is a very good 'philosopher.' Anyway, I do hope you can forgive me for disrupting your discussion. I was rather giddy last night . . . what with the moonlight and all that Errol Flynn swashbuckling and sitting next to a pretty girl."

"A pretty girl?"

"Why, yes. Sharon."

"Oh, yes, Sharon." She turned around gloomily and opened the back door.

"Wait," Creighton called. "What time should I pick you up tonight?"

"It doesn't matter," she replied without looking at him. "You decide."

"The party's at eight o'clock, so I guess I'll meet you around five."

"Five o'clock sounds fine," she agreed despondently and trudged out of the house. Had she taken the time to look over her shoulder, she would have seen Creighton watching her through the kitchen window, a complacent smile across his face.

Creighton held true to his word; he knocked upon Marjorie's door at five o'clock sharp. "Come in," she shouted from the bedroom, where she was putting the finishing touches on her makeup. Pleased with the results, she snatched her best string of pearls and a pair of matching earrings from her jewelry box and rushed into the living room to meet her escort. "How do I look?" she asked anxiously.

The Englishman was standing near the front door, his eyes sparkling. "You're the loveliest sight I've ever seen."

"You can stop acting now, Creighton," she chided while preening herself before the mantelpiece mirror. "You've already got the part."

He approached her from behind and, grabbing her by the shoulders, spun her about, gently. "I'm not pretending, Marjorie. You're positively radiant."

So consumed was she with her own appearance that she hadn't noticed what a fine figure Creighton cut in his white tie and tails. His hair was combed straight back off his forehead, playing up his classic features, and the white silk scarf he wore with his black cashmere chesterfield coat was very smart. At this proximity, she could see why Doris and Sharon were completely wild about the man, for the smell of his cologne was deep, musky, enticing, and the warmth of his hands upon her bare shoulders titillating. Yes, a woman of weaker resolve might easily lose her head over a man like Creighton Ashcroft. Luckily, she was not that type of woman. "You're not too bad yourself," she allowed.

Before he had a chance to thank her, the telephone rang. "Could you get that?" she requested. "I have to switch pocketbooks and put on my jewelry."

Creighton obliged and picked up the receiver. Marjorie listened from the bedroom, where she deposited lipstick, a comb, and her house key into her beaded evening bag.

"Hello? . . . Yes, hello Jameson . . . That's all right, we have a few minutes . . . You did? What did you find out? . . . Mmm-hmm . . . Hard to trace . . . Mmm-hmm . . . Mmm-hmm . . . When will you receive that? . . . That fast, eh?"

She moved back into the living room and put on her pearl earrings.

"No, morning isn't a good idea," Creighton continued. "I don't know when we'll get home tonight . . . noon should be fine . . . okay, we'll see you then." He hung up the telephone with a loud click and approached Marjorie, who was standing before the mirror, frowning at the strand of pearls she had donned.

"What did Robert want?" she asked of his reflection.

"Just to tell us that he ordered an audit of Van Allen Industries."

"And?"

"And he found that during the last year of Henry's life, overall expenditures increased dramatically, the most significant increases being in the areas of office supplies and building maintenance."

She removed one earring and turned her head back and forth, comparing the bare lobe with the ringed one. "Really? Is Robert going to arrest Philips?"

"For what? Paying too much for typewriter ribbons?"

"No, embezzlement."

"There's no proof of embezzlement."

"But you said that there was a dramatic increase in expenses. It's obvious that Philips padded the books and kept the difference for himself."

"I'm with you, dear. It does sound fishy. However, purchasing an abundance of pencils could easily be written off as the result of an overambitious pencil sharpener. The only way to prove that it's embezzlement is to compare the figures in the books with those on the actual receipts, and that's going to take a little more time."

She clipped the earring back on. "Oh," she moaned in disappointment. "Did he tell you anything else?"

"Yes, he said that he contacted the Los Angeles police. They're supposed to wire him a copy of Stella's suicide report. He should have it on his desk tomorrow. I told him we'd check in with him around noon, since we probably won't be back until late."

She nodded and then gazed at her reflection with dissatisfaction. "What do you think of these pearls? Do they look okay with this dress?"

Creighton stuck his hand into the lining of his coat and pulled out a black velvet box. Reaching his arms around Marjorie, he thrust the box in her face and opened the hinged lid. "I think these would go better."

It was a complete jewelry ensemble consisting of necklace, earrings and bracelet, all done in an openwork style, and inlaid with brilliant, colorless stones. Creighton placed the box on the mantle and fastened the necklace about her slender neck.

"Oh, it's perfect," she exclaimed. "I've never seen rhinestones so clear. It almost looks real."

Creighton laughed. "It is 'real.' Those are diamonds, and the setting is platinum."

She gasped. "Diamonds. Oh, I can't—"

"Before you go on and on about how you can't accept it, I might as well tell you that it's not yours to keep. It's only a loan."

"Of course. You can have it back as soon as the party is over."

He took her wrist and placed the bracelet around it. "You don't have to give it back as soon as that."

"Why? How long did you rent it for?"

He laughed again. "I didn't rent it. It's mine."

She clipped on the earrings. "Yours? What is a bachelor doing with women's jewelry?"

"It was my mother's. She left it to me to give to the woman I marry."

Marjorie's jaw fell open and she scrambled to remove the necklace. "Then I shouldn't be wearing this."

He grabbed her hands. "Why not? It's been sitting in a box for over twenty-five years. High time someone wore it."

"But it's supposed to go to your wife," she argued wriggling her arms free of his grasp.

"And it will. However, right now, I don't have a wife."

"But when you do she'll be furious if she finds out that another woman wore it before she did."

Creighton smiled and replied, cryptically, "If I have my way, that shouldn't be an issue."

She relaxed. "Well, if you're not going to worry about it, neither am I."

"Good idea. Are you ready to go?"

"I think so," her eyes darted around the room before coming to rest on the secretary in the corner. "Wait," she commanded, and proceeded to pull a nickel from a box on top of the desk.

"What's that?" Creighton inquired as she plopped the five-cent piece into her bag.

"My emergency change."

"Emergency change?"

"Yes, it's a rule of mine to always carry change with me, for emergency telephone calls. It started when I was a teenager. My father always gave me change before I left so that I could call him if I needed a ride home."

He raised his eyebrows. "Were the boys you saw in the habit of abandoning you without a way home?"

"No, the money was for those times that I wanted to abandon them. If my escort got fresh."

"*If your escort got fresh*," Creighton repeated, looking her over from head to toe. "In that case, here." He reached into his pocket and pulled out a shiny coin. "You'd better bring a dime."

NINETEEN

THEY ARRIVED IN NEW York a few minutes past eight o'clock. It being a soft night, they settled for a parking spot two blocks away from the townhouse and traveled the rest of the way on foot. The street outside the Van Allen house was packed with limousines of every conceivable manufacture. Most of the luxurious automobiles had been operated by chauffeurs who, having nothing else to do while their charges wined, dined, and danced the night away, had gathered around a black Cadillac limousine, smoking cigarettes and listening to a tinny car radio.

"Tonight's question," the radio broadcaster announced, "is in the category of baseball. The question is: 'what baseball player holds the highest single season batting average in baseball history?'"

"Babe Ruth," shouted one driver.

"It's Ty Cobb," corrected the loudest of the group. "Babe Ruth? What the hell's the matter with you, Charlie?" He spotted Marjorie and Creighton and removed his hat. "Sorry for the rough language, ma'am. I didn't see you there."

Marjorie came to halt and nodded vaguely in acceptance of the man's apology. "I hate to tell you this gentlemen, but you're both wrong. The answer is Wee Willie Keeler."

"Wee Willie Keeler?" the loud man laughed. "Why, you're the one who's wrong, ma'am. The answer is Ty Cobb."

"It's Babe Ruth," insisted Charlie.

She stood firm. "It's Keeler. Cobb has the highest *lifetime* batting average, but Keeler still holds the highest for single season."

Creighton stepped back into the shadows and hoped he wouldn't be called upon to settle this dispute, since he cared not a fig for baseball.

"Willie Keeler's way before your time. What could you possibly know about him?"

"Apparently more than you do," she answered sweetly.

The group, with the exception of their ringleader, roared with laughter. "You think you're right, don't ya?"

"I do," she asserted. "I listen to this show all the time, and I haven't gotten a quiz question wrong yet."

"First time for everything," he said to bait her.

"Granted," she agreed, "but this isn't it."

"Lady, if you're right, I'll eat my hat."

She countered his wager. "And if I'm wrong, I'll eat mine."

He looked at her, his wits addled. "Lady, you ain't wearin' a hat."

As if this substantiated her argument, she narrowed her eyes and pointed a slender index finger at him. "Exactly." She grabbed Creighton by the arm and led him down the block.

The boisterous man was left to scratch his head in wonder. "Fellas, life don't make sense," he declared. "A screwy dame like that is let into a fancy party, but *we* have to sit outside."

* * *

The townhouse was ablaze with light. Every lamp in the residence must have been switched on, and rice paper lanterns illuminated the sidewalk and steps that led to the front door. Creighton and Marjorie let themselves in via the unlocked storm door, whereupon the butler greeted them. "Good evening, welcome to the Van Allen residence. Your name again, sir?"

"Creighton Ashcroft. And guest."

He crossed their names off the guest list, and then extended his arm. "Very well, Mr. Ashcroft. If I might take your wraps."

They consigned their outer garments to his care and proceeded into the main foyer, where a uniformed young woman serving glasses of champagne from a silver salver immediately met Marjorie. It was Doris. "Oh, Miss McClelland, how smart you look. Just like a movie star." She thrust her tray toward the blonde woman. "Champagne?"

"Thanks." Creighton reached his arm over and removed two glasses. "Don't mind if we do."

"Mr. Ashcroft, I didn't mean to ignore you. Y-You look very smart tonight, too," she stammered. The girl bit her bottom lip and stared down at the floor as though wishing she could somehow melt into it and disappear altogether.

Creighton decided to aid in her liberation. "Doris, I think that couple near the door could use a drink."

"I'll see right to it." Off she walked, as fast as she could, the glasses upon her salver banging against each other in time with her footsteps.

"And so goes another member of the Creighton Ashcroft fan club," Marjorie commented.

"Another member? You mean there's more than one?"

"Naturally. It is, after all, a fan 'club.'"

"And who else is in this club?"

A flicker of a grin crossed her lips. "Why, Sharon, of course. Who else?"

"Who else, indeed."

They traversed the main foyer and made their way down the hallway. Small groups of people had gathered in various locations throughout the house, talking, drinking, smoking their cigarettes and cigars, but the hub of the night's activities was the ballroom. Located at the end of the hall, the ballroom was not originally constructed as one room, but as three. Someone, either Henry Van Allen or a previous owner, had torn down the dividing walls and replaced them with wide pocket doors that could be opened for large social functions such as this one. The result was a rectangular room of tremendous size, easily capable of accommodating 150 persons or more.

The floor, like that of the hall and foyer, was a white and black marble checkerboard. The walls were dove gray, with stainless steel, fluted pilasters that projected from the plaster at regularly spaced intervals, and from the ceiling, a large metal chandelier provided ample light. Opposite the door, against the long exterior wall stretched a damask-clothed buffet table, its platters filled to overflowing with cheese, fruit, canapés, and hors d'oeuvres. Small, round tables, surrounded by white folding chairs and laid with black tablecloths, were provided for dining comfort and strategically placed along the periphery of the room, leaving the center of the floor available for dancing, the music for which was provided by a ten-piece orchestra.

Marjorie nudged Creighton in the arm and gestured toward the buffet table. "I'm famished. Let's see what they have to eat."

Creighton readily obliged, but before they could cross the dance floor, Gloria Van Allen intercepted them. "Mr. Ashcroft, I'm so glad you could make it." The woman welcomed him by grabbing his hands and giving an "air" kiss by each cheek. She was sporting another black gown, this one in velvet with a scoop neck, a low-cut back, and stiff cap sleeves that put Creighton in mind of bat wings. "Are you here alone?" she purred flirtatiously.

She was wearing even more pressed powder than she had been the last time he saw her, and her standard fake eyelashes had been replaced by a set so large they could have served double duty as lint brushes. He grimaced slightly. God only knew what lurked beneath that makeup. "No," he replied elatedly, "I've brought a date."

Marjorie had left her post and was inching toward the buffet table, her left hand preparing to snatch a carrot stick from a dish of crudités. He grabbed her right arm and yanked her back to his side. "You remember Miss McClelland."

"Miss McClelland, yes," Gloria responded in her overrefined manner. "How did your organization like my donation?"

"They liked it very much, thank you."

"Well, if you play your cards right, there might be more money in store for you. I told my friends about the work you do, and they mentioned some interest in contributing to your cause. I'll introduce you to some of them tonight."

"Umm, that's very kind of you, but—"

"But Marjorie makes it a rule to never mix business with pleasure," Creighton interjected. "And tonight is purely pleasure."

"A wise rule," Gloria commented.

"Gloria," a voice called. "I found him hiding in a broom closet." The voice came from a short, weasel-faced man with a thin moustache and eyeglasses. He was cradling Mal, who looked quite the worse for wear. The bald patch on his rump was covered with a thick, pink ointment that resembled calamine lotion, and a plastic cone had been attached about his neck to prevent him from licking off the solution.

"Oh, my poor baby," she exclaimed, taking the squirming animal into her arms. "Did my wittle Mal get fwightened by all these people? Mal doesn't like parties. The noise makes him nervous. I think that's why he pulled out his fur." She pointed toward his hindquarters.

"He did that today?" Creighton asked innocently.

"No, it happened a few days ago. The day you were here, actually. He must have overheard me talking about the party, and the sheer anxiety of it all drove him to it."

"That must be it," Marjorie concurred.

"Mmm," Gloria mused. "I almost forgot to introduce you, Roger. Miss McClelland and Mr. Ashcroft, this is Mr. Philips, my fiancé."

They exchanged polite nods.

"Fiancé?" Marjorie repeated. "When's the happy day?"

"We haven't set a date yet," Gloria answered. "We wanted to wait a good amount of time after Henry's death. No sense giving people something to gossip about."

"No," Creighton remarked, "the rumor mill doesn't need any help getting started."

"Indeed, after Henry died, I couldn't step foot out my front door without someone whispering about me, but that's the city for you. At least you don't have that sort of problem in Ridgebury."

"You must be joking," Creighton laughed aloud and Marjorie joined him. "Ridgebury is probably worse than the city."

"Really? I always remember it as being rather quiet, but, then again, I never socialized with the townspeople."

"It's just as well you didn't."

"Why? Have you heard something about me?"

"I'd rather not say," he averted his eyes melodramatically.

"Oh, but if you've heard something, I want to know about it."

"All right then, if you insist."

"I do insist! I do!"

"The townspeople think . . . I don't know how to put this except to just say it. They think you killed your husband."

There was a deep intake of air from Gloria and Philips. "Killed my husband?" That's ridiculous. My husband's death was ruled a suicide."

"They claim you murdered him and then made it look like a suicide."

"How would she have done that?" Philips quizzed.

"They say she pushed him from the balcony and then forged his suicide note."

"But why? He was my husband. I loved him."

"That's the subject of another ugly rumor," Marjorie explained.

"Yes, the townspeople believe that Henry was about to divorce you," Creighton elaborated. "Something about him having an affair with a maid or cook."

Gloria's jaw became set and the vein at her temple throbbed. "Leave me for a serving girl?" she seethed.

Creighton had hoped for that reaction. "That's exactly what I said to them. 'Leave Gloria for a serving girl? Don't be preposterous.'"

"That's exactly the word to describe it: preposterous!" she boomed.

"You're preaching to the choir, Gloria," he commiserated. "I know those rumors are ridiculous, but the townspeople seem to take such pleasure in them, and the more ludicrous, the better. I think it gives them something to do."

"Well, they should find another pastime," she judged.

"They should, but there's not much to do in Ridgebury—that's why they still talk about you. After all, you moved out almost five years ago and they continue to circulate the same old stories about the suicide and murder, and the divorce and the ring."

"The ring?" she questioned.

"Yes, didn't I mention that one?" he asked absentmindedly. "They think you stole that ring from you husband's collection. The one that belonged to umm . . ." he snapped his fingers as if trying to recall the name.

"Madame Du Barry?"

"Yes, that's it. Rumor has it that the ring was the most valuable item in Henry's estate, and when you found out it was willed to his brother, you took it out of the safe, hid it away, and then reported it missing."

"If that's true, then I would have to be the greatest magician in the world. The police and the insurance company investigators scoured everywhere and found nothing. Besides, why would I steal a ring I couldn't possibly sell? It wouldn't be very smart of me, would it?"

"No, it wouldn't. But the ring was never found. Where do you think it went?"

She waved her hand. "As I told the police, Henry probably misplaced it. He was always losing things."

"I suppose that's possible," he granted.

"Of course it is! Now, if you don't mind I've had enough talk of gossip, though it is nice to know I have someone in Ridgebury to defend me," she smiled generously at Creighton. "If you'll excuse me, I'm going to put Mal upstairs for his own good."

Marjorie spoke up. "Gloria, I just love the way you've decorated. Do you mind if I come with you so you can give me just a quick walk-through of the place?"

"Certainly not. Come along," she beckoned.

Marjorie handed her champagne glass to Creighton and followed Gloria across the dance floor, leaving Creighton and Philips alone.

"You'll have to excuse Gloria for coming on a little strong," Philips appealed. "She's in a terrible stew; the company was just audited today."

"You don't say? Well, she needn't worry too much about it. It's quite a regular occurrence. Does she have an accountant or business manager to help her?"

"I'm her business manager."

"Ah, then I'd say she's in very good hands."

Philips was aporetic. "I don't know about that."

"What do you have to worry about? You've kept up with the taxes, haven't you?"

"Well, yes."

"And it's not like you've been embezzling."

Philips snapped to life. "Embezzling? Who said anything about embezzling? Is this another one of those rumors you've been hearing?"

"Settle down, old boy," Creighton chuckled. "I was merely trying to lighten your mood with a little joke. No reason to get uptight."

Philips sounded a high-pitched, nervy laugh. "A joke. Yes, I'm sorry. I guess I'm a bit wound up myself."

"I'll say. Why don't you go get yourself a drink, Philips? That should loosen you up."

"Yes, yes. I think I will," he agreed. "A drink will do the trick." He walked off toward the bar, and then glanced behind him. "Will you join me?"

"No, if it's all the same to you, I'll sit this one out."

"Okay, I'll catch you later."

"So long." Creighton sat down at an empty table near the entrance to the ballroom, drank the last remaining sips of his champagne, then proceeded on to Marjorie's glass. There was no need to continue his conversation with Philips; the accountant's reaction told Creighton all he needed to know. Now only two questions remained on his mind. Who killed Henry Van Allen and Victor Bartorelli? And what was Marjorie doing taking a house tour with Gloria?

TWENTY

Marjorie accompanied Gloria upstairs to the master bedroom where, with a pat on the head, they confined Mal for the evening. With the matter of the dog disposed of, they toured the remaining rooms in the upper level, pausing in each doorway just long enough for Gloria to briefly describe the space, and for Marjorie to rejoin with an appropriate comment.

What Marjorie had hoped to unearth from this excursion, she hadn't the faintest idea. A souvenir photograph of the killings? A smoking gun? A diary left open to the page where she confesses her guilt? No, if there were any 'clues' to be found, they would not be in plain sight, not in this house, where secrets were hidden away from prying eyes. For everything in Gloria's universe, right down to her mien and décor, was very carefully arranged to be stylish, sleek, attractive, and coldly impersonal. Marjorie didn't condone adultery, but it was little wonder that Henry sought affection elsewhere.

She followed Gloria downstairs to the billiard and morning rooms, growing increasingly weary of her role as sightseer. Each room was more of the same: the same bichrome palette, the same geometric shapes, and the same aseptic arrangements of objects. The only thing keeping Marjorie from yawning was the search for new ways to praise Gloria's decorating techniques; the final room on the tour, however, gave her new cause to stay awake. Again, it was done in the art deco style, and contained only a squarish sofa and a black lacquer writing desk, the front of which faced the door.

"And this is the study," Gloria announced. "I usually take my breakfast there, on that sofa. Then later in the morning I move to the desk to take care of my personal correspond—" Her voice faltered as her gaze came to rest upon the top center drawer of the desk, which had not been closed completely. "Excuse me one moment." She stepped into the hallway and summoned the butler from his station by the front door; Marjorie strained to listen to their conversation.

"Has anyone been in the study tonight?"

"Yes, madam. Mr. Philips was working in here while you dressed for the party."

"Mr. Philips, you say? Go get Mr. Philips and tell him I wish to see him immediately."

"Very well, madam." The butler headed off for the ballroom and Gloria returned to the study, fidgeting with her hair. "Men! They never put things back the way they find them."

"I hear that complaint from a lot of women," Marjorie said casually.

Philips appeared in the doorway. "You wanted me?"

"Yes," Gloria glared. "I did."

The couple looked at Marjorie in unison.

"I think that's my cue to leave. Thank you for the tour, Gloria. You have a lovely home." She left through the open door, but lingered outside to listen to the beginning of their conversation.

"You left the desk drawer unlocked," Gloria denounced Philips. "And with all these people in the house. How could you be so careless?"

"You're overreacting, Gloria. Who's going to look in your desk?"

"You never know who's lurking about," she warned. "Now give me your key."

Gloria's comment about lurking made Marjorie feel a bit self-conscious. She slipped into the crowd standing in the foyer and hurried back to the ballroom.

Creighton was settling back to enjoy a generous portion of food from the buffet when Marjorie arrived, out of breath and obviously excited. "Perfect timing," he hailed as she approached. "I fixed you a plate. I hope you don't mind."

"Not at all. Thanks." She sat down beside him, and he pushed one of the dishes in front of her. "There's something in the study," she exclaimed.

He stared at her over his forkful of smoked salmon. "*Something*? You're a little old for the ghost and goblin bit, aren't you?"

"Not that sort of something. Something that Gloria and Roger want to hide." She described Gloria's reaction to the open desk drawer.

"What do you think is in there?" Creighton asked.

Marjorie took a paté-laden cracker in her fingers and munched on it. "Your guess is as good as mine."

He took a cracker from his own plate and chewed it, deep in thought. "You say Philips was in there tonight, before the party?"

She wiped her hands on the dinner napkin in her lap. "That's what the butler told Gloria."

"The company's books were audited today."

"You're thinking of the embezzlement angle again," she surmised, cutting a wedge of semisoft cheese into thirds with the edge of her fork.

"Oh, Philips is guilty of embezzlement, all right. I got that much just from talking to him." He snatched a third of the freshly cut cheese with his fork and consumed it in one bite.

"Why, did he confess to you?"

"I'm not a priest, Marjorie." He placed his fork on the table and dabbed the corners of his mouth with his napkin. "Let's just say that Philips could never earn his money playing cards."

"The proverbial poker face, or lack thereof," she commented.

"I tell you Marjorie, I don't think I've ever seen a guiltier man."

She stopped eating. "I believe you, Creighton, but the police can't arrest Philips based on your observations. They need proof."

"I know. We've got to find out what's in that desk," he concluded.

"But how? The drawer is locked."

"We'll have to find a way to open it."

"I'd be more than happy to supply you with a hairpin, but I haven't any."

"I wasn't suggesting we pick the lock, I was suggesting we use the key."

"But Roger Philips has the key."

"Then we'll just have to try and get it."

"But it's on *his person*," she explained.

"There has to be some way to get it," he mused. "I know. You could get him to dance with you. While you're dancing, make lighthearted conversation. Tell some jokes and stories, and then, when you have successfully diverted his attention, you reach down and—"

"No," she interrupted before he could divulge the rest of his plan. "Not even for the sake of sweet justice am I going to stick my hand in a man's trouser pocket."

"You're right. I was out of line."

"I'll say you were."

He apologized and again reflected upon the situation. "What about Gloria?"

"Gloria's his fiancée. She might be able to get away with reaching into Philips' pocket, but I don't see where that would help us."

"It wouldn't." He rolled his eyes. "What I meant is it's her desk, therefore she would have the key to the drawer."

"Oh, yes. That makes sense, but we'd still have to get the key from Gloria."

"Easy enough," he raised his arm and summoned Doris.

"You're sending Doris to get the key?" Marjorie asked incredulously.

"No, just wait."

The young woman hurried to their table, her tray still stocked with glasses of champagne. Creighton helped himself and Marjorie to another glass. "Doris, where does Mrs. Van Allen keep her keys when she's not using them?"

"Upstairs, in her room," she stated artlessly.

"Where in her room?"

"In her vanity table. Bottom right-hand drawer." She frowned. "Why?"

"I think it's in your best interest if I don't tell you," Creighton explained. "This way if you're ever asked, you can honestly say you knew nothing about it."

Doris sighed dreamily. "You *are* the sweetest person."

"Not really. Now, you'd better run along before someone gets suspicious. And remember, we never had this conversation." He winked at her. "Right?"

"Right." She winked back, and went on to ply her liquor on the next table.

"How can you be so sure Gloria doesn't have her key with her?" Marjorie asked.

"Because if she did have her key, she wouldn't have asked Philips for his."

She nodded. "So you're planning to sneak upstairs and steal the key."

"Not quite," he answered haltingly. "I was planning on *someone* sneaking upstairs, but it wasn't me; it was you."

"Me? Why me?"

"You got the tour of the house, so you know where to find Gloria's bedroom. If I went upstairs, I might get lost."

She couldn't argue with such logic. She could, however, try to persuade Creighton to join her in the mission. "I'm afraid to go by myself. What if someone catches me? I could never come up with a plausible explanation for being in Gloria's bedroom."

"Then we'll have to provide you with one before you go."

"I could never say it convincingly, like you do." She placed a hand on his shoulder. "You're a much better liar than I am."

"Thank you." His eyes narrowed. "I think."

"Then we'll do this together. Agreed?"

He sighed, wearily. "Anything for you, Marjorie."

Her smile was fleeting. "I just realized something. How are we going to get upstairs without Gloria's butler seeing us?"

"He won't be there all night," Creighton reasoned. "Once all the guests have arrived, he'll find something else to do."

"When do you think that will be?"

He pulled his sleeve back and glanced at his watch. "It's ten minutes to nine. Most everyone who's supposed to be here is probably here already, so I'd say he'll be packing it in soon."

"And what do we do in the meantime? Sit here and twiddle our thumbs?"

He took on the tone of an old schoolmaster. "Miss McClelland, do you mean to tell me that you're bored? Here, with beautiful music, delicious food, and a copious amount of champagne?"

"No, but we're not here to enjoy ourselves. We're here to work."

"We are working, but don't forget, we're here under the guise of being party guests, and party guests enjoy themselves."

She pulled a face. "You're right, we would stick out like sore thumbs if we sat here all night. It would also make our absence more obvious when we finally do sneak away."

"That's the girl." Creighton stood up and took Marjorie by the hand. "Let's try and blend in."

Amid the strains of "I'm Getting Sentimental Over You," they joined the other couples on the dance floor. "How's this for blending?" Marjorie asked.

He pulled her closer as they swayed to and fro. "Very nice."

"Good, then no one would suspect that we're working with the police."

"Not unless they overhear you."

She lowered her voice. "Oops! I guess I shouldn't talk too much, especially when we're around so many people."

"You can talk, just not about policemen or the case."

"Okay. Since we're trying to blend in, what do people at these functions talk about while they're dancing?"

"I usually don't dance, so I couldn't say for sure, but I would guess it depends on the couple. For example, if we were a young couple in love, I would probably lean forward, like this." He demonstrated by bringing his head close to hers. "And whisper in your ear."

She pulled away. "Yes, well, that doesn't apply to us, does it? So what do the other couples discuss?"

He shrugged. "Small talk, probably. There's the economy. "

"Which stinks," she commented.

"Current events."

"Been very quiet lately."

"The weather."

"It's stopped raining. Thank goodness."

"Gossip."

"The only juicy gossip I know involves our hostess and that would rather defeat the purpose of this little exercise."

"Well, I'm fresh out of ideas. Perhaps you can come up with a new topic of conversation."

"Yes, I think I can."

"I'm afraid to ask. What is it?"

She turned her emerald eyes upward to meet his. "Sharon," she said with a grin upon her lips. "Tell me, do you really think of Sharon as—what was the term Mr. Schutt used—oh, yes, 'womanhood's fairest flower?'"

Creighton looked away, over the top of her head. "She's a very nice girl," he stated blandly.

Marjorie would not be put off. "That wasn't my question."

"No," he agreed, his eyes reuniting with hers, "it wasn't. *Your* question was impolite."

"So that's why you refuse to answer? Because I'm being rude?"

He dipped her, abruptly, and leaning over her, replied, "No, I refuse to answer because it's none of your business."

He righted her again. "True," she admitted, "it isn't any of my business, but the question still gnaws at me."

He was staring at her quite intently. "Why? Are you jealous?"

"Certainly not," she nearly shouted.

"Then it sounds like you're suffering from a case of wounded pride."

"Wounded pride? What do you mean by that?"

"What I mean is that you're the type of woman who's used to having men cater to her."

"That's not true."

"It isn't? The only child of a spouseless father. I'm sure you were the center of his universe."

"That was a long time ago. Things have changed."

"Have they? Are you going to tell me you didn't notice the heads turning as you entered the room? Why, I'll give you my handkerchief right now. Let it drop to the floor and tell me if a half-dozen men don't clamor to pick it up for you." The song ended and the orchestra segued seamlessly into "Please." Creighton and Marjorie paused a moment, then continued dancing.

"No, Marjorie, you didn't ask your question out of curiosity. It rankles you that I might find Sharon more attractive than you. Which raises an interesting question: if I did behave like those other men, if I were to fall all over myself just be near you, if I pushed Sharon aside and devoted my heart to only you, would I, as the song says, stand a ghost of a chance?"

Marjorie's eyes lowered silently.

"No, just as I thought. You already have Robert Jameson as your pet. You don't need another."

"My pet? Sounds like you're the one suffering from wounded pride."

He gave her a sad look. "Rest assured, that's not the case."

"Isn't it? You've done pretty well yourself when it comes to members of the opposite sex. You got a date with Sharon after being in town just a few days."

"Her father arranged it," he argued.

"All right, what about Doris? The poor girl's driven to distraction whenever she's in the same room as you. Then there's Gloria. If I weren't here, she'd probably be dancing with you right now."

"Yes, but unlike you, I'm not interested in my admirers."

"No? You do an awfully good job at pretending."

"It's all part of the game, but those women aren't what I want."

"What *do* you want?"

"You're the writer," he responded glibly. "You claim to have great insight when it comes to people. You tell me."

She stared at his face a good long while, then pulled away from him abruptly.

"What's wrong?" he gibed. "No answer?"

"You're not like most people," she disclaimed before walking off the dance floor. "You're not like them at all."

Marjorie huffed off to the bar, with Creighton following far behind. What was it about him that bothered her so? Was it his presumption to know her thoughts and feelings? Or that his presuppositions about her were correct? (She *was* rankled by the fact that he had chosen

246

Sharon over her, although she wasn't sure it was a case of "wounded pride.") It was as though she were a piece of cellophane, her mind and soul transparent to those scrutinizing blue eyes, and Creighton delighted in his role as voyeur. One could have simply attributed his fascination to a sadistic nature, but when she gazed into his face only moments ago, there was no sign of maliciousness; indeed, what she witnessed there was something altogether different.

He joined her at the bar. "Can I get you anything?"

She acted as though nothing had happened since, in truth, nothing had. "Yes. Thank you."

"More champagne?"

"No, water, please. I want to keep my wits about me tonight."

He ordered a glass of water for her and a whiskey, neat, for himself.

She gulped the water thirstily, then, seeing the butler at the end of the buffet table, tapped Creighton's arm agitatedly. "Our friend is back."

Creighton craned his neck to see the butler replenishing the empty trays of food. He emptied his glass and placed it on the table behind him. "Now's our chance. Let's go."

Arm in arm, they sailed across the dance floor and out of the ballroom. The main foyer was empty, except for two men standing around smoking cigars and discussing the pitfalls of the Securities Exchange Act.

"I say, chaps," Creighton spoke up. "What are you doing out here? Our hostess just broke out a thirty-year-old single malt Scotch. I'd hurry back in before it's all gone."

The men exchanged surprised glances and trotted off toward the ballroom.

"Very clever," Marjorie commented as she scaled the stairs. "Now do you see why I wanted you to come along?"

"I thought it was because you couldn't bear to be away from me," he quipped, taking the steps two at a time.

"And you have the nerve to call me proud." She guided him to a closed door at the end of the upstairs hallway. Grabbing the knob and turning it, she opened the door a couple of inches. It was just enough for Mal to grab a foothold. The dog stuck his front paws in the crack, forced his way though the opening, and shot down the hallway, straight as an arrow.

"Don't let him run downstairs," Marjorie ordered.

Creighton dashed to the stairwell to block the animal's route, but he needn't have bothered. The specialized collar about Mal's neck acted as a blinder, enabling the dog to see only what was straight ahead of him. He scurried past the stairs without giving them any notice.

"There he goes! Oh, Creighton, catch him!"

"Don't worry." Chasing the dog down the hallway, Creighton waited until he was within arm's length of the animal, and then lunged directly for him. The dive was brilliantly executed, but it was ill-timed, for Creighton missed the dog completely and landed face-down on the floor. Mal, stopping to see his would-be assailant stretched out on the carpet, ran over, hopped onto the Englishman's back and stood there like the victor in a wrestling match.

"My hero," Marjorie quipped.

Creighton propped himself on one elbow and glanced at the animal on his back in disgust. "Thank you. It's nice to know you appreciate my efforts."

She walked over and took the dog into her arms, his tongue licking her face happily. "I was talking to Mal. Now stop lounging about. We have work to do."

He stood up and, brushing the lint from his tuxedo, followed her into the bedroom. "There's the vanity table," she pointed across the room.

"You keep an eye on the door," he directed. "I'll get the keys."

Creighton set upon his task while Marjorie stood before the partially opened door, cradling Mal and stroking his head. The dog, however, writhed and squirmed in an effort to break free. With her back to the door, she crouched down and placed him upon the floor, all the while keeping a tight grasp on the leather band around his neck. "We'll be gone soon, Mal," she consoled. "In the meantime, be good." The dog barked, as if in reply, but Marjorie soon realized that he was not responding to her but to the sound of footsteps echoing up the marble steps.

"Someone's coming," she whispered loudly, but there was no answer. She picked up the dog again and swung around toward the vanity table, only to find that no one was there. *Typical*, she thought. *Creighton probably snuck out while I wasn't looking, leaving me here holding the bag.*

Gloria appeared in the doorframe. She gave Marjorie a scathing look and snatched Mal from her arms. "What are you doing here?"

Marjorie felt her heart begin to pound and a cold spot develop at the bottom of her stomach. She opened her mouth to reply, but all she heard was the flush of a toilet.

From the door near the vanity table, Creighton emerged, drying his hands on a white towel. "Hello, Gloria," he greeted casually. "I hope you don't mind me using your lavatory. The facilities downstairs were occupied, so Marjorie suggested I use the one up here."

"By all means," she answered hospitably.

"Miss McClelland brought me up here so I wouldn't get lost, and it's a good thing, too. If she hadn't, you might have needed to send a search party after me."

Gloria was captivated by Creighton's charisma. "Oh, do go on," she laughed. "The house isn't that large!"

"Large enough." He placed a hand on Marjorie's shoulder. "Let's go. We've infringed upon Gloria's privacy long enough."

"It was no infringement. I just came up to change my shoes."

"Thank you. You're most gracious." He grasped the upper part of Marjorie's arm and steered her out the door and into the hallway. "Madam," he addressed Gloria, "I give you back your boudoir." With a bow, he shut the door behind him.

Wordlessly, they ran lickety-split down the staircase, through the foyer and back into the ballroom. Marjorie followed Creighton to the bar, where he ordered another whiskey.

"Can I have some of that?" she asked as the bartender passed him his glass.

He nodded and handed her the glass. "Here. Have at it."

Marjorie took a gulp and then returned the drink to its owner. She closed her eyes and took a deep breath.

"Better?" Creighton asked.

"Much," she affirmed, and then began giggling like a schoolgirl.

"What is it?" he asked, laughing along with her.

"Did you see the expression on Gloria's face when you came out of the bathroom?"

"Her expression? What about yours? I don't know which one of you was more surprised to see me."

She laughed. "Me, probably. I thought you had snuck away while I wasn't looking."

He arched his eyebrows. "That wouldn't have been very gallant of me, now would it?"

"No, it wouldn't, but when I didn't see you, I didn't know what to think."

"I said I'd help you, didn't I?"

"Yes, and you did. Splendidly."

"'Twas nothing for an excellent liar like me."

Marjorie bowed her head in shame. "I'm sorry about that. What I meant is that you have the ability to think on your feet."

"I understood what you meant," he smiled kindly.

Gloria, meanwhile, entered the ballroom. She crossed the dance floor and joined Philips, who was chatting with a distinguished-looking middle-aged couple.

"Our hostess is back," Creighton noted, finishing off his drink. "Time for me to do a little treasure hunting."

"Now?"

"Best to get it over with. I want to put those keys back before Gloria notices them missing."

"You want me to go with you?"

"No. Stay here and watch Gloria and Philips. I don't want them to see me prowling around. If they head toward the door, do something to distract them."

"What if they ask me where you are?"

"Tell them I had to make an important phone call."

She nodded. "Good luck."

"Thanks."

"And be careful," she warned.

Creighton wrinkled his brow. "Why, Miss McClelland, are you actually concerned about my welfare?"

She was worried about him, but she'd rather die than admit it. "No, but you're my ride. If something were to happen to you, I'd have no other way home."

"Oh, is that it?" He grinned. "Don't worry. You still have that dime I gave you, don't you?"

She grinned back at him and watched as he wended his way across the dance floor and out of the ballroom, unseen by Gloria and Philips, who were still conversing with the middle-aged couple. As the band started to play "Lover," she felt a tap on her shoulder.

"Good evening, Miss McClelland," drawled the sonorous voice of William Van Allen.

"Mr. Van Allen."

"Would you care to dance?"

She glanced at her host and hostess. Two other couples had joined the discussion, and it appeared that the group would not be breaking up any time soon. "I'd love to," she replied.

William took her by the hand and they glided onto the dance floor. He proved himself a very competent dancer, sweeping Marjorie across the floor with smooth, graceful steps. "You're not here by yourself, are you, Miss McClelland?"

"No, I'm here with Creighton Ashcroft."

"Ah, yes, Mr. Ashcroft," he exclaimed in recognition. "Well, shame on him for leaving you all alone. Doesn't he realize that you're in the company of wolves?"

"He had an important telephone call to make."

"An important call? What could possibly be so important as to take him away from a creature as lovely as you?"

She smiled demurely. "Business. You know how it is."

"No, I can most proudly say that I do not know how it is."

"You don't? Van Allen Industries must keep you busy," she played dumb.

"Van Allen industries is my sister-in-law's baby. I participate in the running of the company only when it's absolutely necessary."

"How surprising. Since your father started the business, I should have thought that you'd be in charge."

"No, when my father passed away, he left the bulk of the company to Henry. When Henry died, he left controlling interest to Gloria."

"That doesn't seem fair."

"Under different circumstances it wouldn't be, but you see, I have no desire to partake in the operations of the family business. My father and brother knew this, and made alternate provisions for the company."

"You have no desire to take a more active role in something that's your family's legacy?"

"The only family legacy that appeals to me is my share of the money. I know that must sound selfish to you, but I set my priorities a long time ago. The pursuit of pleasure is on the top of the list. Life is too short to spend cooped up in some office, crunching numbers all day. Look at my poor brother, for instance. He threw his entire life into his work. So much so, in fact, that when the market went belly-up, his hopes and dreams went with it."

"True," she reflected, "but you should thank your father and brother. It's because of their number crunching that you're able to live the way you do. If they hadn't done such a good job minding the store, you'd be looking for work right now."

"Work, my dear, is a four-letter word."

"I wouldn't write it off so quickly; you never know what the future holds. If the business was to fold, what would you do then?"

"I have a nice little nest egg to fall back on," he answered enigmatically.

"Are you trying to tell me that a *bon vivant* like yourself actually managed to save some money?"

"No, save is another four-letter word. My nest egg is courtesy of my dearly departed brother. He left me his collection of valuable antiquities. Paintings, sculpture, furniture, firearms."

It was a convenient opening. "Firearms? Was your brother in the military?"

"Far from it. During the war, he finagled his way out of registering for the draft because he was afraid of being sent overseas to fight," he explained. "No, Henry collected weapons because of the glory associated with them, as if their power might rub off on him simply by handling them. If only he knew the horrible sights they had seen."

"I take it you served," Marjorie ventured.

"Yes, I served. 1918, France, against the Argonne-Meuse defensive. I can still remember the smell of the dead bodies, the sound of the rats in the trenches." His eyes were focused on some point in the distance, a time and place far, far away. "When the war ended, my brother asked for my service revolver to add to his collection. A souvenir. The gun that killed a hundred Germans. He kept it in a glass display case in the main foyer of his country house, as if it were something to be proud of . . ." He leapt back into the present, "I'm sorry. You shouldn't hear such things."

She pardoned him. "Tell me, was it your brother's collection I read about in the papers a few years back?"

"I don't know. What did you read?"

"Something about a missing piece of jewelry. Some diamond belonging to a French king."

"Ah, the Du Barry ring. Yes, that was in my brother's collection."

"What happened to it?"

The song ended and William escorted her off the dance floor. "No one knows. It simply disappeared."

"Disappeared? Without a trace?"

"It would seem so."

"And no one has any idea of where it is?"

He led her toward the bar. "I wouldn't say no one."

Marjorie smiled. "You have an idea, don't you?"

They stopped a few feet away from the bar and William glanced about furtively. "Can you keep a secret?"

"Yes," she replied anxiously.

"So can I," he teased.

"After telling me about your experiences in the war, I should have thought you'd be able to trust in me."

He narrowed his eyes and looked her over appraisingly. "All right, if you promise not to tell."

"I promise." She drew the shape of an 'X' over her chest with her hand.

"I think my sister-in-law has it."

"Gloria?" she replied in feigned horror.

"Shhh," he commanded. "Do you want everyone to hear you?"

"What would she want with it? She has plenty of money, and even if she didn't, it's not like she could ever sell it without being caught."

"She didn't take it because of its value," he shook his head. "She took it on principle. She's been dying to get her hands on that diamond ever since Henry bought it. It burned her up to think that my brother bought it as a collector's item and not a bauble for his beloved wife. He never even let her wear it. When Henry died, she probably thought that the ring would be hers. What a surprise to learn that it had been left to me."

"So she took it out of spite?"

"Absolutely. The ring itself is inconsequential. She probably has it locked up in a safe deposit box in that Swiss bank she deals with. For Gloria, it's not the ring itself that matters, it's the knowledge that she pulled one over on Henry. She never lets anyone have the last laugh."

The subject of their conversation suddenly appeared beside them, bearing two glasses of champagne. Gloria handed a glass to William and another to Marjorie. "Here, finish these before they lose their sparkle." She then marched back to the bar to harass the bartender.

"Do you think she heard us?" Marjorie asked, watching her.

"I hope not. If she knew I was spreading rumors about her, she'd kill me." He shrugged. "Oh well, no sense worrying." Lifting his glass, he toasted, "To you, Miss McClelland."

Marjorie lifted her glass to William's. "To you," she rejoined and they drank to each other's health. After only a few seconds, however, William placed his glass on the nearest table, a queer expression on his face.

"What's wrong?" she asked.

"I don't know, but suddenly I don't feel very well."

She set her own glass down next to his. "Maybe you should sit down," she suggested, reaching for his arm.

"No, that's not necessary. I'll be fine." He waved her away, but within an instant grabbed her shoulder with one hand and clutched at his chest with the other.

She placed a hand on his arm. "Oh, my goodness! Are you all right?"

The man could not reply. He gasped and leaned his head upon her shoulder. Marjorie called for help, but the partygoers were too absorbed in their revelry to hear her. William gasped again and leaned his full weight upon the young woman, making it necessary for her to push against his shoulders with both hands in order to prevent him from falling over.

"Help!" she cried again, her voice straining under her heavy load, but again no one paid any attention. The six-foot-tall man lurched forward as though he were going to fall, propelling Marjorie, in reverse, against the nearby table.

Over William's shoulder, she spotted Creighton returning through the ballroom door. She removed an arm from the sick man's shoulder and waved frantically to gain her escort's attention.

The Englishman approached and regarded the scene with a bemused smile on his face. Marjorie, buckling under the heft of her burden, was bent backward over the table, with William's head resting upon her bosom. "Well, well, well. How long has this been going on?"

"He's having a heart attack, you idiot!" she seethed.

"A heart attack?" He whistled. "Boy, when you create a diversion, you really create a diversion."

"Stop your clowning and help me!"

He obeyed and hoisted William, who was still conscious, into a nearby chair. Marjorie stood erect and rubbed her back exhaustedly. Gloria and Philips, having noticed the commotion, were now by Creighton's side. "What's going on?" Gloria demanded.

"It's William. We think he's having a heart attack," Creighton explained. "Call a doctor, quickly!"

Philips summoned Doris. "Get Dr. St. John and tell him what's happened."

Doris nodded and vanished into the crowd.

"Oh, Bill!" Gloria exclaimed, on the verge of tears. "Bill, talk to me."

"It's probably best he saves his strength," Creighton advised. He removed his dinner jacket and draped it over Marjorie, who was shivering.

Doris returned with a balding, tuxedoed man with a white mustache. "What happened?" he asked as he knelt down to take William's pulse.

Marjorie answered. "We were standing here talking, when he suddenly grabbed his chest and nearly collapsed."

"Has this happened to him before?"

"No, never," Gloria replied. "He's always been healthy as a horse."

The doctor gave Marjorie the once-over. "You say you were just talking. Nothing else?"

"Well, we had been dancing," Marjorie confessed.

"Was he out of breath after dancing? Physically exerted?"

"No, not at all."

"Did he seem to be under emotional stress?"

"No, he seemed to be in good spirits."

"His heartbeat is irregular, but it's slow and strong," the doctor commented as he rose to his feet.

"What does that mean?" Philips asked.

"I don't know yet," he answered, peeling back William's eyelids and staring into his pupils. "Dilated. Gloria, is your brother-in-law on any medication?"

"No, I already told you he's as healthy as a horse."

St. John looked up at Marjorie again. "Miss . . .?"

"McClelland."

"Miss McClelland, did he eat or drink anything before falling ill?"

"Yes, he had some champagne. As for anything else, I don't know."

"He ate lightly," Gloria interjected. "Fruit mostly. Bananas, apricots."

"The champagne," St. John started. "How long ago was that?"

"Immediately before he got sick."

The doctor raised an eyebrow. "Is his glass still around?"

"Yes," Marjorie pointed to the table. "It's over there."

"Get it for me, please."

Marjorie walked to where the two champagne glasses were perched, side by side, but hesitated before grabbing either one of them.

"What's the matter?" Creighton inquired.

"One was William's glass and one was mine, but now I can't tell them apart."

"Is there a lipstick mark?" Creighton suggested.

"No, nothing. They're identical."

"Bring them both to me," St. John ordered.

Marjorie complied and passed him the two glasses. He thrust his nose into the first and sniffed. Having detected nothing but the usual aroma of alcohol, he put the glass aside and drew the other glass to his face. He took a deep breath and immediately blanched. "Someone call the police."

"Police!" Gloria cried. "Whatever for?"

St. John took another whiff of the champagne glass. "Because," he stated firmly, "this man's been poisoned."

TWENTY-ONE

As requested, the police were summoned and William, by this time more lucid, was carried to an upstairs bedroom for treatment. Dr. St. John, after reclaiming his medical bag from his car, examined both the patient and the tainted champagne glass. The verdict: a toxic cocktail of champagne and digitalis, which in large quantities would have proved lethal.

Gloria, Philips, Creighton, and Marjorie waited in the foyer for the police to arrive. Gloria instructed the orchestra to continue playing and the servants to carry through with the serving of dessert. However, despite her best efforts to keep the atmosphere lighthearted, the soiree had deteriorated into a somber affair. Partygoers milled about the dance floor, discussing William's poisoning in hushed tones. When the police showed up several minutes later, the scene in the ballroom smacked more of the funereal than the Bacchanalian.

Lieutenant Wilcox was a fair-haired, heavyset, fiftyish man clad in the obligatory rumpled detective's trench coat. He introduced himself and the two uniformed policemen with him and promptly got down to business. "Where's the victim?"

"Upstairs," Philips answered. "The doctor's with him."

"Warren, Sharp," he ordered the two officers. "Take these people inside. I'm going up to speak to the doctor and the victim, if possible."

The officers complied and ushered the two couples back into the ballroom, where, upon their appearance, the music instantly stopped. Wilcox returned shortly, with Dr. St. John in tow.

"How's Bill?" Gloria asked the physician.

"He's stabilized. I gave him a stimulant to get his heart rate back up and administered a dose of activated carbon to absorb the rest of the poison. He's resting comfortably."

"May I see him?"

"After we get all this business straightened out," Wilcox interceded. "Now who was with Mr. Van Allen when he became sick?"

Marjorie raised her hand. "I was."

The lieutenant smiled admiringly. "And your name, miss?"

"McClelland. Marjorie McClelland."

"Marjorie McClelland," he repeated as he scribbled in his notepad. "Are you a friend of Mr. Van Allens, Miss McClelland?"

"No, just an acquaintance. I came here as a guest of Mr. Ashcroft."

"Mr. Ashcroft?"

Creighton waved. "Me, sir."

"First name?"

"Creighton." Recalling the incident with Noonan, he began to spell it. "That's C-r-e-"

"I-g-h-t-o-n," Wilcox completed.

"Very good," Creighton lauded.

261

"I won the national spelling bee in grammar school," the policeman announced proudly. He proceeded to copy the name into his notebook until a female partygoer, anxious to get a good view of the goings-on, bumped his arm, sending his pen sailing off the paper. He looked up to find that guests were encircled tightly around the interview area. "People! People!" he shouted. "Back up, please. Give us some room. Warren! Sharp! Keep everyone back."

The officers pushed the crowd back a few feet, but the front portion of the circle was still within listening distance.

"Now, Miss McClelland, tell me what happened."

"Well," she began, "I was standing by the buffet table, waiting for Mr. Ashcroft to return from making an important phone call, when Mr. Van Allen came by and tapped me on the shoulder. He asked me to dance and I agreed. We finished our dance and were standing near the bar, talking, when Mrs. Van Allen came by with two glasses of champagne."

"Mrs. Van Allen?"

"Mr. Van Allen's sister-in-law. Our hostess," Marjorie explained.

"That is I," Gloria intoned.

Wilcox took a glance at the witchlike woman and rolled his eyes. "Go on, Miss McClelland."

"Mrs. Van Allen handed each of us a glass of champagne, saying we should drink it before the fizz was gone, then went back to talk to the bartender. Mr. Van Allen and I made a toast, and each took a sip of our champagne. Almost instantly, Mr. Van Allen complained that he didn't feel well. A second or two after that, he grabbed his chest in pain and began to gasp for air. I tried my best to keep him from falling over, but he was very heavy. Thankfully, Mr. Ashcroft came back and helped me get him into a chair."

"Were both glasses of champagne poured from the same bottle?"

"Yes," Gloria replied, "I saw the bartender pour them myself."

"Miss McClelland, from the time that Mrs. Van Allen handed it to him to the moment he drank from it, did anyone else touch Mr. Van Allen's glass?"

"No."

There was a great murmur from the crowd.

"That doesn't mean a thing," Gloria repudiated. "That bottle had been open for nearly an hour. Anyone could have tampered with it."

"But only the glass was tainted, Gloria," St. John noted, "not the bottle. Otherwise Miss McClelland would have fallen ill, as well."

"Why should I want to poison Bill?"

"Because you overheard him talking to me tonight," Marjorie asserted.

"What were the two of you talking about?" Wilcox questioned.

"His late brother's collection of antiques. Among which was an incredibly expensive diamond ring, once belonging to King Louis XV. Mr. Van Allen inherited the collection from his brother—Mrs. Van Allen's late husband. Unfortunately, before the collection could be turned over, the ring disappeared. It's been missing ever since."

"I remember that case. It was in all the papers. But what does that have to do with tonight?"

"Mr. Van Allen told me that he believed his sister-in-law had stolen the ring and tucked it away in a safe deposit box in Switzerland."

"Was Mrs. Van Allen within earshot?" the lieutenant asked.

"Yes, she was. In fact, Mr. Van Allen told me to keep my voice down because, as he said, 'if she heard him talking about her, she would kill him.'"

This produced a great outcry from the crowd. "That's a lie!" Gloria shrieked. "For all we know, she put the digitalis in his glass."

"Why would I want to do that? I barely knew him."

Gloria seized this remark. "Precisely. And we barely know you: your background, your upbringing. You could easily be some ill-tempered, homicidal lunatic."

"Really! Creighton, tell them I'm not an ill-tempered, homicidal lunatic."

"Certainly," he agreed. "She's not a homicidal lunatic."

Marjorie cast him an angry look.

"Well, you are a bit ill-tempered at times," he rationalized.

"Nevertheless," Gloria went on, "how can we be sure you didn't tamper with that glass after I walked away?"

"Because I didn't. When Mr. Van Allen comes to, he'll confirm my story."

"Bill's word means nothing. A simple sleight of hand on your part and he wouldn't have noticed a thing."

"You're right," Creighton conceded, much to Marjorie's consternation. "Any fairly competent magician could have easily pulled off drugging that glass of champagne. However, you're forgetting something: motive. Other than your claims of mental instability, what motive does Marjorie have for trying to kill your brother-in-law?"

"I don't know!" Gloria shouted. "But I didn't do it! So someone else must have! You yourself said it would have been easy to drug that champagne without being seen. The area by the bar was very crowded, someone could have dropped the digitalis in the glass as I walked by with it."

The guests eyed each other suspiciously.

"It's a long shot," Wilcox replied, "but I won't rule it out entirely. Did your brother-in-law have any enemies?"

The hope eroded from Gloria's face. "No, he didn't. Bill isn't the sort to evoke hostility." A fiendish glint leapt into her eyes. "But Miss McClelland is."

Marjorie raised her eyebrows. "What!"

"Those two glasses of champagne were virtually indistinguishable from each other. Even Miss McClelland couldn't tell them apart. Perhaps the poisoned glass wasn't intended for Bill, but for *her*." She pointed a finger at the young woman.

Marjorie slid her hand to her throat as though the very thought were choking her. "Me? Why would anyone want to poison to me?"

"You tell us. A scorned lover? A wife whose husband you stole?" She turned to Lieutenant Wilcox. "Miss McClelland is quite the little saucebox. Why, just this evening, I caught her and Mr. Ashcroft upstairs, alone in my bedroom."

Marjorie gasped. "You horrible woman! That's not true!"

Wilcox raised his hand to silence the two women. "Is this true, Mr. Ashcroft?"

Creighton rather fancied this new role as Lothario. Besides, what was he to do? Lie to the police? "Yes, it's true."

The crowd buzzed with excitement. Women shook their heads and clicked their tongues in condemnation of such indecent behavior. The men frowned and tried to look appropriately appalled, but when their wives weren't looking, they grinned at Creighton with a combination of reverence and envy.

"It's not as it seems," Marjorie protested. She hauled off and socked Creighton in the arm. "Tell them the whole story."

Gazing at the men in the crowd with their "attaboy" smirks, Creighton was loath to renounce his newfound popularity. However, damaging Marjorie's reputation would not serve to further his romantic plans. "Miss McClelland is telling the truth. We were alone in

Mrs. Van Allen's bedroom, but not in the way that one might think. I went upstairs to use the lavatory after finding a very long queue for the one down here. Miss McClelland accompanied me as a guide, a modern-day Sacajawea, if you will. There was nothing at all unseemly or untoward about the situation."

There was a great sigh of relief from the women in the room, and Marjorie smiled in vindication. The men, however, bowed their heads in silent mourning. The hero had fallen.

"Not that there *couldn't* have been anything unseemly going on," he added for the sake of the brotherhood.

Marjorie punched him in the arm again, this time hard. "Creighton!"

"Sorry."

The husbands in the crowd shook their heads. Another of their ranks mercilessly gunned down in his prime.

"See that temper?" Gloria imputed. "Violent."

"I told you it would get you into trouble one day," Creighton said under his breath.

"Mrs. Van Allen is just trying to put the blame on someone else," Marjorie declared. "The fact remains that she was the last person to handle that glass."

"Wait one minute," Philips ordered.

"Who in blazes are you?" Wilcox demanded, trying to gain some order in the situation.

"Roger Philips. Mrs. Van Allen's fiancé," he replied, then turned to challenge Marjorie. "Just where would she have gotten the digitalis?"

"From me," a distant voice responded. Gloria's elderly butler pushed his way through the crowd. "My doctor prescribed it for my heart trouble."

"There's people crawling out of the woodwork," Wilcox exclaimed. "Who are you? Her father?"

"No, her butler."

"Did Mrs. Van Allen ever ask to borrow your medication?"

"No, but I leave it on my night table. Everyone in the house knows about it. It'd be very easy to walk into my room and take it, if someone had a mind to."

Gloria's eyes burned through her elderly servant. Creighton whispered to him. "Hope you've saved up, old boy. Looks like you might be retiring ahead of schedule."

"See?" Marjorie declared excitedly. "She had the opportunity, the means, and the motive."

"Miss McClelland, please," Wilcox pleaded. "This is my investigation." He turned to Gloria. "It would seem, Mrs. Van Allen, that you had the opportunity, the means, and the motive."

Marjorie rolled her eyes. "Brilliant summation, Lieutenant."

"Motive?" Philips scoffed. "What motive? William spreading a nasty rumor about his sister-in-law to a party guest? If that were a motive for murder, everyone at this party would be dead."

The room roared with laughter, which Creighton quickly interrupted. "Mrs. Van Allen wasn't threatened by her brother-in-law's theory about the missing ring. She was frightened by his knowledge of her dealings with a Swiss bank."

All eyes turned to the Englishman, including Marjorie's, which were wide with anticipation. "In the study of this house is a desk," he continued. "In the top drawer of that desk are statements from a bank located in Bern, Switzerland, regarding an account in the name of Gloria Van Allen and Roger Philips. The account was opened one year before Henry Van Allen's death and, I think, if you compare the deposits made in that account with the general ledger of Van Allen

Industries, you'll find an interesting correlation. Namely, that while company expenses increased and profits decreased, the bank account grew fatter. In a word: embezzlement."

"This is an outrage," Philips announced indignantly.

"What business do you have snooping about my personal property?" Gloria demanded. "That drawer was locked. Lieutenant, I want this man arrested for trespassing."

Wilcox took her by the arm. "We'll talk about that when we get downtown."

"Downtown?" Gloria shrieked. "Roger, do something."

"Don't worry, dear. I'll call your lawyer right away."

"Might as well call your own, while you're at it," Wilcox suggested, "cause you're gonna be joining us."

Creighton and Marjorie snickered. "What are you two laughing at?" Wilcox questioned.

"Us?" the Englishman replied artlessly. "Nothing."

"Good, because I'm requesting your presence as well, Mr. Ashcroft. There's a little matter of a desk drawer I would like to discuss with you. And you, Miss McClelland, can keep him company."

"Why? What did I do?"

"I haven't figured that one out yet, but I'm sure you did something I should know about." He called to his officers. "Warren. Sharp. Stay here and get statements from the other guests. I'm taking this lot back to the station."

Two other uniformed policemen arrived and ushered the group into the foyer. Marjorie, however, refused to budge. "This is absurd! Call the Ridgebury division of the Hartford County Police and ask for Detective Robert Jameson. He can vouch for us."

"I'll call him from the station." Wilcox nodded to the officers, and they each took one of Marjorie's arms and lifted her off the ground.

"Let go of me!" she protested as she was carried, kicking, through the foyer and out the front door. "I didn't do anything!"

"Yeah," Wilcox commented drolly. "That's what they all say."

TWENTY-TWO

DETECTIVE ROBERT JAMESON CROSSED the threshold of the Manhattan precinct house at 4:00 a.m. to find Marjorie and Creighton seated side by side on a rigid wooden bench. Marjorie's head was on Creighton's shoulder, her mouth agape in a deep yawn. Jameson bowed before them. "Bonnie and Clyde, I presume."

"You know, Jameson," Creighton remarked, "under the right circumstances, you're actually witty."

Marjorie lifted her head. "Where have you been? We called you four hours ago."

"Sorry, I needed some time to get dressed. Like other law-abiding citizens, I was in bed, asleep, when Lieutenant Wilcox informed me of your crime spree. Trespassing? Obstruction of justice? Resisting arrest? Assaulting an officer? What were you two doing? Trying to see which one of you could commit the most misdemeanors?"

"Oh, Marjorie won that contest hands down," Creighton replied. "I had a single misdemeanor. She had three."

"Two," she corrected. "I didn't assault that officer. He inadvertently bumped into my foot."

"With his bum?"

"I told you, he backed into it. It was very crowded in here at the time." Marjorie rose from the bench and stretched. "Now, if you don't mind, I'd like to get out of here before the sun comes up."

"I'll go and see about your paperwork," Jameson offered and headed to the main desk. After displaying his badge, the desk sergeant allowed him behind the counter and directed him to an open office door.

"Well, Creighton, it looks like our little adventure is coming to an end." She slipped into her coat. "Thank you for a wonderful evening. You sure know how to show a girl a good time. Dinner, dancing, *and* a mugshot. Does it get any better than this?"

"Anything for you, Marjorie."

Jameson emerged from the office followed closely by Wilcox; the two of them roaring with laughter.

"They've gotten awfully chummy," she remarked.

"Probably laughing over some joke in *Junior Detective* magazine," Creighton quipped.

The two men shook hands and bid adieu. Wilcox retreated into his office; Jameson rejoined his friends. "Everything's squared away," he announced. "But before we go, I want to say something—"

"Robert, I'm not in the mood," Marjorie interrupted. "I'm tired, I'm hungry, and my hands are stained black from the whole fingerprinting ordeal. So, if you're going to launch into another one of your tirades about proper police procedure, just save it for later."

Creighton smiled. *A lover's spat?* Things were starting to look up.

"I wasn't going to reprimand you, I was going to thank you. Because of your hard work and dedication, we should be able to put

Gloria Van Allen and Roger Philips away for a long time." He took Marjorie's hands in his, "Especially your hard work, darling. I heard how William Van Allen nearly collapsed on top of you. You weren't hurt, were you?"

"No, I was more scared than anything. The speed with which he became ill was terrifying. And when he started to fall, well . . ." She batted her eyes. "I only wished I had a big, strong man like you there to help me."

"What am I?" Creighton griped. "Tom Thumb?"

"Oh, you did just fine, Creighton. But Detective Jameson is more experienced in these matters."

"You're right, Jameson is more experienced in these matters. After all, you've been falling all over him from the first day you met him."

Marjorie slid him a snotty look. "Can we go now, Robert? This whole incident has been horribly upsetting."

"You poor thing, of course we can." He slid his arm about her shoulder and walked her to the door. "And after we take Creighton to his car, you can tell good old Robert all about it."

Creighton, alone in the Phantom, followed Jameson and Marjorie on the lonely drive back to Ridgebury, pouting all the way. It was irritating how the detective could take control of a situation just by his being there, but it was even more irritating to Creighton that Marjorie should succumb to him so easily. She was a fiery, spirited young woman, so different from any other female he had known before; but with Jameson, she became a mere shadow of herself. In his company, she reverted into a retiring, fragile little girl wanting rescuing from the cruel, cold world. In reality, it was not Marjorie who needed protection—she was about as defenseless as a lion in a herd of gazelle—

but Jameson; protection from those smoldering green eyes and that ambiguous Mona Lisa smile.

He tracked the squad car into Ridgebury where it came to a halt in front of Mrs. Patterson's boarding house. Marjorie hopped out of the passenger door before Jameson could even turn off the engine.

Creighton removed the keys from his own ignition and leapt out of the car to join her. "What are you doing? Why don't you go home and get some sleep?"

Jameson stepped out from behind the driver's wheel. "That's what I told her."

She waved her hand dismissively. "It's already daylight, and I'm too excited to sleep. Besides, I want to see Mrs. Patterson. She's probably worried sick about us."

She led them up the front walk and through the front door, where Mary, barefoot and dressed in a white nightgown, was waiting for them in the front parlor. "She's back!" the little girl shouted as she flew into Marjorie's open arms. It was the first time Creighton had heard Mary speak: a testament to her affection for the young writer.

"Of course I'm back. Where else would I be?" She tousled the girl's already rumpled hair.

Mrs. Patterson made her way from her usual spot in the kitchen. "Thank heaven! You nearly scared us to death." She took Creighton's hand in hers and squeezed it in elation. "What happened?"

"Long story." Marjorie glanced down at Mary to imply that it might not be fit for small ears. "I'll tell you later."

Mrs. Patterson nodded. "Mary, go up and get your slippers and robe. You'll catch pneumonia walking around like that."

Mary ran up the stairs obediently and Marjorie watched after her. "Her father go on another bender?"

"Right after you left last night," Mrs. Patterson confirmed. "The worst one yet. He went running through the streets whooping it up. Delirious, obviously. Dr. Russell finally managed to calm him down and help him back home. He knocked on your door to see if Mary could stay with you, but when he saw you weren't around, he brought her over here."

"Poor kid," Jameson commented.

"Mmm," Mrs. Patterson reflected. "You all must be tired and hungry. I have some coffee on in the kitchen. I'll fix you each a cup. And how about some breakfast?"

"Sounds like just what the doctor ordered," Creighton replied.

"Count me in," Marjorie added.

"Detective Jameson," Mrs. Patterson invited, "would you care to join us?"

"Thank you, ma'am, but I'd better check in at headquarters before they start looking for me."

"You're not even going to have a cup of coffee?" Marjorie asked, disappointedly.

"Not right now. But I tell you what, I'll go down to the station, see if there are any new developments, and then I'll come right back here and let you know what's going on. Okay?"

"Okay."

He kissed her on the cheek. "I'll see you in about an hour. Enjoy your breakfast," he bade before walking out the front door.

"I'll put the skillet on," Mrs. Patterson announced as she headed toward the kitchen.

"I'll help you," Marjorie offered.

"No, Creighton can help me. You go upstairs and check on Mary. She's been gone an awfully long time."

"All right," Marjorie agreed and bustled up the stairs.

Mrs. Patterson led Creighton into the kitchen. "Did I see correctly, or did Detective Jameson just kiss Marjorie?" she asked anxiously.

"You saw correctly," Creighton answered nonchalantly.

"Well, why is he kissing her instead of you?"

"Jameson's an okay fellow, but I'm afraid he's not my type, Mrs. Patterson."

"I meant, why aren't you kissing Marjorie?"

"Who said I was interested?" he responded in the most blasé tone he could muster.

"I did. And I've been around too long for a youngster like you to pull the wool over my eyes."

"Is it that obvious?"

"Only to an old relic like me," she explained. "Now, you didn't answer my question. Why is he kissing Marjorie?"

"I've been asking myself that same question lately, and I can only come up with one answer: heredity."

Mrs. Patterson's face looked a question.

"You see," Creighton expounded, "my parents didn't look like Jameson's parents, therefore I don't look like Jameson."

She wasn't convinced. "You're handsome enough. She's just not giving you a chance. Promise me, though, that you won't give up."

"I promise," he vowed.

"Good," she smiled and set about cracking several eggs into a glass bowl.

"You really think I'm the right man for Marjorie? Or is there some other reason you don't want her with Detective Jameson?"

"Heredity," she answered simply.

It was Creighton's turn to be puzzled. "Heredity?"

"Yes. I'm curious as to whether your children's eyes will be green or blue."

*   *   *

They breakfasted on a scrumptious repast of scrambled eggs, freshly baked bread, and homemade strawberry preserves. When they finished, Mary was discharged to the front parlor with a coloring book and a tin of stubby crayons. As the threesome lingered over their coffee, talking about the previous night's excitement, Detective Jameson knocked at the back door.

Creighton and Marjorie waved him inside. He entered, removed his coat and took the seat recently vacated by the little girl. "How's William Van Allen?" Creighton asked the detective.

"Better. His housekeeper said he was sleeping peacefully."

"*His* housekeeper?" Marjorie repeated.

"Yep, he checked himself out of Gloria's house last night and went back to his own apartment."

"Can't say I blame him," Creighton remarked, "given his sister-in-law's penchant for creative beverage-making."

"Did Mrs. Van Allen confess to poisoning the champagne?" Marjorie asked.

"No, neither she nor Philips admitted anything. But they'll change their tune once their lawyers see the evidence. We have enough to convict both of them on the embezzlement scheme, and Mrs. Van Allen on attempted murder."

"And what about the other crimes?" the writer posed.

"Other crimes?"

"Yes. Bartorelli died from a bullet in his head. And Henry Van Allen's suicide is still open to speculation. Or have you already forgotten?"

"No, I haven't forgotten, but I've already exhausted all my leads. Unless a new piece of evidence is dropped in my lap, I'm at a dead end."

"You've exhausted all of your leads? What about the Stella Munson case?"

"There's nothing in there having to do with Gloria, or any of the Van Allens, for that matter." He recited the facts by rote. "On October 13, 1930, Stella's landlady, concerned that she hadn't seen her tenant for several days, went into Stella's apartment to check on her. There she discovered the woman's body hanging from a bedsheet tied to a ceiling light fixture in her kitchen. She had been dead for about a week. A handwritten note, combined with the angle of the rope marks on her neck, led the police to conclude it was a suicide."

"Did anyone notice that Stella was depressed?" Creighton inquired. "What about the landlady? Had she noticed any changes in her mood?"

"Stella didn't know too many people in Los Angeles," Jameson explained. "Even the landlady didn't know too much about her, except that she was an ideal tenant. Quiet, paid her rent on time. And also that she had a mother and sister in New Jersey."

"No boyfriends?" Marjorie asked incredulously.

"None that the landlady could remember, although she did mention a detective who came to the building a few days before Stella's body was found."

"Detective?"

"Yeah, some guy knocked on the landlady's door, claiming to be a policeman. Said he was investigating a case in which Stella might be involved and needed to search the apartment. So he asked the landlady for the key."

"And she gave it to him?"

He nodded, "He showed her something that looked like a badge, so she thought he was legit."

Creighton spoke up. "What did this man look like?"

"Don't know. Landlady didn't have her glasses on. She said from his voice he could have been anywhere from his twenties to forties."

"That narrows it down to about five million people."

"Could it have been Scott Jansen?" Marjorie suggested.

"It's possible Stella hooked up with him again, I guess. Although I don't know why he would search her apartment. Nor have I been able to find any information on him. The name 'Jansen' must be an alias."

"Stafford did describe him as a hoodlum," Creighton reasoned.

"Did you find out anything else?" Marjorie asked eagerly.

"No, and, as I told you, I've run out of leads," said Jameson.

"So that's it. After all our work, the trail has gone cold."

"Marjorie, this case is over five years old. The trail isn't just cold, it's frozen."

"So you're content to let the case go unsolved."

"As far as I'm concerned, the case is already solved. Gloria Van Allen is our murderer. She and Philips were greasing their palms with the company money; Henry found out about it, so she killed him. Bartorelli saw the murder and decided to use his knowledge to gouge his employer for a few dollars. Gloria didn't want a liability like that hanging over her head, so she shot him and, not knowing what to do with the body, buried it on the grounds of Kensington House. Years elapsed and Gloria thought she had gotten away with everything. That is, until last night. Last night, the news of the company audit and William's allusion to a Swiss bank brought back all of her fears. In a sloppy, last-ditch attempt to silence him, she slipped the digitalis into her brother-in-law's glass. Exactly how she committed the crimes and to what extent Philips was involved, I can't say, but the whole thing fits together very neatly."

"Too neatly," Marjorie remarked.

"Marjorie, have you developed a soft spot in your heart for Mrs. Van Allen?" Creighton teased.

"No, I'd have to develop a soft spot in my head first. It's just that the whole thing seems so . . . so . . . anticlimactic."

"What? Having a man poisoned in front of you isn't exciting enough?"

She shook her head, "I mean this woman successfully covers up two murders, and then gives herself away with a botched poisoning. From a writer's point of view, it's very unsatisfying."

"Marjorie," Jameson started, "I warned you when we started that you might not like the way it ended."

"I know, but I didn't take you seriously. I thought you were trying to dissuade me from getting involved."

"So all this time, you've been imagining some heart-pounding conclusion to this whole thing?" He smiled. "Well, I'll prove to you that the end of a case doesn't have to be boring. Tonight we'll go out and celebrate all our hard work finally paying off."

"Capital idea, Jameson," Creighton lauded. "And I know just the place."

Jameson and Marjorie looked at each other. "Actually, Creighton, if it's all the same to you, we'd rather be alone," the detective stated.

"Say no more. Sharon doesn't have to know anything about it. It will just be the three of us. My treat, of course."

"Um, Creighton, I don't think—" Jameson began to debate.

"No arguments. It's the least I can do for my two best friends. You two have become like family to me."

Jameson and Marjorie looked at each other guiltily as Creighton got up from his chair. "Mrs. Patterson, how about you?" the Englishman invited. "Why don't you join us?"

"No, I'm too old. Your dinnertime is my bedtime."

"Are you sure?"

"Yes, you young people go and enjoy."

"All right, then I'll call Andre's and reserve a table for three." He made off for the telephone in the front parlor.

"Well, if we're going out tonight, I'd better go home and try to get some sleep," Marjorie declared as she started to clear the plates off the table. "But first, let me help you with the dishes, Mrs. Patterson."

The elderly woman grabbed her hand. "No, I won't hear of it. You've been up all night. Go and rest before you completely wear yourself out."

Marjorie put the dishes back on the table. "Come to think of it, I am a bit sleepy."

"See there? Now go. You can help me some other time."

"Okay. Thanks for breakfast, Mrs. Patterson," she gave the woman a kiss on the forehead and then pulled her opera coat from the back of her chair.

Jameson got up from his seat and helped her with the garment. "I'd best be getting back to the station. I'll walk you out."

"Where'd you park?" Marjorie asked.

"Out front."

"Then we'll go out that way." She preceded him out the swinging kitchen door.

Before leaving, the detective tipped his hat toward the elderly woman. "Good day, Mrs. Patterson."

"Goodbye, Detective. Enjoy your dinner tonight," she added with an ambiguous smile. "And always remember that things have a way of working out for the best."

"Thanks, I will," the young man replied, mystified, and shoved his way through the swinging door. He caught up with Marjorie in the front parlor, where Creighton had just hung up the phone.

"I got a reservation for seven thirty," he announced. "The restaurant is only a half hour away, so we'll meet here at seven. How's that for everyone?"

Jameson and Marjorie nodded their approval. "Sounds fine," the detective added.

"Good." He noticed Marjorie was wearing her coat. "I hope you're going home and taking a nap."

"Yes, father," she remarked facetiously. "I'm going now."

"Good. I'll walk you home."

"No need, Creighton," Jameson interrupted. "I'm heading back to the station; Marjorie's house is on the way."

"Actually, Robert," Marjorie broke in, "it'd be a good idea if Creighton came along. He let me borrow this jewelry last night and I'd like to return it right away, rather than leaving it lying around. The case is back at my house so, once I take everything off, he can pack it up and take it back with him. If that's okay with you, Creighton."

Creighton tried not to seem too eager to intrude upon their solitude. "Sounds like a good idea to me."

"Good, let's go," she sped out the front door and down the walk.

Creighton and Jameson, eyeing each other suspiciously, trailed after her. Once outside, Jameson pulled his car keys from his coat pocket.

"Oh no," Marjorie replied upon hearing them jangle, "it's such a nice morning. Let's walk."

Jameson silently complied and they strolled to the corner and then across the green toward the McClelland home. As they approached, Marjorie spotted something amiss at the Stafford house, two doors down. "Look at that," she pointed. "He's gone and done it again. Every time John Stafford goes on a binge, he leaves his front door wide open. I'd better close it before he catches his death." She headed toward the house, leaving her male companions to wait in front of the house next door.

"So, Creighton," Jameson started once she had gone, "what's all this about you giving Marjorie jewelry?"

"Jewelry?" he replied innocently, glad to have finally struck a nerve with his sanguine opponent.

"Yes, last night."

"Oh, that jewelry. Yes, I let Marjorie borrow it for the party. I thought it would go well with her dress."

"Borrow it? You mean you just happened to have it lying around?"

"Well, more or less. It was my mother's."

"You let her wear your mother's jewelry? All right, Ashcroft. I'm going to ask you something and I expect an honest answer. What's your interest in Marjorie?"

"Interest? Why, I'm her editor. You know that."

"Professionally, yes. However, I'm talking personally. What's your angle, Creighton? What do you want from her: friendship, or something more?"

Creighton turned the question over in his head. Was it wise to confess his feelings to Jameson? He was a decent fellow; would he do the noble thing and step aside? Or would he follow Creighton's example, and hinder his nemesis's advances?

The Englishman sighed; it was, indeed, a quandary. A quandary that he would have to ponder at another time, for his deliberations were interrupted by a prolonged, high-pitched sound. It was the sound of a blood-curdling scream.

TWENTY-THREE

THE MEN RUSHED TO the Stafford house. Jameson, his gun drawn, entered the residence first, crashing headlong into Marjorie, who was standing near the front door in tears. She threw her arms about the detective's shoulders and buried her face in his chest.

"He's dead!" she cried. "He's dead!"

Creighton moved further into the dusky foyer and peeked through the arched living-room doorway. There, sprawled upon the floor, lay the body of John Stafford. He was lying facedown by the fireplace, his head turned slightly to the right, his lifeless eyes staring vacantly at the trio standing in the doorway. From a deep wound near the back of his head streamed a now-congealed river of reddish-brown blood.

"Looks like he hit his head on the mantle," Creighton remarked. "There's blood on the corner of it."

Jameson gave Marjorie an absentminded embrace, then moved into the living room to call headquarters.

The Englishman took the trembling young woman in his arms and tenderly smoothed her hair with his hand.

"When I came to shut the door," she blubbered, her head against his shoulder, "I called out to Stafford, so that the noise wouldn't alarm him. When he didn't answer, I came in to see if he was all right. That's when I found him lying there. Dead. Oh Creighton, I'm so scared," she sobbed.

"There, there. Hush. I'm here now. I won't let any harm come to you."

She quieted down for a moment before jerking her head upright. "Oh my God!" she cried. "Mary!"

Creighton nodded. "I'll take care of it." He moved into the living room. and addressed Jameson, who was now examining the mantle. "All right if I use the phone?"

"Go ahead," the detective answered as he leaned over Stafford's body. "Just try not to move anything."

With Marjorie clutching his arm, Creighton walked over to the coffee table and picked up the telephone receiver. His long, tapered fingers dialed quickly, then came to rest on Marjorie's shoulder.

Mrs. Patterson answered on the second ring. "Mrs. Patterson," he addressed, "it's Creighton. Is Mary still there with you? . . . She is? Good. Keep her there. Under no circumstances should you let her go home . . . We're at the Stafford place now . . . Something's happened to Mary's father . . . I'm afraid he's dead . . . Must have tripped and hit his head on the fireplace mantle . . . Yes, it's quite unfortunate . . . No, don't tell her yet. It can wait until we get back . . . We'll see you later. Thanks, Mrs. Patterson."

He hung up the receiver. "She and Mary are baking cookies. That should keep her busy for a while."

Marjorie sniffed and nodded. The color had drained from her face and black streams of mascara ran from her eyes.

"If it's all right with you, Jameson, I'm getting Marjorie out of here," Creighton announced.

"No, Creighton," Marjorie protested. "I want to stay. I'm feeling better now."

Jameson shook his head in skepticism. "I don't know . . ."

"Please. If this is related to the Van Allen case, I want to stick around. I've followed the case from the beginning. I want to see it through to the end, no matter what."

Creighton lowered his brow, deep in thought.

She continued. "If I get upset again, you have my permission to take me home immediately."

"Okay," Creighton agreed, "but when we're through here, you're going home and packing a bag."

"A bag?"

"Yes, you and Mary are going to stay with Mrs. Patterson and me until we know for certain that this was an accident. I'll rest a lot easier knowing we're all under the same roof."

Marjorie stomped her foot on the floor. "That's nonsense! Robert, tell him I'm perfectly safe staying at my house."

Jameson glanced at the Englishman irresolutely. "I'm with Creighton. I'd feel safer knowing you're not alone tonight."

"Fine," she sighed. "I'll stay at Mrs. Patterson's. Though I still think I'd be perfectly safe at home."

"You might be," Jameson agreed, "but I don't want to take any chances. I'm not completely convinced this was an accident. Look around the fireplace. There's nothing Stafford could have tripped over. There's no furniture nearby, and the carpet is taut, not wrinkled.

Furthermore, if a person trips—even a drunk person—he generally falls forward, not backward."

"But he did fall forward," Marjorie argued. "He's lying on his stomach."

Jameson shook his head. "He fell forward *after* he hit his head on the mantle. In order to put a gash like that in the back of his head, he would have to have fallen like this." He lifted his leg in the air and arched his back toward the mantle.

"The only way he could have done that is if he were walking backward in the first place, as if backing away from something," Marjorie surmised.

"Or someone," Creighton completed. "Someone anxious to help him along on his journey into the hereafter."

"Precisely," Jameson confirmed. "Now, until we find out exactly who that someone is and why they were here, I don't think anyone is safe."

"I can't tell you who that someone was," Creighton stated, "but I can tell you who it wasn't: Gloria Van Allen and Roger Philips. They were in the city all last night. So there go your prime suspects."

"And your neat little solution," Marjorie added.

"I admit, it throws a monkey wrench into things," Jameson conceded, "but I'm still willing to wager that Gloria's our killer."

"But how?" Marjorie asked. "To drive here from Manhattan, kill Stafford, and drive back would require at least five hours. Gloria and Philips were at the party the entire night, and then at police headquarters until their lawyers bailed them out at three this morning."

"Three o'clock," the detective mused. "It's going on ten now, and Stafford's only been dead a few hours. If Gloria or Philips drove here directly from the station, that would get them here at five thirty, six o'clock at the latest, and back home in time for breakfast. That's still a window of opportunity."

The writer sighed. "You call that a window of opportunity?"

"Watch your fingers, Jameson," Creighton warned. "Looks like Marjorie's about to lower the sash."

"I think it's a bit of stretch, that's all," she argued. "Someone might have noticed Gloria or Philips sneaking back home at nine in the morning. Besides, what possible reason could either of them have for killing John Stafford?"

He threw his hands up in the air. "What reason could anyone have? That's what we'll have to find out. In the meantime, however, I'm still considering Gloria the principal suspect. Need I remind you that she tried to do in her brother-in-law last night?"

"No, you needn't remind me," she plopped down onto the sofa. "But Gloria's attempt to poison William doesn't prove that she shot Bartorelli or murdered Stafford. Any judge will tell you that. The modus operandi doesn't match Gloria's profile. Poisoning is a woman's crime; bloody crimes, such as shooting and smashing some-one's skull, aren't."

"Is that what your female intuition tells you?"

"No, that's what my research as a mystery novelist tells me," she replied smugly.

"Okay, then Philips did the dirty work."

"It's possible, but I doubt it. Gloria's the brains in that outfit, and we saw how rashly she behaved under threat of exposure."

"I tend to agree with Marjorie there," Creighton chimed in. "Philips is the jittery sort. He nearly jumped out of his skin at my mere mention of embezzlement. If he had shot Bartorelli, he wouldn't have had the presence of mind to bury his body and then hide the weapon."

"Ah yes, the weapon," the detective repeated deliberately. "I forgot to mention earlier that I called Wilcox and asked him to get a warrant to seize William's old service revolver. If forensics matches it to the bullet that killed Bartorelli, then I'd say it's curtains for Mrs. Van Allen."

"Mrs. Van Allen?" Marjorie quizzed.

"You said yourself that Henry kept the gun at Kensington House. That means Gloria had access to it."

"Yes, and so did anyone else who came in the front door," said Marjorie. "The gun was displayed in a glass case in the main foyer, like a fire hose. Henry may as well have posted a sign on the case reading: *In event of murderous intentions, break glass.*"

"You're forgetting that by the time Bartorelli was killed, Mrs. Van Allen was in the process of moving," reminded Jameson.

"The perfect time for someone to take the gun. If anyone noticed it missing from the display case, it would be assumed that it had been packed away."

Jameson rolled his eyes. "Talk about a bit of a stretch."

"I'm trying to look at all the possibilities," Marjorie reasoned.

"Fine, but you're wrong. Gloria is our killer."

"No, she isn't."

"Yes, she is."

Creighton drew their bickering to a halt. "Regardless of who's right or wrong, I would say that our plans for a celebratory dinner are premature." He picked up the telephone receiver and dialed. "I'll cancel our reservation, and when we finally do figure out who did it, we'll reschedule."

Marjorie nodded in agreement. "Even if we knew who did it, I wouldn't feel much like celebrating now, anyway, what with Mary's father dead."

Creighton gave her a commiserating nod of the head, and then proceeded to cancel the dinner reservation. "Hello, Andre? Creighton Ashcroft here. Put a stop on those chocolate soufflés. I'm afraid I have to cancel my reservation for this evening . . . Why? Well, let's just say an unexpected guest just dropped in . . . Uh-huh . . . Yes, very sudden . . . Bring him with us? Oh no, we couldn't possibly do that . . . Why not?" He looked down at the body sprawled across the carpet. "He's not at all well . . . No, I'm afraid it's quite serious . . . Yes, I think it's safe to say he's at death's door . . . Put him in a wheelchair? No, I think that would create too much of a scene. Might just put your other patrons off their food. We'll just have to make it some other time . . . Yes, thank you . . . You, too. Bye."

He hung up the phone just as Noonan and Palutsky walked through the living room door. Marjorie surrendered her seat on the sofa. "I know you'll be wanting to turn this place inside out, so I'll get out of your way." She left the living room and continued past the front door and down the hall.

Creighton decided to join her, but not before taking an opportunity to jibe Officer Noonan. "Palutsky," he greeted as he brushed past the two officers and through the living room archway. "Noonan. Any leads on that Homer fellow?"

Noonan screwed up his face in answer.

"No? Well, don't give up, old boy. If anyone can track him down, you can." He gave the burly man a pat on the back and, humming to himself, took off after Marjorie.

He found her in a tiny closet of a bedroom at the end of the hall, taking clothes from a scratched-up dresser and piling them onto an unmade twin bed. "I might as well pack up some of Mary's things while I'm here. She'll be needing clean clothes for tomorrow, and there's some toys she likes to play with."

Creighton glanced around the room dejectedly. It was not at all the way he thought a child's bedroom should look. The walls were covered with yellowed wallpaper scattered with faded pink rosebuds, the hardwood floor was strewn with a discordant mix of multicolored throw rugs, and the only window to be found was positioned beneath a large evergreen whose extensive boughs blocked the sun. Even the few dolls in the room, seated in a child-sized chair, seemed to frown. Nevertheless, even in this world of gloom, Creighton noticed that someone was smiling. In the open nightstand drawer lay a photograph, the corners worn from handling, of an attractive dark-haired woman with wide eyes. She was at the beach, standing near the shore in a white bathing suit; one hand held her bathing cap, the other was waving at the camera. He turned the picture over and read the inscription on the back: *Claire. Asbury Park, New Jersey. July, 1930.*"

"Mary has her mother's eyes," Creighton commented, replacing the photograph in the drawer.

"It's a family trait," she explained as she folded a white cotton petticoat. "Both the Munson girls had very dark eyes—almost black—just like their mother's." She added the petticoat to the pile. "There, that should do it for now."

"Well, if she needs anything else, I can always come back and get it," he offered.

Marjorie set her jaw defiantly. "No, I can do it. I know where everything is."

"Suit yourself," he shrugged. "Shall we go back in the living room and see what Jameson's up to?"

To his surprise, she declined. "No, I think I might heed your advice and get out of here. I'll stop at home, pack up some things and then go over to Mrs. Patterson's. Not that I'm tired," she added quickly, "but Mary might need me."

"You're right, she may," he played along. "If you don't mind, I think I'll join you. This tuxedo is starting to smell worse than Mrs. Schutt's rhubarb pie."

Marjorie smiled her consent and left, taking the pile of clothes with her. Creighton lingered a moment in the cheerless bedroom, then made his way down the hallway, the image of a blithe, carefree Claire Stafford fixed indelibly in his memory.

TWENTY-FOUR

IT WAS LATE AFTERNOON by the time Marjorie finally worked up enough courage to tell Mary that her father was gone and never coming back. But if the writer had readied herself for a deluge of tears, she needn't have bothered. The little girl listened with dry eyes and then skipped happily into the kitchen to help Mrs. Patterson with dinner preparations.

It was not that the concept of death was beyond her comprehension; she had a vague understanding, from what she had been told about her mother, that grown-ups very often left home and never returned. Nor was she not sorry that her father had to leave, for, indeed, she would miss him very much. Yet, the simple fact of the matter was that she was having too much fun to cry. Her few years on earth had been spent in virtual solitude, and now, suddenly, around every corner, were people to smother her with attention. She and Mrs. Patterson had spent the morning baking cookies, Mrs. Schutt had made her favorite chocolate cake, and Dr. Russell brought her a wooden horse he had whittled.

And that was only the daytime. Nighttime brought its own re-wards: the handsome policeman who stayed for dinner gave her a piggyback ride around the house, the tall man who talked funny told her a silly made-up bedtime story, and Marjorie tucked her into bed without making her take a bath. It was like her birthday, but better.

Yet, if Mary's heart was light, Marjorie's was heavy. The death of John Stafford had taken a grievous toll upon her mind. She walked about in a fog, her face tense and pale. As soon as Marjorie had put Mary to bed, Mrs. Patterson drew the young woman a hot bath, fixed her a cup of chamomile tea and ordered her to her room. Marjorie, too exhausted to argue, staggered up to the second floor and stayed there all evening, emerging only once to inquire about borrowing a bathrobe. Soon after, Mrs. Patterson retired, leaving Creighton alone in the front parlor.

Surprisingly enough, the Englishman was not at all sleepy. How-ever, finding the front parlor cold and drafty, he nonetheless with-drew to his bedroom. There, he rolled up his shirtsleeves, removed his shoes and reclined on the bed to give *Death in Denmark* a more in-depth perusal. Upon the completion the first chapter, he heard the creaking of floorboards and a soft, tentative tap on his bedroom door.

He placed the book facedown on the nightstand and went to in-vestigate. Opening the door, he peered out into the dark to see a fig-ure retreating down the hallway. When the light from his bedroom fell upon the figure, it jumped. "I'm sorry, Creighton," Marjorie whis-pered. "I didn't mean to wake you."

"Don't worry, I was awake." He opened the door fully to reveal that he was dressed. "What are you doing up? I thought you went to bed hours ago."

"I did, but I can't sleep." She stepped closer to the bedroom door allowing the light to fall upon her face and torso. Her eyes were tinged with red, her hair was slightly mussed and she was wrapped in an overly large bathrobe in a familiar plaid pattern.

"Is that my dressing gown?" he asked.

She glanced down at her waist as if she had just realized what she was wearing. "Yes, I forgot mine, and Mrs. Patterson is much shorter than I am, so she gave me yours to wear. I hope you don't mind."

"Not at all. You do it more justice than I do. Maybe I'll give it to you to keep." Normally she would have smiled at such a comment, but instead she stared at him blankly, her eyes glassy from an evening's worth of tears. He stepped back from the door. "Do you want to come in and talk?"

She glanced at the bed. "No, I don't think so."

He followed her gaze and realized how his invitation might have sounded. "How about joining me in the kitchen for some brandy, then? It's good for the nerves."

"I've never had brandy."

"Then I'll give you just a little, to help you sleep."

"All right," she capitulated, "to help me sleep."

"Good girl." He went back into his bedroom, grabbed a flask from his suitcase, and followed Marjorie downstairs and into the kitchen.

Marjorie flipped on the light switch and sat down at the table. Creighton retrieved two glasses from the cabinet over the sink, filled them halfway and then placed them and the flask on the table before taking the chair opposite Marjorie. "Drink up. It'll do you good."

She picked up the glass and took a sip, and then another, before putting it down again.

"At least you didn't gulp it down like the sherry," he teased.

She smiled faintly, and Creighton could see that she was starting to relax. "So tell me what's troubling you. Is it Stafford? Or Mary?"

"Both," she answered with a sigh. "I feel so awful about the whole thing. That poor man, the way he was lying there, and now that little girl upstairs is left all alone."

"She's not totally alone. Her grandmother has been notified and she wants to take Mary back to Nutley. In the meantime, she has all of us to watch over her."

"I know that, and she's luckier than most children who lose their parents, but her grandmother isn't going to live forever. Someday she's going to be entirely on her own, with no family to depend upon. Do you know how lonely that is? Well, I do. It's been seven years since my father died, and there are still times when I feel like an orphan."

"I expect every child who loses a parent feels that way. It's been twenty-six years since my mother died. Sometimes it feels like yesterday."

"When does it stop hurting, Creighton?" she begged. "When?"

He frowned. "I don't know that it ever does."

A tear slid down her cheek. "At least we each had one parent to raise us into adulthood. But Mary isn't even five years old yet. What's going to happen to her? How is she going to feel, seeing her friends with their mothers and fathers, when she has none? And what will she do when her grandmother is gone? I have Mrs. Patterson, but who else does she have?"

"She has you, Marjorie," he replied. "She has you."

"Me?" She laughed bitterly. "I'm the one who did this to her. If it weren't for my horning in, her father might still be alive."

"And if you had it to do all over again, what would you do differently? Ignore Victor Bartorelli's body? Pretend you never found it? I don't consider reporting a dead body to the police as 'horning in.'"

"No, but I pressured Robert to reopen the Van Allen case. And because he did, William was nearly poisoned and Stafford was killed."

"Jameson didn't make detective for nothing, Marjorie. He's a smart fellow. With or without us, he would have eventually reopened the case and uncovered the embezzling scheme. It might have taken him a little longer, but he would have ended up in the same place we are now. And, need I remind you, I did my fair share of pressuring, too. As for William Van Allen, if you weren't at the party, he would have shot his mouth off to some other good-looking woman and gotten himself poisoned anyway. And Stafford, well, I hate to say it, but he was well on his way to drinking himself to death."

"But he didn't drink himself to death. He fell, and if I were at home last night instead of at the party, I might have heard something. I might have been able to help him."

"You might also have gotten yourself killed. What good would you be to Mary then?"

"What good am I to her now?" she cried. "I can't put her life back together again. I can't take her hurt away. If I had just been home last night, I could have saved him. But like always, I'm never around when I'm really needed. It happened with my father and now it's happened again." She began to weep.

He handed her a handkerchief and poured some more brandy. "Talk to me, sweetheart. Tell me what happened to your father."

"He was sick. He had suffered a stroke that left him very weak. He had difficulty walking without a cane, and his handwriting was very shaky. When he came home from the hospital, I took care of him. He could do a lot on his own, but I made him his meals, cleaned the house and did the laundry. I also took dictation from him, so that he could still pursue his writing. We lived that way for almost a year— just the two of us. Then, one night in February, they had a dance over at St. Agnes. I didn't want to go, but my father insisted. He said I was too young to be at home taking care of a sick man." She took a sip of brandy. "I went to the dance, and when I came home he was dead. If I hadn't gone, I might have been able to save him, or at least say good-bye." Tears streamed down her face.

Creighton rose from his chair and knelt down on the floor in front of her. "Marjorie, don't you see? He didn't want you there; he didn't want you to see him die. He wanted you to go on with your life, to be young and happy. My mother had a phrase she always told to my brother and me, but I never understood it until now. She said, 'If I could give you just two things, the first would be to give you roots, the last to give you wings.' Your father raised you. He gave you your roots and that night, he gave you your wings—your freedom. It was his last act as a father, to protect you. You didn't fail him. You could never have failed him. Nor could you possibly fail Mary. You're too beautiful a person. Not just your face, but your heart. Your dear, dear heart . . ."

He brushed her tears away and, taking her face in his hands, kissed her, softly, slowly at first and then, finding his lips met no resistance, with a gradually increasing intensity. "Marjorie," he sighed, tasting the salt of her tears upon his mouth.

She slid her arms around his neck and pulled him closer to her. He kissed her again—this time harder, more passionately than he had ever kissed any woman. She reciprocated at first but then, with a sudden capriciousness, pushed him away gently.

She rose from her chair and, as if Creighton had done more than kiss her, smoothed the plaid dressing gown about her hips. "It's late. We should try to get some sleep. We've been awake for more than thirty-six hours now." She cleared her throat, "I'm sorry to have burdened you with my problems. I didn't intend to go on the way I did."

Creighton, still crouched upon the kitchen floor, reached up and took her hand in his. "You didn't burden me."

Like that first day in the drugstore, she gently removed her fingers from his grasp. "What I mean is that I got a bit carried away. I think, perhaps, the brandy went to my head."

In other words, the kiss had been a mistake. Creighton turned his head away in desolation. "Yes," he replied mechanically, "alcohol has a tendency to do that if you're not careful."

Having gotten her point across, she made her way towards the door, and then, apparently deeming it necessary to make some sort of parting gesture, returned to Creighton, placed a hand on his shoulder and grazed his forehead with her lips. "Thank you Creighton. You're a good friend."

At the word "friend," any flicker of hope in his heart was swiftly extinguished, replaced by a profound feeling of emptiness. He swallowed, hard. "Goodnight, Marjorie," were the only words he could bring himself to utter. He listened to the swinging of the kitchen door and the slapping of Marjorie's slippers on the hardwood floor as she walked away from the kitchen and down the hallway.

Creighton returned to his place at the table and pushed aside his flask and brandy glass. No amount of alcohol would assuage his longing, no level of intoxication high enough to numb his pain.

Marjorie was back in her room now, for he could hear the creaking of the floorboards above his head. The sound was faint, haunting, as if it were made not by a flesh and blood woman, but a spirit, a ghost.

He smiled weakly and wondered if this description didn't suit her. He recalled the feeling of her lips as they brushed against his forehead: fleeting, transitory. Certainly, there was nothing tangible about her, nothing to grab hold of and stake claim to as his own. She came to him in turns, alighting suddenly upon his soul and then disappearing as quickly as she had come.

Yes, he thought, perhaps she was nothing more than a phantom, a dream, a vision. And for him, it seemed, that was all she was ever destined to be.

TWENTY-FIVE

MARJORIE WAS SLICING BREAD on the kitchen counter when Creighton entered the kitchen the next morning. He greeted the young girl seated at the table eating oatmeal. "Good morning, Mary." Upon her lap was the same ragged doll she had been carrying the first time he saw her. "And friend."

"Good morning," he bade Marjorie softly.

"Good morning," she rejoined.

"Where's Mrs. Patterson?"

"She went to church. From there she's catching a bus to Hartford. A friend of hers isn't feeling well, so she's paying her a visit. She'll be back this evening."

"I guess we're left to fend for ourselves this morning," he surmised.

"Not entirely." She pulled a face. "Mrs. Patterson left a pot of oatmeal on the stove for us."

"Lovely," he replied facetiously.

"I take it you'll be joining me for toast?" she asked, gesturing to the loaf of bread.

"Yes, I believe I will, thank you."

A small voice came from the kitchen table. "May I be excused?"

Marjorie craned her neck to peer into the little girl's bowl. "Did you and Florence eat all your oatmeal?"

"Florence?" Creighton asked.

"Her doll," Marjorie whispered.

Mary nodded earnestly.

"Okay," Marjorie permitted. "Go upstairs and get dressed."

The little girl scampered out of the kitchen. Now that he and Marjorie were alone, Creighton decided to broach the subject of their kiss. "I'm sorry about last night."

"That's all right, I'm as much to blame as you are. After all, I didn't fight you off, did I?" She gave a quick smile. "Let's just put it down to sheer exhaustion and leave it at that."

"So you forgive me?"

"Yes, I forgive you."

"And you won't hold a grudge?"

"Why should I hold a grudge?"

"Because I had a bad experience when I was a lad. I kissed a girl, Edwina Niedersachsen, without her permission. I apologized afterward and she said she forgave me, but apparently she didn't, because the next day she told the entire upper form what a horrible kisser I was. I couldn't get another date until I went off to university."

"How horrible for you," she exclaimed with more than just a hint of mock pity. "Well, you needn't worry. I promise I won't spread a lie like that around town."

His ears pricked up, "A lie? Are you saying that I'm not a horrible kisser?"

"No, you're not a horrible kisser," she admitted grudgingly.

"Would you go so far as to say that I'm a good kisser?"

"You do all right," she allowed sparingly.

"Just all right? Maybe I can improve. Why don't we have another go then?" He puckered his lips and leaned closer.

"No," she exclaimed, laughing.

"Suit yourself," he shrugged.

She pulled a slice of browned bread from the toaster and thrust it at him. "Here. Go eat your toast."

"Yes, ma'am," he teased and took a seat at the table. Marjorie grabbed her own slice of toast and joined him. "Did you tell Mary that she'll be moving in with her grandmother?" he asked as he poured out their coffee.

"Yes," she replied, smearing some strawberry preserves onto her toast with the back of a spoon.

"How did she take it?"

"She liked the idea. Her only concern was that I wouldn't be able to see her for her birthday. Mrs. Patterson and I were going to throw her a big fifth birthday party this August."

"No reason you still can't. You and Mrs. Patterson can get the balloons and cake together, and I'll drive the both of you down there. As long as her grandmother approves, of course."

Marjorie smiled. "Mary would like that."

Creighton smiled back. "So what's on schedule for today?"

"Nothing," she took a sip of coffee. "Robert put a rush on Stafford's postmortem and the forensic analysis of William's revolver, but, since it's Sunday, he might not get those reports until tomorrow. However, on the off chance he does hear something, he'll let us know."

"Then it looks like it's just the three of us. What would you like to do? Go into town and see a movie, perhaps?"

"No, if it's all the same to you, Creighton, I'd like to work on my book. My notes are hopelessly out of date."

"So you're planning to stay here all day?"

She hedged a bit before answering him. "Umm, no, actually I was planning on working back at my place."

Creighton shook his head. "I thought we discussed this yesterday. Jameson and I told you we didn't like the idea of you staying at your house alone."

"I'm not staying there. I'll spend the day and come back here in time for supper."

"Why can't you work here?"

"Because I left all my notes at my house."

"Then I'll pick them up for you."

She wrinkled her nose. "Creighton, I'm just not comfortable working here. I'm a creature of habit when it comes to writing. I need all my things about me—my desk, my chair, my typewriter. Besides, someone has to go back and feed Sam."

Creighton still had misgivings.

"Don't you have anything better to do than to babysit me all day? What about your house? Isn't there something you could do there?"

"I did receive a shipment of wine yesterday afternoon. I could try to clean up the wine cellar and stock the bottles away, but I don't have to be alone to do that. Why don't you and Mary join me?"

"I'm sure Mary would just love to spend her day in a cold, damp cellar with nothing to play with but bottles of wine," she quipped. "Let me take her to my house. She'd be a lot more comfortable there. She can spread out on the rug with her paper dolls and blocks and coloring books, and if she gets bored, she can always play with Sam."

"She could do those things here," he argued.

"Please, Creighton. I need to work, to help me get my mind off of things."

"Okay," he caved, "but no gallivanting around town."

"I won't."

"And make sure to lock all your windows and doors."

"I will."

"And if you need me I'll be at Kensington House."

"I know. Now, relax. What could possibly happen in Ridgebury in broad daylight?"

Marjorie was ensconced in front of her typewriter, trying to formulate her thoughts into words, but it was an exercise in futility. No matter how hard she tried to focus on her book, her meditations soon turned to Creighton and the incident in Mrs. Patterson's kitchen. She was not upset with Creighton—he was, after all, only a man—but she was extremely cross with herself for having let down her guard. Her father's death was a subject she discussed with no one, not even Mrs. Patterson. Yet, last night she had wept openly, like a child, baring her soul to a man she hardly knew, compelling him to kiss her out of pity. He must think her such a fool!

She banged on the typewriter with both hands, stamping a nonsensical, vowelless word upon the otherwise blank sheet of typing paper loaded in the carriage. Mary looked up in surprise from the tower of blocks she was constructing on the living-room carpet. Embarrassed by her fit of temper, Marjorie smiled. "It's awfully quiet in here. How about some music?"

The writer rose from her chair, crossed the room, and switched on the freestanding Philco radio near the front picture window. The electrical device crackled and hummed before issuing forth the velvet sound of Bing Crosby bragging about his good fortune.

"It was a lucky April shower . . . it was the most convenient door . . . I found a million dollar baby in a five-and-ten-cent store . . ."

Marjorie frowned. She wasn't in the mood for a love song. And the lyrics, about meeting a sweetheart worth a million dollars inside an ordinary storefront, hit a little too close to home. Nevertheless, it was still better than silence, so she raised the volume, returned to her desk, and again stared blankly at the typewriter keyboard.

When the song had finished, the radio announcer broke in with the daily quiz question. Marjorie leaned back in her chair, happy to have even a momentary distraction from her self-loathing.

"Today's question," the broadcaster began, "is in the category of Egyptology. The question is: What Egyptian artifact has been displayed at the British Museum, without interruption, for over one hundred years?"

The broadcaster played "Moon Glow" as he waited for a contestant to call in with the correct answer. Marjorie placed her hands behind her head, deep in thought. *Egyptian artifact . . . what could it be? What could it be? The Book of the Dead? The bust of Queen Nefertiti?* She wandered back to the radio and, as the song reached its conclusion, raised the volume control on the radio so as not to miss the solution to the riddle.

"We have a winner for the daily quiz question," the broadcaster announced when the intermission had finished. "For you folks who missed it, today's question was: What Egyptian artifact has been displayed at the British Museum, without interruption, for over one hundred years? Mr. Howard Kirby of Exeter, Connecticut knew that the answer was the Rosetta Stone. That's right folks, the Rosetta Stone has been on display in the British Museum every day for the past hundred years. It is one of the few items in the permanent collection that is not available for circulation to other museums. Congratulations, Mr. Kirby. Your correct response has earned you twenty dollars and an opportunity to win our grand prize drawing—"

Marjorie switched off the radio in a state of puzzlement. *The Rosetta Stone?*

How could that be? Didn't Dr. Russell say he had seen it in Cairo? The radio station must be wrong, she concluded and then pulled a face.

The station wouldn't ask a question unless they were certain of the answer. Not with twenty dollars at stake. She shook her head. No. Dr. Russell must have been mistaken. He must have seen the stone in London and somehow merged the incident with his trip to Cairo.

The only problem was that Dr. Russell denied ever having been in London . . .

Staring out the picture window, Marjorie searched for an answer, but all she found were more questions. In order to have seen the stone, Dr. Russell must have been in London, yet he claimed not to have been there. Why? For a man to confuse one museum with another was one thing, but for him to forget an entire city was another matter entirely. Unless, of course, he hadn't really seen the stone. Then why say that he had?

In a daze, she wandered back toward her desk. Was there more to Dr. Russell than what met the eye? Had he lied about London in an effort to conceal something? Or was she magnifying the importance of his remarks? She wandered back to her desk chair in a trance. Mrs. Patterson had said that Dr. Russell had been the last person to see Stafford alive. But why should Dr. Russell wish to kill John Stafford? Why should *anyone* wish to kill John Stafford? He possessed nothing except a shabby cottage, a drinking problem . . . and Mary.

She watched the little girl playing on the carpet. *Could it be?*

She felt a dire need to talk to someone—someone to give her a second opinion, to tell her whether she was behaving reasonably. *Creighton*, she thought excitedly.

She grabbed the receiver of the phone on her desk and placed it to her ear. However, as her finger reached for the dial, she realized her error: the telephone at Kensington House had yet to be connected. Marjorie replaced the receiver and assessed the situation. What was she to do? Call Robert? No, he'd send his men to Dr. Russell's house to investigate, and Marjorie didn't want that. If her assumptions were wrong, she'd feel terrible for having sent the police breathing down the neck of an innocent man.

No, she needed to speak with Creighton. She checked the clock on the mantle. Four thirty. The Englishman wasn't due back until six; that left an entire hour and a half of waiting. She would go stir-crazy by then. There was only one clear choice: she and Mary would walk to Kensington House.

She frowned. Creighton had told her not to go out unless it was urgent. But if this didn't qualify as urgent, she didn't know what did. Besides, Kensington House was only a half mile down the road; she and Mary could walk there and back a dozen times before nightfall.

"Mary," she ordered, "get your coat and hat. We're going out."

The little girl immediately began packing up her blocks. "No, sweetheart," Marjorie stated anxiously, "you don't have to do that now. We'll come back for them later."

As per Marjorie's orders, she left the pile of blocks in the middle of the living room floor and wandered off to the bedroom to collect her outer garments. Marjorie pulled her own coat from the closet and recalled her words outside the Stafford home days earlier: *I always wished I had a sister.*

The Englishman, his shirt sleeves rolled to his elbows, stood in the dank cellar of Kensington House surveying his work. Using a large flashlight, he had cleared the area of its cobwebs and loaded part of the shipment of wine into the empty racks, but he was unsure as to the configuration of the bottles. If he wanted a 1934 Riesling, would he be able to locate it? Probably not, for he had gone about his task in the most perfunctory fashion, choosing to contemplate other matters: Marjorie, naturally, being near the top of the list.

Yet, even the memory of her sweet kiss could not rise above his ever-growing agitation. Since he had awoken that morning, Creighton had been plagued by the peculiar sensation that he had overlooked something: some detail, however small, that was of great significance. The feeling was quite vexing—something akin to leaving the house without being certain that the burners on the gas stove have been shut off.

Unluckily, Creighton's source of concern was nothing as simple as an unchecked appliance. It was a murder case, and something, some piece of information in that case, didn't quite fit. If he could only put his finger on it . . .

A series of loud knocks came from the kitchen, and Creighton ran up the few short steps from the wine cellar to find Detective Jameson stepping in the door. "What brings you to this neck of the woods, Jameson?"

Through the open door, Creighton could see that the day had turned blustery and gray, and a light snow had begun to fall. The detective brushed the white flakes from his coat. "I was driving past here

309

on my way to the station when I noticed the front gate was open. I thought someone might have broken in, so I decided to check it out."

"Much obliged," Creighton thanked him. "Why are you going to the station? I thought it was your day off."

He removed his hat. "It is, but I got word from forensics. The preliminary report is ready and is being wired to the station as we speak. I tried calling at Mrs. Patterson's to tell you and Marjorie, but there was no answer."

"That's because no one's home," Creighton explained. "I've been here working all day. Mrs. Patterson is in Hartford for the day. And Marjorie, our stubborn little friend, is at back at her house, writing. She took Mary with her."

Jameson arched his eyebrows. "You think that's a good idea? The two of them alone?"

Creighton shrugged. "I don't see the harm. It's the middle of the afternoon. Plenty of people about. They'll be out of there before dark, anyway. I told Marjorie I'd come by at six o'clock and take her and Mary back to the boarding house."

"I guess writing might do her some good right now," Jameson opined. "She was pretty shaken up yesterday."

Creighton nodded. "It only got worse after you left. When I finally saw her off to bed, it was almost two."

"Well, it's just about four thirty now. Plenty of time until you have to meet with Marjorie. You can come with me to headquarters, if you'd like, and see the forensics report firsthand."

"Yes, I'd like that. I've had enough mucking about in the cellar for one day."

"Okay. We'll take my car and I'll drive you back here later."

"Fine," Creighton agreed, donning his hat and coat. "Remind me to close the gate before we leave."

"Will do." Jameson paused in the doorframe on the way out. "Say, should we stop by Marjorie's house and let her know where we're going?"

Creighton pulled a face. "No, I don't think so. I'll give her a call from the station."

"Are you sure? She'll be awfully mad if we don't tell her what's going on."

"She probably will," he agreed. "However, if we go there in person, she'll just insist on tagging along, which would be fine in any other circumstances, but I don't think Mary should be exposed to any more of this than she need be."

"You're right," Jameson assented as he climbed up the stairs to the ground above. "Poor kid's been through enough."

TWENTY-SIX

MARJORIE AND MARY WALKED, hand in hand, down the desolate span of Ridgebury Road that led to Kensington House. The snow, which had started shortly before they left the house, was now falling heavily, veiling the ground upon which they trod with a thin, white shroud.

"Just a little farther," she stated, more for her own benefit than that of her small companion. "I can see the front gate just a few feet ahead." Indeed, it was the gate, swung open wide in welcoming. Marjorie entered and guided Mary up the tree-lined driveway that she and Creighton had driven on during that mild, early spring afternoon just a week earlier. Reaching the end of the drive, they clambered up the steps to the shelter of the front portico, but the door was locked.

Marjorie lifted the heavy brass doorknocker and brought it down three times in succession. She waited for nearly a minute, but there was no reply.

Of course, it dawned upon her, *Creighton's in the wine cellar. He might not have heard the front door.* Taking Mary by the hand again, she strode to the side of the house. There, at the point where the main driveway and service path merged, stood the Phantom, and, only a few feet away from it, the cement staircase that led to the kitchen. Marjorie and the little girl descended the stairs, and, discovering the door at the bottom unlocked, stepped inside.

"Creighton," Marjorie called. "Creighton, are you here?"

There was no answer.

She moved through the kitchen into the pantry, and peered down the steps to the wine cellar. When her eyes adjusted to the darkness, she could ascertain that someone had, indeed, been working there, for several bottles of wine had been stocked in the racks and two partially filled crates stood in the middle of the room, waiting to be emptied of their contents. Creighton, however, was nowhere to be found.

Where is he? she wondered. Then she recalled having banged upon the front door. *Creighton must have heard the knock and went upstairs to answer it*, she concluded. Choosing to head him off on his way back to the cellar, she made her way through the kitchen and ascended the servant's staircase to the main floor. Mary trailed closely behind her.

"Hello," she shouted as she arrived the top of the stairs. Again no answer. She stepped out into the hall. With the snow falling outside, the room was even darker than she remembered it, yet in the dusky light she could discern a shadow moving near the front door. "Creighton, is that you?" she asked, advancing slowly down the corridor.

There was a flash of light as a gunshot pierced the silence. Marjorie threw herself on top of Mary and they dropped to the floor. Before they could move again, a second shot rang out. A sudden and intense pain tore swiftly through Marjorie's left shoulder and down her arm, but there was no time to linger in agony. As another bullet whistled above her head, she gathered Mary in her arms and, crawling on her knees, scrambled into the nearest room.

Once inside, she relinquished the little girl and rose to her feet. Where were they? What room was this? And was there any way out of it other than through the hallway? She searched the room frantically for a window or door that could serve as an escape route, but to her horror, all that met her eye were rows of bookcases and a sizable stained-glass window depicting a familiar riverside scene. *The library.*

She slumped against a bookcase and prayed, silently. *Mary, blessed mother of God. Mary, blessed mother of God, please help us.* From the hallway, she heard a door creak open and slam closed, followed by the sound of approaching footsteps. *Who was it? The gunman? Creighton? Was Creighton still alive, or had the killer shot him down as well? Oh, God!* Feeling Mary's grip upon her leg tighten, she looked down into wide, apprehensive eyes that, in the wan light of the stained-glass window, resembled pools of liquid chocolate.

Liquid chocolate . . . liquid chocolate. She turned the phrase over and over in her head until it sparked a flame of recognition. *Hot cocoa! By God, that was it!*

Stepping out of her shoes so as not to make any sound on the parquet floor, Marjorie padded to the opposite corner of the room and pressed along the wall with her fingertips until she felt a panel give way. She applied more pressure until the latch of the door released with what, in the eerie silence, sounded like a deafening click.

The writer held her breath as the footsteps at the other end of the hall stopped and then started again, this time moving with greater speed.

As the door of the dumbwaiter swung open, Marjorie hastened back to Mary and bundled her into her arms. It would be tight, but the little girl should just about fit. She crossed the room again and struggled to squeeze the child into the small elevator, but her bulky winter coat got in the way. Marjorie, her heart racing, fumbled at the buttons of the garment, all the while listening as the footsteps stopped another time and then drew closer.

Impatiently, she pulled the child's coat off, popping a button loose in the process. She felt terribly guilty, sending Mary out into the cold without the proper clothes, but it was the only way to secure the child's freedom. Loading her into the dumbwaiter, Marjorie whispered instructions into the little girl's ear. "Listen, Mary, and listen carefully. This elevator will take you to the kitchen. When you get to the bottom, push against this wall, here, and it will open to let you out. Once you're out, you'll be in the kitchen. That's the room we were in before, when we first came into the house. Remember? Run out of the kitchen door, up the steps and down the path to the street. Stand near the street and try to get help. Jump, shout, wave to passing cars, anything. But the most important thing you can do is run. Do you understand? Run and don't look back. Don't wait for me. Don't look for me. Just run. Have you got that?"

Mary nodded, her hands clutching at her doll anxiously. Marjorie attempted to smile reassuringly despite the tears that welled in her eyes. "Don't be afraid, sweetheart. I won't let anything happen to you." She patted the doll on the head. "Besides, you'll have Florence there to help you."

The child nodded again and Marjorie, taking the ropes in her hands, slowly lowered the dumbwaiter. After years of disuse, the pulley squealed and squeaked back into service with a voice so loud as to be audible for several yards away. Marjorie winced, partly in response to the sound of the pulley, partly because of the searing pain that pulsed through her shoulder, but it was too late to stop now. She had already betrayed her whereabouts; the best she could do was to lower Mary as far down the shaft as possible before the gunman entered the room.

She continued to pull the ropes as the footsteps inched ever closer. Then, hearing that the killer was directly outside the library, she threw Mary's coat down the elevator shaft, closed the dumbwaiter door and moved to the other side of the room so as not to disclose Mary's hiding spot. There she waited as the silhouette in the door-frame grew larger.

Creighton and Jameson arrived at headquarters to find Noonan placing a report on the detective's desk. "This just arrived." He waved the piece of paper in his hand.

"Thanks," Jameson murmured, removing his coat and hat and settling down at his desk to read.

"Afternoon, Noonan," Creighton greeted.

The officer looked at him uneasily before answering. "Hi."

Had he been in a better mood, the Englishman might have entered into some lighthearted banter with the policeman, but, feeling even more ill at ease than he had this morning, he plopped into the chair opposite Jameson and waited for him to finish reading before calling Marjorie. Busying himself by looking over the contents of the detective's desk, he took note of a photograph in a wooden frame perched at the corner. It depicted a group of people gathered on the shore of a lake. "May I?" he asked, taking the picture in his hand.

"Go ahead."

Creighton took a gander at what must have been an impromptu family portrait, for the participants were dressed in manner of casual wear: bathing suits, shifts, short trousers. In the center of the group stood a handsome couple, somewhere about sixty years of age. Flanked around them were three younger men and two younger women; everyone in the photo bore the same dark good looks as Detective Jameson, except for one man, fair and blonde, who balanced a raven-haired toddler upon his shoulders.

Forgetting the photograph was in a frame, he turned it over to see if a date had been etched on the back. It was then that he realized what had been bothering him all day.

"Jameson," he invoked, replacing the picture on the desk with a thud, "how long had Stella Munson been living at her last apartment?"

"About two months." He lifted his eyes from the report in puzzlement. "Why?"

Creighton described the photograph of Claire Stafford he had seen in Mary's room.

"So?"

"So, the date on that picture is July 1930. Mary was born in August of that same year."

"And Claire isn't pregnant in the photograph," Jameson guessed.

"Not unless she had a conjurer for a seamstress."

"Someone could have written the wrong date," he argued.

"Possibly," Creighton allowed. "But what if someone didn't? What if the date is correct?"

"Then Claire wasn't Mary's mother."

"Right," he answered with a smile.

"So, the kid was adopted," Jameson inferred. "Makes her sad story even worse."

The Englishman shook his head. "She's not adopted, Jameson. She looks too much like Claire not to be related somehow."

"What are you suggesting? That she's Stella's daughter?"

He leaned in closer. "Think about it, Jameson. Think about it. It all fits. Stella was having an affair with Henry, a very rich and powerful man. By all accounts, Henry was going to end his marriage and

317

sacrifice his financial standing to marry her. Why? Did he love her that much? Or was there another reason?"

"A child?"

"Yes, a child. The one thing that Gloria hadn't given him, would never give him. Then, suddenly, Stella leaves Ridgebury. Why?"

The detective shrugged. "Lover's spat?"

"But why not move to New Jersey with her mother and sister? Isn't that what most women do when they leave a spouse or a lover? Yet Stella, who has no job, no visible means of support, leaves a house that's paid for to rent an apartment on the other side of the country."

"She wanted a fresh start."

"A fresh start? Or did she want to spare her family the disgrace of being an unwed mother? Or perhaps she simply wanted to escape the wrath of a jealous wife." He paused. "Then there's John Stafford. Why was he so euphoric the night he died?"

"Simple. A belly-full of sour mash whiskey."

"Oh, come on, Jameson. He had already had a few sniffles when we saw him the other day, and he was not a happy drunk." He shook his head. "No, something made him happy. Something we told him when we went to see him."

"That Stella was having an affair with Henry Van Allen?"

"That's right. Do you remember his reaction?"

"Yeah, he spit out his beer."

Creighton rolled his eyes. "After that. He stared out the window to where Mary was playing—"

Jameson completed the sentence. "And said that Stella had been holding out on everyone."

"Yes, that 'Stella had been holding out on everyone.' Picture it. John and Claire find out that Stella is pregnant and, whether to ease the strain on Stella or to spare Mary of the stigma of illegitimacy, they decide to go to Los Angeles, pick up the baby, and raise it as their own. Of course, they can't go back to Nutley with the infant. There'd be too many questions. So, they come to Ridgebury and live in the house that Stella has vacated. The townspeople here are surprised when Claire shows up in town with a child, but put it down to forget-fulness on the part of Mrs. Munson, who is under a great deal of strain caring for her ailing sister." He cleared his throat. "Stella, per-haps out of fear or some distorted sense of loyalty, never tells her sis-ter and brother-in-law the identity of Mary's father. Though, from the reports from home, they assume it's Scott Jansen, Stella's boyfriend. Years go by and both Stella and Claire pass away, leaving Stafford to raise Mary on his own. The pressure of raising a child combined with the loss of his wife and his job drive him to the bottle. Things are very grim for John Stafford. Then, three days ago, we come in and tell him that Stella was seeing no other than Henry Van Allen. Stafford sees his golden opportunity. If the child he has been raising is the offspring of Henry Van Allen, it could prove to be very profitable."

"How? Both Henry Van Allen and Stella are dead. Proving that Mary was Van Allen's daughter would mean a prolonged legal battle. Stafford couldn't afford that."

"No, he couldn't. That's why he set about getting his money ille-gally."

"Blackmail?"

"Absolutely. He contacts the Van Allen household, describes his lucrative little business offer and arranges for a clandestine meeting here at Ridgebury on Friday night."

"But why would anyone agree to such a deal?" Jameson asked. "Why not just call the police and have him arrested? That's what I would do."

"Same here, but, then again, you and I have nothing to hide. A person guilty of murder or embezzlement, however, would be very reluctant to involve the police in their personal affairs." Creighton raised his index finger. "Question is: who would have lost the most if Henry had produced an heir?"

"Gloria," Jameson replied, waving the piece of paper Noonan had handed him. "Forensics report. The bullet that killed Bartorelli came from William's service revolver."

"Interesting."

"What's really interesting is where Wilcox found the revolver—stored away in a box in Gloria's house. Supposedly William didn't have room enough for his brother's entire collection at his apartment, so his sister-in-law generously offered to keep some items at her place."

"How very thoughtful of her," he commented. "So, what do we do now?"

"We find out if your theory is correct." Jameson shouted to his officer. "Noonan, get the number of Stella Munson's landlord in L.A."

"You mean the dame who found her dead?"

"No, the person who ran the place where she lived before that, when she first moved out there."

Noonan gave a quick nod of the head and rushed back to his desk.

"While you talk to the landlord," Creighton told Jameson, "I'll call Marjorie. She'll be dumbfounded when she hears all this."

Marjorie braced herself against a bookcase as a familiar face emerged from the shadows. "Dr. Russell!" she addressed the dark figure.

"Dr. Russell. Scott Jansen. I go by many names. Take your pick."

"I knew there was something wrong when I learned that the Rosetta Stone hadn't been in Cairo in over 100 years," Marjorie replied, her voice shaking.

Jansen stepped further into the room, allowing the light to reflect off the small pistol in his hand. "I thought you might have heard that radio broadcast this afternoon. Apparently you did. I went to your house but you had already left, so I followed your footprints in the snow. They led me here."

"You went to my house? Why? To shoot me?"

"No," he adamantly denied. "To keep you from going to the police. To explain . . . everything."

"To explain why you murdered three people? It was you all along, wasn't it? You and Stella were lovers, but you were also conspirators. Conspirators in a plot to steal the Du Barry ring. The idea was to steal the ring, hock it, and leave town before anyone noticed it was missing. That wouldn't be too difficult, since Henry kept it locked in a safe all the time, and as far as anyone knew, he never took it out. Even his wife never wore it. The only catch: your felonious career doesn't include safecracking. So you decide that Stella will cozy up to Henry in order to get the safe combination. It should be easy. He's a lonely man with a shrew of a wife, and Stella is a pretty young girl.

"Stella came through with flying colors," Marjorie continued. "She succeeded in securing both the combination to the safe and a copy of the key to the front door. On the night of Henry's death, you let yourself into the house using the key Stella gave you and went up to Henry's bedroom. You used the combination to open the safe and pocketed the ring. Only you soon discovered you weren't alone in the house. Henry was there, and he witnessed the theft. The two of you struggled, he fell from the balcony. You arranged a fake suicide note and slinked away into the darkness, confident that no one had seen you. Only someone did see you . . . Bartorelli. Bartorelli contacted you a few weeks later and blackmailed you for a share of the ring. You arranged to meet him here under the pretense of exchanging money. But instead of exchanging money, you killed him instead."

"You're right about the plan to steal the ring," Russell confessed. "But I didn't kill anyone. I loved Stella. I really loved her. When she and I met, I was already on the lam. She wanted to steal the ring so that we could run away together. So we could stop sneaking around. I didn't like the idea; I was jealous. I didn't like the thought of Van Allen touching her, kissing her; but Stella told me it would mean nothing to her, that it was me who she loved. So, I let her go ahead with her plan, and within a few months, she had the combination. But she wasn't the same. We weren't the same. Something had come between us. I didn't see her as much as I used to. If I asked, she was tired or had to work late. When I did see her, she was distant, moody. She made me promise not to steal the ring until she gave me the go-ahead. I waited for weeks, but it was never the right time. Finally I decided to confront her. I'll never forget that day. She was upset, crying. She told me that she was leaving town, that she didn't love me. She never loved me. She loved Henry. I vowed to take revenge on Henry Van Allen then and there."

"By killing him?" she accused.

"No! By stealing the ring. You're right. I was there that night. I used the key and safe combination Stella had given me, but when I opened the ring box, it was empty. The ring wasn't there. Suddenly, I heard the front door slam. Someone else had come into the house and was on their way upstairs. So, I closed the safe, ran down the hall, and left by the back staircase. Apparently the person I heard was Henry, because I read about his suicide the next day in the papers."

"You're lying," she accused. "You killed him for taking away your girl. But it was all for naught. Stella killed herself. You thought she had taken the ring, so you went to Los Angeles to search for it. You were the mysterious detective who showed up at her apartment the day after she died. But you didn't find it, did you? And so you came back to Ridgebury to continue the search. But still, you found nothing—nothing until a few days ago, when a drunken John Stafford told you that Mary was Stella's daughter."

His jaw dropped. "How did you know?"

"I thought about a motive behind Stafford's murder, and nothing seemed to fit. Why should anyone want to kill him? And why now, after all this time? What did he know? What did he have? And then it dawned on me. Mary. A few days ago, we told Stafford that Stella was having an affair with Henry Van Allen. I knew Stella slightly and was aware of her less-than-sterling reputation, therefore I was mildly surprised, but not bowled over. But Stafford was shocked. Too shocked for someone who knew Stella as well as he did."

"He hadn't a clue, but I knew. I knew when Stella left that she was expecting a child."

"And you figured that Stella might have passed the ring to her daughter before her death," Marjorie presumed. "Is that why you killed John Stafford? Did he catch you searching for the ring? Did he discover your real identity?"

"I don't care about the damn ring!" he shrieked. "Mary is the reason I came back. She could be my child, Marjorie. She could be my child just as easily as she could be Van Allen's. I told Stella that, but she wouldn't hear it. She said that no baby of hers was going to have a crook for a father. I was angry and hurt. I loved Stella and I lost her. When she left, I was devastated. I tried to track her down, find out how she and the baby were doing. I finally found her, in California.

But I never made the trip out there. She killed herself before I had the chance.

"Months later, after pulling some successful jobs in New York, I was looking for a place to hide when I saw a real estate advertisement for houses in Connecticut. By coincidence, there was a house for sale in Ridgebury. It was perfect. I had squirreled enough money away to pay cash for the place, that way no one would ask any questions about my background. And it was safe here. In all the time I was seeing Stella, none of the townspeople had ever seen me. I stayed in New York during the day and only visited Stella late at night. Stella may have mentioned my name but no one had ever laid eyes on me. It was a great setup – small town, cash transaction. So I decided to give it a shot for old times' sake. I went with the real estate agent to see the house, and as we drove by Stella's old place, I saw a dark-haired little girl playing in the front yard. The minute I saw her, I knew she was Stella's daughter. That's when I decided to take the house." His lip quivered. "You see, I had always hoped that she was mine. And this was a way to be near her, maybe not as a father, but at least to watch her grow. To let her know I care."

"Is that why you killed John Stafford?" she said coldly. "Because you care so much?"

"That was an accident. The night he died, he was very drunk. He was running through the streets like a madman. Reverend Price and I calmed him down some and took him home, but we agreed it wasn't safe to leave him alone in that condition. I volunteered to stay a few hours until he had quieted down, while the Reverend returned to the rectory. Stafford passed out for a while, but not enough to sleep it off. He woke up and started shooting his mouth off again. That's when he told me that his luck was about to change. Seems after you and the police had been there to see him, he figured out that Henry Van Allen might be Mary's father, so he decided to make some money off the deal. He had contacted one of the Van Allens and arranged a meeting with them sometime around dawn. I tried to talk him out of it. I warned him that blackmail was a dangerous game, but he was unreasonable. When I accused him of selling out a little girl, he became violent. He grabbed a poker from the fireplace and threatened me with it. I didn't know what to do, so I hit him. He reeled backwards and slammed his head on the fireplace. I couldn't risk going to the police, so I picked up the poker, placed it back into the caddy by the fireplace, and left."

"It's a touching story," Marjorie quipped. "But you'll pardon me if I suspend my belief while you're pointing that gun at me."

"I don't want to hurt you Marjorie, but I'm not going back to jail. I'm still a wanted man, you see."

"Yes, for murder."

"I admit, I'm many things. Thief. Liar. But I'm not a murderer. Stafford's death was an accident. As for Van Allen and Bartorelli, I have my theories. When I left Stafford's house that night, I noticed something moving in the bushes. Someone had been watching the whole thing."

"So not only was there a mysterious detective visiting Stella in L.A., but also a mysterious lurker here in Ridgebury?"

"No. No mystery there. I saw the person's face as plain as day. It was—"

Another gunshot rang out and Marjorie shrieked as Dr. Russell crumpled to the floor.

TWENTY-SEVEN

CREIGHTON SLAMMED THE PHONE down in frustration. *Confound it! Where is she? Didn't I tell her to stay put?*

Jameson, joined him from the other side of the room, a buoyant expression on his face. "Looks like you were right about Mary," he announced. "We just spoke to the landlord. Stella was definitely in the family way when she moved to Los Angeles."

"Uh huh," he replied distractedly.

"'Uh huh,'" Jameson mocked. "Is that all you can say? I thought you'd be a little happier than that. Do you realize Stella's pregnancy provides another motive for Gloria? Between this and the revolver we found at her house, we have enough to put her away for a long time."

"Hmm? Yes, that's wonderful news."

"Then what's eating you?"

"It's Marjorie. I tried calling her house but she isn't there."

"You know how Marjorie is. She probably got tired of writing and walked back to the boarding house."

"I thought of that, but there's no answer there, either."

"Maybe you just missed her," Jameson said hopefully. "Give it another minute."

"I've already given it another minute!" He jumped out of his chair and began to pace. "No, I have a bad feeling about this, Jameson."

"What do you think has happened?"

"I don't know, but something's wrong." He stopped pacing and ran his fingers through his hair. "Something is very wrong."

Jameson folded his arms across his chest and lowered his brow. Creighton wasn't the type to overreact. "Noonan! Miss McClelland is missing. Put out an APB. Call in Palutsky and have him man the station. When he gets here, go out and search the west part of town. Mr. Ashcroft and I will take the east." Jameson threw on his coat and hat and motioned for Creighton to follow him. "And for God's sake, Noonan, hurry!"

The menacing figure of William Van Allen appeared at the library door, the gun in his hand still smoking. "Alone again, Miss McClelland?" He clicked his tongue several times. "When will Mr. Ashcroft ever learn that the world is full of wolves?"

Marjorie looked down; there, at her feet was sprawled the body of Dr. Russell, dead from a bullet wound in the side of the head. She stood silent for a moment, unsure as to whether she should scream or cry, but then, glimpsing the pistol still in Dr. Russell's hand, dove on top of the body to retrieve it. William, however, was too fast for her. Wrenching her wounded shoulder, he pulled her off the dead man and hurled her across the room. "Now, now, Miss McClelland," he purred, picking up the pistol and sticking it in his coat pocket. "Don't make me have to shoot you again."

Stupefied, she sat up and rubbed her shoulder. She was bleeding heavily, and the blood had soaked through to her coat. "Again?" she whispered, tears of pain rolling down her cheeks. "My God, of course. That's why I heard the front door open and shut, and why it took so long for Dr. Russell to find me. He had only just arrived. But you— you were already here."

"Lying in wait," he smirked. "I wasn't aiming for you initially, but you insinuated yourself between me and my target."

"Mary."

"If that's the little bastard's name, then yes."

"You were the person in the bushes outside Stafford's house the night he died. You're the one he contacted."

"That's right. I don't take kindly to blackmailers, as Mr. Bartorelli can attest. I came out here to silence Mr. Stafford, but your friend here," he poked at the dead man's body with the toe of his shoe, "did the job for me, and very nicely, too. The only problem was, he saw me. So, I drove out here today to see if I couldn't find a way to keep his mouth shut.

"As fate would have it, I spotted him as I drove into town, walking along the side of road. He was following you and my 'niece,' and from the direction you were walking, I guessed that you were heading to Kensington House." He laughed. "The two people I most wanted to remove from the world, both in the same house. It was an opportunity too precious to miss. I doubled back and, using my old key, let myself into the house to greet you when you arrived."

"And the poisoning—the digitalis—was it all an act?"

"Oh, no, Dr. St. John isn't an idiot; if I had faked the whole episode, he would have seen right through it. My only choice was to actually poison myself. I knew Gloria's butler took digitalis for his heart and that he left it on his nightstand. I also knew that digitalis acted as a poison when taken in large amounts by a person who had no history of heart trouble. The night of the party, I smuggled a digitalis tablet from the butler's room and crushed it into a fine powder so that it would dissolve quickly. I kept the powder in a packet concealed in my hand. When Gloria handed me the glass of champagne, I emptied the packet into it. Voila! A horrifying and nearly successful attempt on my life. Although, I did take some precautions. During my research, I discovered that there was, if not an antidote, an element that curbed the poisonous effects of digitalis: potassium. Before my death-defying stunt, I fortified myself by taking a few vitamin supplements and eating foods rich with the stuff: bananas, apricots, spinach, that sort of thing. The potassium alleviated some of the symptoms, but it was still a terrible business."

"Not only did you give yourself an alibi, but you pointed the finger of guilt at your sister-in-law. Brilliant," Marjorie commended.

"Thank you."

"Then you knew from the beginning that we wanted more than friendship from Gloria."

"You and Mr. Ashcroft showed up on my sister-in-law's doorstep at the same time Bartorelli's body was found. The timing was too coincidental. So, I followed you and Mr. Ashcroft to the Pelican Club that evening and saw that you met with a police officer, a Detective Jameson of the Hartford County Police."

"You realized it was only a matter of time before we found out that you murdered your brother. So why did you kill him? Was it for the ring?"

"Not entirely. I knew about Stella's child before Stafford notified me. I knew it from the beginning. Stella had left a note for my brother, informing him of her delicate condition. I intercepted that note and immediately realized that I had to act."

"You knew that if Henry had an heir you'd be cut from his will."

"Precisely, Miss McClelland. So I met with Stella and, under the pretense of being a spokesman for my brother, gave her five thousand dollars to leave town and never mention the child to anyone. She agreed to the offer, took the money and moved out of town. I thought the crisis had been averted, but my brother, the lovesick fool that he was, couldn't leave well enough alone. He had to locate Stella and find out why she had left. He even hired a private investigator to track her down. It was then that the die was cast. I had to get rid of Henry. Permanently.

"I devised a detailed, yet simple plan for his removal. Knowing that the house staff was off on Wednesdays, I came here to Kensington House and telephoned my brother at his office. I told him that Stella had returned and wanted to see him. It worked. Henry dropped everything and drove out here to see her. In the meantime, I grabbed my service revolver from the display case in the hall, forged the suicide note and waited in my brother's bedroom. When he finally arrived, I summoned him upstairs, saying that Stella had fainted and was lying down. What happened next is a blur. Henry entered the room, but he must have suspected something, because he attacked me before I had a chance to shoot. We wrestled for quite some time, each of us trying to get control of the gun. During the course of our struggle, we had made our way onto the balcony. When I realized where we were, I gave Henry a good shove and he fell backward, over the rail, and into the empty swimming pool. It was not as I had planned it, but he was dead. He was finally dead."

"And you had what you wanted—your inheritance," she stated bitterly.

"It was more than just the money, Miss McClelland. I hated Henry. I had always hated him. The way my father coddled him, spoiled him.

I couldn't take it anymore. I had spent my entire life withering away in his shadow, choking under the weight of his existence. Don't you see?" he asked with nary a glimmer of emotion. "He had to die, so that I could live."

"And live you did, but not in the manner to which you were accustomed. That's why you went to Stella Munson's apartment disguised as a detective—to find the only significant piece of your inheritance. After all, work is a four-letter word."

"Clever girl," he purred. "Yes, I had searched for the ring everywhere. The house, the grounds. Then it dawned on me. Madame Du Barry, the most infamous 'other woman' in history. It was only fitting that Henry should give her ring to his own mistress. I flew to Los Angeles as soon as possible."

"You murdered her, too . . ." Marjorie's voice trailed off.

"You disappoint me, Miss McClelland. No, Stella's death was the only true suicide in this whole mess. She was already dead when I arrived, unfortunate soul. However, the circumstances surrounding her death provided me with an excellent means by which to search her apartment."

Marjorie rose to her feet, her eyes focused on the gun barrel aimed at her chest. "So what do you want of me? You already have everything you were after."

"Not quite. I still don't have the ring. The search of Miss Munson's apartment turned up empty. Not that I expect you to be able to help me with that. There are, however, other things you can give me. The girl," he cocked the trigger of the gun. "And your silence."

"Why do you want the girl? She knows nothing."

"Not now she doesn't, but someday she'll become curious. She'll want to know more about her mother and her father. She'll start asking questions."

"Henry might not be her father," Marjorie pointed out.

"I can't take that chance."

"And can you take the chance of putting the police on your trail again? Because that's exactly what you'll be doing. Killing a con artist is one thing, but killing a woman and a little girl is another. Why, the whole town will be out for blood, your blood, and they won't rest until they get it."

"Their bloodlust will have already been satisfied, Miss McClelland. After I shoot you and the girl, I shall put the gun in Dr. Russell's hand and quietly leave. When the police discover that the dead man was not Dr. Russell, but Scott Jansen, they'll assume that it was he who killed Henry, Bartorelli, and Stafford, and that the scene here at Kensington House was a case of murder-suicide."

"And the gun?"

"Purchased specifically for the occasion, and registered in the name of the deceased you see before you." He smiled. "You realize you're obliged at this point to tell me that I won't get away with it."

"Why? You've gotten away with everything so far."

He snickered. "You're very intelligent, Miss McClelland. I may actually regret killing you."

She stepped forward. "Then don't."

"I would love to honor your request, but I'm afraid you know too much."

She inched forward again. Closer, closer. She had to get closer. "Knowing isn't telling. What if I were sworn to secrecy?"

"Miss McClelland, when I discovered you were working with the police, I researched your background thoroughly." William scoffed, "You're simply too honest to cover up something as serious as murder."

"But not too honest to insinuate myself into your sister-in-law's house under the pretense of being someone else."

"That was for the benefit of the police," he dismissed.

"You don't believe I'm eminently corruptible?" She tried hard to smile. "We could replace the pistol in Dr. Russell's hand and call the police. When they arrive, we tell them that you came here to visit Mr. Ashcroft, an acquaintance of yours. Finding the door unlocked, you let yourself in, only to discover Dr. Russell holding Mary and me at gunpoint. Seeking to liberate us, you wrestled with him for the gun and shot him."

"And why would he be holding you at gunpoint?"

"Because I discovered he was the killer, of course."

"And that wound of yours?"

"A stray bullet."

"A wicked plan," he responded appreciatively.

She crept closer to him. "Hopefully it convinces you how valuable an ally I could be."

He raised the gun level with her chest. "I don't need an ally."

"How about a confidante?" she asked coolly. "You'd like one of those, wouldn't you? That's why you've kept me alive this long, isn't it? You could have shot me on the spot, but you didn't. Instead you confessed to me, not for repentance, but because you know that I'm the sort of woman who could appreciate your distinct talents."

Marjorie moved closer still. "It must have been frustrating for you, keeping quiet all this time. Henry's murder was a triumph, your crowning achievement, yet you could share it with no one. To pull it off successfully, you had to resume the role of the foolish spendthrift. Your brother was dead, but you were still living in his shadow. You live in his shadow even now."

She was close enough to touch his arm. "They laughed at you," she whispered. "'Poor stupid William,' they said. They laughed at you the same way your father laughed. They still laugh at you. I've heard them. Gloria, Philips, Hadley—all of them." She slid her hand down his arm and toward his coat pocket. "But I won't laugh at you, William. I'd never laugh because I know." Her hand slid into his pocket. "I know the genius you possess."

William grabbed her wrist and twisted the offending arm behind her back. Marjorie shrieked in agony.

"Brava, Miss McClelland. You nearly convinced me. Nearly. It seems you could use some lessons, perhaps from your mother. She's an actress, isn't she? Lorena Lancaster? I saw her in a play several years ago. She was quite good. It would have been an enormous waste of talent had she stayed away from the world of theater to raise you."

Marjorie, finding no other way to express her contempt, spat in William's eye. With his free hand, he slapped her, hard, across the face and threw her to the floor. "I can see you're not going to cooperate," he commented, wiping away the saliva. "Therefore I won't even ask you where you've hidden the girl."

She got up, blood trickling from the corner of her mouth. "What makes you think she's still here?"

"Because I saw her come in with you, but she didn't come out. That leaves only one way that she could have escaped." He made his way to the dumbwaiter. "Clever girl, Marjorie. Clever girl. Unfortunate for you, however, I'm familiar with every nook and cranny of this house, and I know you couldn't possibly have had enough time to lower her all the way to the bottom." He smiled and opened the elevator door. "Let's take a look, shall we?"

The anger that had been gathering within Marjorie rushed forth in a violent torrent. With a primal scream, she picked up her shoe from the floor and leapt onto the man's back. Using the shoe as a weapon, she pummeled him about the head, the pointed heel digging farther into his scalp with each blow. William bucked, and succeeded in throwing the young woman to the floor. Marjorie, however, would not be put down for long. Taking the scarf from around the collar of her coat, she twisted it between her hands, forming a rope that she looped around her attacker's throat. Bracing herself against a bookcase, she pulled with all her might.

The man fumbled to remove the cord, but Marjorie, despite the throbbing of her wounded shoulder, only pulled tighter. Like an animal in a trap, William thrashed about wildly, trying to break free of his captor. Then, with a gasp, he backed up suddenly, ramming Marjorie against the hard, wooden bookcase. The impact caused the woolen rope to slide from her fingers. It was no matter; she had achieved her primary objective: to get William away from the dumbwaiter.

As William caught his breath, she slipped out from behind him, dashed to the elevator and, with the last bit of strength in her body, lowered the car the few remaining feet to the kitchen. When she felt it reach bottom, she screamed down the shaft, "Run, Mary! Run! Ru—"

The last of her words were drowned out by the blast of a revolver as William quickly discharged two bullets into her back. Marjorie slid, lifelessly, to the floor.

The younger Van Allen stood over the young woman's body like a hunter, admiring his kill. Then, cocking his revolver, he strode out of the library and through the back door, in search of other prey.

TWENTY-EIGHT

MARY SQUATTED ON THE floor of the now stationary elevator car, her knees drawn to her chest. She had pushed against all the walls around her, just as Marjorie had said, but none of them had given way. All she could do now was wait in the pitch-darkness of the shaft and hope that Marjorie would not be too angry with her for failing at her task.

She closed her eyes and tried to ignore the blackness of her surroundings. She wasn't afraid of the dark, but poor Florence was terrified. Mary clutched the doll to her bosom and whispered, "It's okay, Florence. We'll get out of here soon. Marjorie won't forget us." No sooner had she spoken the words than the dumbwaiter began to quickly lower again, causing her elbows to scrape against the exposed stone of the shaft. A few moments later, the elevator stopped moving and Mary heard Marjorie's voice calling to her, "Run, Mary! Run!" followed by two loud bangs.

She pushed against the walls of the chamber until one of them swung open. Grabbing Florence, she sprung from the dumbwaiter, flew out the kitchen door, and scrambled up the stairs to the world above. Stepping foot out of her subterranean prison, Mary surveyed the land around her and struggled to gain her bearings. Marjorie had told her to head toward the road, but precisely which direction the road lay was a complete mystery to Mary. Heedless of the footprints she and Marjorie had created only a short time earlier, she chose to move to the right—unwittingly away from the road and toward the back of the house.

From there on, she obeyed the most urgent of Marjorie's instructions; she ran, as fast as she could, past the pool, through the gardens and into the woods. She didn't stop for a moment, not even to wipe her eyes of the snowflakes that clung to her lashes and blurred her vision. She didn't look back, even though she heard the sound of distant rustling in the brush behind her. She ran, like a frightened rabbit, through the swirling snow until suddenly, she felt herself falling—not *over* something, but rather *into* it.

Her body hit the hard ground with a jolt, knocking Florence from her grasp. Without thinking, she picked herself up and prepared to run again, but there was nowhere to go. In every direction, solid earth walls blocked her passage. Looking up, she saw that she was no longer on land, but beneath it, in a deep rectangular ditch from which there was no exit.

It was the excavated grave of Victor Bartorelli.

Creighton kept a watchful eye on the side of the road during the drive back to town. As they rolled up to the tall iron gates of Kensington House, he noticed something that made him shout excitedly. "Wait. Stop the car."

Jameson brought the vehicle to a screeching halt. "What is it?"

"Look!" The Englishman pointed toward the open gate.

The detective leaned across the hand brake console and peered out the passenger window. "We closed that before we left. Didn't we?"

"Somebody's been here since then."

Jameson swung the car through the gate and started up the driveway.

In the light of the car's headlamps, Creighton was able to pick out the vague outline of tracks in the snow. "Footprints. They seem to go all the way to the house. Maybe it's Marjorie," he added hopefully.

"If it is Marjorie, she's not alone. There are three sets of tire tracks in the driveway. I made two with my coming and going, but someone else made the third." He gave Creighton a sideways glance. "Someone who hasn't left."

As they approached the front portico, the sound of gunshots broke the wintry stillness of the evening. Creighton jumped from the car before it came to a complete halt. "Marjorie!" he roared, then bolted up the driveway toward the front steps.

Jameson put the car in park and ran after him, tackling from behind and knocking him to the ground. Creighton got up, but Jameson grabbed him by the arms before he could flee. "Don't be a jackass!" he warned, restraining the man. "If you go rushing in there, you'll get yourself shot."

Creighton struggled to break free. "But Marjorie."

"We don't know that she's been hurt. Those shots could have been to frighten her. But if you go barging in there, you might get her killed." Creighton relaxed and Jameson loosened his grip. "I'm going to radio for backup and then we'll go in, nice and slow."

Creighton waited helplessly by the front steps while Jameson went back to the car. He stared at the house, his eyes burning a hole through the front door that he so eagerly wished to enter. It seemed like hours before Jameson returned, carrying a flashlight in one hand and a gun in the other.

He passed the flashlight to Creighton and drew the hammer back on the gun. "Let me go in first," he whispered as they approached the door. Creighton nodded and turned the doorknob as Jameson readied his aim.

The door creaked open ominously, and Jameson moved stealthily inside. Finding the doorway clear, he motioned Creighton to follow. The Englishman shone the flashlight into the dark hallway and began moving it to and fro, like a miniature spotlight, to scan the entire room. Seeing nothing but wood paneling, they stepped farther into the house to investigate the other rooms. Jameson motioned to the door on his left, and Creighton highlighted the doorknob with the flashlight. As Jameson turned the knob, they heard a soft, plaintive moan from the other end of the hall.

The two men exchanged worried glances and made their way, cautiously, down the corridor and to the library door. There, Creighton's flashlight picked out the body of Dr. Benjamin Russell. The Englishman knelt down and felt the man's neck for a pulse; detecting none, he looked at Jameson and shook his head.

There was another moan, this time a few feet away from them. In the wan light of the stained glass window, Creighton discerned the body of a young woman, slumped against the base of the wall. He shone the flashlight on her. "Marjorie!" They rushed to her side.

"Marjorie, who did this to you? Dr. Russell?" Jameson demanded.

She gave a faint shake of the head, and then whispered, "William. William Van Allen."

"Where did William go, Marjorie?"

Marjorie's eyes opened wide and she struggled to sit up. "Mary!" she exclaimed. "He's after Mary!"

Creighton knelt down and quieted her. "Shhh . . . don't move. We'll find her." He lifted her gingerly and cradled her head in his arms. "Do you know where she is?"

"The dumbwaiter . . . I lowered her . . . she should be outside by now," she replied breathlessly.

By this time, Noonan had arrived on the scene. He stepped into the room, took one look at the dead body, another at the wounded writer and muttered an astonished, "Jeez." "I'll call for an ambulance," he announced before retreating the way he had entered.

"Where does the dumbwaiter let out?" Jameson asked Creighton.

"Downstairs. The kitchen. There's a staircase on the side of the house." Creighton removed a hand from Marjorie's back to gesture toward the direction of the staircase. As he did so, the color drained from Jameson's face. Creighton looked at his hand and saw that it was covered in blood. In horror, he let his arm sink to the floor.

"Noonan and I will find the girl," the detective explained, trying to retain his professionalism. "You stay with Marjorie until the ambulance comes." Taking the flashlight with him, he headed toward the library door. He paused a moment in the doorframe. "And Creighton, take care of her."

The Englishman nodded solemnly and Jameson took off down the hallway and out the front door, where he met up with Officer Noonan. "Ambulance is on its way," the ruddy-faced man stated.

"Let's hope it's in time," the detective replied anxiously, and ran to the side of the house. "The little girl's missing. She may have come out this way."

Noonan followed his superior to the kitchen door. "A child's footprints," he observed, staring down at the snow. "Looks like they lead to the backyard."

Jameson took note of another, larger set of impressions, sometimes running parallel to, and other times overlapping Mary's footprints. "She's not alone. Van Allen's hot on her trail. Come on," he urged his officer. "We have to get to her before he does." Jameson cocked his gun and took off like a shot, tracking the prints past the pool and into the garden. Noonan pulled a revolver from his holster and took off after him, his stocky body surprisingly agile.

Jameson traced the footprints out of the garden, through a clearing and into the woods, where roots and fallen trees obscured the trail. Hearing the snapping of a twig a few feet ahead of him, he came to a halt and scanned the area with his flashlight. Before him stretched the grave of Victor Bartorelli, and standing over it, the figure of William Van Allen, the revolver in his hand pointed into the open ditch.

Jameson aimed his gun at the man's chest. Noonan, a few paces behind him, did the same. "Hartford County Police!" the detective shouted. "Drop your weapon!"

William did not respond but to smile at his adversaries.

"Drop it!" Jameson demanded again, but the man did not comply. Instead he drew back the hammer of his gun and prepared to shoot. The detective, hearing the click, fired his gun, sending a bullet straight into William's heart.

Van Allen, clutched his chest, the same curious smile on his face, and fell headlong into the grave he had dug five years ago.

Jameson and Noonan put away their weapons and charged toward the grave. Peering downward, they saw the missing little girl cowering beneath a piece of canvas tarpaulin, the body of William Van Allen sprawled before her.

"Stay there, sweetheart," Jameson urged, passing Noonan the flashlight. He jumped into the grave, bundled the girl in his arms, tarpaulin and all, and passed her up to Noonan.

The stocky man removed his coat and wrapped the trembling girl in it, tenderly. "It's all right, angel," the normally gruff officer cooed. "You're safe now. Put your head on Officer Noonan's shoulder and close your eyes, and before you know it you'll be back home."

Jameson watched as Noonan turned and carried Mary back to the house.

"Wait one minute!" the detective shouted, after spying the little girl's doll lying inches away from William Van Allen's body. "You forgot your doll."

Noonan hurried back and Jameson retrieved the toy from the floor of the burial chamber. Apparently shaken loose by the fall, the doll's head popped off and rolled to the ground, discharging a wad of newspaper and a small, shiny object. Jameson leaned down to examine the object and saw it was a golden, circular band, adorned with the largest diamond he had ever seen. He held it in the beam of the flashlight. "The Du Barry ring. Hidden all these years in the head of a little girl's doll."

Noonan smiled at the irony. "Talk about your million dollar babies."

TWENTY-NINE

Wheezing and coughing, Marjorie was finding it increasingly difficult to breathe. She longed to shut her eyes, to relinquish herself to sleep, oblivion, peace, but she couldn't rest until she knew Mary was safe. Creighton's arms tightened around her, and she looked up at him with a smile. "I told you Gloria didn't do it," she said to ease his tension.

He smiled back, tenderly. "You picked a hell of a way to prove it."

"I never was the type to take the easy way out," she replied with a shiver, as a terrible chill swept over her.

Creighton removed his coat and enfolded her in it. Marjorie made a feeble attempt to push it away. "No. The blood. It will be ruined."

"I'll buy another one," he answered, tucking her in tightly.

"No," she argued. "*I'll* buy you another one."

The Englishman chuckled at her indefatigability. "You'll pay for it out of the proceeds of your next book, I suppose. Like the dress you wore to Gloria's party."

"Precisely," she whispered.

"Then you'd better get writing, instead of lying there on your back," he mock ordered. "No more lollygagging about for you. There's work to be done."

"Aye, aye, Captain," she saluted.

From the hallway, they heard the slam of the front door and then footsteps approaching; it was Detective Jameson. "How is she?" he asked of Creighton.

"Hanging in there," the Englishman replied.

The detective gave a brief nod of the head. "We found the girl. She's safe. A few cuts and bruises, but other than that, she's fine. Noonan's with her now in the squad car, waiting for the doctor to come and give her the final okay."

"And William?" Creighton asked.

"Dead. I shot him." He looked longingly at Marjorie. "I want to stay, but I have to contact the coroner's office."

"That's all right, Robert," Marjorie pardoned. "It's your job."

The detective frowned. "Yeah, well, I'll, um, check on that ambulance while I'm at it." He turned on one heel and headed back down the hall.

"Did you hear that, Marjorie?" Creighton asked excitedly. "Mary's safe. She's safe and it's all because of you. You saved her. Now there's nothing to worry about. Nothing to worry about except getting better."

"She's safe," Marjorie repeated, crying. "She's safe. She's safe . . ." The words had a sedating effect upon her. Her job was done. She closed her eyes and sank deeper into Creighton's arms. The pain that racked her entire body began to melt away, and she was less aware of the world around her. She could not hear the sound of Creighton's voice as it called to her, softly at first, then more urgently. Nor could she feel the dampness of his tears as they fell gently upon her face.

She was engulfed within a world of darkness, a darkness that swirled about her, caressing her with velvet fingertips, drawing her farther into its depths. Too exhausted to fight, Marjorie easily succumbed to the shadows and found that despite the absence of light, there was, in this realm, a sense of warmth, security, and absolute tranquility.

At once, there was a blinding flash of light. When the glare evaporated, she found herself in her own living room. She was a girl again, curled upon her father's lap, his sheltering arms enclosing her. He was reading to her, as he often did on cool autumn evenings, telling her tales of princes and princesses, of witches and fairy godmothers. She smelled the must of the aged, oft-turned pages. She listened to the familiar words and the rise and fall of her father's voice resonate deep within her consciousness. How often had she wished to hear that sound again.

Exuberant, she glanced behind her in order to gaze upon her father's well-weathered countenance, but sadly, it was not visible. There were fleeting images of his ink-stained fingers, shards of light that reflected from his wire-framed spectacles, but his face and figure remained in total obscurity.

Marjorie cast about frantically in search of him, hoping to catch a glimpse of those kindly hazel eyes, praying that her hands might meet his. But, as she searched, she realized that the setting had changed. She was no longer on her father's lap, or even in her own house. She had been transported to Mrs. Patterson's backyard, not as she knew it now, but as it used to be, before Mrs. Patterson had become too old to tend the roses, or trim the hedges, before the lawn had turned brown and brittle and ivy had engulfed the white picket fences.

Marjorie sank her bare feet into the thick green carpet of grass. Gone were the silk stockings and high-heeled shoes of womanhood.

Gone were the long skirts, too, for she could feel the golden beams of the sun beating upon her legs. She lifted her face so that it, too, could bask in the warm radiance. As she did, she took note of the sky—a flawless pale azure—and her heart was filled with a sudden sorrow. As much as she wished to remain in this idyllic landscape, she did not belong here. Something, be it memory or longing, was calling her home . . .

EPILOGUE

As is the way of sleepy, New England towns, it was not long before the excitement over the Kensington House incident, as it came to be known, died down and life in Ridgebury went on as it always had. However, for those involved with the Van Allen case, life would never be the same again.

Both the Russell and Stafford homes were stripped of their furnishings and left abandoned until new owners could be found. Mary was released to the care of her grandmother and left town to spend the remainder of her formative years in New Jersey. Marjorie spent several weeks in the hospital being treated for a shattered collarbone, a punctured lung, and three broken ribs before being released to the care of Mrs. Patterson. Detective Jameson received a commendation for his heroics at Kensington House, and called on Marjorie frequently enough that the townsfolk declared them "inseparable."

As for Creighton, he finally moved into his new home, and with the help of his servants, swiftly restored it to the showplace it was intended to be. As promised, he arranged a celebratory dinner to mark the close of the Van Allen case. At Marjorie's urging, he held it, not at Andre's, but in the dining room of Kensington House, and, for his own motives, scheduled it for an evening when Jameson was on duty and unable to attend.

After dining on a sumptuous dinner of champagne, shrimp cocktail, poached salmon, and chocolate soufflé, Creighton and Marjorie retired to the library and occupied the two leather wing chairs that flanked either side of the fireplace. Creighton, bypassing tea or coffee, cradled a large snifter of cognac in his hand. Marjorie, staring pensively at the fire, stirred her cup of coffee distractedly.

"Life isn't fair," she declared. "Poor Mary not only lost her family, but she lost her shot at financial security, as well. Why did they have to return the Du Barry ring to Gloria, anyway? It's obvious Henry gave it to Stella as a gift."

"The police have no proof of that," he explained. "Stella could just as easily have stolen it. She had the combination to the safe."

"It stands to reason that Henry gave her the ring. Stella loved him, otherwise she wouldn't have taken her life. A woman isn't going to steal from a man she loves," she argued. "The only thing I don't understand is why she hid it in the doll's head."

Creighton shrugged. "Apparently she wanted Mary to have it. Whether she told her sister that it was there, or she simply counted on the head popping off, we'll never know."

Marjorie bit her lip. "It's a shame. Mrs. Munson and Mary need that money more than Gloria Van Allen does."

"I don't think Mrs. Munson is too interested in money, otherwise she would have consented to Mary's paternity test." He shook his head. "No, I think she realizes that there are things that money can't buy."

She took a sip from her cup. "You're right, of course. But it would have been nice to have for the future, in case Mary wants to further her education."

"I shouldn't worry about that," Creighton commented cryptically.

"Why not?"

"I opened a small trust fund in Mary's name. She'll receive it on her eighteenth birthday." His voice took on a forbidding tone. "But I wish to remain anonymous in this matter. Do you understand?"

Marjorie nodded, but the expression on her face was something akin to hero worship. "That's so nice of you. I didn't—"

"Oh, no you don't," he interrupted. "Stop it right now."

"Stop what?"

"You know what you're doing," he accused.

"No. I can't say that I do."

"You're sitting there, suiting me up in my shining armor."

"Armor? No, I think it's very kind of you, that's all."

"It's not kindness, Marjorie. It's moral obligation. I am heartily obliged to give back to society what it gave to me."

"But not everyone in your position feels that sense of obligation."

"No, perhaps they don't, but I would expect you, of all people, would be able to understand my desire to set things right."

"Me?"

"Yes, you," he grinned. "Tell me, what did you do with that five-hundred-dollar check Gloria gave you?"

She stared into her coffee cup, and felt her cheeks grow warmer. "I cashed it."

"And then what?" he prodded.

"I put it in my bank account," she snapped hastily, hoping to end this line of questioning.

"You're lying," he accused. "I saw Mr. Schutt the other day, whistling, happy as a lark. He told me that Gloria repaid the debt that Henry owed him, in cash, and had written a formal letter of apology. The letter, as if you didn't know, was typed on Van Allen Industries letterhead."

"And from where would I get Van Allen Industries letterhead?"

"Evelyn Hadley. She gave you a whole stack of it when we interviewed her at her office. So, it would appear that I'm not the only person in this town who feels a sense of higher moral obligation."

"Honestly," she sighed. "There's such a thing as being too smart for your own good." Creighton laughed, but Marjorie would not be put off. "Well, whatever I might have done for Mr. Schutt, it still doesn't compare to the gesture you made to Mary and her grandmother."

He breathed a heavy sigh and regarded her in a fatherly fashion. "My dear Marjorie. You shouldn't place people on pedestals, especially mere mortals like myself. We're bound to fall off of them." He paused for a moment and took a drink of brandy. "And in my particular case, I'd fall so far in your esteem that you'd fire me as your editor."

She giggled. "Don't be ridiculous!"

"Ridiculous? How? Do you mean you wouldn't dream of getting rid of me?" His eyes narrowed and the grin disappeared from his face. "Or do you mean that I couldn't possibly fall any lower in your esteem?"

Marjorie laughed, but she felt uneasy. Was there not just a hint of bitterness in Creighton's tone? In an effort to avoid confrontation, she turned her head and concentrated on a spot in the hearth.

After several minutes, she broke the silence. "I know that the whole town thinks of him as a common thief, but I feel quite sorry for Dr. Russell, or Scott Jansen, or whatever his name is." She continued, "It must be horrible to care so deeply for someone and know that they don't feel the same way toward you."

She had anticipated a response from Creighton—a bit of cynicism, a display of his acerbic wit. But there was nothing, just the sound of crackling logs upon the fire. Through her peripheral vision she saw that he sat motionless in his chair, his pale blue eyes fixed upon her as if in some sort of fugue.

She turned her head and met his gaze, her face a question.

But if there were any answers, Creighton was not willing to provide them. He merely smiled, wearily, drank back the rest of his cognac, and quietly left the room.

ABOUT THE AUTHOR

AMY PATRICIA MEADE (NY) graduated cum laude from New York Institute of Technology, and currently works as a freelance technical writer. Amy lives with her husband, Steve, his daughter, Carrie, and their two cats, Scout and Boo. She enjoys travel, cooking, needlepoint, and entertaining friends and family, and is a member of Sisters in Crime.

If you enjoyed *Million Dollar Baby*,
read the following exceprt from *Murder at the Portland Variety*
by M. J. Zellnik.

ONE

From the moment she entered the lobby of Crowther's Portland Variety, Libby Seale could tell something was amiss. The first clue was the quiet. Normally the building was abuzz with voices, running through a song or dance number on the stage, sometimes accompanied by the piano in the pit. Even if no acts were rehearsing, there should have been the inevitable hammering as stagehands assembled the scenery for incoming acts. And it was dark in the lobby, as if no one had turned on the electricity yet, or even lit any of the gas lamps used to conserve energy when the electric lights—still a novelty in 1894—were off. The only light came through the dull windows of the box office, making the theatre entranceway look grey, despite its bright red carpeting.

Slipping through a side door that led backstage, Libby hung her coat on the peg in the hallway and gathered up her purchases. She was later than usual in getting to the theater and needed to get the fabric and notions she had bought on her way into work into their proper cubbyholes before starting to sort out the mending. Her job as assistant in the costume department at Crowther's meant she helped the wardrobe mistress with any and all of the varied costuming needs of a busy vaudeville theatre, even if that entailed running errands in the hours before work officially began. Today this had included several stops on her way into work to buy the material and trimmings for the new set of dancers' costumes, and she had gotten lost twice trying to find her way around an unfamiliar part of town. But she was in no position to complain, since her status at the Variety was only temporary. She was very much hoping that, when the time came, they would offer her a permanent job. She had arrived in Portland only six months before. In that time, she had still failed to find a secure means of earning her way in the world.

Where on earth *was* everybody? The backstage area was never this quiet the afternoon before a show, especially when new performers were arriving and settling into their small dressing rooms with varying degrees of audible discomfort. Crossing the stage on her way to the costume shop, she saw May hurrying toward the stage from the aisle. May was one of the youngest members of the resident ensemble, "The Dancing Whirlwinds," and Libby had taken a liking to the quiet, sweet girl who tried to act so worldly. In fact, right now, with her fearful eyes and tear-stained cheeks, she looked more like the thirteen-year-old Libby suspected she was than the sixteen-year-old she had claimed to be when Mr. Crowther hired her.

"Miss Seale! Isn't it terrible?"

"What is it, May?"

May looked up at Libby with her big blue eyes. "Didn't you hear about Vera? I mean, Miss Carabella?"

"What is it about Vera, May? Is she still here?" Vera Carabella had been a performer in one of the featured acts, "The Electrical Magic of Signor Carlo," but their run had ended the previous Saturday night.

"She's . . . she's dead!"

With that, May's eyes started welling up, and she grasped Libby's arm to steady herself. "I have to go. The other girls are waiting for me out front, but I left my bag in the dressing room. Mr. Crowther cancelled the show and sent everybody home."

A thousand thoughts ran like lightning through Libby's mind. It felt like she had just seen Vera only moments ago! "What happened?" she asked the girl as gently as she could. "An accident?"

May shook her head. "The white slavers got her! Just like they got some other chorus dancer a few months back." Libby heard the words, but they sounded so far-fetched that her mind refused to make sense of them. Her face must have registered this incomprehension, for May went on, eyes bright and feverish, without any prompting from Libby.

"That's how I got my job here. They found one of the Dancing Whirlwinds in the tunnel beneath the theater, dead! And everyone said that it was white slavers that got her, too! They say they take girls through the tunnels and put them onto ships headed for . . . well, I'm not sure where . . . All the other dancers were so upset that, for a while, no one in the city would come in and audition for the Variety. And they lost some of the other dancers who worked here because they quit." Now that the topic had shifted to matters theatrical, May had lost her fearful look, and burbled like a child. "So, when Mr. Crowther put out the word that there were positions in the chorus open, I . . ."

Libby had to break in, "But what about Vera, May? What happened today?" She tried hard not to sound exasperated.

"The police were here when I arrived. They said some workmen in the tunnels found Vera's . . . body this morning, right in the same spot where they found Polly . . . that was the other dancer, Polly. And then one of them—a policeman—said to watch my back. Then, when they thought I was gone, I heard him say to the other one that girls like dancers and actresses had to expect this sort of thing." She looked indignant.

Before Libby could frame the multitude of questions that popped into her mind, the girl started off toward the Whirlwinds' dressing room. "I have to go! I'll see you tomorrow, Miss Seale."

Mechanically, Libby made her way to the wardrobe room, released her armful of packages in a heap on the table, and sank into a chair.

She couldn't quite believe Vera was dead. While they hadn't been close friends, she had gotten to know Vera well over the magic act's four-week engagement at the Variety. Libby was too busy to become friendly with most of the featured performers, but circumstances, in the form of a backstage accident, had brought Libby and Vera together. The very first week that "The Electrical Magic of Signor Carlo" was playing the Variety, Mr. Maynard, the theater's bookkeeper and office manager, had spilled a brand new bottle of India ink all over the front of Vera's costume, ruining it beyond repair. Vera had been frantic at the loss of the gown, which was only a year old. It had been made for her at great expense in San Francisco, and she had been enthusiastically grateful when Libby (until six months before a seamstress for a large and fashionable New York dressmaker), had managed to whip up a stylish and sophisticated new dress overnight.

Libby would have been the first to admit that the gown itself could never have been called high fashion, since the front of the peacock blue skirt was cut away in a wide swag to reveal Vera's shapely legs. Even so, it had an air of elegance that lifted it (and presumably Vera as well) out of the realm of the vulgar. Vera had been delighted by it, and she and Libby had been fast friends from that moment on. Libby now found some small measure of comfort at the thought that the dress she'd made had brought the doomed performer some happiness, for perhaps one of the last times in her life.

At that moment Hatty Matthews, wardrobe mistress, came through the door carrying a load of costumes that was every color of the rainbow and almost as tall as she was. Hatty was in her early fifties, with jet black hair (enlivened by a few strands of silver just above her forehead) and classically Asian features. Though she was tiny, she had the strength of an ox, as well as a nononsense but motherly disposition that endeared her to Libby and everyone at the Variety. Her husband, now deceased, had been a British soldier stationed in Hatty's native Hong Kong, but when exactly she had come to these shores, Libby didn't know.

"Oh, good, Libby, you're here." Hatty said, putting down the mending with a sigh and flopping down on a chair. Her English was nearly flawless, but since she had learned it as a British colonial, one could hear traces of middle-class British pronunciation nestled alongside the Eastern coloration of her l's and r's.

"Hatty! Did you hear about what happened to Miss Carabella?"

The older woman gave a sad sigh and pushed her spectacles up on her nose. "Oh, yes, it's tragic. The police were here all morning, talking to Mr. Crowther in his office." She looked at Libby with concern. "You were friendly with her, weren't you?" Libby nodded. "I was going to ask you to stay and help me with the mending, but if you would like to go home, that's certainly all right."

"The mending!" Libby blurted out. "How can you think about mending now?"

"Life goes on," Hatty said quietly. "Best not to let the bad things keep you from doing what needs to be done."

"May told me it was white slavers. It . . . that . . . sounds like something out of a penny dreadful! Surely there aren't really white slavers right here in Portland?" She had read about all the crime and mayhem here in America's "wild frontier," but with all the worries and fears she had about being on her own in a new city, it had not occurred to her to worry about an illegal trade in kidnapped women.

"Ah, sit down, my dear, and I'll tell you what I know. You have heard of the Shanghai tunnels running under the city, I assume?"

"I think so." When she had first arrived in Portland and was doing piece-work for local tailors, one of them had regularly received deliveries of imported silks and other materials via a basement entrance to his shop. He had explained to Libby that many of the cargo ships delivered their packages via the tunnels that came up from the harbor. "They're those tunnels that go down to the waterfront, aren't they?"

"Exactly." She added dryly, "I'm sure you have noticed that it rains a bit in the Pacific Northwest. The tunnels were built to make it easier to deliver cargo in inclement weather. Or so they say. I wouldn't be surprised if they were really built to make it easier for smugglers and thieves to navigate the city underground."

Hatty went on to tell Libby of the criminal gangs that preyed on both men and women, drugging them and spiriting them down to the waterfront for nefarious purposes. In the case of the men, they would wake up on a strange ship at sea, only to find they had been sold to the captain of a vessel in need of a crew. Since many of the boats were headed for China, the term "Shanghai" became common parlance for the crime ("to Shanghai") as well as the tunnels. If Hatty had any personal feelings about the fact that it was the land of her birth that was being slandered by this slang, she kept them well hidden.

The fate of the women abducted was murkier, and all Hatty knew were the rumors . . . that attractive girls were sometimes abducted from the seedier bars in the area, taken on ships far away from their homes, and from anyone who might rescue them, then stranded in remote parts of the world, unable to return home. The saddest part was that, once a girl had been ruined in this way, she was effectively unable to ever return home, even if she could find the passage, since her reputation and virtue would be in shreds.

"So our theater basement has an entrance to these tunnels?" asked Libby, fascinated. "May said something about another body being found under the theater a while back. A dancer here . . . ?"

Hatty cut her off, anticipating the rest of her question. "My, my, no wonder you're so upset. Please, don't go thinking this sort of thing happens all the time at the Variety. But yes, it's true enough. I suppose it would have been a little over two months before you started working here. There was an unpleasant incident involving one of the showgirls here, but it was something she brought upon herself. Her name was . . . well, she called herself Polly Pink. She was . . ." She squeezed her eyes closed, apparently trying to come up with a delicate euphemism, "a gay girl from the streets trying to move up in the world, and people here thought that's why she was killed. They say she must have let a man into the theater after hours, someone she knew from her previous line of work, and he drugged her, then dragged her into the tunnels through the basement, intending to sell her to the white slavers. They found her dead down there with the drugged rag still over her face. Apparently, her killer had used too high a concentration of chloroform in his attempt to subdue her, and she died."

The more Hatty told her, the more apparent it became to Libby that there was a whole world of unsavory characters and criminal activity that she never read about in the papers. It made her wonder whom one could trust to get an honest assessment of any city or town. As she looked out the small grimy window at the city street, Portland seemed newly menacing, as if she had never really seen it before.

Lost in her reflections, it was a few minutes before she realized that Hatty was no longer speaking. Instead, the costumer was looking at her with a mixture of pity and exasperation. But when she spoke her voice was kind. "There isn't any point dwelling on the crime, Libby. Let's get to work; these aren't going to mend themselves." With that, she looked meaningfully at the pile of costumes.

Hatty was right, of course. Best to move forward and throw herself into her job, rather than endlessly analyze the circumstances that led to Vera's death. With difficulty, Libby turned her thoughts to the tasks at hand.

A few moments later, as she was diligently darning a torn stocking, Hatty asked her if she had gotten the new buttons and ribbons. With a start, she remembered her purchases, though it seemed like days ago that she had bought them. "Oh, Hatty, I got the loveliest yellow brocade for the new Rickshaw Ballet costumes, and I found some dear little pearl buttons reduced for quick sale at Prager Brothers, which might work on those spats . . ." For the first time since she had arrived at the theater that day, a sense of normalcy returned.

The rest of the day passed slowly, the theater almost empty without any of the performers. The one loud interlude in the day occurred when Signor Carlo, the magician whose assistant Vera had been, flounced into the theater and proceeded to mourn her melodramatically. Ostensibly, he was at the theater to supervise the moving of his trunks to the railroad depot, but having waved the bored and taciturn movers towards the dressing rooms, he flopped down in the middle of the stage, practically begging for attention. He spotted Libby, who had been drawn out of the wardrobe room by all the noise, hovering in the wings.

"Oh, Miss Libby! My Vera, *la mia bella,* she is gone!" He jumped up and grabbed Libby to his chest in an expansive Mediterranean hug. "You have heard what those monsters, those animals, did to her!" Theatrically, he bowed his head for a moment of silent reverence. But just a moment.

Then he commenced a tirade espousing the theory that whoever had done this awful deed was obviously trying to sabotage him. The rant encompassed everything from the horrible backstage conditions at this theater to the fact that Portland had always shown too little respect for the great talents of Signor Carlo. Libby, who had seen him perform, found the word "great" a bit of an overstatement. In her opinion, Carlo (who called himself "Signor" although Vera had confided to Libby that the closest he had ever been to Europe was New Jersey) had almost no talent whatsoever. The fact that he put on a likable-enough act was primarily because he was canny enough to make Vera's blatant sensuality the center of attention.

It was common knowledge among the types of men who frequented theaters that a magic act was a good chance to see a beautiful, scantily-clad woman contorting herself into boxes or behind nearly-transparent screens as the magician worked his illusions. All Signor Carlo's tricks had required Vera to wriggle her body to and fro: he made doves fly out from beneath her dress and found a shiny gold piece behind first one ear, then the other.

The highlight of the act was the "electric chair" trick, in which Vera supposedly allowed 20 volts of electricity to course through her. With elaborate showmanship, Carlo waved a magic wand, to which an electric light bulb had been attached, up and down over Vera's seated body. Sure enough, as the bulb grazed Vera's arms and shoulders, it lit up seemingly of its own accord. As he raised the wand, her hair rose up with a crackle and her shapely legs, tied to the chair, shuddered slightly. Carlo worked this magic, complete with patter about the awesome danger of electricity when not properly controlled, and the crowd was always silent, fascinated.

The one night she had sat out front to watch the show, Libby had glanced around the audience during this trick and noted with a smile that the men down front seemed particularly enamored of it, or more likely of the cutaway slit up the front of Vera's blue dress. Several of the men were regular stage-door Johnnies, who filled Vera's dressing room after every evening performance. As Carlo waved his electric wand, Vera had aimed a few winks directly at this crew, but Libby suspected this was all for show. Not once in all the weeks Vera had been in Portland had Libby seen her accept any offers for late-night suppers or drinks. Vera knew how to play to the men and accepted their flowers and compliments, but she was wise enough to know that to favor one man in particular would be to lose the adoration of the throng. Libby realized now that, after all of the men had left every night, Vera was left in her tatty dressing room with nothing but a lot of overflowing vases. She wondered sadly if, beneath the glamorous façade, Vera's life had been lonely.

Recalling the magic act's true star, she suspected that Signor Carlo, who was still reciting his litany of woes, was in even worse shape career-wise than perhaps he realized.

"And tell me what I am to do now?" Carlo was saying. "I have to go back to San Francisco and find a new girl, and then take all the time to train her, and—*il Dio mio!*—it is all too horrible to think about. Not that Vera did so very much in the act, you understand. As long as there still is a Signor Carlo, the act will rise again! But yet, she had a certain style, my Vera."

He slumped against the proscenium arch, then glanced surreptitiously at his watch. "Where are those moving men? I must be at my train in five minutes! There are nothing but lazy, no-good people in this city. They must hurry ... I will stay in this city not a minute longer than I have to! It is a lawless place that would do such a thing to my *carissima*. What sort of a city is it that treats Signor Carlo this way?"

Without waiting for an answer, he rushed through the wings toward the dressing area, yelling about having a train to catch. During his entire speech, Libby had not said a single word, not that Signor Carlo seemed to notice. All the way from backstage and up the stairs, she could hear him instructing the porters how to carry his trunk, yelling about its delicate contents and swearing that he would have their heads if they dropped it. Libby noticed that whenever he got angry or flustered, his Italian accent slipped from thick to nonexistent. With a sigh, she headed back to her sewing.

TWO

MRS. PRATT WAS ALREADY at the breakfast table finishing a piece of lavishly buttered toast when Libby came downstairs the next morning. From the looks of it, it was the tail end of what had been a hearty breakfast, complete with eggs and bacon. Libby, who unsurprisingly had not slept too well, practically recoiled at the sight of the greasy bacon platter. She was also unprepared, in her sleep-deprived state, to cope with Mrs. Pratt's current state of excitement.

"Tsk, what is the world coming to? We'll all be murdered in our sleep one of these days, I'm sure." Mrs. Pratt paused, but only for a moment, to place a cup of coffee in front of Libby. "Terrible, terrible." She was pointing to the front page of the newspaper, and before she even looked at it, Libby knew what story Mrs. Pratt must be up in arms about. Sure enough, even from across the table, Libby could see the far-left column of the *Portland Gazette* proclaiming: *Cold-Blooded Murder In The Shanghai Tunnels.*

"Oh, my dear, I'm so glad you came down for breakfast before I left for church." A devout Irish widow, her landlady went to mass daily, praying for her departed husband (and, Libby assumed, for the continued health and well-being of her pampered housecats). She pointed to the headline, as if Libby would have missed it. "I assume you'll be starting to look for a new place of employment first thing this morning?"

Libby didn't answer, but since Mrs. Pratt didn't pause to wait for one, the omission was not noticeable. Mrs. Pratt continuing speaking as she picked up one of the cats and stroked it with increasing vigor.

"Oh, but this town used to be such a safe place, before all these outsiders and foreigners came to town! Back when my dear Brendan was still here, God rest his soul, he would say to me, 'Maggie,' he would say, 'when they bring that railroad all the way to Portland, it's bound to bring trouble along with it.'"

Behind that reference to "outsiders" lay a distrust of almost anyone born outside of the United States (or Ireland). Here on the West Coast, Libby had found, anti-Chinese sentiment was a powerful force. Libby often heard casual slurs against "those wicked Chinamen with their secretive ways," as if they were deliberately stealing jobs from white men. And even as Portland's matrons shopped in the local Chinatown for imported fabrics and porcelain with which to decorate their overstuffed parlors, they never wavered in their belief the Chinese had nothing to offer America. Just yesterday, while shopping for the trim for the Rickshaw Ballet costumes, she had heard a sales clerk refer to all the Chinese as "Yellow Devils." It was this forthrightness, this open display of prejudice in Portland that she found particularly shocking. Back in New York, she had not been exposed to it on such a regular basis.

Sometimes Libby wondered if Mrs. Pratt's distrust of "outsiders" extended to non-Christians—she had never actually mentioned to her landlady that she was Jewish. At first Libby had assumed she must know, but now she was pretty certain the fussy older woman had no idea. There never seemed an appropriate moment to bring the subject up and find out for certain, and so she let the matter slide, from day to day and week to week, telling herself that she was sure it wouldn't make any difference. Now she wondered if she was being naïve. Though she had been shielded from them growing up in an insular Jewish neighborhood in New York, Libby knew there were people in the world who reviled the Jews as much as the locals did the Chinese. She gave a small, sad sigh. Intolerance and violence everywhere, she thought, dark reflections of all the bright and shining marvels this century could offer.

"Aye, he was a wise man, my Brendan." Mrs. Pratt paused, lost in nostalgia, and then gazed intently at Libby, finally noticing she hadn't spoken at all. "No, I don't suppose you can afford to just quit your job, can you, Dearie? But you will promise me you'll come home straight from the theater every night, won't you?"

Libby actually smiled at the earnestness behind the plea. Mrs. Pratt certainly could talk her ear off, but her heart was in the right place. She appeared to genuinely care about Libby, and the slightly hectoring tone she used actually endeared her even more to her, as it reminded Libby of happy mornings at home with her mother. The thought prompted a pang in Libby's heart. When, if ever, would she sit across the breakfast table from her mother again? Libby spoke for the first time that day, her voice slightly scratchy, "I promise, Mrs. Pratt, I will be careful."

"You're not getting sick, are you?" Mrs. Pratt reached over and felt Libby's forehead, gazing at her intently as if trying to diagnose the problem. "You didn't actually know this . . . showgirl, did you? At the theater, I mean?" Her landlady's tone grew sympathetic. "She was a friend?"

"No, I didn't know her very well at all," Libby lied, a forced lightness in her voice. It was simpler to lie, and she really didn't feel like discussing Vera right now.

Mrs. Pratt looked unconvinced. "I'm sorry, Miss Seale. I should have seen you were upset. Father Callahan will understand if I miss mass today. I'll stay here and sit with you."

"No, please. I'm really quite fine. Please don't change your plans for me." All Libby wanted was a chance to drink her coffee in peace, and perhaps see what the paper had to say about Vera.

"Well then, I'll be off to mass, but you eat your breakfast and don't give the cats any of that milk!" She pushed herself up from the table and left, cats mewing at the door after her.

To quiet them, Libby placed her saucer of milk down, as she did nearly every morning, and lifted up the newspaper. To her surprise, she found she couldn't bear to read the story about the discovery in the Shanghai tunnel after all. Somehow seeing the news of Vera's death printed in black and white would make it so much more difficult to bear. Putting the paper down, she sliced herself two thick pieces of Mrs. Pratt's excellent, homemade oat bread, topped them liberally with butter and cheese and placed them in the warming oven. While she waited for them to toast, she scanned the front page for anything other than the story about Vera to occupy her thoughts.

There was little in the paper that would qualify as good news. The most prominent story on the front page was devoted to the ragtag collection of unemployed men and drunkards in California who had banded together, calling themselves "Coxey's Army" after the Midwestern folk hero who'd sworn to march on Washington and demand jobs from the US government. It wasn't just California either; the whole country was in the grip of a depression, and all across the West, drifters and unemployed men swore to reclaim their jobs back from the foreigners and unfair bosses.

She moved on to a story about the continuing Pullman strike. President Cleveland was once again threatening serious action if the striking railroad workers didn't get back to work. Somewhat mitigating the harsh tone of that particular piece was a small article next to it, which suggested that Congress was about to make the first Monday in September a legal holiday in honor of all laborers. She skimmed both articles, munching absentmindedly but contentedly on her toasted cheese bread, without really absorbing any of their content. It took all of her concentration not to glance at the story jumping out from the left side of the page. Finally, buoyed up by a full meal, she felt she could face reading it.

She needn't have bothered. Despite the eye-catching headline, the story was little more than filler, and contained no more information than she had herself, and in some cases not even that much. Most of the text was devoted to the mayor's statement to the effect that this horrible crime was indicative of the general decline of morals in the city. Clearly, an increase in law enforcement downtown was sorely needed, and if reelected, he would address that very issue in his second term. The mayoral election was only a few months away now, and to Libby's eye it looked as if the mayor was using Vera's death merely as an opportunity to grandstand. The article didn't mention Vera's name until the last paragraph, and they couldn't even get that right, referring to her as "Vera Carbello, a dancer employed by the Portland Variety." With a sense of disgust, Libby tossed the paper aside and went back upstairs to prepare herself for work.

The boy came out of nowhere, barreling directly towards her as she turned the corner from Third onto Taylor. He clutched a large sack to his chest, dripping what looked like it might be blood, but before Libby could take a closer look, the boy sprinted past her. A block or so behind him she spied a commotion, as several men chased after him. A ruddy-faced, overweight man in a bloodied apron stopped to catch his breath, shaking his fist at the retreating figure, shouting, "Catch him! That's over three dollars' worth!"

She had been walking from her tram stop slower than usual, almost dawdling, since she was not looking forward to another long day fending off memories of Vera, but abruptly all sluggishness vanished. Dropping her bag where she stood, Libby sprinted off after the boy. She had a commanding lead over the crowd of men down the street, and she could see the boy breathing hard as he ran only about thirty feet in front of her.

She reacted completely without conscious thought, with a reflex born of her childhood experience watching over her father's fruit stand on Rivington Street. As a young girl, she had often chased after some youth who had pilfered an apple or pear, aiming to hold the thief by the collar until her father could catch up. Back then, there were few boys she couldn't outrun, and she was almost always successful in catching them. But as she ran down Taylor, beginning to gasp for air, the thought entered her mind that perhaps this particular race had not been a good idea. Even at ten, her father had disapproved of his daughter running through the streets, and (losing steam now) Libby was forced to admit she was no longer the runner she had been at ten. Her overworked lungs felt trapped inside her constricting bodice, and her skirts felt incredibly heavy.

But it did feel good to be using her body, to be pushing herself to her limits. Despite her hammering heart, the thrill and excitement of her exertions were helping to dissipate the heaviness she had been carrying around all morning over her friend's murder. Even as it became clear Libby had no real hope of outrunning the young thief, the attempt was helping dispel the sense of impotence she had felt ever since hearing about Vera's death.

The boy turned onto Front Street and headed for the docks, and Libby finally came to a ragged stop. She knew she would never catch him now. The waterfront, with its big ships and piles of cargo and supplies, would provide an endless array of hiding places. Of all the areas in the city, the blocks along the Willamette River were universally considered to be the most dangerous and lawless. She reckoned the boy would have no trouble finding a safe place to hide in exchange for part—or all—of his loot.

A crowd was gathering around Libby. The men who had been running behind her had also given up on the chase and were catching their breath and straightening their clothes. One of the men who had been most actively chasing the child, a big disheveled fellow in workingman's clothes, weighed in. "Little devil headed for the docks. No way to get him now."

She heard the murmur of high-pitched voices and snatches of conversation on all sides, evenly divided between comments about the thief ahead and her own inexplicable and unseemly behavior. "Did you see that?" "He was trying to bunco the butcher!" "Who on earth is that girl?" "Well, I never!" But Libby ignored them, or tried to, suddenly very self-conscious about her impromptu, and very public, sprint. A burly police officer, distinguished by his dark blue serge jacket and official-looking badge, joined the excited mass of people and, noting only one breathless woman in the center of a crowd of men, made his way towards Libby with a scowl.

As his large hand tapped her shoulder, she flinched reflexively. "Would you like to tell me what's been going on, Miss? Exactly why were you running down Taylor Street like some madwoman?" The policeman towered over her, and Libby felt like a little girl again. It was almost as if her father were suddenly there, reprimanding her as he used to. *What were you thinking, Libbeleh! You bring shame to our family!* But this time she had no reason to feel guilty, did she? And yet when she spoke she sounded nervous. "I was trying to catch that boy. I assumed he must have stolen something, and when he ran past me . . ."

"You mean you had no idea what, if any, crime had been committed and yet you took it upon yourself to chase this alleged criminal?" Libby realized the murmuring crowd had quieted down, and she felt very exposed, as if everyone around her could tell she didn't belong here. This wasn't her father's fruit stand on the Lower East Side, and she certainly wasn't a young girl anymore, free to run in the streets like a child.

By now, the fat man in the bloody apron, who turned out to be a butcher, had caught up to where the crowd was loitering and marched up to the officer. "Same boy got ten dollars' worth of prime steak from Allan and Lewis last week. And nobody puts a stop to it! I don't know what this city is coming to." The butcher shook his head in disgust, though whether at the crime itself or police incompetence it wasn't clear. "I heard about Allan and Lewis, and Sym's Wholesalers the week before that, and I was sure I was ready if the boy set his sights on my store. I instructed my apprentice not to let anyone sign for credit unless that person was known to us by sight. But before we could ask him to sign for it, the boy just took the load of steaks I had wrapped up and started running away. I didn't even realize what was happening until he was halfway down the block."

"Yes, I see." The officer gave a great sigh, indicating his displeasure at the thought of having to write up a report on this sort of thing. Libby took the opportunity to turn away and quietly leave, but the policeman raised his hand, motioning her to wait while he finished with the butcher. "I suppose you'll have to come down to the station. Not that I suppose there's much hope of getting the boy now." He turned to Libby, "And you . . . I have half a mind to take you downtown as well. Creating a public spectacle that way." He suddenly realized that the crowd around them was watching eagerly, waiting to see if the law would really go so far as to take a young woman into custody for chasing a thief. As if sensing this would not be a popular move, he grumbled after a long moment, "Very well, go along. But I trust this is the last time I'll see your face at one of these disturbances."

Libby's face was burning, and she kept her head down and headed off in the direction of the Variety. She was mortified, wanting only to disappear. What *had* she been thinking, running down the street like a banshee? Why did she constantly do exactly the opposite of what she ought to do? *To come home in such a state, Libbeleh! Always with you it is something.* Why couldn't she respond to life's struggles with the calm strength of her mother? Her mother, who had always gently (or sometimes not so gently) tried to keep her from making the mistakes that would inevitably bring down the wrath of her iron-willed father.

All her life, Libby's mother had cautioned her against being so impulsive, and all her life, it seemed, Libby's father had been disappointed in her. She recalled a steady stream of grim lectures from him that ran right up to the terrible night, just days before she had run away from New York. *Whatever you have done, you must somehow try to make it right. It is your duty, no matter how painful. Your behavior dishonors our entire family . . .*

She had to go back home sometime. She knew that. But she was still not ready. Every fiber of her being told her that if she went back now, nothing would have changed. If she went back now, she would only run away again. Running away from New York had been just as instinctual, if just as wrong, as her behavior today, when she dropped her bag and sprinted after that thief.

The thought of her bag made her realize she had left it lying in the middle of the street. She had to retrieve it before she continued to the theatre, even if it meant that (once again) she would be late. And what if it were gone? Oh, that would be the last straw! Nervous, she turned to head back and found herself face to face with a man, quite a good looking young man, regarding her with a crooked half smile. In his arms he carried the large carpet bag she had just remembered.

"Yours, I believe, Miss? You seem to have forgotten all about it in . . . your haste," he said, rather formally, but his eyes still smiled.

Libby blushed slightly and reached for the bag with a subdued "Thank you." He held on to the bag and gave her an appraising look. She steeled herself for the inevitable lecture about her unladylike behavior which would come next, but he surprised her.

"It's a pleasure to see such . . . civic mindedness in a woman," he deadpanned.

She wished he would just give her the bag and let her go. "It was probably foolish of me to have reacted that way when the boy ran past me. I don't know what I was thinking."

He seemed to realize she thought he'd been making fun of her. "No disrespect intended, I assure you. I was being sincere." To be fair, Libby recognized there was no disapproval in his voice, which carried discernible traces of the East Coast. He bowed his head sheepishly, "And, I must add, I would have been no help. I can make no claims to athletic prowess. While you . . ." he paused. "Well, if they ever get around to holding that modern Olympics they've been arguing about over in Europe, you for one will be all ready to go."

So he *was* making fun of her, but lightly. She surprised herself meeting his eyes with a smile. "I fear the modern Athenians are no more liberal in their views than their forbears, and I suspect they won't allow women to compete." His crooked smile reemerged. "At any rate, I really must be going," she added. "May I have my bag, Mr. . . . ?"

His smile became a full-fledged grin, as he swept his hat off his head with his free hand, "Peter Eberle, Miss . . . ?"

"Libby Seale."

"You're from New York?" It appeared he had noticed her accent, too.

"Yes." She smiled.

"Well, Miss Seale, I'm glad to see the New York schools provide a solid grounding in Ancient History. And I insist upon walking you to your destination, in case you are tired from your Olympian labors and need a helping arm."

At that, she actually blushed. What an odd conversation this was to be having, thought Libby, with a complete stranger at the intersection of First and Taylor. This Mr. Eberle was flirting with her in a most outrageous fashion, and what surprised her more was that she was tempted to flirt right back. Almost as if she was Vera and flirting came naturally to her. At the remembrance of Vera, she suddenly felt ashamed of herself, for no other reason than that she was standing in the warm sun, smiling and being happy, while poor Vera was not yet in her grave. But she couldn't simply walk away from this kind young man. That would be more than impolite, so she hurried to change the topic to something safe and ordinary as they walked slowly down the street towards Crowther's. "Tell me, are you from New York as well?"

"New Haven, Connecticut . . ." He held up his hand to forestall her next comment, "No. No, I didn't go to Yale. My father is a groundskeeper there. But I did used to tag along with him to the campus and sneak into whatever lecture was going on in the main hall that day. I suppose you might say that I have a Yale education without the all-important Yale diploma. And of course, as a result of my haphazard course of study, I only know a little bit about a great many topics. But it's a type of education which serves me well in my present line of work." Once again, he answered the question before she could get it out. "I'm a reporter for the *Portland Gazette*, covering everything from farming implements to international affairs. And street crime as well, which I suppose brings me to you. I was up at Third when I heard a commotion, saw a boy racing past clutching something bloody, smelled a story and . . ."

Well, thought Libby as he went on and on. He's sweet, but he does like the sound of his own voice. As Peter continued talking, she took stock of him. He was on the slim side, not that much taller than she was herself, with green eyes and straight brown hair that refused to stay off his face.

". . . imagine my surprise when I saw this pretty, well-dressed young lady take off after him. That made it a rarer, and much more interesting story." He pretended to sigh sadly. "If only you had caught him, I could've put you on the front page: *Gallant Maiden Comes to Aid of Butcher in Distress*." Despite her avowal to be no more than polite, Libby couldn't suppress a laugh. "Still, give me an exclusive interview and I'll put you on page two." Finally, he stopped.

Libby decided she had better extricate herself, as gracefully as possible, while she still could. "Oh, I'm sure there must be many things going on in Portland far worthier of paper and ink." She reached out her hand for the bag, which he had continued to hold. "I'd better hurry to work before I become even later than I already am. I really am grateful to you for seeing after my bag, but there is no need for you to carry it any longer. I'm almost there, at any rate."

He gave a little mock bow. "Seeing as you won't give me an interview, you might at least do me the honor of allowing me to escort you door to door." He popped his bowler back onto his head. "I'll be happy to carry this to wherever it is you work."

"I'm quite capable of carrying it myself."

"I'm sure you are. I'm sure you're capable of many, many things." There was that disarming smile again. They began to walk again. "What is it that you do, Miss Seale? Something tells me there's very little call for lady runners in Portland."

She shot him a look, but decided not to be baited back into a discussion about her earlier antics. "I'm a seamstress . . ." it was out of her mouth before she realized, "at Crowther's Portland Variety."

Peter's reaction was exactly what she feared. His eyes glinted at the name of the theater. "Where they found the body of that showgirl yesterday."

She had no doubt a barrage of questions was about to follow that simple statement of fact, and so she cut him off with, "But I'd really rather not discuss it."

He hastened to assure her, "No, no . . . of course not. I understand." But she could tell he was disappointed.

Libby couldn't help herself. "And it wasn't 'a body' . . . I mean, it wasn't just some body." She heard her own voice thicken. "She was a lovely woman, a true friend. Miss Carabella. And she wasn't a showgirl . . . she was a magician's assistant."

Now he looked abashed, and she was sorry for her outburst. He hadn't meant to be insensitive, she knew that. Very likely he hadn't been the one to get Vera's name wrong in that morning's article. She wished she could think of a way to ask him without making it sound like an accusation, but there wasn't. Or she couldn't think of one.

Both were silent for a bit, but they continued walking together side by side. The theater was only a short block away now. It was Peter who broke the silence. "Almost there. Need someone to vouch for your tardiness?"

"No, really, I'm not that late. But thank you." They were at the stage door now, and Libby gathered her belongings from Peter's outstretched arm. "You've been very kind, carrying this for me."

"It was a pleasure running into you," Peter said, tipping his hat. Libby didn't smile. "I'm sorry. I promise—no more jokes."

Libby started to open the stage door.

"Wait . . . Miss Seale. The Choral Society at St. James Church is having a musical evening this Friday. Would you be interested in joining me?" There was a puppy dog eagerness in him that was at odds with his jaunty and cocky sense of humor.

She couldn't. It was too risky. Already she liked this young man far more than their brief acquaintance should have allowed. The word "yes" lingered on the tip of Libby's tongue, but instead she said, "Oh, I'm so sorry. Right now . . ." she half cocked her head towards the inside of the theater, as if to remind him about what had just happened there, "I just don't feel I can think about socializing. I'm afraid the answer must be 'no.'"

Peter's face fell, but before he could say anything more, she said goodbye and slipped through the stage door.

Today the theater was alive with activity. The arrival of some new acts, a troupe of Scandinavian gymnasts as well as "Little Anita, Child Contortionist," seemed to be the cause for more frivolity and laughter than usually attended a change in the bill. Libby guessed it had more to do with a need to put the unhappy news of the day before as far from their minds as possible. No one talked openly about the murder, although there did seem to be more hushed conversations in corners than usual. Libby felt very alone.

Late in the afternoon, a very stout lady strode imperially into the wardrobe room, holding in front of her small straw valise and an oversize hatbox from which protruded—Libby couldn't quite believe her eyes—two curved horns. Her presence, if not her bulk, overwhelmed the small space, as she announced in a thick German accent and Wagnerian tones that could probably be heard throughout the theater, "This is the costume room, yes? I am Frau Blumentraum, singer of opera and light musical interludes, direct from Bavaria, Germany!" The woman sounded like she was reciting from a program note, then Libby realized that she most likely was.

"You must be the new first act closer! I'm Lillian Seale, the assistant wardrobe mistress, but please call me Libby."

"*Ja.*" Frau Blumentraum accepted the invitation regally. "Libby, my Viking helmet needs a good polishing." She handed the hatbox to Libby. "And a good polishing, lots of polish, you understand. Not just to wipe it over." Libby nodded and tried to hide a sigh. "And this," she went on, referring to the little straw suitcase in tones of pure disgust, "is not my bag."

Libby was sure there must be a reason the soprano felt it necessary to impart this information to her, but after a long and tiring day she couldn't make it out, nor was she particularly in the mood to try. Perhaps the blank look on her face telegraphed this to the large German woman, for after a moment, Frau Blumentraum went on.

"I moved aside the screen in my dressing room because I needed more space for my makeup," she paused significantly, and Libby had time to reflect that however much makeup Frau Blumentraum had it wasn't going to be enough, "and there, in the corner of the room, was this!" She once again held forth the offending bag, making it clear she expected Libby to take it and, judging by her tone, preferably burn it.

Libby took it. "Thank you, Frau Blumentraum, I will have your helmet back to you before this evening's performance."

The singer stood her ground. Libby had no idea what she was waiting to hear, but the claustrophobic nature of the room with her scowling figure in it caused Libby to add, "I'm sorry you've been inconvenienced."

Frau Blumentraum didn't look exactly happy with this meager apology, but nonetheless she pivoted on her heel and swept out of the room.

Alone, Libby took a closer look at the straw valise and realized, with a catch in her throat, that she did recognize it after all. Like a photograph, an image came into her head of Vera packing trinkets and tubes of makeup into it her last Saturday night. It was the very last time she had seen the performer alive.

She had gone up to Vera's dressing room during intermission that night to give her a mended petticoat, so it could be packed away with the rest of the costumes for the magic act. Reaching the upper corridor where the dressing rooms were located, she heard giggles, and peering ahead down the dimly lit corridor, she saw a crowd of Dancing Whirlwinds hovering around the door to Vera's dressing room. This was hardly unusual, since to these local girls Vera represented a glamour and worldliness that was totally new and fascinating. Libby wondered what was causing the excitement this time.

Entering the dressing room, she discovered it was Vera's new underwear (trimmed with swirls of lace and woven through with yards of lavender ribbon) that had occasioned the fuss. Vera turned this way and that in front of her mirror, modeling the dainties to the delight of the girls. She hadn't yet noticed Libby's entrance, so Libby had a good long moment to watch how intently Vera stared at her own reflection. Libby's first thought was that Vera was just showing off, but then she noted how genuinely happy Vera looked and how unconscious she was of the crowd watching her every move. There was a certain radiance emanating from her which Libby almost hated to interrupt, but intermission was drawing to a close, and from the state of the dressing room, it looked like Vera hadn't even begun to pack.

"All right, girls," Libby smiled, "back to your own dressing room." The throng of girls, still sighing and whispering, began to withdraw. Vera looked up at Libby and smiled, then glanced at the folded petticoat she proffered.

"Oh, Libby, thank you." Vera started to unbutton her costume. "Now I can start packing."

"Would you like some help, Vera?" Libby asked, not yet ready to leave the warmth and friendliness of Vera's small dressing room. She realized with a start that she would miss her new friend, miss her amusing anecdotes about life on tour and her ready smile. Before starting work at the Variety, Libby had never been exposed to free spirits like show folk, and though sometimes their odd behaviors were inexplicable to her, she enjoyed their refreshing lack of constraints and their easy way with friendships.

"Oh, you are a treasure, Libby." Vera stepped behind a folding screen to dress.

Libby placed the petticoat in the waiting steamer trunk and began to fold Vera's other clothes. "That's a lovely new ensemble, Vera. Though I would say that corset is a little more Paris than Portland."

"Oh, well, it is closing night," Vera's voiced was muffled a bit by the covered screen, "and I'm feeling special." Vera emerged, dressed. "Besides, I think you underestimate Portland. I've performed here dozens of times, but I only recently realized what a lovely, lovely city it is." Vera was beaming as she sat down at her mirror to do her makeup and switched on the row of naked electric bulbs mounted above it. "Why, you know, if I ever decided to give up the theater, Portland is just the sort of town I would like to settle down in."

Something in Vera's tone caused Libby to look up from her packing. "Are you planning to give up the theater anytime soon?"

Vera continued to smile enigmatically. "Well, one can't go on as a magician's assistant forever. I've been on the road since I was . . . well, perhaps it's time to look for a more permanent booking."

Libby watched as Vera carefully plucked a pot of rouge from the numerous pots, jars, and tubes packed neatly in the straw valise which lay open on her dressing table and proceeded to touch up her makeup. In the bright glare of the electric lights Libby could see fine lines at the corners of Vera's eyes, and the thin, papery skin beneath them. Why, she's older than I thought, thought Libby. Probably closer to thirty-five than thirty. It occurred to Libby that Vera's departure from the stage, whenever it occurred, might not be a matter of mere choice.

Her heart suddenly bled a little for Vera, who was through with her makeup now and was writing in the little locked diary she kept on her makeup table, humming slightly to herself with the sweet unselfconsciousness of a little girl. She had never realized how dependent Vera must be upon those commodities no amount of skill or charm could gain her more of: youth and beauty. What did women like Vera do, she wondered, when their looks could no longer command flowers and compliments? Had Carlo indicated to Vera that he would be looking for a new assistant? But Libby dismissed the thought, for if that was true, she couldn't imagine that Vera would look so composed and even joyous this evening.

Vera had finished her diary entry, tucked it into the valise with her makeup, and shut the case with a snap. "Why, Libby, you've finished almost all the packing! Thank you!" She rose from her seat and clasped Libby's hands. "I want to tell you how much it's meant to me, becoming friends with you. I'm sure that's one of the reasons Portland has been such a happy place for me this time. Please say we'll stay friends, even though tonight is closing."

"Or course, Vera! I look forward to seeing you again too, the next time you're in Portland! Do you think that will be sometime soon?"

By way of response, Vera grabbed Libby in an expansive hug, crying, "Oh, before you know it! I am sure of it." A polite knock at the door interrupted the moment, and much to Libby's relief, Vera broke the hug. "Come in!" she called out gaily.

A tall young man holding a bouquet of roses entered through the doorway, "I . . ." He noticed Libby. "Oh, hello." Vera stepped in to make introductions, her eyes shining as she took the flowers.

"Gerald Williams, this is Libby Seale. She's the wardrobe mistress here and one of my dearest new friends in Portland! She made me that lovely dress I wear onstage." Gerald made appropriately complimentary noises, but he looked a little uncomfortable. Libby suspected he wanted to be alone with Vera, especially since he had come back to see her while the second act was still in progress. Most of the men waited until after the show was over.

Libby decided to take pity on him and made a hasty exit on the pretext of checking on the chorines. She didn't even stop to say goodbye to Vera, not wanting to interrupt her while she had a gentleman caller, and assuming she would have a chance later to say a proper goodbye.

Of course, that chance had never come, and thinking about it now, Libby wanted to cry.

She dragged her mind back to the straw bag in her hands. Even closed, she could picture its interior, lined with cornflower blue silk and filled up with neat rows of everything that had been dear to Vera. But when she undid the clasp, the top of the valise popped open on its own. The contents had been shoved in so haphazardly that they had been pressing on the lid. Either Libby was misremembering the methodical way in which Vera had packed it, or Vera must have reopened it sometime later and searched through it in a hurry.

Libby started to look through the bag—there were the tubes and pots of makeup she'd remembered, plus a soiled towel, a small wooden jewelry box, and some old theater programs. Then she realized that even though Vera was dead, she still had no right to paw through her private things. It ought to go to Vera's next of kin, whoever they were.

Libby decided to turn it over to Mr. Crowther right away. She made her way to his office and knocked firmly.

As heavy footfalls headed for the door, she heard Crowther's distinctive growl, "I thought I told you there's no way we can do it right now. We'll have to wait until . . ." The door was pulled inward and stopped as he saw her standing there. "Miss Seale . . . I'm sorry, I thought you were someone else. What is it you want?" He remained standing in the doorway, making no effort to invite her into his office.

Crowther scared Libby a little, although if asked, she couldn't have said exactly what she was afraid of. But there was an undercurrent of violence in him, a sort of violence that reminded her all to well of someone she'd rather not be reminded of. She brushed aside her memories and managed to speak without letting the tremor appear in her voice. "Mr. Crowther, Frau Blumentraum found some of Miss Carabella's belongings that had been left in the star dressing room. I wondered what to do with them."

There was a pause, then he asked carefully, "What exactly did you find?"

With a question in her voice, she replied, "It's a small straw suitcase. It has some makeup in it, plus some theatrical memorabilia and the like. I don't believe any of it is valuable," she added, in case that was what he had wanted to know.

His look of interest faded. "Do whatever you like with it. I don't care." And he shut the door.

Libby was relieved. Crowther's presence was always unpleasant. Of course, she now had no idea what to do next. She still felt she should make some effort to deliver the valise to Vera's next of kin or heir, or someone who would cherish these mementos, but she didn't know how. Who would know something like that? It suddenly occurred to her . . . the police. They were probably digging around looking into Vera's past and would be sure to know what family Vera had, if indeed she had any. Perhaps, too, the contents of the bag might provide some clues.

She decided that first thing tomorrow morning on her way into work, she would deliver the bag to the man in charge of the investigation.

She was just gathering up her coat and preparing to leave for the day, when Jack Reilly came into the costume shop. "Miss Seale, I —" Libby jumped, her pulse racing. She hadn't heard him come in. "I'm sorry. I didn't mean to frighten you. I guess we're all a little on edge today. Thought I'd let you know there's going to be a funeral service for Miss Carabella tomorrow at three, up at Lone Fir cemetery. Can you go there before you come into work?"

"Of course, Mr. Reilly." She was surprised he would even ask.

"Oh, good." He seemed relieved. "You'll have to be the official representative from the theater, since all the performers and crew have to be here before three for afternoon call. Mr. Crowther insisted, since he had to cancel Monday's shows, we can't cancel another. Say, are you all right? You look a little pale."

She nodded dimly. She didn't really think Jack meant to sound heartless, but she supposed that to him Vera was just one in a never-ending stream of guest artists, not really a person at all. His job as stage manager was to deal efficiently when any problem arose and then move on quickly.

"Well, thank you. Enjoy your evening." He walked off to cope with the next item on his list.

She left the Variety with a heavy heart and began her journey home.

www.MidnightInkBooks.com

From the gritty streets of New York City to sacred tombs in the Middle East, it's always midnight somewhere. Join us online at any hour for fresh new voices in mystery fiction, book club questions, author information, mystery resources, and more.

Midnight Ink promises a wild ride filled with cunning villains, conflicted heroes, hilarious hazards, mind-bending puzzles, and enough twists and turns to keep readers on the edge of their seats.

MIDNIGHT INK ORDERING INFORMATION

Order by Phone:
- Call toll-free within the U.S. and Canada at 1-888-NITEINK (1-888-648-3465)
- We accept VISA, MasterCard, and American Express

Order by Mail:
Send the full price of your order (MN residents add 7% sales tax) in U.S. funds, plus postage & handling to:

Midnight Ink
2143 Wooddale Drive
Woodbury, MN 55125-2989

Postage & Handling:

Standard (U.S., Mexico, & Canada). If your order is:
$49.99 and under, add $3.00
$50.00 and over, FREE STANDARD SHIPPING

AK, HI, PR: $15.00 for one book plus $1.00 for each additional book.

International Orders (airmail only):
$16.00 for one book plus $3.00 for each additional book

Orders are processed within 2 business days. Please allow for normal shipping time. Postage and handling rates subject to change.